RJ BAILEY

NOBODY GETS HURT

SIMON &
SCHUSTER

London · New York · Sydney · Toronto · New Delhi

A CBS COMPANY

First published in Great Britain by Simon & Schuster UK Ltd, 2017
A CBS COMPANY

Copyright © RJ Bailey 2017

1 3 5 7 9 10 8 6 4 2

Simon & Schuster UK Ltd
1st Floor
222 Gray's Inn Road
London WC1X 8HB

www.simonandschuster.co.uk
www.simonandschuster.com.au
www.simonandschuster.co.in

Simon & Schuster Australia, Sydney
Simon & Schuster India, New Delhi

A CIP catalogue record for this book
is available from the British Library

Australia Trade Paperback ISBN: 978-1-4711-5720-2
Paperback ISBN: 978-1-4711-5719-6
Ebook ISBN: 978-1-4711-5721-9

Typeset in Sabon by M Rules
Printed and bound by CPI Group (UK) Ltd, Croydon, CR0 4YY

Simon & Schuster UK Ltd are committed to sourcing paper
that is made from wood grown in sustainable forests and supports the Forest
Stewardship Council, the leading international forest certification organisation.
Our books displaying the FSC logo are printed on FSC certified paper.

This book is for Clare Hey, with much love, gratitude and best wishes.

SECURITY INDUSTRY ASSOCIATION REGISTER

SIA LICENCE NUMBER: 51774040/SRW
SURNAME: WYLDE
FIRST NAME: SAMANTHA
MIDDLE NAME: RAE
D.O.B.   30.06.1981
HEIGHT: 1.75m (5'9")
WEIGHT: 62kg (9st 11lb)

MARITAL/FAMILY STATUS: Widowed. One child.
DISTINGUISHING MARKS: Bullet wound (entry and exit) above right hip. Scar on left ribcage, beneath breast (8cm). Brown mole on right shoulder.
EXPERIENCE/QUALIFICATIONS: Joined army at 18. Combat Medical Technician, 1st Battalion Princess of Wales's Royal Regiment (tours of duty, Iraq and Afghanistan). Early Service Leaver/Medical Discharge (pregnant). Graduated ISS Masterclass Course (2009) with SIA accreditation. European Firearms Licence (Shield Security Associates, Slovakia, 2011), Defensive Driving Certificate (Aegis Security Training, Wales, 2011). AGENCIES: Creative Security Solutions (London),

Hippolyte (London), ISS (Zurich).

LICENSED ACTIVITY: Personal Protection, Close Protection, Defensive Driving.

ROLE (Front Line/Support): Front Line

LICENCE EXPIRY DATE: 05.02.2021

LICENCE STATUS: **SUSPENDED**

REFERENCES: Contact SIA

NOTES: No Russians (personal reasons)

PROLOGUE

It started with a cold-blooded murder. An execution, as he called it. I remember the details very clearly. You tend to do that when the man telling you the tale is pointing a shotgun at your stomach. Especially when it is quite obvious that, once story time is over, he will pull the trigger. It concentrates the mind. Anyway, all this happened one night in Northern Ireland. County Tyrone, he said, twenty years ago, in the 1990s. That was the start of all the hurt that was to come.

It is almost midnight when they bring the treacherous bastard in. Marie Ronan hears the crunch of tyres on thick gravel and looks down at the scuffed pine table, with its collection of timers, from old British World War Two models to the latest Czech electronic number. There are also two revolvers, one of them a Smith & Wesson, the other a battered Webley of some vintage. There is no time to put them away. And no point, if that is the Brits out there. She throws a cloth over the pile, a motley collection that had arrived by ship the previous week, reportedly from Estonia, and fetches the shotgun from the cottage wall.

She sits, places the gun across her lap, pulls back the twin hammers and waits. The headlamps strobe briefly across the drawn curtains in the centre of the wall. She hears the car halt, the engine die, and a door slam. Silence. Then the whistling.

It is Anjel. He always was a cunt for the whistling, that Anjel McManus, even though it is always a tune that only he could recognise. Probably some Spanish shit. He has been brought up in Spain – hence the mad name – and he only came to Ireland as a teenager. She eases the shotgun's hammers back down very gently.

Within moments, the room is full of bodies, and the oxygen sucked from it. She feels as substantial as a pipe cleaner next to the two burly men who come in first: Anjel, with his jet-black hair and swarthy, rough-hewn face but blessed with the most beautiful eyes; Sean Logan, her younger brother, is behind him, stooped by the low ceiling, his baby face with its incongruously full moustache devoid of its usual grin. He has a cut above his right eye. The third man is hooded with a black plastic bag, slashed across the nostrils. His hands are tied behind his back and his legs sag as he walks.

Bringing up the rear is Ronnie Corrigan. Older than the rest of them – into his forties – he has a rep that stretches back to the Troubles of the early 1970s. He is one of those that Tony Blair calls 'Men of Violence'.

Chairs are pulled out and the hooded man is pushed down into one, a belt strapped round him. His head lolls. She can only imagine what is beneath the shiny black plastic.

'Jesus, Anjel, you scared the living daylights out of me.'

'That was my doing,' says Corrigan, in a low voice that is meant to be soothing, although to her it is laced with something sinister. Or perhaps that is simply because she knows his role in the traditional scheme of things: one of the group known as the Squad, the internal security men, punishers of those who step out of line. 'My apologies. We had no option.' He points over his shoulder towards County Armagh, a few miles to the east. 'Bit of trouble.'

'Can we get a cup of tea, Marie?' asks Sean.

'Are you all right?' she fires back.

He touches the cut on his forehead. 'Me? Aye. Just need a cuppa.'

Anjel, who had rented the cottage for her, puts the kettle on, and from beneath the cupboard fetches a half-bottle of whiskey. Marie scoops stubby glasses from the dresser without being asked.

The hooded man moans.

'What did you bring him here for?' she hisses at Anjel. 'I thought we agreed—'

'As Ronnie said. No option.'

Ronnie Corrigan remains standing and impassive. Marie knows he and his young wife – still in her twenties – have just had a baby daughter, not two weeks old. It doesn't seem the right time to be congratulating a man on bringing new life into this world, not with what is about to happen.

'We picked him up at a meet with his fucking handler,' Sean chips in. 'Some TRU piece of shit. We had to be sure, y'see.' The TRU is the Tasking Research Unit, the deliberately anodyne name given to one of several organisations that handle planted agents and cultivated informers – commonly known as touts – within the nationalist cause.

Marie knows without asking that this particular TRU handler is no more.

'What we didn't know,' says Anjel, sloshing out the drink, 'was he'd already given away the place in Monkton. We nearly walked right into it.'

They all take a glass and automatically raise it in silent toast and drink. Marie is glad of the burn, snapping her back to the reality of her situation. 'This is not good. Bringing him here. Not if Monkton is blown. What were you thinking? Have you finished yet?'

It is Corrigan who answers with a shake of his head. 'Barely started.'

He reaches over and yanks off the makeshift hood.

Marie gasps at the state of the face, the split lips, the eyes closed by ugly swellings. There is blood matted in the hair on the left-hand side, as if an ear is missing. But that isn't what causes her stomach to heave. It is that she recognises him, despite all the damage to the face. Jamie Brogan.

'Jesus, Anjel.'

The prisoner opens one eye a few painful millimetres. It is garishly raw beneath the lid. 'Marie? Is that you? God love me, Marie—'

Corrigan backhands him round the head. His neck whiplashes back and forth. 'Let's hope so, because nobody here does.'

'Is this official?' Marie asks. She knows that there is a procedure to be followed, with final permission for any punishment resting with the Army Council. 'Are youse all on the level?'

'There's no time for any bollocksy red tape,' says Corrigan. 'This is urgent. He's one of us.'

He meant a member of the Freedom for Ireland League, which raises money in America for the cause. Which means money for buying guns, be it from Libya, Lithuania or Liberia. Since the ceasefire, the donations had slowed to a trickle. But that doesn't mean there isn't still a sizeable amount in FIL's war chest.

Jamie's voice is a tremulous whine, far removed from the soft baritone that had once whispered in her ear, hoping to distract her with sweet words while he slid a hand up her sweater. 'I'm innocent, Marie. Swear to God. And I haven't given them anything. You know me—'

'Anjel—' she begins.

'Hush now. Is there another room you can wait in?' Corrigan asks, quietly but firmly.

'Marie, listen, Marie, there's been a mistake—'

Corrigan punches the tout so hard that the chair tips over and Jamie Brogan's skull rings like a bell on the stone floor. 'Get him up, clear that shite off the table, turn on those cooker rings and get me a kitchen knife.' When he turns to Marie all semblance of civility has fled from his face. 'You can watch if you want, it's all the fuckin' same to me. Right?'

She glares at him for a second, but he turns away, dismissing her from his mind.

'You be fuckin' careful with that shite,' she says, pointing at the pile of timers. ''Cause next week you'll be comin' around whinging to me for a wee proximity bomb or two. Won't ye?'

Anjel takes a step towards her, but Marie grabs her cigarettes and lighter from the table and strides from the oppressive room, out into the cool night air, slamming the door behind her. She walks past the parked Mondeo the men had arrived in, down to the fence. From the dark hills beyond comes the bleating of sheep. She looks up at the sky, sprayed with shimmering stars, innocent witnesses to all this. Marie shivers, wishing she had brought a coat, but there is no way she is going back in there, not yet.

A long, piercing wail fills the air as she hurries through the gate, down the rutted road, to where the hedgerows swallow her and blot out the sight and sounds of the cottage. There is a loud squelch underfoot and she swears. Cowpat. Should have fetched a coat *and* a torch. She moves to the edge of the lane and wipes her shoe on the grass beneath the bushes.

Jamie Brogan. There had been two boys at the time, 'circling like sharks that smell blood in the water', her ma used to say. Jamie Brogan and Bobby Ronan. Jamie had been the handsomer, the silver-tongued charmer. Bobby was intense, serious, his great-grandfather one of Michael Collins's Twelve Apostles – the forerunner of the Squad – so he had family tradition to uphold. Her mother favoured Jamie, not tainted back then by any association with the lads of the IRA. Her ma knew Bobby Ronan was going to be an *óglaigh*, a volunteer, come what may. It was his destiny.

Marie moves further into the welcoming gloom and lights a cigarette, the tip unsteady as she holds it to her lips. In the far distance, among the stars, she can see the winking of aircraft lights. They appear to be stationary. Helicopters perhaps, searching for the men now a few hundred yards away in her cottage. Trying to prevent the inevitable.

It isn't just Jamie who will suffer. The blight on a

tout's family, the stain, lasted for generations. His ma and da, his lovely old nan, his young sister Mavis, they would all be contaminated by this night.

How many times had she stepped out with Jamie? Four at the most, and he never did get much further than a bit of tit through a bra. Bobby, though, he didn't push it, he almost let her make the first move. And, in the end, it was Bobby Ronan she had chosen. And Bobby who had been shot by members of the British Army's out-of-control Military Reaction Unit six days before their wedding. Assassinated.

That's when she had said she would like to help. Wait a while, the men said. You are still grieving. It makes you reckless. Now, she said. I want to do it while it still burns in me. At first they had wanted her for the honeytrappers, young women who flirted with the soldiers at the hotels and invited them back for a party. After beer, crisps and wine, the Lads would arrive, give them a good beating, then lie them face down and shoot them. But she couldn't do it, because when you got that close they changed from fuckin' pig-shit Brits into gormless, daft-as-a-brush boys just looking for a wee bit of company. The ones she wanted to hurt, the hard bastards, they weren't dumb enough to go off with some bit of skirt to an unknown address.

So they sent her to America, to Boston, as the young, pretty face of the Freedom for Ireland League.

It was when she came back, clear-headed, her grief

now a cold, hard thing in her, that she had discovered that her dainty hands with their overlong fingers were wonderfully dextrous. That she could thread the smallest needle, twist the tiniest wire, create the most compact of detonators, build the deadliest of bombs.

She lets out a small scream when she feels something soft brush her neck.

'Steady, Marie. It's only me,' Anjel whispers, putting the coat over her shoulders. 'It's getting cold now.'

His breath is clouding the air. She shudders as she realises just how chilled she had become. She gets a whiff of the linseed oil on him from the windows. A glazier is a good job to have if you're an IRA man. Blow them out. Put them in. Repeat as advised.

'What time is it?'

'Past one.'

'Oh, Anjel.' She falls against him and he wraps his thick arms around her and pulls her in close. She can smell wool, sweat and whiskey. 'Is it done?'

'Aye. More or less.'

She untangles herself and they begin to walk slowly back up the track. She takes his arm. Her and Anjel had done the bold thing two or three times, although they weren't officially stepping out. But Anjel was from good stock, it would be a grand match. His mother, Caitlin, had been an IRA girl, his father an ETA lawyer/activist. That was freedom fighter royalty, that was. It was why Corrigan had taken him under

11

his wing and green-booked him into the organisation with almost indecent haste.

'Are you sure?' she asks. 'About him?' Marie knows what has to be done to touts. They are carrion, feeding on the carcasses of the dead. But the thought that they could get it wrong appalled her. 'Jamie—'

'We knew there was a tout, didn't we? Who else knew about the shipments that the bastards kept intercepting?' The last four shipments of explosives and weapons had never even made it to Ireland.

His voice is hard, full of certainty. 'Marie, he's given you up. It's you he's touted.'

She halts, her arm slipping from his as he takes an extra pace. A terrible iciness spreads over her face. 'What?'

'Not by name. So he says. I don't think he's lying. He's past lying now. He's told them there is a woman bomb-maker who supplies the active service units. That she designed the Manchester bomb. He was stringing them out for the name.'

'That's desperate. The Manchester bomb wasn't mine,' she says crossly, as if it really mattered. But it would have put Jamie's standing up with the Brits. And the price he could charge them.

'Maybe not. But you know how hungry they'll be now, don't you? Like fuckin' wolves.'

'Aye.' They begin walking once more. Her brain is spinning, faster than the whirling teacups that Jamie

Brogan had taken her on that time when she'd been sick down his best trousers. And, now, the wee bollix of a gobshite . . .

She manoeuvres them round the cowpat, her eyes better adjusted to the dark now, as they emerge from the sunken lane.

'So what do we do? What do I do, Anjel?'

'You cash in the money and get out of the country. Run.'

'What money?' she asks.

'Don't come the maggot with me, Marie Ronan. The FIL money you've got stashed.'

She doesn't contradict him.

'I'm not stupid, Marie. Every time they pull those arms shipments, the weapons are pieces of shit. Not what we paid for. Something is going on. Someone is feathering their nest.'

There is fear laced through her voice when she speaks. 'Don't let Corrigan hear you.'

'I'm not worried about what you or Corrigan or anyone else is doing. I'm worried about you. They'll be pulling the prick of every tout they have for this one. And we know they have men on the inside down there. In the Gardai, too. They might even think it's worth blowing a tout or two for youse.'

She has to agree. It was true that the British Special Forces didn't have much respect for Irish sovereignty. Well, none at all, in fact. And that they always played

13

the bigger picture, deciding when it was prudent to protect their man or worth letting him 'have his tea', as they said, if the prize was big enough. She would be a big enough catch that they'd risk losing a few tiddlers along the way.

They are at the gate, the cottage now in view once more, deceptively serene, the new synthetic slate roof gleaming silver in the moonlight. She hesitates, not wanting to go in, no desire to see what is beyond that door.

'When?'

'Well if it was up to me, I'd have you packing your bags right about now.'

She feels a stab of fear. Her heart twitches in her chest, as if it has received an extra jolt of electricity. That could be a euphemism. Would it be easier just to get rid of her? To let young Marie 'have her tea'? She's not worth the bother, the heat she'll bring down. Let her pack, give her tickets, then put her in a car and when she's just thinking about being somewhere sunny for a change . . .

Anjel reads her mind. 'Hey, Marie, don't you go worrying. You're solid, you are.'

'Where then? Where will we go?'

'We?' he asks with a grin. 'There's two of us now, is there?'

'Don't joke, Anjel.'

'We could try Spain.'

She has never been, but she has an image of blue sea and sky, shades brighter that you ever saw in Ireland. A cold beer on a hot beach. But something tells her it isn't that part of Spain she'd be seeing. 'The ETA lads?'

'Aye. It's what they did with my mother when some cunt shopped her. History repeating is what this is. But they sent her to our friends in ETA, out of harm's way. It'd do for you, Marie. I still have relatives over there. You'll be safe.'

'And you'd visit?'

'I'll take you over myself. Settle you in.'

She'd met some of the ETA men, of course, fighting for the freedom of their Basque homeland. Serious, dark, dour men with furrowed brows who seemed to suck all the light from a room. They had listened intently while she had explained new ways to create death. Thanked her when she had finished, like it had been a talk on flower arranging.

'They'll appreciate you. And what you can do.'

Anjel reaches out and lets her red hair fall through his fingers, looking into her alabaster face, letting his mood soften enough to allow a little of her pale radiance to touch him. He is standing there, the ugly smell of another man's blood and piss and singed skin in his nostrils, in front of a rare beauty, and for a few seconds, he almost forgets the horror of what has happened on the pine table. And the terrible thing he has done. Is still doing.

'Don't worry. You're special to all of us, Marie. *Neska polita.*'

'Don't you start talking dirty to me in your secret language, Anjel McManus Garzia.'

'It means "beautiful girl". You'd better get used to it. They'll love you over there.'

'I don't know. What do I know about Basques? Look, I still have friends in Boston, in FIL. They'd look after me. You'd visit me there? In America?'

'Of course.' A grin flashes in the night. 'I'm not going to let you go, Marie. You're the best fuckin' ride I ever had.'

She laughs despite herself and punches him on the arm and at that moment the cottage windows glow brighter momentarily, and, what seems like minutes later, there comes the flat bark of a handgun. The sequence is repeated two more times.

Anjel snakes an arm around her waist and pulls her close. 'There,' he whispers softly into her ear. 'It's over.'

But it wasn't over. It was just the beginning of a cycle of killing that would continue long after peace had been declared and weapons destroyed. That night marked the start of a wave of violence that would eventually sweep me up in its lethal path, depositing me on a lonely mountainside and a meeting with a man intent on committing yet more murder. Including mine.

PART ONE

ONE

Port Hercule, Monaco – present day

The last of the day's races had finished and with it went the ear-splitting thrum of big-bore exhausts bouncing off tower blocks that had battered the principality for the last few hours. Now the only engine sounds came from members of the public who had paid handsomely to have a few laps of the circuit, racing up Avenue d'Ostende to Casino Square – the strange tearing-linen sound of venerable racing cars, the high-revving shriek of a LaFerrrari or an Audi R8, the throaty growl of a Maserati or Lambo with a heavy-footed owner at the wheel.

The main business of the day – the classic car duels around the street circuit that makes up the Historic Grand Prix of Monaco – was over, the final chequered flag dropped, and the city was coming out to party. The girls were sliding off their 'Opium Beds' at Nikki Beach on the seventh floor of the Fairmont, men were checking dress codes and selecting just the right multi-dialled fat-faced watch for the evening. Cocktails were being shaken, cards sorted at the casino, reservations made for Twiga or La Trattoria, invitations to private parties confirmed. And a significant number of the latter were for my boat.

I say 'my' boat. I doubt I'm ever going to have the forty million euros or so needed to order a vessel like *Kubera* from the Benetti dockyards in Viareggio, Italy. And if I ever had forty million euros, I doubt I'd use them to buy a lurid gin palace like *Kubera*. To me, it looked like a good way to get rid of a few more million euros just in upkeep. There was a lot of chrome and mirrors and wood on *Kubera* and, therefore, a lot of staff to polish it all on a daily basis. After all, the hoary old joke was that BOAT was really an acronym for Break Out Another Ten grand. Superyachts are really just an obvious way for the super-wealthy to display the size of their bank balance to each other, a floating version of a pissing contest.

Mind you, I preferred the traditional styling of *Kubera* to some of the other yachts in harbour. The current trend seemed to be not so much boat as destroyer or frigate, more like ocean-going stealth bombers than anything you'd actually have fun with. It was a case of not only *Mine's bigger than yours* but also *Mine could survive WW3*. Or start it. But the rich are different. As my friend Freddie put it: 'Not every-one who is rich enough to have a superyacht is a cunt. But every cunt who is rich has to have a superyacht.' She could be quite poetic for an army girl, that Freddie.

The first guests were arriving and I slipped along the deck to take up my position. There were two levels of invites for this after-race party. The regular ones looked like ordinary business cards but were made of metal and so heavy I suspected they were created from some pocket-stretching element at the far reaches of the periodic table. Obscenelyrichium or some such. That little rectangle got the holder onto the middle and upper decks where canapés and champagne circulated and a DJ pumped out a soundtrack of electro-pop and soft Euro-house, the same music that would be played that summer from open-air bars in Ibiza to Stygian clubs in Moscow. The soundtrack to the privileged at play.

The second invite was a gold pin containing a small transmitter that would register the wearer's details on the smartphone in my hand. The man – and they would all be men, was my guess – would then be allowed to access the door behind me and slip below deck to witness the whole point of this gathering. Everything else was just expensive window dressing.

I watched the first guests arrive, 70 per cent of them women, all looking a little shorter than planned as they had had to shuck their deck-threatening Marc

Jacobs cowboy boots, their Aquazzura high-heeled sandals, and their Mulberry Marylebones at the foot of the gangway. There, a bow-tied crewman slipped each pair inside a soft velvet bag embossed with a gold number and handed a matching disc over to the barefoot contessas. There were some scowls of disappointment – most yacht owners with style simply budgeted to have the well-heeled teak-wood decks relaid at the end of the party season, rather than humiliate their guests.

At least the women got to keep their handbags. It was easy to spot this year's must-have, a mid-size number (after a season of bags so large they could double as suitcases, followed by minuscule clutches that could barely take a lipstick, let alone the detritus in my own bag) called an 'Ornella' (as in Muti, the Italian actress). It was present in a Pantone-like palette of colours and a variety of species of hide. As well as their Ornellas, Birkins or Lorens, some of the women were carrying those pocket-sized dogs that seem to have lost the power to walk.

OK, so there was perhaps an undertow of jealousy in my assessments of the incoming guests. Most of them looked pretty damned gorgeous, almost all clad in Chloe and Nikki de Marchi, displaying enviable cleavage and toned stomachs, the skin in a fetching shade of never-worked-a-day-in-my-life tan. I was wrapped in a black suit that made me look like an usher at a funeral costumed by Primark. And it was getting hot in there. I watched one blonde beauty sashay by. Her bum looked like two small but firm watermelons having a head-butting contest. I probably had an arse like that once, I thought, maybe fifteen years ago or so. Although back then my arse was covered in camo and dodging Iraqi bullets. Maybe these women had the right idea after all.

There were fewer of these party girls than there would be in two weeks' time, when the Formula 1 roadshow strutted into town. Monaco's Historic GP attracts a different crowd from its glitzier sibling, which is more a media-circus-cum-party with a sometimes-inconvenient grand prix motor race at its core. But some of the Riviera's gold-gatherers (they'd never do anything as vulgar as dig for it) realised that there was a better calibre of men to snare at the Historique – less flashy, more sophisticated, with deeper pockets, genuinely interested in motorsport and with the odd million or two to drop on the right vehicle. Or woman. At least, that's what my research notes had told me.

I checked my level of alertness. It had shifted from yellow to orange and I knew someone was behind me before he spoke.

'You been down to see Eve today, Alison?'

I turned to the voice over my shoulder without any hesitation and was quietly pleased. Alison wasn't my real name, just my 'legend' for this job, but I'd managed to get my reaction times to the point where it might as well have been.

The speaker was Jean-Claude, one of the team hired by the host – like me – to beef up the security for this event. He was in his forties and had that enviable French elegance that Englishmen try so hard to copy, but fail. This man's cardigan would never slip from his shoulders, nor his sunglasses slide down off his head, and he would age slowly and gracefully, the lines on his face only serving to make him more Belmondo handsome. He looked as though if you boiled him down to his constituent parts, he would be nine-tenths ego, but during the many pre-event briefings he had slotted in as a part of the team, only speaking when he had something pertinent to say and happy to do his share of mundane duties. I liked him, though he liked himself more.

'No,' I said.

'She looks beautiful.' His voice was ripe with appreciation and I swear he had a button in his pocket that could turn on the twinkle in his eye. I was grateful I was immune to such charms, at least when I was working.

'She'd have to be,' I said, 'to go to all this trouble.'

A commotion near the rear of the boat interrupted us. A woman screamed, not in fear or pain, but frustration.

'Lost invite?' I suggested.

'Or lost shoes. I'll go and see,' he said.

Another DJ started up on the boat to our port, sending over a faster rate of BPMs at a slightly higher volume. Our man on the decks responded with a nudge on the sliders. I wondered if we were about to witness a decibel war more suited to the peacock boats – with the emphasis on the word *cock* – that usually lined up opposite the GP start line. That was where you docked if you really wanted to get noticed.

Kubera, however, was berthed at the quieter end of things, outside the Club Nautique, part of Norman Foster's Monaco Yacht Club complex, which looked as if an Art Deco ocean liner had slid along the Avenue President J.F. Kennedy and juddered to a halt just at the exit of the famed tunnel. The imposing Monaco Yacht Club itself was a bastion of formality – its dress code included copious instructions on the correct amount of pocket handkerchief to reveal from the top pocket of the club blazer – but the rowing club was much more egalitarian and relaxed about such things. Again, it was all in my briefing file. This lot, the people paying my wages, were nothing if not thorough.

I shook my head as a proffered tray of champagne flutes slid by. The server obviously didn't know the no-drinks-for-security rule. The first of the buyers who were on board for business, not pleasure, had detached himself from the growing throng. As he passed our host – my employer, Vijay Jagajeevan Thakri, known as 'VJ' – they exchanged knowing nods.

The man looked like a younger Ralph Lauren, with longish grey hair swept back, one of those yacht club blazers on, dental-white trousers and blue deck shoes. The tan was deep and permanent and, judging by the web of lines around his eyes and mouth, as much from wind as sun.

His right hand touched the lapel that held the gold pin and I looked at my phone. It beeped and told me this was Jeff Torelli. A brief biog popped up – Harvard Business School, Redwind Hedge Fund, which successfully bet on the 2008 sub-prime mortgage crisis and had made a killing on dollar–pound speculation during the Brexit referendum, blah, blah – and a photograph. It was him all right, but then I would have guessed that by the force field of invulnerability that he radiated, the sort that money really can buy. He had reached the stage in life where he considered himself bulletproof and probably recession-proof, too.

'Welcome, Mr Torelli,' I said as I stood aside, pushing open the door as I did so. A breath of refrigerated air played over my neck and shoulders. It felt good. Even though I was in the shade, the heat of a fine Riviera day hadn't yet abated and my black suit wasn't helping. I was glad I'd been liberal with the deodorant.

'Balraj is waiting below to introduce you to Eve.'

Balraj was VJ's Sikh BG – bodyguard. I'd expected someone like VJ to have more than one CPO. But then I saw the sheer bulk of Balraj – muscle, not fat – and watched how the big man moved and reckoned the Sikh was worth two or three regular Close Protection Officers.

'Thank you,' said Torelli, looking right through me. I knew he'd have trouble picking me out of a line-up in ten minutes' time. The little people probably didn't even form an image on his retina.

VJ watched his guest disappear through the doorway. The host was in his thirties, with a handsome face made round by his love of high living. One day gravity would exert its pull and that moon would collapse in jowls, but for now he looked every inch the self-made Indian millionaire. Well, self-made once you factored in the fortune that his parents made from importing basmati rice into Europe. VJ himself had gone into steel using their cash, buying up a number of moth-balled plants in the UK and Europe, and it looked as if he had done very well out of a risky move.

VJ stared at the doorway for a few more seconds. I stepped in front of it and pulled the door closed once more. VJ inclined his head to me and dived back into the party, scooping up a tumbler of Amrut Fusion, his favourite whisky, as he went. The volume and the crush were rising now and some of the earliest arrivals moved to the upper deck, where, for those who had come prepared, two large, white hot-tubs waited. The interiors and fittings on *Kubera* were by a swanky outfit here in Monaco, although to me they seemed to be channelling Peter Stringfellow chic, circa 1990. Maybe it was ironic. There were no books, simply lots of giant TVs and some dubious art. That's the thing about the rich – they want everything to look super-neat. Books can be messy. And you might have to read one. And reading isn't high on many oligarchs' or multimillionaires' list of recreational activities. People ask me if I envy my wealthy employers. 'Not when you see them up close,' is what I say. I know how rich I'd like to be. Just wealthy enough so that I didn't feel the need to buy a yacht.

Laughter drifted over from the neighbouring boat. It was then that I spotted her. She was standing towards the rear of the upper deck, dressed in a simple white shift dress, her hair piled up, what looked like a Bellini in her hand. A little taller than she'd been when I lost her, somewhat more elegant and poised. I felt a horribly familiar stabbing sensation in my stomach, as if some maniac were sliding a blade in and out, in and out. I looked down, half-expecting to see a spurt of arterial blood.

'You OK?'

It was Jean-Claude. My mouth was too dry to speak. I was afraid my voice would betray me.

'What's up?' he asked.

I looked at him, then back at the other boat. The young girl had disappeared, my view of her blocked by other partygoers. 'I thought I saw ...'

'What?'

What? Alison Cooke didn't have a daughter, missing or otherwise. I had slipped out of cover. Unforgivable. I put the shields back into place.

'An old friend. The daughter of an old friend,' I improvised. 'On that boat.'

He frowned at me. 'Alison, stay sharp. You need to keep your attention on *this* boat.'

I glanced over again. The girl was in view once more. She had her head thrown back, laughing at something a bronzed young man had said to her. I could see now it wasn't Jess. Nothing like her, really, apart from very young, very pretty. And that wasn't so rare around these parts. The pain in my abdomen departed as quickly as it had arrived.

'Of course.'

'You do remember why we are here?' I resented the tone. Jean-Claude was just a hired hand like me. 'It isn't to run into old friends or daughters of old friends.'

Don't fucking lecture me, I wanted to say. Instead I said, 'I'm on it.'

'Stay on it.'

I tasted blood when I bit my lip. The irritating thing was, he was right. I'd let my attention wander. PPOs aren't meant to think of anything except the job. But then, I wasn't really a PPO any longer, was I? I was counterfeit through and through.

I refocused my energies on the task in hand. It had happened a lot to begin with – I'd see Jess in every bus queue or on every tube train, in the back of a taxi, pushing a supermarket trolley or trying on shoes in Office. It had tailed off recently – down to once or twice a day – but it was still like a bucket of cold water in the face when I realised I'd been duped yet again.

Behind me the door opened and Jeff Torelli reappeared. He straightened his blazer and headed off, no doubt to find VJ.

'I'm fine,' I said to Jean-Claude. 'Just an unexpected sighting. Threw me a little, that's all.'

Jean-Claude pulled a face that suggested I was paid to deal with the unexpected and looked at his watch. He stepped aside as another client approached, this one coming up on my phone as Andrei Tass, big in fertilisers. After he had gone below, Jean-Claude leaned in. 'It'll happen soon, eh?'

I looked at my wristwatch, a 28mm Omega Seamaster. It was somewhat flashy and overengineered for my taste or requirements – the chances of me finding myself 300 metres under the sea were slim – but it was a gift from a Russian oligarch for services rendered. Although I'd wrecked his home, cars and garage, he'd seemed remarkably grateful, all things considered. Then again, it was his ex-employees who had nearly killed me in a dark, cold basement. So perhaps it was just guilt at work. Whatever the motive, it was a handsome watch, ticking down nicely to the main event of the evening.

'Yes,' I agreed. 'Very soon.'

TWO

Zürich – eight days earlier

Colonel d'Arcy was in unusually philosophical mood as he looked down over the railway tracks from the thirtieth floor of the Prime Tower. 'What do you English think when you hear the word Zürich?'

Neat, privileged, smug, colonically irrigated, clean (at least physically, if not morally), I thought. But it was a rhetorical question, so I kept my mouth shut.

'The Gnomes of Zürich, no doubt. An ordered city, with no litter. And lots of banks.' He turned to face me. 'But look at those train tracks. As wide as the Mississippi.'

I was sitting in front of his desk, he was standing at the window, so he had a better vantage point than me. All I could see was sky and distant snow-dipped mountains. 'They speak of a different past. Down there, in District Five, between here and the Limmat River, there were turbine manufacturers, shipbuilders, soap producers, brewers and yoghurt makers. Yes, shipbuilders. The Schiffbau produced paddle steamers for the world, from the Swiss lakes to the Amazon basin. You know what it is now?' He let his lip curl. 'A *jazz* club.'

He invested the word with the sort of disdain with which one might have said 'child molester'.

'The Spanisch-Brötli-Bahn was the first railway on Swiss territory. It connected Zürich with Baden in 1847. Do you know why it was so successful?'

I shook my head, biding my time. He would get to the point eventually.

'A Spanisch-Brötli, or Spanish Bun, is a pastry traditionally made in Baden but prized in Zürich. The wealthy lake-dwellers liked these pastries so much that servants would be sent out very early in the morning to fetch them from Baden, twenty-five kilometres away, by foot. Every day. The train builders boasted that, if the tracks were laid, buns could be delivered to Zürich in just forty minutes. Investors flocked. It was probably the first and only rail investment in the world driven by a love of pastry.'

He laughed at that, his shoulders shaking at a story he must have told a hundred times.

'Why did you move from Geneva?' I asked. It was where he had been based when he trained me in the finer points of personal protection. Or bodyguarding if you prefer.

He looked serious now. 'Geneva? I was fossilising there.'

He didn't look like a fossil, but he did look like a mummy. His great dome of a bald head was dense with wrinkles. His mouth looked like he'd borrowed it from Boris Karloff. It was a good job old men don't use lipstick. It would fill those lines like water flowing into a delta, spreading across his face. His ears were like large handles on either side of his head, but as transparent as parchment. How old was Colonel d'Arcy? He could be a careworn sixty or a well-preserved ninety. What was his nationality? I had no idea and the wayward accent was slight and gave no real clue to his origins. Armenian, some said. Others insisted he was descended from French nobility. All I knew for certain was that he was still somewhere near the top of his game. Which is why I needed him.

'You look thin,' he said as he sat down. I breathed a small sigh of relief that his history lesson was over. 'Is it the cigarettes?'

'I'm not smoking,' I said. Not much, anyway.

'You need to look after yourself.'

'I do.'

'Really?' He gave a little sigh of disappointment as he looked at the notes on his desk. 'So, you lost your SIA accreditation.'

My Security Industry Association status was

actually suspended, rather than revoked, for two years. It was a serious hindrance to getting a job in the UK. Apparently I'd brought disgrace on the close-protection business. 'For the moment.'

'You kidnapped this man and tortured him?'

'Torture is an emotive word.'

'What would you rather say?'

'I thought Ben had set me up by getting me a job with a family that others wanted to discredit. Business rivals.'

'And had he?'

'He admitted that he had.' After a bit of light persuasion. More threat than any actual *torture*.

'There was something else?'

'I thought he might have some knowledge of the whereabouts of my daughter Jess, who was—'

'Taken by your ex-husband, her father, and his young girlfriend.'

I nodded in appreciation of the depth of his knowledge. My ex-husband Matt had pitched back into our life at a very inopportune moment, just as I was involved in an elaborate scheme to discredit the Sharifs, my employers. And while Jess was being a turbo-charged adolescent. In the midst of that, he was demanding full access to our daughter, even though he had walked out of her life years before. Given his background as a drug-taking and drug-dealing hedonist, I wasn't too keen on that arrangement. So he simply took her, persuaded her to come with him from my friend Nina's house. Yes, I should have stopped him. In my defence, I'd like to say I was busy fighting for my life at the time.

'A year ago now?'

Stab, stab, stab. 'Yes.'

'You took your time coming to me. This Ben, the man you abducted, he actually knew nothing of the Jess business. Is that right?'

It was. I had threatened – well, terrified – a man who was innocent. At least, innocent of anything involving my daughter. I was blinded by hate and panic. Still, no lasting damage was done to him. Not physically at least. 'You are well informed.'

'I like to keep a distant eye on my protégés. I worry about you, Sam. I worry about all of you. But you, especially. After the wars you fought in, the death of your husband Paul, the loss of your daughter . . .'

I didn't exactly fight. I'd been a battlefield medic. My second husband, Paul, an undercover cop with the British Nuclear Police, had been gunned down on the streets of London, but there remained some confusion as to who exactly was responsible. Islamic terrorists or avenging Albanians? It probably didn't matter a whole lot to Paul who did it, but it was another scab for me to scratch at.

'So you have been running around Europe, looking for Jess?'

'I have.' The trouble was, the 'sightings' of Jess and her father Matt came thick and fast, thanks to the power (and sheer perversity and mischievousness) of the internet. Like some deranged maze rat, I had crisscrossed the continent, to the frustration of both the British police and Europol, who thought I was just creating confusion in their ranks and their ever-so-logical approach to the investigation. Ibiza, Amsterdam, Cyprus, Berlin ... dead ends all of them. A good proportion of the sightings were either hoaxes or just wishful thinking on someone's part.

'And now you would like me to help?'

I kept my voice low and steady, not always a given when talking about Jess. I wanted, needed, this man to take me seriously. Not dismiss me as a grieving mother prone to ranting and flights of fancy. 'It's very simple, Colonel. You have a network of eyes and ears, better than any police department's. If you put Jess on a watch-for list ... well, I'd be surprised if a man with Matt's history and predilections didn't pop onto your radar sooner or later.'

The Colonel stroked his chin. He didn't look convinced by my thesis. 'Possibly. Yet he appears to have gone to ground rather effectively.'

I ignored that, because it wasn't what I wanted to hear. Nobody can hide forever in this day and age. 'And where there is Matt, there's Jess.'

His sparse eyebrows went up. 'Again, possibly.' He

made a pyramid with his hands. 'You have to face up to one thing ...'

'She's alive,' I said firmly. 'Matt's a twat. But he's not a murdering twat.'

The Colonel allowed himself a little smile at my language.

'I can pay,' I said.

I don't know if he had pre-checked my bank accounts, which were severely depleted by my travels, or if there was a telltale note in my voice, but he shook his head. 'How, exactly? I fear you have used a lot of funds on your wild-goose chases.'

I was getting tired of him being a know-all. Although that was his skill set. It was, after all, why I had come to Zürich. This was a man who traded in information. 'I can work.'

'Without an SIA accreditation? Anyone worth their salt would run a background check to discover why you lost your badge. Bringing the industry into disrepute is one thing. But the police were involved, I believe. What were the charges again?'

I was sure he knew perfectly well. 'It came down to one charge in the end. Kidnap with intent to cause grievous bodily harm,' I admitted. 'But the sentence was suspended ...'

'Nevertheless, it doesn't look good, Sam.'

'No,' I had to agree. That Ben Harris, the man I kidnapped, was head of my agency – my ultimate employer – probably wasn't going to help, either. And the fact that I hadn't been thinking straight – blinded by grief and anger – was no defence. On top of that I didn't regret my actions. No remorse at all. If I thought it would bring Jess back, I'd go into the kidnap and torture business full time.

'And putting Jess on a watch-for list isn't cheap. You'd have to keep it live for weeks. Perhaps months.' *Or years*, I sensed he had wanted to add.

'How much?'

'For six months, say, twenty thousand euros.'

Twenty thousand? I felt like that German airship after it burst into flames and plummeted to the ground. The *Hindenburg*, that was it.

He caught my expression. 'I don't run a charity.' He cleared his throat. 'I'm sorry.'

I looked down at the bag at my feet, full of USBs containing pictures of Jess and Matt and grainy images of Laura, the treacherous bitch who had masqueraded as my au pair so she could help him snatch Jess from me. I had intended to hand them over to the Colonel for the watch-for list. Instead, they would be coming home with me. I reached down for the bag, preparing to leave.

'There might be one thing you could do for me. To pay your way.'

I let my fingers brush the holdall's handle and straightened up again. 'Oh, yes?' He knew I wouldn't think that 'one thing' was sexual. Colonel d'Arcy was not that sort of man. 'A PP kind of thing?'

'There's two, in fact, but one has been delayed.' He frowned at his screen. 'Client has a morbid fear of flying. So has decided to cross the Atlantic by boat.'

'How long does that take?'

'A week, perhaps more, but they aren't even under way yet. We'll come back to that. What I have immediately isn't quite personal protection though. So your suspension won't be an issue.' A slight grimace crossed his face as he reached for a file to his left and flipped it open. This was something outside his normal remit, I was sure. He glanced up, studied my face for a second, and cast his eyes down again. 'You'd be perfect, I think. And you can use your initial fee to defray some of the watch list costs.'

I had a sudden feeling a blow job might have been the easier option. 'What is it?'

He extracted a photograph from the file and pushed it across to me. It was a picture of the sort of unfeasibly large boat that men use to signify to the world the size of their bank accounts, the smallness of their penises or the number of people they have ground into the dust on their way to that yacht.

'Nice,' I said, not really meaning it. I reminded myself not to turn sour-tongued on him. It was very easy for the bitterness I felt inside at the hand life had dealt me to leak out.

'Forty million euros worth of nice.'

'Really.'

He smiled at how unimpressed I was.

'Is this what the client is crossing the Atlantic in?'

'No, no. This is a completely different kind of job altogether. Tell me this, Sam. How well do you know Monaco?'

It isn't unusual not to be told all the finer details of a job you've been hired for. I've been ordered to turn up at Heathrow where I would be briefed on the plane, or waited in lay-bys at dawn for a pick-up to take me off to some secret location where a celebrity wedding or a party was taking place. If they pay you well enough, they can be as secretive as they like.

So, as instructed, I pitched up at Nice airport and took a taxi to Villefranche-sur-Mer. There I checked into the Hotel Welcome – room 28, a corner deluxe – unpacked, opened the bulky package in my name that was lying on my bed and waited to be contacted.

It wasn't a hardship. I had a lot of reading to do (these days briefing documents have gone back to being presented on paper, rather than vulnerable emailed PDFs) and a cute balcony to do it on, overlooking the glistening waters of the beautiful bay.

I spent the next day watching a slab-sided cruise ship send tenders full of slightly dazed passengers to catch trains to Nice or Monaco or to wander the front exclaiming at the extortionate prices in the seafood restaurants. Low cloud rolled in over the Cap opposite, blotting out the sun and bringing a rain squall with it, sending the day-trippers into those restaurants they had recently been complaining about. A half-hour later the sun peeked out again, the Italianate villas over the bay, their cypresses standing like exclamation marks, glowed ochre and saffron, the sea twinkled and sparkled, the streets of Villefranche began to steam themselves dry and I went back to my spot on the balcony and my stack of files.

I liked working, even if that only meant background reading. It was morphine to me. It allowed me to put the constant pain of Jess's absence into a compartment. It was still there, I was fully aware of it, but I could function. Without activity, the agony could be excruciating, from the first stirring in the morning when the brain zipped up to speed and delivered its cold truth – she's still gone – to the final slip into (sometimes drink- and Zopiclone-induced) oblivion.

When I'd had my fill of the minutiae of Monaco's Historic Grand Prix and the construction of super-yachts, and once the last of the tenders had chugged the passengers back out to the *Bollocks of the Seas* or whatever the ship was called, I went down and sat in the little chapel that Jean Cocteau decorated for the local fishermen. It was empty, the interior cool. I had read in the hotel brochure that during the making of *Exile On Main Street*, Anita Pallenberg had taken refuge here to escape the madness of the Rolling Stones. That had been one of Paul's favourite albums.

I slipped into a pew and, embarrassed before a god I didn't actually believe in, I had the temerity to pray for the safe return of my daughter, just as wives had sat a century ago and prayed for the safe return of their fishermen husbands, in the time before day-trippers became the local harvest.

The next day went much the same. Breakfast on my balcony, lunch at Palmiers, dinner in the cave-like L'Aparté, which was built into the Rue Obscura, one of the town's covered streets. I didn't smoke at any location and had one glass of Bandol with dinner. I hadn't yet spotted who was watching me, but I was damn sure someone was. And I didn't want them to see my bad habits.

It was at breakfast on the third day, in the square behind the hotel, that he showed himself. I was impressed that I hadn't clocked him before. He was a little shorter than me, but wider, and probably a little younger, too. His fair hair was cut short, his smile was playful and the pastel colour of his jacket suggested he was American, as indeed he turned out to be. As my hot chocolate arrived, he sat himself down opposite me, took off his sunglasses and ordered a coffee. His eyes had the sparkle of sobriety and clean living. 'So,

Alison,' he said affably, as if he believed the name on my phoney documents was actually my real one. 'I'm the Keegan you've been reading about. Ready to go to work?'

THREE

Monaco – present day

By now a dozen people had gone below deck, for between five and twenty minutes each. Several of them subsequently engaged in conversation with VJ in a fashion that managed to be both animated and subdued, as the pair tried not to draw attention to themselves. This was meant to be a social gathering, after all, and not business.

Elsewhere, the party had peaked as the excitement of being on *Kubera* had subsided and it became clear that some of the bandied-about names (Nikolai von Bismarck, George Spencer-Churchill, Suki Waterhouse, Lennon Gallagher) weren't going to show and that DJ Henry wasn't the same as DJ Henri. It settled into a calmer rhythm as the rate of slugging back the champagne, vodka martini and gin gimlets slowed. A small number of the most restless guests – those with event-ADD, a well-recognised syndrome along the Riviera at that time of year – had left to grab their shoes and move on to the next boat or bar. It was as if they had a permanent hunger they could never sate, no matter how big the martini glasses or glittering the guest list, they were convinced the grass over the hill was even more gold-plated. It could be exhausting, living the High Life. It was tiring enough just looking on.

That still left upwards of eighty people on board, not counting crew and security. As guests drifted by, heading for the foredeck, they left behind snatches of conversation, like glacial erratics dotting the landscape.

'... *the trouble with the Monegasque boys is their only ambition is to become a croupier at the casino ...*'

'*I saw him at Jimmyz. Wasted. White powder all round his ...*'

'*The brakes on the E-type were always shit.*'

'... *just too expensive to divorce ...*'

'*Don't talk to me about Cannes.*'

'*Let me introduce you to my dealer ... he's just off Dover Street.*'

'*Oh, that kind of dealer ... I thought you meant ...*'

'*I'd fuck him. And then I'd let you fuck him ...*'

'*I've set up a new company. I'm a Lifestyle Curator, if you know anyone who needs one ...*'

I wondered if I needed a Lifestyle Curator, whatever that was. I suspected not. I beckoned Jean-Claude over.

I needed to breathe some different air for a while. 'You mind if I go down and take a look at Eve?'

'Not at all. I'll mind the shop.' I handed him the phone. 'You seen Keegan?'

Keegan was the American from Villefranche, the gangmaster who had placed us on *Kubera* as part of the security detail.

'No,' Jean-Claude said. 'But he'll be here somewhere.'

'I hope so.' Keegan had a key part to play in the next stage of the operation.

'We have done this sort of thing before,' he said.

'I'm pleased to hear it. I'll just give her the once over. I won't be long.'

Eve had come aboard in Barcelona, taking up residence in what was normally the sports deck. A couple of RIBs and wetbikes had been offloaded to make room for her. Since I last saw her, lights had been rigged to show off her body to full effect, which had been polished, preened and buffed to within an inch of its life. She sat there mute and imperious, millions of dollars resting on surprisingly skinny tyres.

Balraj was standing to the rear of the vehicle, arms folded across his imposing chest. He beamed when he saw it was me. 'Come to see what all the fuss is about, Miss?' He always called me that. Made me feel about thirteen.

I inhaled the heady esters of varnish and polish. A

woman could get high in that confined space. 'What do they think? The buyers?' I asked him.

'What do *you* think?' He raised an eyebrow as thick as a moth caterpillar.

She was a Bugatti 35B, painted in the standard blue livery, and she was known as Lady Eve, in tribute to the mistress/wife of William Grover-Williams, the man who won the first Monaco Grand Prix back in 1929 and went on to have a career as a Special Operations Executive agent in occupied France. That much was in my file.

There was also the suggestion that Williams once raced this very car, much later, when he substituted for an unwell Louis Chiron at a non-championship race at Circuito Lasarte near San Sebastian in Spain. The claim was unsubstantiated, but I could understand why VJ would want to keep it in circulation – the presence of the legendary Williams behind the wheel of a Bugatti could easily add a few hundred thousand euros to the estimate at auction. Not that this was going to go on the block. It was to be a very private sale.

'She's beautiful,' I said, and for once I was serious.

'You should hear her when she starts up.' He kissed the fingertips of his right hand. 'Such a sweet sound.'

'Any takers?' I asked.

'Several of them certainly want her. You can see it in their eyes. Like lust. But whether that will translate into an offer ...' He shrugged his massive shoulders. 'We shall see, Miss.'

The sale was to be by sealed bids, left by the prospective purchasers as they departed *Kubera*. Over at the salons of the Fairmont Hotel such cars were going under Bonhams' hammer the very next day, making perhaps twenty million euros in a few hours. And a lot of commission, which VJ did not want to pay. Hence the clandestine sale.

I walked around, looking in at leather seats that were cracked and scuffed, with wisps of stuffing poking out like hair from old men's ears. Apparently new seats would actually lower the value. I touched the bodywork and got a little static shock that made me jump. Maybe the car was telling me it was out of my league. Bloody cheek. It wasn't even a league I wanted to play in. 'I'd better go back up top. You expecting anyone else?'

'Petro Groysman.'

Now that was one Ukrainian with very deep pockets and a garage full of supercars. He was rumoured to have a Bugatti 'Tank' as raced at Le Mans in the 1930s. A 35B with Eve's pedigree would bookend that nicely. VJ would hope he would show.

'You all right, Balraj? Can I get you anything?'

'No, Miss. Thank you for asking.'

I went back up top and stepped outside, retrieving my phone from my colleague and taking up my position once more. The sun's strength was waning and a breeze was riffling the waters of the harbour, but the words I heard from a passing waiter ten minutes after my return up top suggested that things were about to hot up.

'*Can you smell smoke?*'

FOUR

I watched VJ in conversation with one of the buyers, a man who had made his fortune promoting Mexican wrestling in South America. My employer was looking increasingly desperate as the prospective purchaser slowly shook his head. Unhappy with that gesture, VJ broke off, abruptly swung away and strode over towards me. 'Has Groysman appeared yet?'

'No, sir.' I made a show of double-checking the list on my phone. 'He might be on the yacht, but he's not been below yet.'

'Shit.'

He looked like tears might course down those plump cheeks at any moment. He pulled out one of those bling-tone, jewel-encrusted Vertu phones, dialled, and walked out of my earshot. His shoulders were hunched in tension. One second he looked like a man basking in sunshine without a care in the world. Anyone who glanced over now would see an anxious character sitting under a cloud that was firing lightning bolts at him.

I checked my watch. Not much longer of this shift now. Later, I would put a call in to my old friend Freddie who was liaising with Colonel d'Arcy while I was on assignment. Like me, Freddie had been an army medic and I trusted her with my life. More importantly, I trusted her with my daughter's life. If the Colonel turned up anything on Jess and I couldn't react, there was nobody I'd rather have in my place than Freddie.

I felt a familiar toxic pool of hatred congeal in my stomach. It was Matt-shaped. My first husband, a cute guy who turned into a drug-addled knobhead before deciding that he deserved to have his daughter back. What the fuck was he thinking? That he'd pluck a ready-made family off the shelf, since he couldn't have kids with the treacherous Laura (his fault, not hers: he'd had a vasectomy when he thought life was nothing but banging bimbos in Ibiza).

'Can you smell smoke?' the waiter asked me.

I sniffed, and at that moment I heard the boom of an explosion, the shattering of glass. Now I could not only smell smoke, I could see the stuff, spiralling up from somewhere near the waterline. More glass broke, this time champagne and martini glasses being dropped. The louche, the sophisticated and the elegant were instantly as jittery as meerkats sensing jackal.

VJ strode quickly towards the rail, his face creased

with worry as the breeze wrapped tendrils of smoke around him.

The second low boom came from starboard and, again, thick grey smoke spewed up, sullying the air. I could hear shouts of alarm coming from other vessels. Our own guests were starting to move aft, as solid as a phalanx of Roman soldiers. I raised a hand and caught Jean-Claude's eye. I indicated he should get everyone off, without a stampede. It would only take one person to fall and there would be carnage. He gave a hand signal back in fluent irritated. *What the hell do you think I'm doing?*

The insistent screech of a smoke alarm kicked off, followed by a second and third, like an electronic choir: danger, danger, danger. Seconds later the deep bass of the music stopped abruptly. Even the DJs had realised something was amiss and the smoke wasn't just incompetent special effects.

VJ was in front of me, aiming to move past. I put a hand on the door.

'Let me past,' he demanded.

'Sir, just think. We don't know what's going on. There's crew down there. They'll take care of it. There might be a fire,' I said, pointing to the twin streams of smoke. *Might?*

'We have sprinklers,' he said. 'State of the art. I have to put the covers on Eve before they deploy.'

The door behind me opened and a thick cloud of

fumes swept over us. From it, Balraj emerged, his frame shaking with his coughing and spluttering. His face was streaked with soot. I pulled the door closed after him.

'Eve?' VJ asked his man.

'The tarpaulin is on,' the Sikh said.

If he was expecting thanks he was mistaken. 'And sprinklers?'

'Not yet.'

'Is there a fire down there?' he asked. 'A real fire? Flames?'

'Not that I could see. No flames.'

That didn't mean a thing. 'You need to get off the boat, sir,' I said. 'For your own safety.'

VJ ignored me and tried to push past.

I barred his way with a shoulder to his chest.

The captain came over the Tannoy, his Aussie voice as calm as ever. 'Ladies and gentlemen, we seem to have an incident in one of the galleys. It is nothing to worry about, probably someone just cremated the toast, but if you'll just make your way off the vessel in an orderly manner, just in case.'

Most were getting off, all right. Orderly didn't have much to do with it, however.

I heard the wail of a police siren over the alarms.

'The captain is right, sir,' I said. 'It's time to evacuate.'

'Don't talk rubbish. I'm going below,' said VJ.

I looked at Balraj; his eyes were red from the gritty smoke that had filled *Kubera*'s lower decks. 'He shouldn't,' I said to him.

VJ jabbed a finger at me. I resisted the urge to grab it and twist. 'Balraj, get her out of the way.'

'Balraj, take him ashore. It's only a fucking car.'

'Only a fucking *car*?' An outraged VJ pulled back his hand as if to slap me.

It was an impulse on his part and his arm snapped back with impressive speed. But I was faster. I punched four stiff fingers into his solar plexus. Assaulting my employers was becoming a habit. As VJ staggered back, his eyes bulging and his mouth making guppy movements, Balraj grabbed my forearm and squeezed. I felt my hand go numb and a stab of pain accelerated up to my shoulder.

'What the hell are you doing?' he demanded.

I twisted away and stepped out of his reach. I transferred my weight to the balls of my feet. If the Sikh wanted a fight, he could have one. But first, I tried reason. After all, he was a big guy to try to take down and, unlike VJ, match fit. 'We're on a boat, standing above a car full of petrol and an engine room with God knows how many gallons of fuel there, next to other boats similarly loaded with flammable material, with smoke pouring out, and he wants to go and check his fucking investment?'

'Balraj ...' VJ gasped.

'You're a BG,' I said, with as much feeling as I could muster. 'Guard your Principal's body, not his bank account.'

I heard a police whistle sounding three sharp trills from the harbourside.

Balraj made up his mind, turned and scooped up VJ into a fireman's lift and headed aft. VJ began kicking his legs in a petulant fit. I managed to keep a straight face.

The door behind me swung open once again and two crew appeared, faces blackened, coughing. 'Sprinkler system has failed,' one of them said.

'What will you do?' I asked.

'Captain's going to take her out to where the harbour fire boat can get to her.'

'OK.'

At that point a group of three cops appeared from the stern, ran past me and took the ladder in double-quick time, en route to the bridge.

The crewmen went off to deal with the lines that secured us to the jetty. Jean-Claude took their place in front of me. 'All OK?'

I felt the deck tremble beneath my feet as the engines started. We were casting off, much to the relief of our nervous neighbours. 'Will be soon.'

'Seen Keegan?'

I nodded. 'Yup. Don't worry, he's here.'

We were nosing out of the berth. On the decks of

our flanking vessels anxious partygoers applauded us, wishing us good luck. But the smoke seemed to be diminishing now. I watched as several police cars, their blue lights pulsing off the shiny frontage of the yacht club, pulled to a halt.

Jean-Claude reached around beneath his jacket and pulled out a Beretta 90two automatic pistol and held it out to me.

'Just in case.'

I hesitated for a minute. I didn't sign up for any shooting. It's not my thing. Not since I left the army. Not since I got shot a while back. That didn't mean I didn't know a thing or two about them. And guns do have a way of changing a situation. I took the Beretta and made sure the safety was clicked on – I like weapons with an old-fashioned manual lever, so you can be sure you won't blow a hole in your thigh – and tucked it into my waistband.

'Now for the tricky bit,' he said.

FIVE

Any vessel longer than 50 metres is required to have a pilot to enter or leave the harbour at Monaco. *Kubera* was thirty-eight metres in length. So no pilot needed. Which was just as well; pilots would probably ask some awkward questions about why the boat only *appeared* to be on fire.

The first thing I did was insert nostril plugs and go below. I located the smoke cylinders that had been hidden earlier in the day and doused them with a fire extinguisher. In truth, they were pretty exhausted anyway. I then made sure that the explosive charges that had been set to blow out windows had all detonated, so there would be no nasty surprises to come. All checked out. Keegan had been as good as his word when he had briefed me in Villefranche and all the gear supplied had been top rate. Most was from companies that supply special and covert forces. You don't get this kind of kit on Amazon.

Eve was still sitting under her lights, her sleek form

58

now shrouded by a thick green rubberised cover, dusted with a grey film of smoke particles. I felt *Kubera* pick up speed and steadied myself. I imagined VJ standing outside the yacht club, watching his pride and joy pass through the breakwater and then lift as she picked up her skirts and ran away from him. Anger and anguish would overwhelm him, meaning it would be a good few minutes before he realised what had really happened.

We had stolen his boat.

After I'd finished I collected an envelope that I had secreted behind an access panel, pulled out the Beretta and threaded my way up to the bridge, ignoring shouted questions from the remaining crew. Nobody tried to stop me. A 90two does that to people – it is the kind of gun that looks like it means business. Before I went onto the bridge, I dropped the magazine from the butt and checked it was loaded. I hesitated. It was. Did I want to be waving a loaded gun about?

But what if you have to fire a warning shot?

If you have to fire a warning shot, things really have gone tits up. I rammed the mag home again. I kept the safety on, though.

I looked at the shore. We had passed Monte Carlo Beach and the Monte Carlo Country Club (both of which are technically in France, not the principality) and *Kubera* was now speeding on east. Round the cape, past Menton and we were in Italy. Home and dry.

I stepped onto the bridge and took in the scene. Jeff, the Australian captain, was standing with his hands on his hips, defiant despite the gun that was being pointed at him. He was dressed in a white shirt with *Kubera* stitched above the breast pocket and shorts that stopped just above his knee, showing tanned legs with sun-bleached hair. Despite the uniform, he looked more like a surf bum than a skipper. But skipper he was, and a mighty pissed-off one judging by the look on his face.

At the wheel was one of the trio of Monegasque cops who had run by me – actually this was Marco, an Italian hired because he knew boats and these waters. The second cop and Jean-Claude kept their weapons levelled at two other *Kubera* crewmen, a couple of Croatians who clearly didn't want any trouble. Standing in front of Jeff was Keegan, who had removed his policeman's hat. It was his gun Jeff was facing down.

'What is this, mate? Piracy? You think we're in bloody Somalia now?'

'Just be patient, captain,' said Keegan evenly. 'We mean you no harm.'

'You've got a bloody funny way of showing it.'

Marco turned and spoke to Keegan. 'OK, out of French waters.' We all knew in borderless Europe that didn't mean much, but it did signify we would be dealing with officials sympathetic to our cause.

Keegan let the tension leach out of his body and the gun barrel dropped an inch or so. 'Sorry, captain. It's just business, that's all.'

He probably shouldn't have ended that sentence with what could be construed as a provocative smirk. Jeff decided to construe it that way. The skipper stepped forward as if he was going to pull Keegan limb from limb. He certainly had the height, but Keegan was pretty bulked up under the policeman's uniform. I saw the Glock in Keegan's hand twitch up.

'Jeff,' I said, walking into the centre of the bridge and sliding between him and Keegan. I had pocketed my pistol and now I handed him the envelope. Over the past couple of days I had made sure I had said hello and chatted to Jeff, so that he would have a familiar face undertaking this particular task. As a temporary hired hand you have to work hard to make sure you are noticed.

He looked at me like I was something he'd found floating in his lavatory bowl. 'What's this?'

I held out the paperwork. 'This is a repossession order, legal in Italy and most other countries, to retrieve *Kubera* and the Bugatti. All official and above board.'

'What?'

'The boat doesn't actually belong to VJ. Never has.'

He snatched the envelope, ripped it open and did a quick scan of the contents. Then he let it fall to the floor. 'Bandogs, huh?' I assumed this was some sort of Australian slang for bailiffs. He shook his head in disbelief and I could see a vein pulsing in his forehead. 'I still think you're jumped-up fuckin' pirates.'

'No,' said Keegan slowly. 'We're retrievers.'

After things had quietened down a little, I went out on the hot-tub deck. I stood at the rail and watched our silvery wake churn up the darkening sea. Strings of lights were appearing along the shoreline and the first stars peeked out from between the scattered clouds.

I felt more favourably towards *Kubera* now. Sitting in harbour she had looked like just another vulgar plaything, a gilded fish almost out of the water. Out here, slicing effortlessly towards Genoa, she could show what she was really built for.

Jeff had accepted the situation once Keegan explained that the 'retrieval' of the yacht included a severance package for captain and crew. Something VJ was unlikely to offer. Turned out Jeff didn't even know *Kubera* was up for sale.

VJ had lost a fortune with his gamble on old steel plants. Everything he once possessed was in hock. The yacht was owned by a bank in Singapore, the Bugatti by an insurance fund in New York. They weren't really his to sell. Which was why the Bugatti sale had been off-the-books. And why his terms of sale had included a buy-back option within twelve months, before, he hoped, New York found out what he had done. But collectors weren't interested in buy-back clauses. They wanted to own their baubles, no strings attached. VJ was treating them as high-class pawnbrokers. It was little wonder there had been no takers.

Ever since the 1980s, whenever such a situation arose, banks and insurance companies had turned to a small group of what came to be known as retrievers. They were really upmarket repo men, debt collectors, bailiffs or, as Jeff put it, bandogs. But taking the goods from the recently rich and powerful was not the same as kicking down a door in Dartford or Detroit and swiping the flat-screen TV. It involved getting past security systems and guards and, very often, required elaborate operations like the one we had just pulled on VJ if nobody was to get hurt. Such undertakings were expensive, and retrievers usually asked for between 10 and 15 per cent of the resale value of goods. There were some very wealthy retrievers around who had yachts that they actually owned.

'Look what I found.'

It was Jean-Claude, holding out two glasses of champagne. I hesitated.

'It's over. Off duty now.'

I took the glass, clinked his and sipped, enjoying the little kick the first alcohol for a week gave me. Enjoying and worrying about it. I shouldn't be so in thrall to it. Not in my line of work.

'Sorry I snapped at you earlier,' he said.

'I deserved it.' It was the truth.

'We all have momentary lapses. You did well.'

'Thank you. Although I am feeling a bit sorry for VJ now.'

Jean-Claude leaned on the rail next to me. 'That's because you see him as your boss, your Principal. We just see him as a mark, someone to be taken down.'

'Still . . .'

'What if I told you something not in the briefing file. That he was a RoHo Roller.'

'A what?'

'I still have friends in the Sûreté. If this had been a normal party on *Kubera*, he would have made sure at least one pretty girl stayed behind for one last . . .' He held up the glass of fizz. 'The next thing she would know, she'd wake up in a state room, underwear missing, her insides feeling as if someone had been using a cheese grater on her.'

'Nice image.'

'Nice guy. He uses machines on them, sex machines, and films it on that fancy phone of his.'

I felt VJ's champagne turn to acid in my stomach. 'RoHo is Rohypnol?'

'Or something similar,' said Jean-Claude.

'Nice.'

'It was how we managed to get Balraj on board with this whole thing. He had no part in it, in the drugging and filming, but he is not a stupid man. He knew that VJ was up to something unsavoury. We just told him what that was and he came onside.'

The whole charade of Balraj carrying VJ off the ship had been prearranged. He was never going to let him go below. My stab to VJ's pudgy solar plexus was just an improvisation on my part. Now I wish I'd prodded him a little harder. 'VJ was lucky the Sikh didn't toss him overboard. It wouldn't be the first time a Sikh bodyguard had turned on their employer.'

'And you didn't choose to tell me about his little hobby?'

He shook his head. 'Keegan and I agreed. You had to behave entirely natural around him. We thought this information might ... colour your judgement. And, therefore, affect your behaviour towards him. Bust millionaire is one thing, but a man who likes filming unconscious girls being penetrated by a Robo-Fuk machine?'

I laughed despite my disgust. I really hoped he had made that name up. 'You were thinking I might swing him around the poop deck by his skinny dick?'

'Something like that. But by taking away his toys, we have saved many young women from such an unpleasant experience.' He gave me a smile that showed some expensive dentistry. 'Feel sorry for him now?'

'Well, I'd definitely unfriend him.' I took another hit of the champagne, reasoning that Veuve Clicquot was an innocent party in all this. I pulled some wind-blown hair out of my face. Jean-Claude's coiffure had, of course, barely moved. 'However, you are not Robin Hoods, are you? You didn't do this to right such wrongs. That was a fringe benefit. And you'll be a wealthy man now, I suppose.' Jean-Claude was on a percentage with Keegan. I was on a fixed salary, a third up front, the rest on final sign-off of the job.

He gave an unapologetic shrug. 'When I retired from the Sûreté I bought a vineyard near Beaune. Last year my *vigneron* died and I brought in a young lady from New Zealand. Very progressive. Very expensive. I am in a rich man's game without being a rich man. You?'

'Mine's all accounted for too,' I said. 'At least the first tranche.' I had already spent the initial retainer/expenses on the watch list and it would be months before all the monies finally came through – the companies who hire the retrievers usually don't pay the full amount until all sales of recovered goods have been completed.

'Why don't you sign up for another job with us in the meantime?' he asked. 'Keegan would be happy to have you.'

It was my turn to raise my shoulders towards my ears. 'I'm not really a retriever. This was a one-off. I prefer looking after people to stealing from them.'

'I have done your job,' Jean-Claude said. 'Looking

after the rich and pampered. My God, it's boring. Yellow status, orange status, clear to go, emergency evac. I don't know how you do it. With us, we never know what is next. There is a Gulfstream in Hong Kong that needs to be retrieved, a garage full of Ferraris in Dubai, a house in Barbados to be cleared and sold while the so-called owner is off skiing, a Takashi Murakami lifted from a secure vault. There's real adrenaline in that. And good money every time you pull a job off.'

'And between jobs?'

'I make my wine. And drink it.'

'That last part sounds more up my street. But I've had my share of excitement,' I said, truthfully.

'In the army?'

That, and in a garage in north London with men coming to kill me. But I didn't really want to be there again, not even in conversation. It could have ended very differently. With me dead. 'Yes. I think fundamentally we do different things. I'm there to stop the client getting fucked. You lot are there to fuck the client.'

'That's rather a reductive way of looking at it. In many ways we are the good guys – you keep the status quo, protecting the interest of an elite. We redistribute the wealth a little.'

'Back to the banks and financial institutions. That's not much of a redistribution, is it? As I said, not quite Robin Hood.'

'*Touché.*' I might have imagined it, but he appeared to move a little closer when he asked the next question. 'And is there a man in your life?'

Oh, for God's sake. I wondered what his idea of a 'wrap' party for a job entailed. A quick roll in the sack with a suave Frenchman? I put some air between us.

'I am only interested. I'm not *interested*,' he said, catching my repositioning. 'Marco is more my type. If you understand.'

Well I'll be damned, I thought. My gaydar must be faulty. 'There is a man. Sort of.' Tom Buchan. At least, that was the handle he was using when I met him. He had taken on several others since. But he was still Tom to me.

'You don't sound very certain.'

'It's complicated.'

'I used to be a cop.' I wondered if his being gay had anything to do with him leaving the Sûreté at a relatively tender age. 'Complicated is second nature to me.'

It was probably because I had finished the champagne, on an empty stomach, that I told him about Tom and Paul, my late husband. How they had rescued a young girl from a gang of rapists in Kosovo, but how Tom had let one of them, a mere boy, live. Now that boy had turned into a vicious gangster who had pledged to track down the British peacekeeping unit that had murdered his brothers, uncles and cousins on a lonely hillside. He had done just that to four of them, including Paul who, I now believed, had been executed for what happened all those years ago. So, Tom and the surviving members of the K-FOR patrol were in hiding, living under assumed identities until Leka, the Albanian warlord hunting them, was put somewhere where he was no longer a threat. Preferably with his brothers, uncles and cousins.

Jean-Claude pursed his lips in thought when I had finished. 'My sympathies are with the British soldiers, of course. I think they did the world a favour by killing those men.'

'They felt they had no choice. They had broken the NATO mandate by intervening.'

'Oh, I think there is a greater moral imperative than that.' He drained his own glass. 'Would you like me to ask my friends at the Sûreté if they have anything on this Leka? After all, he might be dead and your friend can breathe easy. Albanian warlords have a very finite lifespan.'

'Would you? You can always get a message to me through Keegan. He has all my details.'

'It would be my pleasure. And where is your man now?'

I stole a glance at my watch. With a bit of luck, I thought, packing for the early-morning flight to Cristoforo Colombo airport. 'Come on,' I said, and pushed off the rail. 'I'd like to see what Genoa looks like from the bridge of a forty-million-euro yacht.'

Most of the retrievers went off to party in the bars along the narrow rat-run *i vicoli*, the web of alleys connecting the Old Town of Genoa to the port. I checked into my hotel and, after a quick shower, took myself down to the lobby bar rather than watch TV in my room. Keegan was there, nursing an open bottle of champagne. He had changed into a white open-necked shirt and pale-blue trousers with loafers. With his dark hair swept back he could pass for one of the locals. He gestured for me to sit down.

'I thought you'd be out with the others,' I said.

'I'll catch them for dinner. I'm here to persuade you to come along.'

'Thanks. But I'm going to turn in early,' I said.

'Well, I wanted a word anyway. Jean-Claude told me you are giving up the retrieving game.'

'I never really started it,' I said, taking the glass of champagne he had poured me. 'It was simply a favour. Cheers.'

Well, not a favour. Just a way of earning cash to fund the Colonel's watch list. But I didn't feel like going into all that. I really did want an early night.

'Cheers.'

We drank. Out of habit I scanned the room, right to left, looking for anomalies. Apart from the elegantly attired woman perched on a stool at the bar who rented by the hour, nothing stood out.

'I don't get you,' Keegan said, picking at a bowl of crackers. 'And that bothers me.'

'There's not much to get.'

He laughed. 'You're kidding, right? You telling me you have a nice, uncomplicated life? A missing daughter. A boyfriend under a death threat? J-C filled me in. It's not really a story of everyday folk down on the farm, is it?'

I drank some more, enjoying the buzz. I had to be careful. I didn't want to meet Tom with a hangover. It always got things off on the wrong foot. 'It is what it is. Not what I chose.'

'Look, I have a crazy idea. Why don't you come and work for us? It's a pretty good life. Travel the world. Steal things from people. Things that don't belong to them.'

'Sounds like fun,' I admitted. 'But as I told Jean-Claude, no. Thank you.'

His fingers drummed on the table while his brain turned over. 'So, this Albanian J-C told me about. Quite a tale. Seems like your guy is in pretty deep shit. I know what these Balkan guys are like. Terriers with a bone. What's the Albanian called again?'

'Leka.'

His brow furrowed in thought. 'You know, the name almost rings a bell. What if we could get the

71

skinny on him? Maybe neutralise him somehow. How about that?'

'Why would you do that?'

'Because we like you.'

'Bollocks.'

He laughed. 'OK, because we often need a woman in the set-up for a retrieval and qualified, trustworthy ones are few and far between. They've got the looks but not the brains, or ... well, you know. You have both.'

'Is that flattery I see before me?' At my age, even after fifty years of feminism, I was still susceptible to a compliment from a good-looking guy. Call me shallow. I can handle it.

'No. It's the truth. I'm offering you a simple business deal.'

I let out a sigh. 'So you are saying, using Jean-Claude's contacts, you'll find out about Leka and let me know if he constitutes a real threat.'

'That's about the size of it.'

'And figure out a way to make that threat go away.'

'If it's possible, yes.'

'And if you do, then I come and work for you.'

'You got it.'

I hadn't had enough champagne to make me completely reckless. Just a little. 'I'll tell you what. You find out about Leka, and I'll *consider* coming to work for you.'

Keegan looked at my empty glass and signalled for another bottle. Then he held out his hand. 'It's a deal.'

I took it, cursing the drink in my bloodstream and wondering what I had let myself in for. I wouldn't have to wait too long to find out.

SIX

Northern Italy

Tom had hired a car at the airport. I had told him to source an Alfa, but it turned out he'd gone for a Fiat Panda with a shitty semi-automatic gearbox. I let it pass and we drove south, more jerkily than I would have liked. He had some romantic idea about staying at Portofino, maybe at the Splendido. I squashed that like a bug. He'd be disillusioned by the miniature Chanel and Gucci boutiques squeezed into the old fisherman's net stores. Also, I was well aware that Portofino was just the place that people with PPs frequent. I was in no mood to bump into former colleagues or clients while tucking into risotto on the terrace of the Splendido Mare.

Besides, my funds wouldn't last long there. Portofino is the kind of place where it's always best if someone else picks up the tab. So I told Tom to keep the Fiat on the E80, heading for Pisa.

'I've seen the Leaning Tower,' he said grumpily as the turn-offs for Portofino slid past.

'Me too,' I said. I gave him what I hoped was my best enigmatic just-you-wait-and-see smile. He just shook his head in mock despair. I liked that about Tom. Recent events had made him more phlegmatic and accepting of what came his way. He used to have this theory that Trouble, with a capital T, was always following him around. I think he was learning to accept that shit happens and it happens to most people. Look at me.

Stop that. Self-pity is not an attractive look for a date night.

Friend Nina in my head. Nina right. Again.

I had been toying with Lucca, but in the end I opted for Forte dei Marmi. It was May and I reckoned the beaches wouldn't yet be lined with oiled bodies sequestered in overpriced – but I had to admit, elegant – *bagni* or beach clubs, and that we'd get tables at Lorenzo or L'Enoteca at Pietrasanta, up in the hills among the marble quarries that gave Forte its name. I had been there as a PPO to a pop star's wife when Armani and his partner threw a party at their villa on Roma Imperiale, all laurel hedges, sprinkled lawns and Olympic-sized pools with a spray of international glitterati patrolling the grounds. But I got to see a little of the resort beyond the gates and walls of the lavishly porticoed private villas.

Forte wasn't that much cheaper than Portofino, but it had the sort of passionate dedication to indolence I needed. And we could always live on the pizzas from Pizzeria Orlando, which, as I recalled, stayed open till three in the morning, and eat cheap pasta at the Nelson Club. It was also, the Russians aside, very understated. You might be an Agnelli or a Juventus star, but it was all about dressing down and keeping a low profile. That included ditching the PPOs, so I was unlikely to meet anyone on the Circuit there.

The suite I had booked at the Byron overlooked the main drag and its row of ninety-odd beach clubs. The room was a duplex, with the bedroom on the upper level, with one of those beds piled so high with cushions, it takes ten minutes to get them all off before you strike pillow. And if you aren't careful, you spend the rest of the stay tripping over them.

I sat on the edge of the mattress and bounced in the time-honoured way that tells you very little at all. Tom sat next to me and put an arm round my shoulders. I felt myself stiffen a little. I wasn't used to letting another human get so close.

'How do you do this again?' I asked.

'You relax. Christ, it's like you're made of iron.'

I untangled myself, stood and went downstairs, opened the French doors to the terrace and stepped out, letting the breeze blow across my face. I had a little thumping behind my eyes from the champagne that I was trying to ignore. With Keegan's considerable help we had finished off the second bottle. The walk back to my room was less than steady. But I had been alone, despite Keegan's no-doubt chivalrous offer to escort me.

Would I tell Tom about his offer of work? No, because it might be nothing, just post-caper bluster on Keegan's part. I'd divulge the deal I had made with the retrievers once I had something concrete. But part of me was annoyed for letting myself be manoeuvred into a position where I might be in Keegan's debt.

Tom had followed me down and was standing a few paces behind me. Across the road the sun was dropping, the shadows lengthening, the daybeds on the beach were emptying, the sand groomed once more by the army of rake-wielding *bagnini*. Soon a languorous *passeggiata* would start on and around the pier just to the north of us, as fiercely competitive as any F1 race, only a lot slower.

I heard Tom clear his throat. I knew what that meant. I waited while he summoned up whatever reserves he needed in order to tell me some bad news. 'Sam. I've been seeing someone.'

I folded my arms and closed my eyes. Of course. Intermittent Lover Syndrome. How could I expect him to wait for my erratic phone calls? He had probably hooked up with a nice, uncomplicated woman with a proper job and a stable background. Me? I came with more baggage than Terminal Five.

I was aware he was behind me, hovering. 'Don't,' I said.

'Don't what?'

'Put your arms around me and nuzzle my neck.'

'You are a scary mind-reader.'

'Who have you been seeing?'

'I thought you'd be pleased.'

'Really?'

'Her name is Rachel. The thing is, she's good. Bloody good.'

'Spare me the sordid details.'

'Sam! Jesus.' He spun me round and waited until I opened my eyes. Part of me was already wondering where to hit him first. 'She's good at *listening*.'

Listening? He'd be telling me he had found his *soulmate* next and I'd have to retch.

'I got her through OCC7.'

This was part of the Organised Crime Command of the National Crime Agency, charged with preventing criminal activity organised by foreign nationals on UK soil. They took a special interest in death threats and potential assassinations. As Tom was a target for action by a disaffected Albanian drug lord, it was part of their remit to keep him alive. But to supply him with women?

'I never thought I'd do it. See a shrink, I mean.'

'A shrink?' Something flooded through me. Not exactly relief, more recrimination and embarrassment at my stupidity.

'Well, strictly speaking, she is a psychotherapist. She's been helping me with all that *Trouble-Will-Always-Find-Me* bullshit.'

It used to be his mantra, the feeling that, if he stuck in one place too long, bad things would happen. But trouble *has* found you, I thought. I found you. Which is much the same thing.

I unfolded my arms. 'That Trouble-Will-Always-Find-Me shit, the constant moving on, that might just have kept you alive.'

I couldn't believe I was defending his paranoiac tendencies.

'She knows that. It's more to do with interpersonal relationships. Learning to trust. And to accept what has happened. To deal with the past, not bury it so deep it festers.'

Ah. I saw where this was going.

'You know my father was in Northern Ireland?' he asked.

That wrong-footed me. 'I didn't know you had a father. I mean, obviously you did. But we've never talked about our families.' Apart from Jess. Otherwise, I had good reason not to speak of my miserable bastard of a deceased father, nor the meek, scared mouse he turned my mother into over the course of their marriage.

'Well, I still have a dad. Lives in the Isle of Man. When I was growing up, after he had left the army, he

79

had this funny habit of always going through doors sideways. You know, left shoulder first.'

'To offer up as small a target as possible?' I asked.

Tom nodded. 'And another thing. He always sent us on ahead into a darkened room to switch on the light. He was OK if the switch was just inside the room, but if he had to cross it . . .'

'He'd done a lot of house-to-house?'

'I guess so. He never talked about it and, to be honest, for all I knew as a kid, every dad did that. But, yes, he'd done two tours in Northern Ireland. Had a rough time. You can imagine – it was a very dirty war. And he'd lived with what he found in those rooms when he was doing house clearances – booby traps, dead snouts, some of whom had been tortured, traumatised women who had watched their boyfriends, brothers or husbands get tapped. Sometimes they found nothing, sometimes nothing but bloodstains. Fifty years he had lived with all that. Five decades of night sweats and fear of the dark. Until he went to therapy. Now he's only angry that he didn't do it a long time ago.'

'He can probably have therapy for that.'

He spun away. 'I knew it was a fuckin' waste of time. I'm saying it helped him, it's helping me, it might do something for you.'

'Tom, I don't have PTSD.'

He was back in front of me in one long stride. 'No? Then why do you do this fuckin' stupid, dangerous work? Eh? It's not normal. And even if you haven't got combat stress, what about Jess, eh? She's your version of the darkened room. You need to come to terms with what's happened.'

'You really expect me to answer that? She's my *daughter*. She's been *taken*. There's nothing to come to terms with.'

I saw a fleeting moment of vindictiveness in his face. 'Then how come—'

'What?'

The expression faded as quickly as it had arrived. He ran a hand through his hair and gave a hollow laugh. 'This isn't going quite as planned. I'm sorry. I was just saying, it might do some good to talk about it. About Iraq, Jess, Matt, what happened in that garage. You know? Just talk it out instead of slamming shut like a steel trap and internalising it all.'

I took a deep breath. There was part of me that just wanted to walk out the door. Call the whole thing off. Another part liked it better when I thought he had a new girlfriend. At least he couldn't lecture me from that moral high ground then. But I also knew he was right. Caring and sharing wasn't me. You don't meet many touchy-feely PPOs.

'Can you do me a favour?' I asked.

'Of course.'

'Go to the bar and have a drink? Maybe we can start this over. I just need a little time. Alone.'

His eyes narrowed suspiciously.

'I'll still be here when you get back,' I said, probably not too reassuringly.

'Fifteen minutes?'

'Thirty would be good.'

'OK. See you in half an hour.'

I watched him scoop up the room key and his wallet and exit without looking back. After he had left I let out a long sigh. Men. Women. Relationships. War. Rum.

I went to the minibar and mixed myself a Havana Club 7 with a diet Coke and went back to the terrace. Hair of the dog, I told myself. A handsome, elegant couple in their thirties, dressed entirely in white, were cycling slowly towards the centre of town, probably for an *aperitivo* somewhere they could be admired. I marvelled at the uncreased linen – she a floaty dress, he a suit – they were wearing. They were the epitome of *la bella figura* that the Italians strive for.

The British don't get the beach clubs of places like Forte. Why pay up to 350 euros just for the privilege of lying on a sunbed under an umbrella? After all, sitting on the sand at Southwold or Broadstairs or Pembrokeshire is free. But Brits also lug umbrellas, windbreaks, towels, picnics, children and other bulky paraphernalia down the beach, arriving red-faced and panting. After a few visits to Forte and Sardinia, I understood perfectly. What the Italians are paying for at a *bagna* is freedom from this sort of donkey work. The quest for *la bella figura* trumped all else.

Maybe Tom was right, I thought, as I sipped the rum. Maybe I did need my head testing. But I didn't need telling what to do about Jess. Finding her was a given, no matter how long, how much money or how many people I had to hurt along the way. I thought about the phone hidden in the lining of my bag. On it were all those precious messages from Jess. The ones I listened to which help get me to sleep some nights. Even hearing the short, sharp 'Oh, mum', 'You don't understand!' and the 'Whatever' messages helped. Just the sound of her voice, petulance and all, was a comfort. But now wasn't the time to curl up with Jess.

I looked down and my glass was empty. Another?

No. I stripped off my clothes and went into the bathroom. It had a walk-in shower with an oversized head and controls that would have baffled Captain Kirk. I eventually managed to set it to a bearable temperature and stepped in. For once the shampoo was in generous grown-up-sized bottles and I lathered up and then stood under the rainshower spray for a good five minutes.

I felt something give in my back. I rotated my shoulders and pushed them up towards my ears. They actually moved freely for once. Another muscle or two popped and I did a few side stretches. I had been coiled up so tight, it was as if I had been shellacked.

Like an armadillo, as my masseuse used to say. Back when I had a masseuse. But now I could feel the fibres beneath my skin slackening. Maybe there was something to this relaxing lark after all. And if Tom was right about that ...

No. No trick cycling. Not yet. Maybe when it's all over and I have Jess back. What was I frightened of? That too much self-analysis might take the edge off. In truth, that I might lose the anger that drove me on. 'Feed the rat,' as climbers say. That's what I needed to do. Keep giving scraps to the rodent gnawing at my insides.

I grabbed the body wash and soaped all over. I tugged at my pubes as I did so. Could probably do with a trim ...

I heard him pad into the bathroom on bare feet and step into the cubicle behind me. His breathing was shallow and I realised he was going to try to make me jump in surprise. 'Don't you know better than to sneak up on a woman with PTSD?' I turned and he put his hands on my waist. 'I might have thought you were ISIS scum and broken your neck.'

'You never fought ISIS.'

'I haven't got PTSD either.' I looked down. 'And I see you've brought your little friend with you.'

'Hey, less of the little.'

'Tom, do me a favour?'

'Another one?'

84

'Yes. It's sort of son of the first one. For the next half-hour or so ...' I put a soapy finger to his lips. 'Just shut the fuck up.'

Later, I decided we'd eat in the glass box that was the Byron's restaurant, overlooking the pool and gardens. I didn't feel up to a fashion face-off at Bistrot or Osteria del Mare. I thought Tom would find the wine-list-sized selection of different mineral waters amusingly pretentious, but he waved it away, and went for the real thing, huffing over a list of Chianti that filled several pages. In the end he jabbed a finger at one in the middle of the list. 'That one, please,' he said to the server.

'And some water would be good. Tap is fine,' I added.

The waiter gave the merest hint with his expression that perhaps tap water wasn't fine when they had Veen and Tasmanian Rain on offer, but he smiled anyway.

'You OK?' I asked.

'Yes. Of course. I just ...'

I waited.

'I find it hard to relax in these places.' He picked up a piece of cutlery and waved it at me. 'All this. You know what I mean ... all this flummery.'

When I had met Tom he had been living on a canal boat. He was what is known as a constant cruiser, a peripatetic inhabitant of the waterways, slated to move on every few days. He missed that life. He was right, he was more about mooring rights than Michelin stars. But there was nothing wrong with a little flummery once in a while.

'You seemed to be having an OK time just now,' I said, my eyes flicking back to the hotel.

The smile he gave me back looked strained. I was aware that, whereas I felt as floppy as a filleted flounder, there was a rod of tension running through Tom. We appeared to have swapped places, me loose and easy, him stiff and unyielding. As the waiter poured the wine, Tom wouldn't quite catch my gaze. Damn him, I thought. I had sunk beneath the waves, to that place where I felt comfortably numb, where my constant pain was a small, distant thing, and he was forcing me to surface and breathe the harsh air of real life. As he made to drink, I reached over and gripped his wrist.

'Tom, what is it? You pissed off that I wouldn't take your therapy idea seriously?'

'No. I expected that. I had to try.'

'And I'm not dismissing it out of hand. I'll think about it. Promise.' Jesus, I must be relaxed. 'Is it this Leka business? Has something happened?'

'No.' He took the glass with his other hand and gulped. 'Not with me. I talked this over with Freddie, and she said it was best—'

'You talked what over with Freddie? Have you two been plotting something behind my back?'

His gaze bored into the table. 'Not really.'

The word 'intervention' popped into my head. 'Yes, really. What was it you decided was "for the best"?'

Another clearing of the throat. 'That you heard this in person. And from me. After all, what difference would twenty-four hours make? And if you abandoned your job down here, well . . .'

I leaned in across the table, knocking over my glass of water, and hissed. All the good that the last hour had done me disappeared, like a caged bird finding the door open and fluttering off as fast as its wings would carry it. I felt the springs inside me re-coil. 'What the fuck are you talking about, Tom?'

'Thing is, Sam . . . Jess has been in touch.'

SEVEN

London

Saanvi was an old schoolfriend of Jess's. Her parents had a house on Highbury Fields and I insisted Freddie drove me straight there after the pick-up from Heathrow. 'Shower first?' she had suggested. I demurred. She sniffed to show this was a bad idea, but for once didn't argue. As usual the M4 was snarled, the Hangar Lane Gyratory System refused to gyrate, so we had plenty of time to talk. Or rather, for me to rant.

'What gets me is he waited to tell me until *after* we had had sex. Like it slipped his mind or something. Jesus, I thought he was better than that.' I went on in that vein for quite some time, before concluding: 'But he's like every other bloke, isn't he? Sex first, everything else can wait.'

Freddie changed lanes as we moved over to come off the A40. The building containing a storage company that always had strange or witty installations on top – a fighter jet, the Tardis, a Trabant – had an EU flag apparently shot full of holes and a tattered Union flag. 'That was my idea,' said Freddie.

For a moment I thought she meant the flags but then the truth dawned on me. I glanced at her but she was apparently concentrating on positioning herself for the off ramp. Her hands gripped the wheel like a bird's feet on a perch. She had grown out her hair from the pixie cut she had favoured during our days in Iraq. She looked softer, more feminine, even when, as now, she was devoid of make-up. I looked like I'd not only been dragged through a hedge backwards, I had brought said hedge with me. I hadn't slept since Tom's little revelation.

'I told him it would be best to delay telling you.'

'You did what?' I spat and the last word was dripping with so much venom, I was surprised her left side didn't go numb.

'Told him to wait. Not to blurt out the news immediately.'

I spoke through teeth that were not so much gritted as cemented together. 'And what was the thinking behind that?'

'Sam, we only heard about this less than forty-eight hours ago. I knew you'd drop everything if we told you – thus voiding whatever contract you had.'

I had told Freddie a sketchy outline of the retrieval operation, where I'd be, how to contact me in case of emergency. All she knew was the job was helping me pay for the search for Jess. She approved of that, because wages had been thin on the ground since I lost my SIA accreditation.

'And Tom wouldn't have had a chance to mention his therapy . . .'

'Oh, yeah. That was a high point. Christ. How dare you assume you know what is best for me?'

'OK, in retrospect—'

'No, not in retrospect,' I said. 'It was a bad idea from the moment you had it. Jesus.' I crossed my arms as aggressively as I could.

'Jesus nothing. We informed Connie straight away.' Detective Constable Connie Farnham was the FLO assigned to my case. Although why I needed a Family Liaison Officer when my family had been stolen from me I wasn't sure. Anyway, she was the interface between me, the police here and Europol. Her main job was to gather evidence that might be useful to the investigating team, whether from me or Jess's teachers and circle of friends. It wasn't Connie Farnham's fault nothing had been turned up and that Jess's trail was cold. Although I often acted like it was. 'She's on it. There was – is – little you can do. So I thought you deserved some fun.'

'Fun?' I made it sound like 'pus' or some other unfortunate bodily secretion.

'You know, sometimes a girl just needs—'

'Yes, thank you,' I snapped. I was in no mood for Freddie's vulgar aphorisms.

Traffic congealed on the approach to the junction for IKEA. I looked out of the window, amazed at the change in light from the Riviera. We were capped by a leaden sky, the grey uniformity broken by splodges of dark clouds, like liver spots. I was feeling pretty liverish myself. How could he agree? Tom? He knew this was the most important thing in my life.

I had pretended to forgive him, waited until he had fallen asleep after he had consumed the lion's share of the red wine, then left the hotel, took the Alfa and drove down to Pisa to get on the first flight to London. Let him figure out the rest. The nine missed calls on my phone suggested he was still trying.

'He's a bloke,' said Freddie, as if this would be news to me. 'He knew the way it worked. He could tell you the news and watch you go straight back to London. Or he could have a shag first and you get the flight the next day. I suggested that you'd welcome the chance to have your brains banged out.'

'Thank you, Dr Freddie.'

'Welcome. My bill is in the post. And, you know, he's stuck around for you.'

'He's living under an assumed name in Nottingham. He's hardly stuck around.'

'He's been there on the rare occasions you've needed him.' She shot me one of her fiercest glances. 'You are lucky to have Tom. Someone who will come at the drop of a hat like he does. A proper fuck buddy. And then some.'

Is that what he was? I suppose so. I just wasn't used to framing it in the current vernacular.

'You ever consider he is risking his life every time he breaks cover?'

There was some truth in that assertion. We had to be careful because we had no idea if the Albanians were still after their revenge. So we acted like we were drug dealers or spies, with cut-outs, letter drops and burner phones. No emails, no regular post, no landlines. If it was a love affair, it was a very strange one. But Freddie was right. I might not see him for two months but if I got a message to him and said I was in Biarritz or Barnet and needed him, he'd drop everything and come running. Was that risking his life? Possibly. Just because we hadn't seen any sign of the aggravated Albanians, didn't mean they weren't out there.

And the thought had occurred to me: they don't have to find him. They just have to watch me. He would turn up eventually. I comforted myself with the thought that I was very unlikely to be on their radar.

We drove in silence for a few miles while I seethed, albeit with a little less commitment to the cause.

'Sorry,' she said softly. 'I wasn't thinking. About Tom, I mean.'

I was in no mood to let her off the hook. 'The

problem is, you *were* thinking. Too much. It's very simple. Anything happens that has something to do with Jess, you tell me right away. No ifs and buts and no pause while I get some dick.'

'It was just a thought.'

'A bad one.'

She stomped on the brakes as we came up to a speed camera, maybe a little harder than necessary. She was back on the attack.

'The truth is, you've been moping and miserable and running yourself into the ground. There has been no light in your life at all. It's all shade. No *fun*.' The word sounded better on her lips. 'Look, if I didn't love you, I'd have to say I wouldn't like you very much right now.'

'What?'

'You know what I mean. And just think it through instead of sticking metal pins in Tom or me. Two things might have happened if I had called. One, you walked straight off the job and came home. Two, you decided you were too professional for that and you stayed, but with your edge gone. And that would have been dangerous. Am I right?'

I thought about it. Would I have turned to Jean-Claude and said, sorry, something has come up, I'm off? 'I'd probably have stayed. On balance.'

'Right. But, the knowledge would have eaten into you, distracted you. Maybe made you fuck up on something important.'

93

'You figured all this out?'

'I'm figuring it out with hindsight,' she said. 'It's true though. And it's true I told Tom to let you relax, unwind from the job, before he broke the news.'

She smiled as we ascended the flyover at Brent Cross. It was what they called an infectious grin and I envied her for it. Freddie could probably disarm a jumpy jihadist with a quick flash of her teeth. I turned away slightly. I was in no mood to be disarmed.

'I still can't believe he did it.'

'He wouldn't have if you had looked like that.'

'Thanks. And I didn't mean the sex.'

'I know. There's some make-up in the back. Help yourself.'

'I'm fine,' I grunted.

'Only if you want to make small children run away from you screaming.' She broke out her best West Country accent. 'You look like shit, my lover.'

I spent the rest of the journey trying to un-shit my face.

Saanvi's parents owned the lower two floors of an impressive pile right on Highbury Fields. He was, as I recalled, a surgeon or maybe a dentist, and had already left for work. His wife was obviously office-ready too, impeccably turned out in a two-piece powder-blue suit and groomed to within an inch of her life. I felt like a corpse next to her.

We sat in the living room, the three of us. Its ceiling-height French doors overlooked a garden the size of a small municipal park. Two gardeners were turning over a bed under a wall of yellow London stocks. I could hear the scrape of violin practice from above. Saanvi's younger sister. It all looked like an idyllic set-up for family life in the capital. Something I would never know, even if Jess came back. I had made my life choices and they had blown up in my face like a roadside IED.

Missing: two husbands (one dead, one absconded) and a daughter. Whereabouts: unknown.

Saanvi was sitting in a button-backed leather armchair, knees together, hands on her lap. I was amazed by how much the girl had changed, blossomed. She looked like her mother, but with quite startling brown doe-eyes and even sharper cheekbones. She had acquired poise and a pair of breasts in the year since I had last seen her, when she had been hanging around my living room with Jess. She was wearing her school uniform, but it looked all wrong on her, as if she were an adult going to a fancy-dress party. Was Jess also changing into a gamine young lady? Or was she some Bohemian wild child being dragged around drug dens and flophouses by my no-good ex?

'Thanks for waiting for me,' I began.

'Are you sure you don't want a tea or coffee?' the mother offered.

95

'No, thank you, I won't keep you longer than necessary. And Freddie's waiting on the lines.'

'Very well.'

I turned my attention to Saanvi. 'I know you must have told this a dozen times . . .'

'That's OK,' she said quickly. 'I'm glad to help find Jess.'

'So, from the top. When did you hear from her?'

'It was twelve fifty-three. In the morning. Wednesday morning, that is.' The precision was no doubt due to the time display on her phone.

'She should have been asleep then,' said her mother through pursed lips. 'And there is a "phones-off" policy at midnight in this house. I was passing Saanvi's room when I heard the ping of an incoming message and went in to investigate.'

Saanvi glanced at her mum. 'I told you. I just knew something was going to happen, so for once I left it on.'

Nobody in the room believed that but I was relieved the mother let it pass.

'Have you still got the phone?'

'No. The police lady took it.'

That would be Connie. 'Do you have a copy of the text?'

I was relieved when she nodded. 'They copied all my contents and data over to a new phone. An iPhone 7,' she said proudly. 'I only had a 5S before.'

I made a mental note to find out who paid for the

new handset. It wouldn't be fair if it were the family that had footed the bill. 'And it was the first time you had heard from her?'

'Yes, the first text in a year.'

'But you didn't recognise the number?'

'No. But I recognised the sign-off name. Poobag.'

'Poobag?'

'It's a sort of nickname.'

First I'd heard of it. 'It's not very nice.'

'It's meant in an affectionate way. We called each other that when we started secondary school, like a little gang. *Hi, Poobag*, that sort of thing. It's what the tattoo says . . .' the voice trailed off.

'What tattoo?' I asked.

Saanvi froze. Her mother came over and sat on the arm of the chair and stroked the girl's hair. It was oddly intimidating, as if she might grab a handful at any minute. But her voice suggested otherwise, it was as soft as velvet. Which was even scarier. 'Do you have a tattoo, darling?'

'No, of course not.' She looked her mother in the eye. 'I wouldn't. Not without asking. And I know what the answer would be.'

'But Jess has one?' the mother asked on my behalf.

A short, sharp nod was the answer.

'Jess is underage,' I said. 'And not just underage. Three years short of eighteen. And when you say "it's what it says" . . .'

97

'The tattoo is in Sanskrit. Or Thai. Or something like that.'

I looked at her mother, whose face had collapsed into concern. 'Can I change my mind about the coffee if you don't mind?'

It was a few seconds before she nodded and left.

I took a deep breath. 'Saanvi, what you say to me is just between us. I will not pass anything on to your mother, I promise. I don't care if you have the Stars and Stripes tattooed across your arse.' That got a smile out of her. 'All I care about is Jess. I don't even care about the Poobag tattoo.'

Something in Saanvi's expression told me I should care. Her lower lip began to quiver.

'When did she get it? This tattoo.'

'About six months ago.'

Which meant six months after she disappeared. I felt the certainties of the last few minutes of conversation crumble like ash. I took another, deeper breath, and tried to calm the storm of anger swirling round my brain. It wouldn't help. 'Shall we start again? You said the other night's text was the first time you had heard from Jess.'

Saanvi swallowed hard. 'I said it was the first time I received a text.'

It was an effort to keep my voice level. 'So she's called you?'

'No.'

'Tweeted?'

A look of disdain briefly distorted her features. 'Nobody tweets any more.' That was also news to me. I was learning a lot. Just not what I wanted to know.

'Look, Saanvi, I'm an old woman. Over thirty. I'm not up on the latest social media. We could play guess-the-platform all morning. How did she get in touch?'

'Snapchat.'

'Snapchat,' I repeated, sounding like a particularly dull three-year-old.

'It's—'

'Even I know what it is, Saanvi. The images delete after ten seconds.'

'Up to ten seconds. You can choose shorter if you wish.'

Marvellous. 'How many times did she use it?'

'Twice, I think.'

'And did you reply?'

'On the chat screen, yes. I asked where she was and if she was OK.'

'And did she reply?'

'No.'

'Did you tell Connie, the policewoman, about this?'

She shook her head, her face clouded with guilt. 'I'm sorry. Jess said to tell no one.'

'You said she didn't reply.'

'It was written over the photos. You can put text on top of the pictures. "Please don't tell anyone," it said.'

'And is there any way to retrieve the photos?'

'If you take a screen shot you can keep them.'

I'd heard that part, of course. It was how embarrassing photos, which the sender thought were as ephemeral as mayflies, suddenly found eternal life on the internet.

'And did you take a screen shot?' I asked.

But I already knew the answer. 'No.'

'Are the images stored on a server?' I was getting desperate now.

'I don't know. I don't think so. Millions of photos are sent every day ... I'm sorry, I have to get to school.'

'I know. Look, I'll tell the policewoman to check your phone for anything from Snapchat. But don't worry. I'll say you forgot to mention it.'

'Thank you.'

'It might be the files are still there. I've heard nothing is ever really deleted.' Saanvi nodded as if it might be true. But perhaps she was just playing along, trying to make me feel better. 'Could you see anything in the background of the pictures? Anything that might give me a clue to where it was taken?'

'The first was a close-up of the tattoo. It's on her ankle. The second was ...' Her eyes were suddenly studying the polished parquet floor. A leaf-blower started up in the garden outside so I had to raise my voice slightly.

'Go on.'

She looked back up and met my gaze, the words coming fast, as if she was keen to get rid of them. 'In a bar or a club. Kissing a boy. It was very blurred. A selfie, I think.'

I tried to keep my voice level, but it sounded as brittle as dried flowers. 'Thank you. Can I see the copy of the text now?'

My ribs felt crushed and it was difficult to expand my lungs, as if someone had just turned up gravity to eleven, as I took the phone off Saanvi. The message wasn't very long and felt like it was hurried, at least judging by the number of spelling mistakes and predictive-text glitches. It mainly asked how other girls were and if they were looking forward to Indonesia – I'd almost forgotten she was meant to go on a school trip there – and it wasn't until the last line that I broke in two and the tears came.

It's all OK here, but I really miss my mum.

PART TWO

EIGHT

Saturday

Dear Diary . . .

Isn't that how you are meant to start?
   *Feels silly. But I'd rather put this down on
paper than on a computer. You never know who
pokes around in your computer. I bought this
book in the market two weeks ago. I keep the key
to the lock around my neck. Feels strange to be
handwriting again, though.*

I MISS my Poobags.

And my mum.

Monday

Matt says I can't even text to say that I am safe and OK and that my texts could be traced. So I have sent some pics using Snapchat to the Poobags. They got ten seconds of me and my new tat. And the cute guy I met. I was going to tell them where I am anyway and then blank it – I'm in ▬▬▬ *! Ha, ha. But I didn't. Anyway Matt … he won't let me call him DAD, not in public at least. Says it makes him look OLD. Like he isn't.*

Why all the secrecy? He says if they find out where I am he'll go to jail. For KIDNAPPING me. He didn't kidnap me. I just thought it would be cool to have an adventure with him and Laura (especially as Mum was being so strange). But he says that because I am underage what I think DOES NOT MATTER to them. He says once he has convinced the courts I should be with him and that Mum should get treatment (I don't think she is ill. But she could be weird, couldn't she? And she was drinking loads), then we can go back home. Hooray! I didn't think I would be away sooooo long though.

Rained today, crazy rain that looked and felt like you were under a waterfall. I went out for two seconds and got SOAKED. Sun out now, everything steaming.

Tuesday

Very hot here today. And the air conditioning is crap.

I feel a bit better today. I think I was homesick. But I am getting to like this place. We have a little house on the outskirts of town. It's built of stone and bamboo and has a thatched roof and best of all ... an outdoor shower. But nobody can see you, it's off the bathroom and you can only see sky when you are under it. The only thing is the floor gets slimy and there's some gross BUGS in there. Maye the housekeeper goes in with a stick before I get under, just to get rid of anything. She says my scream can wake the dead. There's one spider the size of my hand that lives in the garden. It's glittery blue on top, with a long black body. But it's meant to be harmless. Laba-laba, Maye calls it. I'm SO brave. Apart from the cockroaches. Urgg. We live here with Laura who is kinda like my friend and my teacher rolled into one (and Matt's girlfriend). She used to look after me when Mum was off doing her bodyguarding. They have decided I have to 'keep up with my education'. So I have lessons every day in the usual stuff – Maths, English, History, Geography. Laura talks to me for a bit and then there are learning modules on her laptop that I do. But

Matt says I am mainly studying at the University of The World. He says we are all brainwashed to become little exam machines – robots that walk through GCSEs then A-Levels and then do a degree for some job we don't even really want.

He says I am meant to be a free spirit.

But after lessons Laura and me go to the beach. She has taught me to surf and she says I AM REALLY GOOD.

I told him I missed Mum and he told me that she isn't very well. She has Post-Traumatic Stress from the army. He said Paul being killed sent her over the edge. Those were his exact words. But she already had it from being in the war. It's sad. She's had a sad life. Matt says he has ways of telling her I am OK without giving our location away. So that's good. At least she won't be worrying TOO much.

Thursday

I forgot to write about the tattoo! It took weeks of working on Matt. Laura said it was cool but Matt thought I should wait. And I just had this fanny fit (as my mum calls them). I said I'd been dragged around Amsterdam and Ibiza and Athens and left alone at night to cook my own dinner and treated like an adult on most things. But not this. So I showed him the design I'd got from this little parlour down the road. I told him it said 'Friends' not Poobag. And he said yes. He even paid. It was less than a tenner though. And it didn't hurt.

I'm a liar. It did hurt. But no worse than the dentists. And it sort of went a bit crusty and yellow, but Laura looked after it. OK now.

And what about the BOY?? The one with his arm round me. The pool is at the Four Seasons, which is just up the road. Got to go now.

Friday

OMG I am SO STUPID.

I feel like screaming.

I told Laura about the messages I sent to the Poobags on the phone. I thought I could TRUST her. But she told Matt. And he went SHIT CRAZY. Stopped me surfing. Switched off the satellite TV. Took away the iPAD he got me (which anyway is so old it doesn't even have a camera). I went down the bar with Laura to apologise and he sent me away. Dieter, his partner, gave me a Coke when Matt wasn't looking.

Dieter. You don't know him. He's Dad's partner in the bar. He's hot for an old guy. I *think he's about twenty-five. Maybe thirty. He mostly wears cut-off jeans and a Bob Marley vest with armholes so big, he might as well be naked. They have this bar just back from the beach, behind one of the fish shacks. It's funny, when the customers come in Dieter is all friendly. Hey, guys, where you staying? he asks them. He told me if they say, down the road at The Four Seasons or The Ritz Carlton, then he charges them double for drinks. They can afford it, he says.*

Now I'm going to see if Laura will let me watch Girls *on her laptop.*

Very, very hot again, I am SO sweaty.

NINE

Bedfordshire, England

I pulled my Golf to a halt at the side of the row of hangars that constituted One-Eyed Jack's fiefdom. As I got out, I could hear his voice bellowing across the old airfield. 'Chrissake, Lennie, you don't have to be a cunt all your life – you can take today off.'

As I walked around I could see the object of his abuse. The hapless Lennie was a tall, spotty young man dressed in a pair of new-looking overalls. He and Jack were either side of the open bonnet of an old Ford Escort Mexico. Jack looked up, saw me and grabbed a rag.

'Lennie, go and get a cup of tea, will ya. We'll carry on in five.'

Lennie, clearly still stung by the verbal whiplash, sloped off to one of the far hangars where the tea and coffee were kept. Jack turned to me. 'And this woman here,' he shouted after the boy, '*she* knows the difference between an alternator and a generator.'

Did I? Jack was responsible for modifying most of my clients' cars for speed or protection or both. I recalled some long lecture about the different ways of generating electricity in the engine bay. I'd only been half-listening. But I assumed something as old as a Mexico had a generator.

'Is that real?' I asked of the Escort, knowing the sporty versions went for over forty grand.

'Mostly,' he smirked.

Once he was certain Lennie wasn't around, Jack approached me and held his arms out. We had spoken but not seen each other since the night I had brought bad people to this airfield who had threatened to harm Jordan, his son.

Jack was not only old enough to be my dad, I'd have preferred it if he had been. The outstretched arms were anything but threatening and as they came round me and the familiar combination of oil, grease and Swarfega filled my nostrils I felt myself go. Tears burned my eyes and my sobbing was hard enough to crack a rib, but still he held on. I felt his hand go up and down between my shoulder blades, like he was burping a baby.

'I'm sorry,' he said at last.

'For what?'

'Last year. Giving you up.'

'Jesus, they'd have found me sooner or later. I'm sorry I involved you.'

He pushed me away, holding on to both my shoulders. 'So we're both sorry. But that's not why you're crying now.'

I sniffed and composed myself a little. 'No.'

'This isn't the Sam I know of old.'

'No. She's M.I.A. for the minute.' I thought of Freddie's comment, about how she loved me but didn't like me at the moment. It stung harder than I had imagined, now I'd had time to digest it. 'It's Jess . . .'

'You have news?'

'Not exactly. Well, yes. Look, I need to see Jordan. I need his geeky brain.'

'Yeah, I think he brought that one in today. Come with me.'

The lad was sitting in his office out the back of the hangar that housed mostly Italian cars in various states of undress. He smiled when he saw me and turned down the music that sounded like the mating calls of a couple of angle grinders. Jordan had suffered some oxygen starvation at birth, which left him with a slight defect and an arm that didn't always play ball, but he knew his way around a computer in a way I couldn't comprehend.

While Jack fetched me a coffee, I explained to Jordan about Saanvi, Snapchat, the iPhone 5S and Connie Farnham, the policewoman.

'There might be something on there,' said Jordan, in a tone that suggested he didn't hold out much hope.

'The computer guys the cops use are pretty good at this game. But if your woman could find out if they have used something like Dumpster or FonePaw iPhone Data Recovery to look for .nomedia files.'

'Would Snapchat keep the images? You know, stored in some giant mainframe in Greenland?'

'Hold on.' He tapped on a keyboard with his good hand and the screen filled with rows of tiny writing. When he read his voice was slippery with the sibilance his condition sometimes lent his words. 'This is from its terms and conditions. Listen to this: "You grant Snapchat a world-wide, perpetual, royalty-free, sub-licensable, and transferable license to host, store, use, display, reproduce, modify, adapt, edit, publish, create derivative works from, publicly perform, broadcast, distribute, syndicate, promote, exhibit, and publicly display that content in any form and in any and all media or distribution methods."'

'Wow.' That seemed to cover all the bases. It said: everything you do on our site is ours to keep forever and do with as we like. 'What's your point?'

'The point is … why would you have to grant all those rights to images that don't exist?' Jordan said.

'So they do keep them?'

A shrug. 'Who knows? They say not. There's 700 million messages a year. That's a lot of storage.'

'But?'

'I'm just sayin', is all. Maybe some get kept.'

'Could you hack them?'

He chuckled at the thought. 'Hack Snapchat? Fucksake, Sam, I'm not that good. You'd need ... you'd need more resources than I've got and even if you got in, how would you find a couple of images among 700 million?'

'I guess.'

'Your best hope is that they are still on the original phone.'

I stood up and did some stretching. I needed some exercise. It had been a while since I'd had a good run or lifted any weights. Jack came back with the coffees and a Coke for Jordan. I drank in silence and they were wise enough to let me.

I was at a loss what to do next. One thing kept me together: Jess is out there, even if she has got a tattoo that says 'Poobag', and she misses me. That thought kept me breathing.

'Look, there is the possibility she posted somewhere else. There is a piece of kit called IAR. That's Image Approximation Recognition. They say it was developed by GCHQ but I think that's just bollocks. But if you sketch a version of the image, then feed it into the web, it comes up with all approximate matches.'

'Jesus.'

'So this friend of Jess's, could she do a sketch of the photo?'

'Like an identikit?'

'Yeah.'

'I'm sure Connie could get a police artist to talk it out of her.'

'Thing is, it doesn't work with common set-ups. A selfie, for instance. I mean, there's how many photos of people grouped together grinning into a phone camera? But maybe someone showing their foot? You'd only be down to millions, not billions.'

'So still a needle in a bleedin' haystack?' said Jack.

'Needle in a field of haystacks,' Jordan admitted. 'But worth a try.'

'Anything is worth a try,' I said, trying not to sound quite as despondent as I felt. 'Can you do this?'

He shook his head. 'No. You need a lot more crunching power than I've got. And my guess is the cops won't have the time or the manpower. Sorry, maybe I shouldn't have mentioned it.'

'No, it's good you did.' Another ray of light, another sliver of hope.

'And if you do get an image, you can get it scanned for metadata. There's often info hidden in the photo.'

'Such as?'

'Where, when, what phone.'

'You mean like co-ordinates?'

'Yes. There might – not always – but there might be a GPS tag on there.'

'So if we do get a picture, we could tell . . .'

'Exactly where it was taken, yes.'
The ray of light exploded into a supernova.

I have a favourite tree on Hampstead Heath. After a run, and before a swim in the lido or the Ladies' Pond, I usually sit and stare at it. I used to jog along the canal at Islington, but I'd rented that flat out. When Paul died – when Paul was *murdered* – I abandoned Chiswick because of all the ghosts. Something similar happened at the canal. I could no longer bear to be in the flat alone. I was always waiting for the sound of her key in the door, a blast of tinny music, the request for a fiver or tenner. Jess should have been everywhere, but she was nowhere. It was like someone had taken a bite out of my soul and spat it out somewhere I could never retrieve it.

So I moved to a few streets away from Freddie, a two-bedroom apartment in a modern block on Highgate Hill. The rent was scandalously high, but then so was the rent the agency was charging for my place. It evened out.

The morning after seeing Jack, I sat on the bench looking at my tree, waiting for my heart rate to drop. It stood alone and remote in the centre of a triangular plain of grass, which was still glossy from the spring rains. The backdrop was of lush oak and plane trees and could have come from a Gainsborough. My tree, in contrast, was as white as sun-bleached bones.

My phone rang. It was Connie, getting back to me after I had reported on my conversation with Jordan. She came straight to the point. 'There's nothing on there. No .nomedia file.'

'You sure?' I asked.

'I got the Hi-Tech Crime Unit boys to look at it. I told them there was suspected child pornography on there. That always gets their attention. If anything was on there, they'd have found it. Nothing.'

'How can that be?'

'They said young Saanvi had downloaded an App called Scourge that made sure nothing was left to find. It takes out all your history, leaving no trace. Paedophiles love it apparently.'

And schoolkids with nosy mothers, no doubt. 'OK, thanks. Any luck with the text she sent?'

'That's going to take longer to get a result.'

'Well at least the country code tells us where she is.'

'That could be a false flag. SMS texts can be routed in all manner of ways.'

Of course they could. 'But you've asked Sweden to co-operate?' Sweden had surprised me. Matt liked his places warm. Like in the 30s. But he also had a thing about Swedish women. Maybe he and Laura had split up and he'd gone fishing in colder waters.

'We have. But it takes time. They have to contact the MNO—'

'The what?'

'The Mobile Network Operator. It can determine which tower it came in to and which tower it came out of. But there are hoops to jump through before we can access carrier records. I'm sorry. We'll keep pushing.'

I hung up and stared at the lonely tree once again. It looked as if it had died in an instant, a lightning strike flaying it of leaves and bark. Its ivory branches reached up to the heavens as if they were arms thrown up in agony. Why was it my favourite tree? Because of what it reminded me of.

Me.

TEN

Zürich

'You want me to do *what* exactly?'

'Get into Telia's Swedish records and find out about the text message. Hack Snapchat and see if those two photos of Jess still exist. If not use IAR to try and locate duplicates on other servers. All the details you need are in that folder.'

Colonel d'Arcy twirled a Mont Blanc pen the size of a fat cigar around his fingers. 'I thought your wonderful Scotland Yard was on to this?' The tone suggested he thought the Met anything but wonderful. But then a man in his business wouldn't approve of any cops. It was in his interest to suggest people were better off going private.

'There's a lot of heel-dragging going on.' Jordan had been right. The thought of putting a whole team on the IAR programme searching for a tattooed foot had been blown out of the water faster than a Trident missile in launch mode. 'I don't think finding Jess is a priority. It's a domestic. If Matt had taken her to join ISIS we'd get a lot more press and a lot more sympathy.'

The latter was in short supply outside my immediate circle. Most of the people who commented on the @ findjess account that my journalist friend Nina had set up in the aftermath of the kidnapping – which is what I thought of it as – considered it all my own fault for being an absent parent. The *Daily Mail* had run a lurid piece about the life of a female bodyguard, as they insisted on calling me, and how it was incompatible with responsible motherhood. I was told by a producer on *Crimewatch* that I didn't have a sympathetic face or manner. Fuck you, I said. Possibly proving her point.

'That is a tall order,' said the old man, rising creakily to his feet. He went to the window and looked down at the city. I hoped he wasn't going to give me his virtual tour of Zürich again. 'And expensive.' He turned, pointing the pen at me like a dagger. 'Even if it's possible. I don't know about these things. I'm still getting to grips with Morse code.' He gave a laugh like a rusty saw.

I suspected he was as tech-savvy as I was cyberignorant. But it was a useful pretence. And anyway, he was a prince at outsourcing appropriate skills. 'But of course you know a man who does know about such things?'

The Colonel nodded. 'Several. As I say, none of them cheap. There are risks involved.'

'How much?'

'Risks?' he asked.

'Money.' I didn't care about risks.

'I don't know. Not off the top of my head. I suspect there would be no firm quote. The price would depend on how long it takes and the number of people needed to mount an attack on these corporations. It could be very high.'

He was making it sound like I was going to fund D-Day. 'But I've got more to come from the Monaco retrieve.'

'Oh, yes. Of course you have. Once Keegan gets paid from the insurance company and he pays me. But that could be . . . a while.'

'Can you advance me?'

The returning smile was weary, as if he was hearing the question for the millionth time. He probably was. The answer had the dog-eared feel of an old paperback. One that had been left in the rain. Then pissed on by a passing dog. 'I do believe there are very reputable banks and lending houses in this city. I am sure they would accommodate you.'

I got up. Another wasted airfare. 'Stick it up your arse, Colonel.'

He laughed at that. 'A very English response. Don't be in such a hurry, Sam. Let's consider our options.'

He walked from the window and sat back down, put on a pair of frameless glasses and opened the folder I had brought him. He looked down the first page. 'It's not much to go on.'

'It's all I've got.'

'Give me a moment. I need to consult Henri down the hall.' Henri was his son.

The Colonel left the room and I crossed the Plain of Deep Pile to the window, taking in the view across to the lake. I heard my phone buzz in my bag. I ignored it. Probably Tom. I'd spoken to him once, just to tell him where the hire car was. I had probably been a little hard on him. His heart was in the right place. As was, Freddie would doubtless say, his cock.

I wondered if I had shot myself in both feet there. I liked Tom, he had a good, solid feel, both physically and emotionally. Freddie and Nina hardly ever agreed on anything, apart from the fact I needed to take myself in hand. But they both agreed Tom was good for me. What was bad for me was not even knowing where Jess was. Maybe those internet trolls were right. I should just accept the situation. That Jess was being raised by her father. Just move on.

To kiss boys in nightclubs and get tattoos?

But who was I to say she wouldn't have done that anyway? I was hardly a Tiger Mum. I never helicoptered over Jess like Saanvi's parents did with her. Perhaps Jess would have jumped the rails anyway – they were pretty bent and twisted what with one thing and another. But I couldn't do 'just move on'. I had panic attacks when I realised I couldn't picture Jess's face or imagined her changing into a young woman without me being there to witness it.

The Colonel swept back into the room, a box file under his arm, Henri trailing behind. Henri was in his twenties and dressed like an accountant. Which is more or less what he was, although it was likely the business would be his one day. Assuming the Colonel really was mortal. 'Henri, tell her.'

The son had a voice so soft I had to lean forward to catch the words. 'We have someone who'll do it. A German.' He adjusted his glasses, pushing them back up his nose. 'Goes by the name of Gorrister. Not his real name, I suspect. But I am afraid he wants ten thousand up front.'

'Dollars?'

'Euros,' said the Colonel.

'Shit.'

'He is worth it,' said Henri. 'In my experience he gets results. We usually use him for accessing financial records that others would rather were ... kept under wraps, shall we say.'

The Colonel sat and opened the box file. Then he turned on his computer. 'I just need to check a couple of emails. Thank you, Henri.'

After his son had left, he began tapping at his keyboard, his face immobile as he read the screen.

'He's a nice young man. Henri, I mean. Is he your designated successor?' I asked, although I couldn't imagine the words 'One day, son, all this will be yours' coming from Colonel d'Arcy's mouth.

'We'll see.' The Colonel's eyes flicked up, as fast as a lizard's. 'He hasn't enjoyed quite the life we have.' Too soft, was that what he was saying? 'An MBA from Lausanne Business School is not quite a stint in Iraq or Algeria, is it?' the Colonel confirmed. 'But, don't worry.' He gave his wheezy laugh. 'I'm not going anywhere for a while. Now give me a moment.'

In other words, shut up. Eventually he took off his glasses and rubbed his eyes. 'So, the good news is, I can advance you the money for a job.'

'Not another retrieval?'

'No, this one is right up your street. I mentioned it last time you were here, but it wasn't greenlit then. PPO needed. Client has to be in Luxembourg for an emergency board meeting. Client lives in New York. And is afraid of flying.'

I remembered now. 'So what am I meant to do? Row across the Atlantic?'

He put his head to one side and gave me a quizzical look. I suspected he thought I should be more grateful. 'They'll come by sea.'

'Not that much of an emergency then.'

'The fear of flying dictates the transport. It means time will be of the essence once the client reaches this side of the Atlantic.'

'Why do they need a PPO?'

'Well, apparently there are parties who would rather the Luxembourg meet didn't take place.'

'What kind of parties?'

'The unpleasant kind.'

'The armed and dangerous kind?' I asked.

He showed me his palms in a what-can-you-do? gesture. 'You could say that.'

'Surely the client could bring their own home-grown muscle?'

'Apparently not.'

I thought for a moment. 'Even if I liked being an armed guard – which I don't – I'm not licensed to carry a weapon in France. And I won't be approved in the current climate.' Nor, it went without saying, with my SIA suspension. 'I don't want to end up doing five years in a French prison because I had to carry a pistol. Just on the off chance there'll be trouble.'

'That's not your problem. We have a FITLO.'

A FITLO was yet another of the acronyms the world of close protection loves. Firearms Trained and Licensed Operative. 'French?'

'Hungarian.'

I had a mental flash of a bullet-headed thug like Bojan, the Serbian who once tried to stab me in what was his idea of a fair fight (although only he had a knife). 'Who is he?'

'George Konrad.'

Europe is awash with gorillas with guns. They were mostly hitmen. That was where the easy money was. Offing someone's rival for cash, no questions asked on either side except who, where and how much? But the real thing, the FITLO, was a rare bird, because his or her job was to stop the hit. Some did it because it was morally more attractive than mere assassination, others because it was more of a challenge. And then there was the financial benefit of it being a less crowded field. 'George Konrad? I don't know him, do I?' I asked.

'Unlikely. He's good, so I am reliably informed, and that's all you need to know.' His eyes flicked to the screen. 'Very good, so they say. You'll be in charge of driving and choosing the route. He'll be there in case a situation arises.'

The PPO world not only loves an acronym, it loves a euphemism, too. A 'situation' in this case meant some bastard opens fire on us. With real bullets. 'I have control of all transportation? Right? No arguments?'

'I'll make it clear to him.' You might think that two professionals assigned to look after a Principal would agree on most things. It was rarely the case. Even deciding which road to take could cause arguments. It was much better if tasks and responsibilities were assigned beforehand. Compartmentalisation was the key to the harmonious and safe transport of a client.

'Where is the client now?'

'Somewhere in the Atlantic aboard a private yacht. They'll be dropped off in France in a couple of days.'

'Where in France?'

'Do you want the job?' he asked.

I was intrigued, but I gave a noncommittal shrug. 'I assume a landing as close to Luxembourg as possible?'

'Well, no. Don't assume that. The coast towards Belgium is still very tightly patrolled, thanks to the refugee problem.'

A few tumblers clicked into place in my still-addled brain. I found a little cubicle for Jess and parked her there. There was something else he wasn't telling me. It made no sense not to land close to the destination. Unless . . .

'What's the PoFU?' Potential for Fuck Up.

'A Red Notice.' Colonel d'Arcy said this as if it were a golf handicap. But his eyes were darting about. I'd never seen him look properly shifty before. He usually stopped at mildly evasive.

I found myself wanting it spelled out. 'An Interpol Red Notice?'

'Yes.'

'Anything else?'

He cleared his throat. 'The client is also carrying an outstanding EAW.'

'A Europol Arrest Warrant?'

'Yes,' he snapped. 'So it will all have to be under the radar.'

It would be best under the fucking ground – tunnelling to Luxembourg. A Red Notice was only a request to detain a suspect. The EAW was trickier. That required the police force of a member state to arrest the suspect. So if we came up against a cop with a computer, there would be an instruction to detain. And then what have I got – a Hungarian willing to shoot his way out?

'What's Konrad's OD when it comes to the police?' The Operational Directive established any ground rules. I just hoped there were some.

'I'll make sure he knows it's the same OD that applies to all my people. To put his hands up and go quietly. He's not there for cops. He's there for ... any others.'

That was something at least. A gunfight with cops was never a good idea.

'And before you ask, we don't know who the said "any others" are.'

Not so good. 'You had time to prepare any fake documents?'

'No, but that will be the first port of call after landing.' He knew what my next question would be. What was the EAW for? Rape? Murder? There are some things that are beyond the pale even for a PPO.

'The warrant is for bribing a trader at Deutsche Bank to rig the Euribor rate.'

The needle barely gave a jerk. Insider trading and market manipulation was the norm with many clients. Few of them got extremely rich and kept clean hands. Every yacht in Monaco harbour was built with somebody's tears. Or somebody else's money. I didn't know much about finance, but knew the Euribor as some sort of exchange rate set between European banks. Like the better-known Libor, it could be manipulated to give traders an edge. And a big profit. 'How serious is it? The offence?'

He tried to sound dismissive, as if it were nothing. 'It's an unsubstantiated historical allegation.'

'How long ago?'

'Four years.'

'How seriously will the cops take it?'

The Colonel shrugged. 'You can never tell. At the moment, as you know, bankers and investors are pariahs to some sections of the press. But on the scale of banking offences that have been committed in Europe? Small beer. However, there is always a risk of running across a policeman who thinks he is Eliot Ness reborn.'

'Did he do it?'

The Colonel's wrinkled visage gained a few more crevices as he frowned. 'Who?'

'The client. The man we've just been talking about

for fifteen minutes. Did he bribe someone four years ago?'

The glint in the Colonel's eyes illuminated the garden path I had been led up. 'Didn't I say? Why you are perfect for the job? The client isn't a "he". It's a "she".'

ELEVEN

London

'I don't have long. I'm meant to be shivering on a beach somewhere in Normandy sometime tomorrow night.'

'You only call when you want something.'

'I know. Today I wanted lunch. With you.'

Nina narrowed her eyes suspiciously. We were sitting in a restaurant in east London, surrounded by fellow customers on MacBooks and iPads and being ignored by tatted-up waiters and waitresses. We were so much older and less hip than the rest of the clientele, they had probably decided we'd just come in to find somewhere warm to curl up and die, like cats who know that their time has come.

It was my idea to meet for lunch, Nina's choice to dine at Hogget. She had decided to move east, declaring the rest of London a dead zone for decent restaurants and bars. Sclerotic, she called it. Whereas, young fresh blood flowed through E1 and E8. You couldn't book at Hogget, and it was so popular – having been open for all of three weeks and with a positive Jay Rayner review under its belt – you had to turn up immediately after breakfast to be sure of a lunch spot. So we sat on our rickety mismatched chairs and tried to ignore the giant steel ducting that was hanging over our heads.

'So, can you do some digging for me about this client? Elizabeth Irwin. I trawled the internet. Very little out there. Rich, lives in New York. It'd really help. Help get Jess back too.'

That was a low blow. I knew Nina felt guilty because Laura and Matt had abducted – or more likely enticed, prior to abduction – Jess from Nina's house while she was in her care. For the longest time she couldn't understand why I didn't blame her. Because it wasn't her job to stop my fuckwit ex-husband taking Jess. That was my job. I'd failed, not her. But sometimes, you can play on guilt like one of those twiddly jazz guitarists Paul, my husband, used to like. Paddy McTheny or something like that.

'And this client of yours, she bribed someone to make a shitload of money?' There was something about Nina's Scottish accent that could cut through a restaurant's hubbub like a laser through steel and a few heads turned.

'I think it's called capitalism.'

'Ach, it's a modern form of rape and pillage.'

'Has someone explained our concept?'

I looked up at a hirsute server whose eyebrows had so many rings in them you could run a curtain pole through and make a set of drapes for his eyes. 'Yes. But give us a minute.'

When he'd gone, Nina asked: 'Why didn't you let him explain the concept?'

'I thought you were the trencherman Londoner, fearlessly patrolling the cutting edge of cosmopolitan dining. The concept is that they take some food, preferably mixed with ingredients foraged from railway sidings nearby, fix it up as small, sharing portions and then charge you the same as if they were full-sized plates. Then the moment I've started eating they'll keep coming round and asking how everything is so you can't actually enjoy it.'

'Cynic.'

'You've done this to me too many times. I hate sharing. I want my own food, please.'

'It has bigger plates.' She waved the coarse paper menu at me. 'Look. Left-hand side. Under "For the Pig-Faced". You can have a great slab of meat all to yourself. Just don't ask for any of mine.'

It wasn't under any such thing. And they had fish.

'Are you OK, Sam?' she asked.

'As well as can be expected. Why?'

'It's just that ... everything makes you so angry.

Out of all proportion. They do small plates. It's not a tragedy. Syria is a tragedy.'

I knew she was right. It didn't take much for the stopcock on the well of fury somewhere around my stomach to open up. Sometimes it gushed pure bile.

'Losing Jess, that was a tragedy,' I said.

'Yes. I'll accept that. But Sam, this anger will eat you hollow.'

'I know, I know. And before you suggest it, I am not seeing a shrink. I'm trying to channel the anger. Hence this job in France. I can justify it as part of getting her back.'

Nina reached across and squeezed my hand. 'OK, but we are here now and you have work to do. So you have to babysit this woman in France. Can you tell me more?' she asked.

So I did, or at least the edited highlights. I even managed to avoid biting her head off for using the word 'babysit'.

'You'll drive over to meet this woman?' Nina asked when I had finished. 'Mrs Irwin?'

'No. I'll fly. I want to be using a car with French plates and a non-hire number. There'll be one waiting for me not far from the pick-up spot. Then it's off to have a new passport made. That's probably a few hours' delay. Then off to jolly old Luxembourg on a route of my say-so.'

'You alone?'

I wasn't certain what she meant by that. 'The decision is mine alone, yes. But I've got some muscle with me. Name of George Konrad.'

'Muscle?' Her voice was laced with suspicion. Or was it excitement? 'What kind of muscle?'

'The kind designed to keep us out of trouble, not get into it.' At least I hoped so.

'How long do you think it'll take, this little jaunt?'

'Depends where she comes ashore. If I used main roads, five, six hours. Seven tops. Plus however long it takes for the Colonel's man to do the passport. But I probably won't be using the autoroutes.'

'Why not?'

'With both an EAW and a Red Notice out on her? Why do you think?'

'But it isn't that serious a crime, is it? Aren't they all at it? Bankers and traders?'

'It might not be, but we think it might be designed to tangle her in red tape. An arrest is an arrest. It tends to make things complicated, no matter what the charge.'

We ordered from the be-ringed server, who was disappointed that I didn't want to have fun with their sharing concept and asked for a sea bass to myself and a bottle of Godello for us both. I wasn't on duty yet.

'Look, Sam ...' Nina played with her cutlery and her face set itself into 'deadly serious'.

'Listen, I know what you are going to say. Smuggling a wealthy fugitive across France, wanted by the law and God knows who else. It's stupid. I should get another job. But the money is good. And, as I said, if it helps bring Jess back—'

'What I was going to say,' she interrupted, 'was that it'll make a great story. Fantastic copy for the magazine. Bodyguarding a fugitive across Europe. I'll change the names, of course.'

My jaw must have dropped because I found it was almost brushing the 'repurposed' wood that constituted the tabletop. 'You are *not* coming. Understand? Jesus, what do you think this is? The British Army? That you can embed in my unit? I'm only telling you so that someone knows where I am should anything happen.' In fact, I'd briefed Freddie too, but it was better each felt they were the sole repository of this information. 'No, forget it—'

'All right, hold those bloody horses. I didn't mean that. I was just thinking I could interview it out of you when it's all over. Maybe you could just take some notes as an aide-memoire. And as I said, we'd change all the names. Including yours.'

'Nina, this isn't your sort of piece. I thought you were at the sharp end of journalism.'

'Yes, well, things change, don't they? Most of what I used to do, the comment and analysis, you can get for free on the web now. Bloody newspapers are into "citizen journalism". Which means let any Tom, Dick or Mary have a go, and look – we don't have to pay them!'

Bonus. Another couple of years, it'll be robots doing it. I'm not kidding – bots do most of the stats compilations for the papers now. And after nobody outside the KKK predicted a Trump presidency, political punditry is seen as something like casting the runes. You might as well go back to haruspicy. Reading entrails,' she added helpfully. 'So, I'm trying to move across to the mag. Colour pieces. Interviews. The soft end, as you'd probably say.'

'I see.'

'It was just a thought . . .'

'Sorry. No.' I made it sound as final as possible, the way a belligerent Frenchman might. 'I can't do it. Even with names changed. Too risky.'

Nina huffed. 'I thought you wanted some background on this woman.'

'Not that badly.'

'Well, if I do some digging, what do I get in return?'

We were interrupted by the arrival of the wine and subsequent fuss, which was probably just as well, because I'd calmed down a little by the time we resumed. 'I can see what you are thinking. But let me tell you – my job is to make this trip as dull as possible. To make sure nobody gets hurt. Not so much as a splinter. A few days of tedium is a very acceptable outcome. If there's even a whiff of "good copy" I've fucked up.'

I held up my glass and after a brief hesitation Nina

clinked hers against mine. 'Then here's wishing for the most boring trip, ever.'

I think it is called tempting fate.

'You are like an armadillo!'

I smiled at the familiar complaint. After the buzz of lunchtime wine had worn off, I had gone to see Elsa who, during my peak PPO days, would give me a massage twice a week to help keep me supple. She reckoned I had a tendency for my skin to glue itself to the underlying tissues whenever I was tense. Hence the jibe that I had a covering like an armadillo.

Elsa was no normal masseuse. She wasn't blonde or pretty or young. She didn't try to push expensive exfoliants or miracle creams on her clients. Her 'studio' was the front room of her house in Finsbury Park, bare but for the table I was lying face down on, a rack of towels and a corner sink. Not so much as a scented candle. There was no new-age piano or flutes or pan pipes and, thank Christ, no bloody humpback whales. Just the sound of Elsa grunting as she dug her fingers deep and the occasional whimper from me.

Elsa was Dutch, and I am not sure what kind of masseuse she trained to be. I know she had a lot of professional dancers and musicians as clients, helping them get over the inevitable strain their careers put on their bodies. Her approach was certainly novel. I often found myself folded like a pretzel with my face between the two great pillows of her breasts while she coaxed my muscles in her heavily accented English.

'Come on, come on. You know you're not meant to be there. Float away like a balloon. That's it, that's it. Goooood. Thank you.'

I just kept my eyes closed and let her get on with it, because when she had finished – after an hour and a half – I always felt springier and far less armadillo-like.

This time she worked away for close to the two-hour mark, a lot of it seeming to involve excavating under my shoulder blades. When she had finished she let out her usual 'Soooooooo,' that signalled she had done all she could.

'Thank you,' I said, savouring the cessation of pummelling and stretching and prodding by lying there for a few moments.

'You were very tight.'

'I did relax for about five minutes a few nights ago.'

'Well, you are as ready as I can make you for another of your trips. Then I suppose I have to put you back together.'

'I'll try not to fall apart too much.'

She walked over and rinsed the oil off her hands in the corner sink. 'Your muscles feel good. Now I can get to them through your skin. Well toned. '

'I've been training,' I said.

'But, I am a little worried. From what you say.'

We had spoken for about ten minutes at the start

of the session. I couldn't even recall what I had said. 'Worried about what?'

'I am not sure you are fully ready.'

I raised my face from the hole in the massage table and looked at her. 'I don't think I can get much fitter at my age.'

'Not in the body.' She pointed at her temple. 'But in here.'

'Mentally?' I asked.

She nodded. 'I think so. I think you need to work on up here as well.'

'Fucking hell, Elsa,' I said. I sat up and swung my legs off. 'Not you as well. Why does everyone want me to get my head tested?'

'I am just saying. I know how focused you used to be when you came here before. I don't get that now. I get the sense you are not as sharp as you could be. In the mind.'

I dismissed her with a shake of the head. It wasn't what I wanted – or needed – to hear. I was, in fact, annoyed at her for expressing thoughts that, were I a weaker person, might dent my confidence. But, sadly, time would prove her right. I just wasn't ready for what was coming my way.

PART THREE

TWELVE

Normandy, France

There was a knock at my door before seven in the evening. I looked at the kit laid out on the bed and made sure there was nothing incriminating before I said, 'Enter.'

George Konrad had the shaven-headed look of the typical East European hardman, a goatee and some serious jowls that made his face look pear-shaped. His cheeks were pitted with the evidence of a bad case of acne or chickenpox. He had, though, a pair of clear green eyes that sparkled with a self-aware humour. They suggested he knew that he was a walking cliché. My job is always to blend in the background. Maybe people like him think it's better to play your trump card right away. *I'm dangerous. Don't fuck with me.*

He had on smart black trousers and a matching polo shirt with the Lacoste crocodile on it. It was pretty loose on him, but I could see he kept himself in shape by the tightness of the sleeves around his biceps.

'George Konrad,' he said, holding out his hand, but his eyes went to the bed. He ran his gaze over my Ready To Go gear. I didn't like his staring at my stuff and I stepped between him and the goods on display. As I did so I took his hand, noting the strength of the grip, and gave him my name. The real one.

'Were you a Girl Guide?' he asked, peering over my shoulder. '"Be prepared?"'

'I think that's Boy Scouts.'

He moved around me to pick up a set of restraints from the gear and he sensed my body tense. 'Sorry. I wouldn't like you touching my stuff.' He tossed the straps back onto the pile. 'Looks like you got it all covered.'

It wasn't anything out of the ordinary for a PPO – spare batteries, travel plug, solar and regular chargers, camera, lightweight jacket, wash kit, broad-spectrum antibiotics, a Uvistar combat tourniquet, antiseptic spray, analgesics, butterfly sutures, tampons – which double as efficient blood-absorbers for a different kind of bleeding – a supply of various currencies, two phones, both with the FMF (Find My Friends) app, so one can always locate the other, nylon jacket, field dressings and haemostatic packs. Plus the MLA fast-strap restraints, in case someone had to be taken out of the picture. Ordinarily I might have included a can of

Mace, but not when flying. Airport security isn't keen on tear gas of any description. But carrying a pepper spray with 2 per cent of added CS gas was legal in France, so I could always pick up a couple of canisters along the way if I felt the need.

'You check your phone?' There was an odd accent at work here, part-European, part-American, and something else I couldn't quite pin down.

I nodded. The message had come through that the car was in place, about half a kilometre from the hotel we were in, parked on a *place* in Fermanville, not far from the Hôtel de Ville. The keys would be on the front nearside tyre.

The hotel was situated between Barfleur and Cherbourg. The rendezvous point with the client was to be a beach – basically, a shingle-strewn gap in the cliffs – five kilometres out of town, just after midnight. It wasn't yet seven.

'You know, I thought I was flying solo on this one.'

'Is it a problem?' Some men on the Circuit really are lone wolves, happy to do the driving and the PPO work. Others, like me, feel more comfortable if the two tasks are separated.

He shook his head. 'Nope. It's a load off my mind having you. I don't have to figure out a way to get into the ladies' bathroom every time she wants a piss.'

'That's true. And you're more use without your hands on a wheel.'

'You want to get something to eat?' he asked. 'Might be the last meal that doesn't come film-wrapped for a while. And coffee in a proper cup.'

So he knew about road trips. That was good.

'And now we are two, we can talk about the split in our duties, perhaps.'

Another person who liked things well defined. I thought that was promising, too. 'Sure. Give me fifteen minutes to pack this up, I'll meet you downstairs.'

After he had gone, I re-dressed, putting on the Kevlar-reinforced ProTex bra and Under Armour knickers. Over the top went dark jeans, a long-sleeved T-shirt and a suede jacket that had seen better days but was just about smart enough to cover all the bases I might meet on this trip – I wasn't expecting tea at the Ritz or dinner on a yacht. The jacket also had plenty of pockets for phones and the Petzl folding hunting knife I had bought earlier in the day. It had a particularly nasty blade. The French were a lot more relaxed about knives, too.

Before leaving the room, I examined myself in the mirror. I looked OK – I wouldn't go further than that – in that I was pretty relaxed and ready to go. It was good to be back doing something I knew about.

I picked Konrad up in the lobby and we found a restaurant close to where the car was waiting for us. It took a while to select a table, because neither of us wanted to have our backs to the door. Force of habit.

But as he was the strong-arm element, I let him have prime position, with the room and the exits in view. Not that anything was likely to happen until we had the client under our wing. But pre-emptive strikes are always a possibility, so I kept my status hovering at the border between yellow and orange.

We ordered Virgin Marys, a bottle of Badoit and the *fruits de mer*. No alcohol. Konrad put a packet of Gitanes and a box of matches on the table before him and then ignored them. I watched him shift a little until he was comfortable. Something was digging into his back.

'If you don't mind me asking ... what is it?'

He knew what I was referring to. He stroked his beard, cupping his mouth to keep his voice low. 'You know guns?'

'I know which end you point at people,' I said, somewhat disingenuously. I knew a little more than that, thanks to the army and an intensive course in Slovakia back when I was qualifying. The Colonel had insisted, even though the chances of using or needing a firearm in the UK were close to zero.

He rubbed a finger along the side of his nose, as if considering whether to reveal his innermost secrets – gunmen spend hours agonising over their choice of weapons – or just tap it and tell me not to worry my little head about such things. I hoped he wasn't going down the patronising route.

It took him a minute to make his mind up. 'This one here –' he meant the one against his spine '– is a Ruger .38 Special LCR.' He said it in exactly the same tone as he had ordered drinks, albeit a little softer.

LCR stood for Lightweight Compact Revolver. 'The polymer and aluminium one?'

If he was impressed he didn't show it. 'That's it. It's fifty per cent lighter than the all-stainless-steel model. And it has a light trigger pull for a double-action.'

He stopped and smiled.

'What?'

'You just want to check I know what I'm talking about.' It wasn't a question as such.

The Virgin Marys arrived, so I didn't reply.

'Cheers,' I said, lifting up the drink to my lips.

'*Eskerriska.* So you are testing me?'

'No. I always like to hear a professional speak. It's comforting. Also it puts me on the same page if anything happens. I won't be shocked when you pull out a bazooka.'

'Pistols only, I am afraid.'

Handguns were fine by me. Submachine guns, assault rifles and anything else fully automatic make me nervous. Guys with AKs and the like tend to spray the room and see what they've hit afterwards. I was hoping this guy had a little more finesse. 'You use an ankle holster too?'

'When I'm in the car, yes. The Ruger is hammerless,

so nothing to catch on clothing. It's a smooth ...' He shook his head and gave a little smile. 'There I go again. And before you ask, I've got something with a little more ... what's the word?'

'Clout?'

'Punch.'

The Ruger was good for close work, but didn't have much in the way of real stopping power. I didn't ask him what the other handgun was. I was just satisfied he had one. I changed the subject. 'What's your accent?'

'All over the place. Hungarian, Scottish—'

'Scottish?'

'Mother's side. I've got some ginger in this beard when it gets long enough. And I've spent a lot of time on film sets, so there's American in there too.'

'You act?'

'They'd have to be pretty desperate. Sometimes, I'm third thug from the left. But no, I'm an armourer. I make sure the actors know how to hold a musket or a Sten and how to handle blanks. So that they don't blow each other's heads off for real.'

'So where does the BG gig come in?'

He stirred the Virgin Mary, making the ice rattle.

'Sometimes you get sick of play-acting. I mean, really sick. The real thing keeps me sharp. And sane.'

Half the crustacean population of the Atlantic Ocean arrived on a vast platter and we began to tear them limb from limb. 'What do you know about the job?' he asked.

'I'm just the driver.'

'That's not what I heard.'

I didn't ask exactly what he had heard. He might just be digging. Or he might have talked to the Colonel. It didn't matter to me. 'This time, I'm just a driver. Any idea who the opposition is?'

'Apart from the cops with their Red Notice?'

'Which could be a stitch-up,' I said. 'Just to delay her.'

He cracked a crab claw open and sucked out some of the meat. 'Could be,' he agreed eventually. 'Although it was there on the Europol bulletin, so I think we assume it's kosher. But, look, I'm not even sure there is any other opposition. I think there's just a feeling that accidents don't happen.'

I must have looked blank.

'Good crabs.' He dipped into the finger bowl and wiped his hands on a napkin. 'You know the best crabs I ever had? Velvet crab soup. We used to fish for them off a pier as kids and hand them to the chef. He'd fry up onion, leek, garlic, fennel seeds and thyme, then add tomatoes, white wine, stock. You'd blend the crabs whole, shells and all, sieve them, then add to the liquid. Bring to the boil, remove from heat, add cream, maybe a little white crab meat. Delicious.' He caught my look.

'What?'

I shook my head, partly in admiration, partly in surprise. I hadn't realised I'd picked up Gordon Ramsay by mistake. 'Nothing. I've never met a gourmet gunman before.'

'I'm not a gourmet. I just like decent food. I mean, this is good but . . .' He cleared his throat, perhaps suspecting he was about to become a food bore. 'Anyway. Enough about crabs. Back to the business in hand. Luxembourg? You know about that?'

'I know that's where we are going. A board meeting, so I was told.'

'Kind of.' While he considered whether to tell me, he began to dismember a langoustine. 'You know what an NOP is?'

I ran through all my PPO acronyms and then a few more. PON – Person of Note – I knew, but not the reverse of it. 'I don't. Not On Purpose is my best guess.'

'Close. It's Nothing On Paper. It's a bank account, or accounts, where everything is kept up here.' He tapped the side of his head. 'No statements, no tax returns, nothing. One person at the bank is charged with knowing all the financial information of a particular client. They report in person to both client and bank, so there is no paper trail. No emails, nothing.'

'That's crazy.' It was like that novel *Fahrenheit 451* that Paul gave me to read once, where books were kept alive by each member of the rebel underground memorising one great work of literature each. Some people got to recite *The Great Gatsby*, others *Pride and Prejudice*. I always felt sorry for whoever got *War and Peace*. Maybe they split that one. Paul also cajoled me into watching the underwhelming movie of the book; mind you, sometimes I missed being cajoled. 'Doesn't sound like a sane way to run a business.'

'Nobody ever said tax avoidance schemes were rational,' he replied.

'But surely it's also illegal?' I felt very naive saying it. Clearly it wasn't a service Post Office Savings would offer.

'It is now. There's something called the Foreign Account Tax Compliance Act that, as an American citizen, she should comply with. But some historic arrangements with private banks were exempt from the change in July 2015, when anonymous NOPs and bearer shares were made illegal, if the holder had dual nationality. Mrs Irwin has dual citizenship.'

'With?'

'Ireland, I believe. Although I suspect she doesn't spend a lot of time hanging out in Ballybackass of nowhere.'

'You've done your homework.'

He gave a sly smile. He knew it was unusual for someone in his line of work to be quite so diligent in researching the background to a job. 'These days, according to the Luxembourg rules, someone, somewhere, has to know the names of whoever owns the cash or shares. But there were loopholes.' He gave a what-can-you-do shrug. 'There's always loopholes if you know the right people. If there's one thing the Panama Papers showed . . .'

He had managed to shuck the spiny carapace of the langoustine and tucked in.

'It's that with the right money you can get away with murder. Sorry, bad choice of words. You can get away with fleecing friends, families, institutions, whole countries.'

'Colonel d'Arcy told you all this?' I asked, a little peeved that he should have more information than me.

'A little. As you said, I do my homework. It means you don't have to keep asking the client stupid questions.'

Ah, the client. Mrs Elizabeth Irwin, widowed, left very wealthy by her late husband, on the board of a couple of museums, contributor to several charities. She didn't sound like the sort of person who used these NOPs. But then again, as Konrad said, the Panama Papers threw up all sorts of apparently upright citizens who had squirrelled their money away in less than wholesome places.

'So she needs to go and see her NOP guy? I thought the mountain would come to Mohammed.'

'Usually would. Normal procedure, the bank's guy gets on a plane and they meet in an airport lounge in Dubai or a bar in Miami, or wherever. It's difficult, though, when you are in a coma after being knocked down in a hit-and-run accident.'

He let that sink in. It took its time. 'The account supervisor or whatever he is called?'

'Yes, the man with it all in his head.'

'Jesus,' I said. 'Accident?'

'Crossing the road after work, hit by a big four-wheel drive. Didn't stop. Now in hospital pissing into tubes.'

'Shit. And, as you said, some people don't believe in accidents.'

'Right. And if it wasn't an accident, they probably didn't intend him to even survive to live like he is, a vegetable. It was most likely a murder attempt. So, I suspect the client is taking out an insurance policy just in case the next step is a tragic accident befalling her. That's you and me, by the way. The insurance.'

'What about her own security?' I asked. 'A woman like that must have her own . . .'

'Goons?'

'BGs, PPOs,' I said.

'They missed the boat. Literally. Two of them, never turned up for the crossing. Sailed without them.' He finished the rest of the crab. 'Hence the call to Zürich for emergency replacements.'

'And that doesn't worry you?'

'Somewhat. But it might be for the best – it's always comforting to have someone with local knowledge.

The Americans probably wouldn't even know the rules of the road.'

I didn't like it, though. The NOP guy gets hit by a car, two PPOs miss the sailing? 'Why didn't they fly out? The muscle?'

'I think she fired them. You would, wouldn't you?'

'I guess so.'

He examined the carnage before him, dipped his fingers in the lemon water and wiped his hands on a napkin. 'I'm done here.' He nudged the Gitanes packet. 'Mind if I have a cigarette?'

'Mind if I join you?'

'You'd be very welcome.'

We moved outside to the terrace and smoked two each, not saying much, lost in our thoughts. Eventually he said, 'How about we get the car now, drive back to the hotel, check out and drive down and look at our very own Omaha Beach.'

I glanced at him through the last wreaths of my smoke. 'Omaha? Hardly. At least I hope not.'

'I worked on *Saving Private Ryan*. Tom Hanks's Thompson was one of mine. Nice guy.'

All this seemed a long way from Hollywood film stars and re-enactments of D-Day. If it were me, I think I'd stay with replicas and bank the pay packet. At least nobody would be shooting real bullets at you. But then again, it was possible that men like Konrad needed the adrenaline that the work gave you. And

I was one to talk. What the fuck was I doing there, smelling the breeze off the ocean, wondering where a woman who was worried about her secret fortune was right now? I could tell myself I was doing it all for Jess, but part of me *wanted* this.

'What's your real story?' he asked.

'How do you mean?'

'Everyone on the Circuit has something inside them, a little kernel of hate or addiction or love that brings them back.' He looked at me. 'We're all damaged in some way.'

'Apparently, you know more about me than I do. You tell me.'

'I heard lots of things about you. Dead husband, missing daughter, some trouble in a garage in London. It's hard to know what's true and what isn't.'

I laughed. 'Thing is, it's all true.'

He gave a low whistle. 'Wow. I guess some of us are more damaged than others.'

'Fuck off,' I said softly, but with feeling.

'Sorry. I meant . . . some of us carry a heavier burden. My English . . .' An apologetic shrug. 'It doesn't always work right.'

'Yeah. Forget it. OK, let's go see what wheels they left us. Let's hope it comes in black.'

We settled the bill. I checked the Seamaster. It was after nine and the streets were growing dark as we walked towards the car's location, but the air was still warm. I refused a third cigarette but Konrad lit up. 'Last one for a while,' he promised. I didn't have to ask why. It wasn't because he was worried about passive-smoking risks for me or the client. It was so he would always have his hands free and never have to worry about dropping a lit fag in his lap in the heat of the moment.

I had asked the Colonel for a French car and something with a boot, rather than a hatchback, which ruled out the Citroen DS5 that I would really have liked. The Colonel had sourced me a Peugeot 508 GT Line saloon, which was nice and roomy for three people, with enough space in the rear for the Principal to lie down if need be. Not the fastest car on the road, maybe, but more anonymous than, say, a BMW M5. And besides, I was hoping to avoid any high-speed chases. Slow but steady would be my watchword. I saw it as soon as we turned into the *place*, parked at the southern end of the square, well away from a brightly lit brasserie.

I found the keys on the wheel and pointed the fob to unlock it. Konrad put a hand on my wrist to stop me.

'Not yet,' he said. 'Give me a minute.'

He hoisted the knees of his trousers, got down on the ground and began an almost melody-free whistling. From his pocket he took out a compact Maglite and examined the chassis. He ran his hands around the bumpers, too, and the wheel arches. The whistling stopped abruptly.

'You found something?'

'Nope.' He pulled a clump of mud out of the wheel arch. 'OK, open her up.'

I pressed the button. The car flashed its sidelights and the interior lit up. I opened the door and was hit by the new-car smell of leather, plastics and faux-wood. I sat in, adjusted the rake of the steering wheel and moved to fire it up. 'No. Before you start the engine.'

He leaned inside and looked under the dash, checking all the panels were tight.

'Pull the bonnet release, can you?'

Another quick inspection around the engine bay and he slammed it closed.

'Trunk.'

'Boot,' I corrected. It took me a while to find that one.

'Sorry, we'll be doing this every time we have left it unattended. I need to check.'

'For trackers?'

'Yes. I've got a GPS and RF detector I'll run over it too. But I'm also looking for something nastier. Used to be they used mercury tilt switches,' he said. 'Easy to spot. Now they use the same technology that puts a spirit level in your iPhone.' He held thumb and forefinger a few millimetres apart. 'Tiny. But the first corner you lean into ... Boom.'

'You honestly think ... ?' I began.

'*Ez dakit,*' he said softly, before switching back to

English. 'I don't know. No stone unturned, eh?' He brushed dirt off his hands, then his knees, and walked to the rear of the vehicle.

'Right. No stone unturned.' I watched a cohort of jerky black shadows diving above the lights on the square, scooping up a final meal of insects. Bats. My insides felt as if there were a couple of them trapped inside me, flapping about. I hadn't figured on worrying about bombs.

'Sam,' Konrad said. 'Come here a second.'

I got out and walked around to the rear of the Peugeot. At first I couldn't see what he was referring to, just the yawning black hole of the boot's interior, but then he flicked the Maglite's beam on, just for a second, long enough for me to take in the curled-up body and the grey pallor that only death can lend to human skin. The delivery driver, I assumed.

'Welcome to Omaha Beach,' said Konrad softly.

THIRTEEN

Monday

Rubbish day today. Laura told me we were
going to have brunch up above the rice paddies.
That's over on the other coast, up in the
mountains. It was a beautiful drive, but I knew
something was going on. She was all tense the
whole way. We had a driver with us, Putu, who
works in the bar. He laid out the blanket while
we looked down over these ridiculous terraces
carved into the mountainside. The view was
spoiled by all these ships anchored off the coast,
dozens of them. Laura said some of them were
waiting to get into port, but others were waiting
for 'orders' about where to sail next. She said
they could be there for months. Some of them
were really rusty and looked like they had been
there years. Anyway, while we were eating Laura

told me she was going back home for a bit. That was her news.

How long is a 'bit', I asked.

She doesn't know. Her dad is ill and she has to go back to help her mum. I sulked for a while but I suppose she has no choice.

We've got another few days before she goes. She has got me another tutor, she says, a nice English girl called Sarah. But it won't be the same.

I feel so ALONE.

Monday (2)

I forgot to write about The Boy, didn't I? The one in the picture I sent to Becca, Saanvi and Aileen. He's not like my boyfriend or anything. He was called Eric and that picture was taken in the bar. He's eighteen and on a gap year with some mates. They are from Reading. (I suppose I'll miss the festival.) Anyway, he was a bit drunk on Bintangs even though it was only like five o'clock in the afternoon, and messing about being jokey and he put his arm round me and we took some selfies (I've got my phone back btw, yay). Anyway, Dieter came and yanked him off me. Told him to behave. Gave him a slap round the face. Not hard. But they said they are never coming back to the bar, ever. Dieter told them they were barred anyway. I saw Eric in the market when I was out with Laura a few days later but he just blanked me.

Can't blame him. Dieter can be a bit scary.

There's lots of too fit Australian boys around though. Spicy!!!!!!

I met Sarah my new tutor. She has locks and cornrows. She's nice. BUT SHE DOESN'T SURF.

Thursday

Had to go to hospital today. We went to the monkey temple at the bottom of the island. It's nice – looks like something out of that Tomb Raider or Zelda. Anyway, I went with Matt and he said, watch the monkeys. Don't take any food or they'll steal it. I didn't have any food with me but one of them jumped on me and put its hands around my neck. It was going for the diary key. They go for anything shiny.

I fought it off and Matt kicked it but the f-ing thing bit me on the hand. I had teeth marks and blood. Matt insisted I go to the hospital. They said the monkeys PROBABLY don't have rabies. Probably????? Not so far they said. Always a first time I think. But all I got was a tetanus jab. So my arm hurts now. The nurse was really nice and

*very pretty and Matt was chirpsing with her. I
told him he was just so embarrassing. He thought
it was funny.*

Saturday

*I've been following the Poobags on Facebook.
Not contacting them. Just looking at their posts.
It doesn't help. It's like they've forgotten all about
me. I'm not doing it any more.*

FOURTEEN

Normandy, France

It turned out that the brightly lit brasserie on the square still had an old-fashioned wooden telephone booth, with a concertina door for privacy, out the back. The place was busy with yacking locals and I barely earned a glance when I strolled in and ordered a coffee at the bar. I took the opportunity to scan the room. Only a woman near the door, fully dressed in an overcoat and a scarf, made my gaze linger. The café was warm enough that you wouldn't sit there in outdoor clothes unless you were looking to make a quick exit.

But then she began to sneeze into a handkerchief and gave an almighty blow that had fellow customers looking at her askance. I agreed with them. She should be at home in bed, not spreading germs. Nobody else raised any alarms, so I downed the coffee, paid and sidled off to use the phone. I dialled the Colonel but there was no answer. I waited two minutes and tried again. Nothing. I strolled back to the Peugeot, slid into the driver's seat and looked across at Konrad. 'No answer.'

'You think he's set us up?' he asked. 'The Colonel?'

I had considered that. But I shook my head. 'He wouldn't dare. Either for business or personal reasons. I don't think he'd do it to me and if word ever got out that he was double-dealing . . . there wouldn't be much of an empire for that accountant son of his to inherit.'

He thought on that and delivered his verdict with reassuring confidence. 'I agree. The Colonel depends too much on his reputation to play games. And he'd know I'd come looking for him if he fucked us.' He didn't make that sound like it would be a social call for *kaffee und kuchen*.

'I don't want to try his mobile. Or use mine, just in case. Someone could be watching with a spot mic trained on us. I'll ring again tomorrow, once we are on the road. At least we know that there is opposition now.'

'But why kill this guy?' he asked, more to himself than me.

'Maybe just to frighten us.'

'Harsh,' he said. 'Killing one of the cogs just to put the wind up us.'

'Worked though, eh?'

He grunted. He didn't want to admit he was rattled. Me, you could use for a maraca, that's how rattled

I was. 'More likely to frighten Mrs Irwin,' he said. 'Maybe into bolting.'

We both pondered that. A frightened client can be very unpredictable. Might even turn round and head back over the Atlantic. But might also panic and do something really stupid. Like not listening to either of us.

'Any likely candidates in the café? Just watching to see our reaction?'

I shook my head. I had given it a good scan. Nothing had caused the hairs on my neck to stand to attention nor my stomach to flip. A good PPO doesn't ignore a good old-fashioned instinct that something isn't quite right. But the café seemed clean. 'Not that I saw. Family groups, friends. No ones or twos, no obvious out-of-towners. And yes, I checked the plates of the cars outside. And for anyone sitting around waiting for the entertainment to start. Again, nothing suspicious.' There is a simple surveillance rule when you are looking at people. Ask the question: what are they doing there? Is there a reason for that person being in that place? If it isn't obvious, look again. But nobody triggered that response.

'So either they didn't stick around to admire their handiwork ...'

'Or they're too good for me to spot,' I said before he could.

'I'm hoping for the first one.'

Me too. 'What do you want to do with him?' I asked, throwing a thumb towards our lifeless companion in the boot. 'We can't take him to Luxembourg. And he's beyond needing the hospital.'

I had checked. He was still warm but cooling fast, and there was no pulse. He'd been shot once in the temple. No exit wound. Of course I should go to the police, but only if I wanted to get my client arrested on the Europol warrant. That wasn't in my job description. And I had a gunman with me. Maybe fully legal, maybe not, but the cops would certainly be interested in him.

'I vote we put him somewhere that will keep him overnight and you can get the Colonel to retrieve the corpse down the line. There'll be people who will miss him. They deserve a body to bury.'

I'd never met a gunman who cared about friends, wives, lovers or family before but he was right. Dumping him at sea or burying him in a shallow grave would be callous in the extreme.

'The bullet to the head is going to be difficult to explain away,' I said.

'He's a driver. He'll die in a car smash that causes terrible cranial injuries. Nobody will be looking for a bullet. Anyway, someone will make sure it is no longer there by the time he has the accident.'

He made it sound like he had done this kind of thing before. A lot.

In the end we drove to the beach where we had arranged to pick up Mrs Irwin, the Principal. During the journey mercury tilt switches – and their modern, compact replacements – and plastic explosives were at the front of my mind, but no bomb disturbed the peace or added to the night's death toll. On the shore we found an upended, rotting rowboat that clearly hadn't been moved for some considerable time. It would make a reasonable temporary casket. Carrying the body down the path to the shingle was no easy task. All dead people are heavy, but this one was well over six foot when he was alive. I was grateful for whatever workout regime Konrad used, because he took the bulk of the weight.

It was gone ten by the time we had finished the gruesome business and the only noise was the hiss of the incoming tide on the stones and my ragged breathing. I needed a shower. I wanted to scrub my skin raw. Even then I'd have trouble getting the smell of death, and the corpse's aftershave, out of my nostrils.

I stole a glance at the luminous hands on my watch. 'We've got time to get back to the hotel and pick up our stuff,' I said.

'No we haven't,' he said. He had put on a pair of aviator sunglasses. He caught my look of disbelief and said: 'When they come ashore waving their flashlights, it won't fuck up my night vision.'

'They won't be here for over an hour,' I pointed out.

Konrad pointed out to sea. 'Listen.' I did so. Above the thump of the waves I could just about hear the thrum of an outboard, growing louder by the second. 'They're early.'

Not only that, there was twice the number we were expecting.

He had on a college sweatshirt under a Superdry nylon jacket, jeans and trainers so bright their glow cut through the darkness. I swear the stars dimmed. Acid yellow was the closest I could guess to the colour. As the kid helped Mrs Irwin out of the beached RIB, Konrad identified the supernumerary for me. Myles.

'Who?'

'Her son.'

'Son?' Nina hadn't said anything about a son when she had finally briefed me on the woman I would be escorting. 'What does he think this is? Spring break? Did you know?'

Konrad shook his head. 'Nope. I knew there was a son. I didn't expect a mother and child reunion.' He caught my expression at the phrase. 'They don't live together.'

'Is there anything else I should know?' I asked, exasperated.

'No. He probably thinks it's just a European holiday.'

Not that many holidays began with a clandestine

landing on a deserted beach where, as it happens, there was a dead man hidden under a boat.

I introduced myself to the client as the two crewmen took the RIB back out to sea. There wasn't enough light, despite Myles's sneakers, for me to get a good look at her. She had on a headscarf wrapped tightly over her hair and knotted under the chin and a pair of large-framed sunglasses. I didn't think she needed to worry about paparazzi and I doubted she was concerned about her night vision. But sometimes they just act as a security blanket. That's the reason you see celebs wearing them on rainy days.

The crew had left her luggage, two large Louis Vuitton cases, on the damp shingle. Myles was making do with a small backpack. Or maybe one of the LVs was his. Neither of them showed any sign of picking up the cases. And Konrad wouldn't want to be caught in the open with his trigger finger around a kangaroo-skin handle.

Which left me to play bellboy.

'Hi, I'm Myles. With a "Y".'

I ignored him and turned to his mother. 'We thought it was just you coming over, ma'am,' I said, hoping I didn't sound tetchy. But I was tetchy. One cold, dead driver, one unexpected warm body. Neither had been on my call sheet for this one.

'Change of plan,' she replied in a raspy voice that suggested a serious current or past cigarette habit. Just like that. Bring an extra person along, the more the merrier. 'And don't call me ma'am. Ruth will do.'

'I thought . . .'

'Ruth is the name in my new passport. Or will be. I thought I'd better get used to it.'

That's thinking ahead. 'As you wish,' I said, but I had no intention of using a Christian name. Keep it professional. 'I need your mobiles, please. Cellphones, I mean.'

That got me more bristles than a toilet brush. There always were. These days people always act as if you have asked for their genitals on a plate when you want to take their mobiles away.

'No way,' said Myles, less than helpfully.

'Why is that?' asked Mrs Irwin, her voice cool enough to make ice cubes.

'Security, ma'am. Any call you make might give our position away. Phones can be remotely hijacked.'

Myles made a 'huh?' sound, as if he didn't believe me.

I ploughed on regardless. 'Texts and emails can be intercepted. And I bet you've got something like FMF on there so you and your pals can all keep track of each other. That's why I need the cellphones. You'll be off the grid for a while. Twenty-four hours or so. You'll live.' That was meant for Myles. He didn't seem convinced human survival was possible without Pokemon Go or Minecraft or whatever was the current *jeu du jour*. 'I'll give you the SIM cards for safe keeping.'

Nobody moved.

'I can't force you to hand them over. I can only advise you on the best course of action, Mrs Irwin. And you are paying for that advice.'

Konrad broke the resulting silence, his voice low and urgent. 'When we turned up here, someone had murdered the driver who delivered the car. I think it's fair to say that whoever that was knows you are here. It's a good idea not to make it easy for them. Phones make it easy, believe you me.'

I cursed myself for not discussing with Konrad how – even if – to break the news to the client. But I had to admit it was more effective than my attempt at phone fear.

'It's true,' I said glumly. 'Bullet to the head.'

'Get the fuck out of here,' said Myles, as if Konrad had just told him I had four nipples rather than a man had been murdered. I wouldn't have broken it to them quite like he had – if at all, there, on that beach – but that cat was out of the bag now and scampering down the road.

'That's very much what I'd like us to do,' I said, brushing hair from my face as the breeze strengthened. Maybe it was the situation, and the body nearby, but the air seemed distinctly chill now. 'We need to get out of here, ma'am. And we need to stay secure.'

'Give her your phone, Myles,' Mrs Irwin said. 'They know what they are doing.'

From the corner of my eye I saw a light out at sea, sweeping as if searching for something. 'How reliable were the crew?' I asked her.

'Considering what I tipped them, they'd better be damned reliable.'

That didn't sound much like a ringing endorsement to me. Money doesn't buy loyalty. Well, it does until a thicker wallet walks through the door. Or the cops. I picked up the two cases. 'We should get a move on.'

I ushered them, *One Man and His Dog* style, up the beach. Konrad hung back, alternating between watching our backs and checking nobody was blocking our fronts. How he could see much through those bloody sunglasses beat me. But something about his body language – and the gun in his right hand, held close against his body so as not to draw attention to it – reassured me a little.

'Hold up.'

We waited in a breeze that had matured into a wind as Konrad performed his inspection routine on the car.

'What's he looking for?' Myles asked.

'He lost his lucky rabbit's foot,' I said.

'I'd thank you not to be quite so sardonic with my son,' said Mrs Irwin.

Clearly, I was going to have to bite my lip with Ferris Bueller's mum around. 'Sorry, ma'am.'

At some point I was going to have to break it to her that the price for her little jaunt had probably just gone up. Not doubled, but by a good percentage. Because, for starters, two people were much harder to look after than one. Especially if one of the pair is not a child but not yet an adult.

'All clear,' said Konrad.

I put the luggage in the blessedly empty boot and opened the rear car door for our wards to get in.

We headed back to the hotel in silence. Konrad sat in the passenger seat up front, with the client behind me and a fidgety Myles next to her. She took off her sunglasses and scarf; I discreetly studied her reflection in the mirror but it told me little other than I had a tired woman on my hands.

I pulled up outside the hotel, killed the ignition and said to Konrad, 'We should go in one at a time.'

The lad, though, had spotted the welcoming lights of the bar next door. 'Can I get a drink?' he asked.

'No,' we all said at once.

'But it's legal here,' he whined. So he was under twenty-one. Surely he hadn't come all the way to Europe just to get wrecked? And presumably he had been able to drink on the boat over.

'You go first,' I said to Konrad. As he opened the door and the internal lights came on, I gave Myles a quick once-over. He had a square face with a neck that suggested plenty of sports, flawless skin and teeth. Lots of teeth. Wide and white. All-American teeth. There was something of the genetically cloned about him, as if he had been bred to be the captain of the school football team. Gridiron football, that is.

The courtesy lights flicked off as the door closed and I made a mental note to disable them. They could ruin night vision and also give anyone who cared to watch a good look at us.

'I'm sorry, you can get a drink when we get to our final destination.'

'I'll be the judge of that,' said Mrs Irwin firmly.

She hadn't been much of a judge so far. We were heading to get a fake passport for her and she had gone and brought along the boy. I bet the inker in Saint-Lo that the Colonel had employed wasn't expecting that. And I would put good money on Myles having a passport in his own name. Which he would have to show at any hotel we stopped at. So, no hotels. I would have to drive straight through to Luxembourg. When we stopped for breakfast I'd make sure I popped something from my first-aid kit to keep me awake. My body wouldn't thank me, but I'd pay it back later.

'Yes, ma'am,' I said. 'You, of course, have jurisdiction over your son.'

'Thank you.' It was as sharp as a sherbet lemon.

I poured as much concern into my voice as it would take. 'Except if it involves your safety, or the safety of the group, Mrs Irwin.'

'I told you, Ruth will do,' she replied briskly.

'Yes, ma'am.'

'This man who was killed? Was it definitely murder? Not an accident?'

'I don't think so.' Not unless he shot himself in the head, climbed into the boot and then disposed of the weapon, because there was no sign of it. 'It fact, I'd put money on it not being an accident.'

'Then that's bad news.'

'It is. You have any ideas about who might be trying to stop you making this journey, Mrs Irwin?' I asked.

'Not a clue.'

I doubted that. She would have some inkling, if only a sneaking suspicion, even if she didn't want to face up to it.

I checked my phone surreptitiously. There was a voicemail from Nina, but I was low on battery on both my phones. I had assumed nobody was out to track me, but I didn't want to get into an argument about why I still had a phone – well, two phones – and they didn't. I lifted the central armrest and found the charging slot and connected the iPhone. On the Android – one-handed and under my jacket so as not to rub it in to my phoneless charges – I texted Nina: *Will call later.*

I used my new knife to saw off the buckle of the seat belt and then shoved it into its slot. That way, the car's computer wouldn't go apoplectic every time

I pressed start, binging and bonging to remind me I wasn't buckled up. Seat belts slow you down. Many a driver has been trapped for a split second by a belt. Just enough for someone to shoot them through the side window. Of course, that was assuming you didn't have a collision where you needed the belt, but my instinct told me it was better to stay mobile on this one than be strapped into a seat.

Konrad reappeared and I popped the boot again. I got out and intercepted him. 'Let's not dwell on the driver, eh? It's just sinking in with Mrs Irwin. We don't want to spook them too much.'

He shrugged. 'Fine by me. I covered the bill, by the way. Cash, before you ask.' I'd used my Alison Cooke passport from the Monaco caper to register; I assumed he'd also used one that didn't have his real name on it. 'Let's get out of here.' There was impatience in his voice. We both wanted to put some distance between us and this town. Oh, and the body under the boat.

I handed him the knife. 'I assume you don't want a seat belt?'

'No. Not now we know it isn't a day at the park.'

'Walk in the park,' I corrected. 'Day at the beach.' Whatever the phrase, it wasn't going to be either of those.

It was my turn to fetch my stuff. I had repacked my gear before we went for dinner, so, with a final, longing look at the shower, I grabbed the RTG bag and left the room. It was going to be a long night.

Ordinarily I would have gone along the coast road, the D116, or the slightly faster inland route, the D901, to Cherbourg and then struck south towards the N13. But there was no ordinarily about this. We had to avoid any cops and we had to assume we had been blown by whoever the opposition was. And I really wanted to know if anyone was following us. So I picked up the D24, which would wind us, in a series of doglegs, to Valognes, where I would pick up the D2. There was no place for anyone to hide on such a road. If we'd picked up a shadow, I'd see them. There was only one problem. What if they *wanted* to be seen?

Nobody spoke for a while and I kept my eyes on the mirror as much as the black tarmac that shone like patent leather in the Peugeot's big halogens. I could see Konrad was watching the door mirror on his side. I used the electronic control to angle it so he had a decent view of the road behind. He grunted his thanks.

The road was in pretty good shape, the headlamps picking out tall hedgerows that sometimes crowded in alarmingly, so that two cars abreast could only just squeeze by each other. Ambush country. But I didn't think we were up against that, not yet. How could they know I'd come this way? No, my main problem with how narrow the road was involved me clattering into another vehicle, given that I wasn't braking much and no longer had a working seat belt. But this wasn't a route favoured by lorries and I reckoned that there would be little agricultural machinery out at that time of night. The last thing I wanted was a head-on with a Massey-Ferguson or whatever the French equivalent was, but I considered that was unlikely.

So I kept up a steady speed, just a notch above entirely sensible, and tried to take the bends as smoothly as possible. I didn't want carsick passengers either. Luckily the 508 had suspension set for comfort, not handling, so she sailed round most of them in a stately fashion, despite being shod with unforgiving run-flat tyres. Which I hate.

'Can you tell me the arrangements?' Mrs Irwin asked.

'We are to stop in Saint-Lo and get you some papers. Only one set has been arranged, I am afraid.'

'Myles and I do not have the same surname. So his passport should not set alarm bells ringing.'

Well, that was something. And might explain why he wasn't flagged up as her son in Nina's research. Although Myles, with that spelling, wasn't such a common a name. Hoteliers might remember it if asked. I was still disinclined to use official lodgings.

'OK, after we get the papers, then we go directly to ... where we are going.' I was too superstitious to say it out loud. It's an old PPO habit: you don't advertise where you are going, even when it's bleedin' obvious. It means that when it really matters, you don't let slip the route or final destination. PPOs still live by that old poster: *Walls have ears*. These days it's ceilings, floors and windows, too.

'Luxembourg.'

'Yes.'

'When do you expect we will be there?'

I looked at Konrad. 'I'm mainly going to use roads like this. It's slow, but safe.' At least, I hoped so. 'We'll be in Saint-Lo at first light. We can have breakfast while the papers are done. Then, by tomorrow evening, with a bit of luck, we'll have you at your meeting.'

'You will share the driving?'

'No.' Konrad answered for me, just in case I thought that a good idea. 'You can't be the firepower and the driver at the same time. You end up compromising both.' I was glad to hear that definitive dismissal. If he ended up driving it meant I was disabled. Or worse.

'I'll be fine,' I said. 'I've done this before. Why don't you try and get some sleep?'

We drove on in silence, although Myles seemed to twitch and sigh a lot. Screen withdrawal symptoms, no doubt. After fifteen minutes I pulled over in a passing place and switched the car's engine off, killing the lights. The engine ticked as it cooled. The impenetrable blackness of the countryside seemed to thicken around us.

'Why have we stopped?' asked Mrs Irwin eventually.

'Just a precaution,' said Konrad.

A car came in the opposite direction after five minutes and I closed my eyes as the headlamps raked our cabin. I am sure Konrad did the same behind his sunglasses.

I waited another ten, thinking about the phone call I was going to make to the Colonel. I'd call from the inker's place, on a landline, and I'd still have to use some sort of code to tell him the driver had a headache he wasn't going to recover from. *It's the vet here. I am afraid your cat is very unwell.*

I'd think of something better than that, I was sure.

Once I was certain nobody was on our tail, I restarted and turned left at the next crossroads. Konrad leaned forward and looked at the heads-up satnav display. I was going to circle back as well, just in case.

There was, though, another possibility. Maybe they didn't need to follow us. Maybe they already knew where we were going. After all, if they knew we were getting a car delivered ...

But I put that thought aside until the next morning. Things usually looked better in daylight.

Usually. Not always.

FIFTEEN

'I could do with a coffee.'

They were the first words that Konrad had spoken for some time. I was travelling west, above Saint-Lo, the red smudge of a sunrise filling my mirror. The address I had been given for the inker was in the eastern suburbs of the town. I wanted to come in from the west, just in case someone was expecting us. The obvious approach, given our origin point, would have been from the east.

'If you think that is OK,' he added.

Coffee sounded good. My eyes were full of sand and I could feel my energy levels dropping. Those roads were tiring and the constant vigilance, not to mention the doubling back and the long diversion to the west, had taken it out of me. Konrad, though, looked box fresh.

I studied the rear-view mirror. Myles's head had lolled to one side; he had his mouth open and was snoring. 'Ruth' had her head back against the headrest, but

I couldn't be sure she was asleep behind the sunglasses. Now it was light, I got a good look at her face. She was attractive in a severe way. Her face looked as if it had been hewn out of a solid block of alabaster to give it cheekbones and a firm jawline. Red hair poked out from beneath the headscarf, just a shade too bright to be her natural colour. Even a few surreptitious glances were enough to tell me she'd had work done. Possibly a lot of work. Certainly expensive, for she didn't have any of the usual trout-in-a-hurricane features that shouted SURGERY. How old? In her mid-forties, Nina had said. Young to be pricking and plumping at her face, but that's rich Americans for you. Can't leave well enough alone.

I slowed as I approached the rear of a Renault van decorated with a logo showing a bunch of smiling carrots. I pulled round it. Its side was covered with more drawings of happy, happy vegetables. 'There'll be a town with a market somewhere around. Where there's a market …'

'There's a market café,' Konrad finished.

He played with his phone. 'Marigny? Says here Wednesday is market day. And today's Wednesday.'

I punched the name into the sat nav. Twenty-one kilometres. 'It'll do.'

He turned and examined our cargo. Satisfied they were asleep, he asked: 'How'd you get into this business anyway?'

'I thought you'd checked me out?' I asked.

'Only your PPO record.'

'I was a Combat Medical Technician. Iraq, mostly. Afterwards I just fell into it. You?'

'I was in the thirty-fourth Bercsényi László. You know them?' There was a pride in his voice I hadn't heard before. 'Hungarian Special Forces. Then the movie business started coming to Budapest and Prague. Hollywood and the BBC came calling whenever they wanted to recreate old Paris or Victorian London. So you get Tom Cruise or Johnny Depp, wanting to see the sights and the nightlife, and studios getting very nervous. They still thought of us as the Wild East, full of gypsy thieves. So, they hired local muscle. Ex-special forces like me. From there, hanging round the set, it was easy to get the job fixing up the guns.'

There was a queue of traffic into Marigny and Konrad stopped talking as we slowed. He rolled up his right trouser leg, revealing the holster strapped to his ankle. A crawling line of vehicles was a good place to sandwich me in and try a snatch. If that was what they wanted. Or spray the car with bullets, if that was their preference. Konrad began to watch for anything that might be the initiation part of a move against us. I did the same for my side.

Most of the vans and cars turned right, so we took a left and drove around the other side of town. I parked up in a side street and turned the engine off. I looked at my watch. It was coming up to six-thirty.

'Early for tourists to be out and about,' he said, reading my mind. What were we to the casual observer? They'd be unlikely to think: oh, look – a professional BG/gunman, a PPO, an American millionairess and her rangy son. But then again, they would probably remember us as strangers in town for a day or two if anyone came asking. We didn't exactly blend in.

'We'll have to take that chance.'

I left the car and opened the rear door. Mrs Irwin's eyes snapped open as cool and fresh morning air hit her. 'Are we here?'

'Comfort break, ma'am,' I said. 'We won't be too long.'

'Coffee?'

'Coffee,' I agreed.

'Good.' She shook her son on the shoulder. She spoke with real affection, as if he were a slumbering prince. 'Myles. Myles, darling. Wake up.'

He gave a start, a snort and then smacked his lips together. It obviously took him a few seconds to place where he was in the world. He pulled himself upright in the seat. 'Wassappening?' he asked.

'Coffee. Rest rooms,' I said.

'Will there be somewhere for me to freshen up?' Mrs Irwin asked.

'Probably.' I wasn't making any promises. I was not

in familiar territory. 'If you don't mind, we'll see how we go.'

'Of course.' She grabbed her handbag and exited in a smooth, elegant movement. She was wearing a dark-grey trouser suit, and when she stood the wrinkles seemed to fall out of it. I smoothed my own clothes as best I could. Once we had gathered, the four of us strolled down the pavement trying to look nonchalant.

'You have spoken to the Colonel?' Mrs Irwin asked.

'No. I'll do it later, I promise. Myles, listen . . .'

A grunt came back.

'You and your mother, please could you not speak in the café any more than is strictly necessary.'

'Why not?' he asked with a distinct undertow of irritation.

'Just in case someone wonders what two Americans are doing so far off the beaten track. Your country-men come for the Normandy beaches to the north. I doubt Marigny has many must-see sights for them, so you'll stand out. That goes for you too, Mrs Irwin, if you don't mind.' I waited for her to correct me with a Christian name I was never going to use. She let it pass. 'Unless your French accent is good.'

She shook her head to let me know it wasn't. 'What about you?'

'Passable,' I admitted. 'But there's a tradition of English speaking bad French all over France, from the boom years of property buying. They're no longer a novelty.'

Café du Marché was just what I expected it to be, with scuffed wood panelling, bentwood chairs and a zinc bar. It was busy, mostly with traders hitting early-morning brandies, and we got few glances as I ushered our party towards the rear. I knew Konrad was worried about exits, but going deep inside meant we were hidden from view in case anyone was window-shopping for us. He had rolled down that trouser leg so he no longer looked like a gunfighting Mason with a grievance, but when he sat he would make certain his right leg stuck straight out so he could grab the ankle gun if need be.

I found us a table behind a coat rack that shielded us further and was a few paces from the kitchen, which gave us an escape route if necessary. Konrad made sure he could see the front door, to check comings and goings and, as I expected, he kept that ankle within easy reach. But we both knew it was all more a set of familiar precautions than anything really useful. We had no idea what our opposite numbers looked like. Or what they wanted. He would have to go on instinct if anything started.

I ordered four coffees and assorted pastries from a waiter whose look told me he had better things to do than listen to me mangle his language. Konrad said something in fast, fluent French I didn't catch. The waiter scuttled off.

'I told him to move his fuckin' ass or I'd give it a good kicking.'

'And we were meant to keep a low profile,' I said.

He shrugged. 'It's what they expect.'

'I am going to use the washroom,' Mrs Irwin said in a low voice.

'Hold on. I'll come with you,' I said.

There's nothing unusual about two women going to the bathroom together. That is unless one of them goes in first and checks both cubicles to make sure there are no nasty surprises waiting. While she had a noisy piss, I threw water on my face and tried to make myself look more awake than I felt. I remembered I had neglected to take my Pro Plus or the Ritalin I kept as emergency back-up when mere caffeine won't do. But perhaps it was best I didn't rely on artificial stimulants until I really needed them.

Mrs Irwin came out and joined me at a mirror that looked like it had scabies. From her bag she extracted three tubs of cream, two lipsticks, a fancy palette of eyeliners and some wet wipes. She used the latter to scrape off whatever remained from the previous day, examining the black smudges under her eyes with a frown. They weren't going to come off with wet wipes.

'I would like you to cut my son some slack,' she said to the mirror.

'I'm just doing my job, ma'am,' I said.

'Can you do it with a much more consolatory tone?

190

Please. He's just a boy. He had a rough crossing. He's tired. After he has had a rest, you'll see a different side of him. He can be fun. Funny.'

'I'm sure.' I wasn't, but I'd have to take her word for it. 'He was a surprise addition, though.'

'I appreciate that and I'm sorry. But he's here now and I'd appreciate it if you'd deal with the new situation in a civil manner. He's worried about me, even if he doesn't show it. About the arrest warrant.'

'Me too.'

'I didn't do it, you know.' Now she looked at me properly, trying to gauge my reaction.

She offered me the packet of wet wipes and I took one. I dragged it over my cheeks and forehead. 'That's not my concern,' I said, keeping my voice idling in neutral.

'I didn't bribe anyone. Manipulate the Euribor rates. I play the markets, sure, but I do it above board. It was someone trying to cut a deal who gave the authorities a long list of names. Mine was just one.'

'It isn't important to me what you did or didn't do with the rates,' I said. 'The police notice just makes the job trickier.'

'I just want you to know, that's all. The sort of person you are dealing with. The charge is a total fabrication. A smear. It is easy to pay enough to make sure a name goes on a list. A ploy designed to stop me going to the meeting.'

She fixed me with a stiletto glare, waiting for a response.

'I understand. And I agree, it isn't hard to throw mud at a wall and wait for it to stick. But why would anyone want to stop you getting to Luxembourg?'

'Who knows? I am a very rich woman, on paper at least, Miss Wylde. Is that right? Wylde?'

It was good to have my real name back. 'Alison Cooke' had been an alias created for the *Kubera* operation, just in case someone had thought to check out my previous history. And in case anyone came looking for the retrievers later with the thought of doing them harm. 'With a Y, yes.'

'And as you know, you make enemies on your way to that position. Not all of whom are rational. Perceived slights can grow into personal vendettas.'

I shifted to a more placatory tone. She was in a very defensive mode. I didn't think it would take much to get her hackles rising. 'Ma'am, if you have any idea of who it might be, no matter if it is embarrassing or illegal, you really must tell me. And Konrad. He has to assess what we are up against.' And maybe whistle up some reinforcements.

'Miss Wylde, let me assure you I have done nothing embarrassing or illegal,' she said, giving me a quick flash of those hackles. 'I simply need to attend to some business.'

I was about to ask more about the business when the

door opened and a mother and young daughter came in. Once I had checked they were what they seemed, I left Mrs Irwin to her expensive make-up. I'd put on a smear of Chanel lipstick. It didn't improve matters much, but it would have to do.

I sat back down and moved my chair so I could see her come safely out of the lavatory, which she did two minutes later, just as the coffee and pastries arrived. I placed some euro bills on the table, in case we had to make a hasty exit. It was probably too much but I wouldn't be waiting for the change if we had to abandon the café. And I didn't want a waiter chasing me down the street demanding another euro or two while we were trying to make a swift exit from Marigny. We ate and drank in silence.

When we had finished, I pointed to the bar and said, 'That payphone there is too public. I'd best wait until the Post Office opens.' There was a good chance that the PTT in a town like Marigny still had old-fashioned booths like the one I had used in the brasserie. 'With a bit of luck that'll be eight o'clock on market day.'

'I'm going to take a turn round the square,' said Konrad, rising from his seat.

'Sure?' I asked.

'I like to be ... what's the word ...'

He rarely struggled with his English vocabulary, so I waited a beat before I helped him out. 'Pre-emptive.'

'Yes, pre-emptive.'

After he had gone I ordered more coffees and placed some extra notes on the stack.

'Can I speak now?' Myles asked.

I looked around. Nobody had given us a first, let alone a second glance. 'Sure. Just keep it down.'

'What's he doing?' he hissed. 'Your scary friend?'

'Checking everything is as it should be.'

'What does that mean?'

'He'll have a sniff around, see if there's anyone who might be looking for us. You can tell sometimes. People who have a different agenda, who aren't in town for a string of onions or cheap shoes. They have tells sometimes, like poker players.' In truth, you had to be very, very lucky to spot them. But maybe Konrad was just that. Unlike our delivery driver.

'Do you think we are in much trouble, Miss Wylde?' Mrs Irwin asked.

I decided I had best be honest. 'Yes. I think there is trouble. I don't know how far into it we are yet.'

I had the fresh cup of coffee to my lips when I heard the distinctive sound that told me we were in pretty damn deep. I looked around the room. Nobody else had so much as cocked an ear. Maybe they weren't tuned in for those sounds like I was. But I knew immediately what I'd heard. Gunshots.

Three of them.

PART FOUR

SIXTEEN

I could tell by the pallor of Konrad's skin that he was hurt, but his face was absolutely still. He was standing at the entrance to the alley that led from the rear of the café. His right hand was in the pocket of his windcheater. His left was gripping his waist. I couldn't see any blood on his fingers. That didn't mean there wasn't any.

'You OK?' I asked.

'*Min egiten du,*' he said, before remembering he was talking to an English speaker. 'It'll keep.' Then, quietly: 'Must be gettin' old.'

'Don't say that.' I meant it. I didn't want a gunman who thought he was losing his edge. Not when we had armed opposition out there. Dammit, though, he shouldn't have got himself shot. But it was no time for recriminations. 'I'll take a look at it as soon as I can. You OK to walk?'

A weak smile. 'Run if I have to.'

'Let's hope it doesn't come to that.' I wasn't joking.

If we ended up running, then we were in deep shit. I glanced down at Mrs Irwin's shoes. She wasn't going to challenge Usain Bolt in those heels. Myles's eye-bleedingly bright sneakers might just come into their own, though, but I knew we were going to have to dump them at some point. Too damned memorable.

Mrs Irwin and Myles pressed forward, starting to crowd me, and I waved them back, unsure whether it was safe to step out into the street. Plus I wanted room to manoeuvre if need be.

'Take your shoes off,' I said to Mrs Irwin. 'Please. Just in case we have to move quickly. There's cobbles out there. I don't want you turning an ankle.' I certainly didn't want to have to do a fireman's lift on her.

She did as she was told. I turned back to Konrad, who was resting his weight against the wall. Shit. I had a sudden unwelcome thought. *I don't want to die here. I don't want to die not having seen Jess again.*

'Is the Peugeot compromised?' I asked.

'It was,' he said, with a sharp intake of breath I didn't like the sound of. 'It isn't now. I saw two flies, paying undue attention to it. I swatted them away.'

'How are they?' I meant had he hit them in the exchange of gunfire. Three shots, I had heard. I assume only one got him. Where did the other pair go? And who else had heard them and recognised them for what they were? 'Do they have any men down?'

He ignored that. 'We should get going. The cops

will . . .' Another gasp. 'They'll know. That there's been gunfire. They probably won't know from where yet.' It is always surprisingly hard to pinpoint where gunshots have come from. You only have to see videos of cops under fire from a sniper to realise it's a while before they can get a bead on the location of the shooter.

We walked briskly out, as unobtrusively as we could, Konrad in front, me behind. I spotted a small hole in the back of his jacket. Exit wound. So the bullet either passed through his body or simply took a chunk out of his side. Either way, the hole was good news. Well, better news anyway.

'Myles, eyes front,' I said. His head was swivelling like he was at Wimbledon.

An old guy with his enormous belly barely contained by his blue overalls stopped to watch us, filling his pipe as he did so. It looked like he could smell our . . . well, fear was too strong a word. Or maybe it wasn't. Someone called his name and he turned to greet an old friend. We were forgotten.

'Up on the left,' I said. 'Window.'

Konrad shook his head. 'I don't think so.'

A young woman appeared and tossed keys down to a teenage boy, who let himself into the house.

Konrad dropped back a pace. 'We can't make the first move. Too many innocent people. They'll have to show themselves.'

We reached the car without anyone yelling for us

to stop or put our hands up. I blipped it open from a safe distance and Konrad told me to hold my horses. Although it clearly pained him he went through his routine – underneath, under dash, engine bay, boot. From the boot he extracted the punchier gun he had been talking about, although I didn't get a clear look at it. But it had some heft to it judging by the grunt he gave. I grabbed the smaller of my two first-aid kits from my RTG bag and tossed it to Myles.

'Satisfied?' I asked Konrad.

'Clean as a whistle,' he said, and we climbed in, taking up position as before.

'I think I'm about to drip on the expensive uphol-stery.' Konrad raised his left hand. The palm was bright scarlet.

'It's wipe-clean,' I said.

He laughed.

'How badly are you hurt, Mr Konrad?' asked Mrs Irwin.

He glanced at me and managed a half-smile. 'If only we had a medic who could tell me.'

'Yeah, if only . . .'

I pulled out of the street and set about getting out of yet another town with indecent haste. It was becoming a habit, I reflected, as we powered on up the tree-lined hill that led towards Saint-Lo. Luckily all the traffic was coming into town and the road ahead was pretty clear.

'I'll find somewhere we can stop and take a look,' I promised. 'You OK, Myles. Myles?'

The boy looked paler than Konrad. He swallowed hard and nodded. Ah, the blood.

'It's not as bad as it looks,' I said. It was our stock phrase in Iraq, used no matter what the situation. *It isn't as bad as it looks. You'll be OK, it hasn't hit anything vital. Chopper will be here in five. You'll be running marathons again before you know it.* Ordinary, everyday lies.

Konrad gave a wheezing laugh. 'That's OK for you to say. It's not your blood.'

'Sorry. I'm sure it's painful.'

'I've had worse,' he snapped.

The tone told me just how much it hurt. I know what it is to have a bullet wound throbbing in your side. It is deep and painful and seems to vibrate through your entire skeleton. I had caught one in Afghanistan, when I was carrying Jess and before I had decided whether to keep her or not. The bullet – the thought of what it might have done to her in the womb and the fierce protectiveness that triggered – rather made my mind up, about both having Jess and leaving the army. I couldn't seem to stay away from them though. Bullets weren't done with me yet, it seemed. Plus there was another source of pain for Konrad: his pride. Gunmen aren't meant to get shot, they are meant to do the shooting.

I checked the mirror. Only a lorry labouring after me. 'How did you leave them?' I asked. 'The flies?'

'Why are you so worried?'

'Because it'll slow them down if you got one in any of them,' I snapped. 'You know that. Or you should.' I took a deep, deep breath. 'Sorry. That was the adrenaline talking.'

He nodded to show it was OK. The analysis could come later, but he would be aware that this was a situation we shouldn't have found ourselves in. 'Put it this way. They won't be doing much tap dancing from now on.'

Leg shots. At least we didn't have dead bodies. Living, they could make themselves scarce. Dead, the police have a habit of finding them and making a fuss. With leg wounds they were going to need some sort of medical treatment and they were unlikely to opt for the nearest Outpatients. Chances were he'd bought us some time.

'Good. Can you hold on for a while?' I asked.

'As I said, I'll keep.'

I heard Mrs Irwin make a squeaking noise that might have been disgust. She met my eyes in the rear-view mirror.

'Men. Why can't they just admit it hurts like fuck and be done with it?' The swear word should have sounded strange, but I had a feeling it was, or had been, second nature at one time. But, judging by the look on her son's face, not for a while.

'It's the Bruce Willis in me,' said Konrad. 'I worked with him once. One of the *Die Hards*. The one set in Russia. Nice guy. Anyone mind if I smoke?'

Nobody did. He had earned a cigarette. He opened the window and let the blue fumes trail out behind us. He kept the Gitanes in his left hand, which meant he had to twist slightly to let the slipstream snatch the smoke away and to flick the ash out of the window. But he wanted his right free.

'Myles, open that first-aid pack, there should be a field dressing. Green pack, FD-W written on it.'

'Got it.'

'Rip it open, hand it to Mr Konrad. He'll know what to do.'

I gave the gunman a sideways look and he nodded. With the cigarette dangling from the corner of his mouth he rolled up his polo shirt. I could see a splodge of blood, some of it already congealing. Taking the bandage, he ripped off the protective strips that covered the sticky surfaces of the dressing. I used my right hand to help him press it home.

'Son of a bitch.' He turned to Mrs Irwin. 'It hurts like fuck.'

A smile flickered across her face and those chiselled features softened a little. It suited her. 'That's better,' she said.

A red light on the heads-up display flashed at me. 'Shit.'

'What?' he asked.

'Left rear tyre is deflating.' And making a rattling noise as it did so.

'Doesn't feel like it,' he said.

'These are run-flats. It will feel like it when the last of the air goes. You see any spikes on the road back there?'

'No. Not that I could see.'

'It might just be bad luck.' There was certainly enough of it around.

'Don't you have a spare?' asked Myles.

'Nope. You're just meant to nurse the car to a garage, where you'll be charged a fortune to replace the damaged tyre.'

'That sucks.'

A second warning lamp. 'Right rear. We've run over something, either deliberate or not.'

Konrad flicked the cigarette out of the window. 'I don't believe in coincidences like that.'

Nor me. Not when the rear tyres blow and the fronts don't. Which was what the dash display was indicating. I listened for, and heard, another rattling sound. Odd. 'You did check the tyres?' I asked.

'Yes.' He almost succeeded in keeping the tetchiness from his voice. 'But not tread by tread. We didn't have that sort of time.'

True. His inspection would have spotted one of the larger devices cops use to split or spike the tyres of fugitives. But there were also small percussive caps that could be hidden in the tyre tread that could cause a blow-out. You had to check every inch of the wheel to find them.

'Will we have to stop?' asked Mrs Irwin.

'Usually you have a limit on run-flats. Do not exceed eighty kilometres an hour or so. But even if we stay at that, they're only good for ninety or a hundred clicks before we'll be running on rims.'

I was just thinking we could still put some distance under our belts when I felt the accelerator soften under my foot. I pressed down, gently and then harder, eye on the rev counter. Not much happened.

'Fucking computers,' I muttered.

'What is it?' asked Myles.

'I'm guessing there's a limiter kicked in.' The OBD – the On Board Diagnostic chip – had sensed we had a double deflation. It had gone into 'nanny' mode. The speed was dropping. We were barely at sixty. The lorry from Marigny was catching up with us.

'We need two new tyres. I can't get us to Luxembourg like this.'

'You sure?' asked Konrad.

'I'm sure.' My turn to be tetchy. I didn't like this one bit.

'They'll know that we'll need to stop,' said Konrad pensively. 'If it was a deliberate ploy.'

'I don't think they gave us a double puncture just as a parting gift, do you?'

He shook his head.

'So they are probably waiting somewhere up the road for us.'

'I would have to agree,' Konrad said in a weary voice.

'I thought you shot the other guys?' asked Myles, his voice laced with worry. His mother, I thought, was commendably calm.

'I took out two of them,' Konrad explained with measured patience. 'They didn't hand me a cast list for this particular production.'

Or a shooting script.

'If it was me,' I said, 'doing this, trying to screw us up, I'd stake out the next few garages along the route. Knowing we'd have to call in sooner rather than later.'

The lorry, which had been filling my rear-view mirror for the past two minutes, pulled out and, in a cloud of black particles and clashing gears, accelerated past. I braced myself, but it really was just an innocent truck. Behind me the nearest cars were mere dots. For now.

'I've got an idea. If you care to hear it,' said Konrad. He was talking through clenched teeth now.

'Go on.'

'I know all routing decisions are yours.'

'Yeah. I'm doing just peachy up to now. Go on. Fire away.'

'I did a German version of *The Four Musketeers*

near here. Thirty kilometres, maybe less, there's a big chateau they used for filming some exteriors and a ballroom. Actually, it's not big – they just made it look like that. I know the location scout that sourced it. I might be able to get us in there while we sort some tyres. In fact, there's a film service unit in Le Mans I could call. It supplies vehicles to movies. From 2CVs to tanks.'

'A tank might be good.'

He laughed at that and regretted it. He gripped his side again. 'Terrible mileage. These guys could help, though, no questions asked. And we'd know their hands are clean.' He meant they were unlikely to have been tapped by whatever black hats were ranged against us.

'Le Mans is a fair distance from here,' I said, thinking out loud. 'It'll take time to get them up here.'

'Not too long, once they've sourced the right tyres. They've got a van with all the gear on to do the change.'

He didn't say anything else. He didn't have to. What was going through his mind was busy yelling itself hoarse around the cabin: *do you have any better ideas?*

Truth was, I didn't. 'Does the chateau have a landline?'

'Last time I was there it did. We've just got to hope they're not making the sequel there.'

'I don't think there is a Five Musketeers,' I said. I

could feel the bumps in the road more keenly now. The rear axle was juddering with each pothole as it lost the cushioning of air in the tyres. The Bridgestones were running on the stiffened sidewalls.

I twisted slightly so I could look at Mrs Irwin for a second. 'It'll make us late. Stopping off. But it means I can treat his wound properly, rather than in some service station toilet. How do you feel about that? The delay, I mean.' I was fairly sure she'd be indifferent to where I administered first aid.

'Delayed by how much?' she asked.

I could only take a stab at that. 'Twelve to twenty-four hours. I can't be more specific.'

'Better late than dead.'

It was a moment before we all realised it was Myles who had spoken. Konrad turned and gave him a smirk. 'Well said, young man.'

I looked at the dash clock. It was still surprisingly early. Most of France was still having breakfast. Why did I feel like I'd done a day's work already?

'We'll make the calls,' I said.

I wasn't taking any chances with the phones. I sent Myles to buy a throwaway burner from a phone store when we reached the outskirts of Saint-Lo. While he did so I checked the tyre sizes. At the same time I ran my hands round the two rears. Each had a serious hole, but not the jagged kind they would have displayed if we'd run over a Pit-BUL or a similar vehicle-stopping device. Something subtler had been used. But if it was an explosive charge, I would have heard it. There was another possibility – a Riptor device, a self-boring circular blade that burrows like a parasite into the tyre. As used by MOSSAD. If that was the case, the evidence might well be inside the tyre. That rattle I had heard maybe? For the moment, that was immaterial. Something had chewed out the tyres and the condition of the Bridgestone's sidewalls suggested that, even at the much-reduced speed, we couldn't go on indefinitely.

Then I got an approximate location from Konrad for the Musketeers chateau and put it into the satnav. It was more like forty kilometres. Which was an hour or more with us limping along. Konrad reckoned he would be able to pinpoint it once we were in the immediate vicinity.

The first call Konrad made was a success. 'OK, there's nobody in it,' he said when he had hung up. 'I've got the gate code. There's a caretaker who may or may not be on site, but there's a keybox with the same code in reverse round the side of the house. And if it's the same caretaker, we'll be OK. He's a good guy.'

'Good.' I knew something else was coming.

'One drawback.'

I hazarded a guess. 'They're charging us. Through the nose.'

209

'Yes.' He looked resigned to the fact. 'Because they always do, don't they?'

Because when the chips are down, the bill always goes up. Desperation is not a good bargaining position. And we were desperate. 'We'll pass the charge on to the Colonel.'

'Who'll pass it on to me,' said Mrs Irwin.

'Well,' said Konrad, letting himself slide down the seat into a more comfortable position, 'in which case we are indeed fortunate that you are a very wealthy woman.'

The next few kilometres passed in what I guess was a frosty silence from the rear.

The chateau was at the end of a long poplar-lined drive. It had those slated Disney-style turrets with high windows where princesses are usually kept, steeply pitched mansard roofs, apertures flanked by pilasters, a sweeping staircase to the entrance and plenty of frou-frou plasterwork dotted with coats of arms. It wasn't 'little', as Konrad had suggested, and it appeared that the exterior had been piped in a patisserie, not actually built at all. It looked the part for a bit of swordplay and skulduggery. Inside, though, it smelled musty. No musketeers of any description had been swashing or buckling for quite some time. Which was fine by me.

We based ourselves in one of the smaller salons, which was furnished with brocaded chairs, heavy gold and red drapes and over-ornate sideboards, mirrors and clocks. It wasn't hard to imagine the Sun King lounging on a chaise longue complaining about the Protestants or his demanding mistresses. There were four such rooms downstairs, a mirror-lined ballroom and a cellar kitchen.

We piled our gear against one wall. I finally got a good look at the cannon Konrad was using. It was a Czech FK Brno, a pistol chambered for the 7.5mm bottlenecked, claimed to be second only to the .44 Magnum in power. I didn't want to be in the same room when that went off. The other guys were lucky he had only fired the Ruger. A shot in the leg from the FK and they'd be amputees for sure.

I let the Americans go off to explore the place and find a room to rest up in. I pulled a dust cloth off a highly polished table and laid it on the carpet. A cloud of dust erupted as I did so, making me sneeze.

'Get on the table.'

'You sure?'

'Blood wipes far easier off shiny walnut than it does carpet.'

He put the FK on a nearby chair, climbed up very gingerly and lay back. The table gave the politest of groans as it took his weight. I cut away some of the polo shirt to reveal the crudely applied field dressing.

'How many approaches to the house?'

'Only one—' The last word segued into a wail as

I ripped the soiled bandage from his body. Blood did indeed spatter the wood, coalescing into little globules on the wax surface. 'Ow. That really did fucking hurt.'

'Sorry. I figured if you were thinking about business you wouldn't be thinking quite so much about how that was going to sting.'

I used a magnifying glass to examine the exposed flesh and muscle and picked out a few strands of fabric that might fester. He was lucky, there was little debris in there. Then I cleaned out the wound, squirted a blast of antiseptic spray, and sprinkled in some antibiotic powder. I used a haemostatic-sealing pack and applied a fresh dressing. I then wound a strapping bandage around his midriff, just to keep everything in place.

'It's not deep and it's good and clean. More a gouge than a bullet channel. It skittered along your side and out the back of your jacket. A stitch won't help, I don't think. No shrapnel or fabric fragments I can see. Some powder burns on the skin. Guy was close, huh?'

'I could smell his breakfast on his breath. I managed to knock his gun aside, otherwise you'd be looking at a PAW.' A Penetrating Abdominal Wound would have had a whole different outcome. 'Second one was a way away. He missed.'

'So four shots?' I asked.

He nodded.

'I only heard three.'

'And there'll be some people who say they heard fifty. The cops are probably looking for someone with a machine gun as we speak.'

That was true. The public was notoriously unreliable when it came to details such as how many shots were fired.

'Any thoughts on who they were?'

'I don't think they were A-team. I took them too easily. This apart, I mean.'

I wasn't sure whether that was good or bad. At least the top guys tended to work in predictable ways, within a set of parameters we all knew. If we were up against a bunch of amateurs, anything could happen.

He swung his feet off the table and slid to the floor. He did a couple of side bends and then some twists.

'It's gonna hurt.'

'It won't slow me down.' A little chippy inflection crept in and the Hungarian accent showed itself.

'Never said it would. Here.' I gave him a strip of painkillers.

'Thanks. Good job.'

I went to look outside while he selected a new shirt from his case. The floor-to-ceiling French doors of the salon overlooked a terrace and beyond that once-formal gardens that were busy embracing a modish informality and a section of the road that led to the house. Nobody could get up there without us seeing. Not in daylight, anyway.

'You OK to hold the fort?' I asked him. 'I'll go and make those calls.'

'Sure. I'll see if I can find a boiler room, get some hot water going.'

I found a phone in the anteroom of the ballroom. It looked old enough to have been used by Louis XIV or one of his flunkies to summon the troops and the receiver almost took two hands to lift it to my ear. I jammed it between shoulder and chin and dialled. The Colonel answered immediately. 'You there already?'

'Not quite. There was a problem with the delivery. The postman fell ill.'

I hoped he understood that. I'd spent hours choosing it.

'How ill?'

'Doesn't look good. He's lying down on the beach you told us about.'

'Is he cold?'

As the grave, I wanted to say. 'We covered him up. I suggest you send a medical team down.'

'I will do.' There was a little sigh that managed to convey irritation. Like this was all my fault. 'Where are you now?'

'Still a good few hours away from the destination. Some car trouble.'

'Same cause?'

'We think so. My cousin . . .' I couldn't think what to say next. 'My cousin caught a chill. Nothing more than that. I've given him some aspirin. We'll fix the car and be on our way, either tonight or tomorrow. My money is on tonight. But I might not be able to call in on our calligraphic friend.'

I didn't want to go to the inker now. My instinct was he would be blown. Either dead like the driver or with someone watching the house. Or maybe both. Belt and braces.

He spoke between clenched teeth. The profanities would come when he hung up. 'We can sort any formalities at the other end.'

They'd do her a false passport in Luxembourg, so she could extract cleanly. All I had to do was make sure nobody asked for one between here and there.

'Where are you, exactly?'

I hesitated. My instinct was against giving away specifics over an open line. So I only gave him the rough location of the chateau, just to be going on with. There was a pause at the other end and I heard computer keys clicking.

'I have no qualified mechanics in the immediate vicinity to help with your car.'

He meant there was no armed back-up to be had in the vicinity. Not that could reach us in time to be useful. 'OK. We'll be out of here as soon as we can anyway. I'll call again if I get the chance.'

'And Sam.' His voice softened just a little as he said my name. 'That guy we talked about. The specialist

Henri recommended. He has one of the photographs you were interested in.'

I felt a flutter in my stomach. 'Which one?'

'The tattoo. Shall I get him to email it?'

Yes, yes, yes.

'No,' I said quickly before I blurted the opposite. 'Not now. It'll be a distraction. When I'm done here.'

'Very well.'

My voice went very small when I asked the question. 'Was there any metadata on it?'

'None that he can find. Yet. He's still looking. And you're still paying, if that is OK.'

'Of course it is.'

'Good. Stay in touch. I'll deal with the other business.' He meant the dead delivery driver.

My hand was shaking when I broke the connection. Two more calls to make. I dialled Nina.

'Where are you?' she asked.

'On the road.'

'So is it as dull as you hoped?'

I wasn't going to disabuse her of that notion in case she revisited the idea of writing a piece. 'Duller.'

'Well surely my voicemail spiced things up a bit.'

'Fuck. Sorry, I haven't had a chance to listen to it.'

'That boring, eh?'

'It takes a lot of work to make sure nothing happens. Got anything else for me on my charge?'

'Well, there's three things. The first is a negative,

I'm afraid. Nothing I can find on why she has a fear or flying. Secondly, my people at the *FT* say she isn't part of the Euribor scandal. Not that they can find.'

'Odd.'

'Yes. And thirdly, you can be grateful of one thing, that the son isn't with you.'

'What son?'

'Mrs Irwin's son.'

'Myles?'

There was disappointment in her voice. 'Oh, you know about him? Took me a while to put two and two together. You know, that they were related. What with having different surnames. Strange coincidence though.'

'What is?'

'Mother and son. Them both being wanted by the law. If she *is* wanted by the law, that is.'

I suddenly wasn't worried about whether she had or had not rigged the Euribor rate. 'Hold up. The son. He's wanted?'

'Well, not exactly. He and several others are being investigated, pending further action.'

'What's the charge?'

'Rape.'

SEVENTEEN

Saturday

Laura went home yesterday. It was very emosh at the airport. I cried, Laura cried, the check-in girl cried. Dad/Matt didn't seem as upset as I thought he would be. He said they'd Skype and WhatsApp and all that. And Laura asked me to as well, just to keep up on the news on the island. Dieter said he and his girlfriend Aja (who is really, really beautiful) would take over the surfing lessons. But I don't have any friends my own age. There is an English language school here. I suggested to Matt I could start there but he said not until the court case is over. He says that won't be finished until Mum gets out of hospital. HOSPITAL? She's being treated for her PTSD he said. It's sad, but good if it helps her get better. He says she's promised the doctors that once she gets out she'll stop the bodyguarding. And her drinking. I'd like her to do that. Both, I mean.

Tattoo still hurts a bit.

Monday

Dieter and Matt have put a new pizza oven (it's not actually new – they bought it at an auction of some place in town that was closing down) in the bar and bought two mopeds for Putu and his friend Tjokaran to ride about town delivering them. I think Matt thinks they are going to become Domino's. Which is a bit stupid, because there is already a Domino's here.

First lesson with Sarah. She has given me homework! I have to read a book. Jane Austen. She says she is her favourite author. It was bad enough when Mum made me watch a film with Keira Knightley on TV.

Wednesday

OMG, the pizzas are shit.

EIGHTEEN

Normandy, France

The others had decamped to the kitchen. It wasn't so much a cellar as a semi-basement, with windows set high into the walls. Light slanted through them onto stone-flagged floors, a cast-iron cooking range you could feed an army from – or an army of movie extras – two huge American-style fridges and a battle-scarred pine table that could seat twenty. An electric kettle was creaking its way to boiling on a steel prep surface. The three of them looked a little lost in the vastness of the place.

On the wall above the hog-roasting-sized fireplace was a security camera screen with a feed from the gate at the entrance to the chateau's drive. So we could see anyone who arrived. If they bothered to come in the front door, that is.

I wouldn't say the atmosphere was jolly when I walked in, but they all seemed to have relaxed a little. I hoped that had nothing to do with the bottle of cognac sitting on the table in front of Myles, which was placed next to his tablet. I hadn't realised he had one of those in his pack. Did those things have GPS in them?

'Look what I found,' he said, waving the bottle by the neck.

'Put it back,' I said. Mrs Irwin bristled a little at my brusqueness, but I was past caring.

Myles looked crestfallen.

'Let the kid have a slug,' said Konrad. 'Where's the harm now? I've found the hot water. We can all have a shower. Or a bath, if you insist on being very English. There's no milk, but coffee and tea. Some canned food. Pizza in the freezer out back.'

'Pizza.' Myles said it like he had just been offered truffled lobster. 'What kind?'

'The frozen kind,' I said.

'Is something wrong, Miss Wylde?' The mother was more perceptive than the son, I'll give her that. And, for the moment, than my wounded shooter. I recognised the little skip in his step. He'd been shot and lived. The rest of the day always seemed like a bonus after that.

I moved over to where the gunman was sitting. The big FK was an arm's length away from him. I pushed it closer to him. Only then did he catch the look on my face. He sat up a little straighter.

'What's up?'

'I think it's time for a little show and tell. I'll have that coffee if you're making.'

I watched him get up, the upper body held a little stiff. I don't care what he said, that gunshot would slow him down, at least for the next twenty-four hours.

I stared at Myles while Konrad sorted us out with drinks. His eyes kept flicking to the wall behind me, where the screen showed the front gate. It was as if he was expecting someone.

I didn't speak again until the coffee was in front of me. 'OK, leaving aside my personal feelings, is it possible the subject of whatever is happening here is not you, but fallout from what Myles has been up to?'

'What are you talking about?' asked Mrs Irwin.

'I'm talking about rape,' I said, making the word as ugly as possible. It isn't difficult.

'I see,' was all she offered in return.

'Alpha Chi Tau, is it? I got that right?'

Myles was reading the label of the cognac bottle like it held the secret of eternal life. His body was set into full surly, uncooperative mode. I had a powerful urge to go over and give him a good shake. Except I knew it would probably progress to more than that.

'Well, it's something Greek.' I turned and addressed Konrad. 'The fraternity at the college that young Myles attends has an initiation ceremony. Well, it has lots of them. Hazing, it's called, isn't it?' No answer from

Myles. 'But in this particular episode, the wannabe member has to find them a girl to gangbang at one of the parties. Apparently the unwritten rule was – is, for all I know – that she had to have the sort of sexual history that would suggest she might welcome such an event. The initiate was charged with making a film that could be edited later to suggest she was complicit. If she did complain, there was a settlement and an NDA clause. A non-disclosure agreement. In other words, silence was bought. The university has a reputation to protect.'

Konrad simply frowned and looked at the boy as if he was pond life. Well, he might evolve into that one day.

'Is that about right?' I asked.

A shrug.

I took a deep breath before I continued, just to tamp my temper down, which was flaring in spurts, like the gas burn-off at the top of an oil rig. 'They got away with this for a few years. You know American universities are notoriously reluctant to report rape claims that involve fraternity houses. Especially if the frat house has rich sponsors.'

Now my eyes flicked to Mrs Irwin. She kept her gaze on me, steady and burning. It was like looking into the sun.

'Except one of the girls from last year, who went to the campus police, the college authorities and then the real police, killed herself. The parents did some digging and—'

'It's bullshit,' blurted Myles. 'Total bullshit.'

'Which part? That a girl was humiliated and raped or that she killed herself because nobody would believe her?'

'It was never rape,' said Mrs Irwin coldly.

'Well, it's sometimes a tricky interpretation,' I said with a tact the situation didn't really deserve. 'But the journalist I have just spoken to seemed convinced it fitted any definition we care to make.'

The lad stood up and was about to head for the door. 'Myles, sit down,' Mrs Irwin snapped.

He did so and began to unpeel the foil from the top of the cognac. 'She was game for it,' he said softly.

'Myles, you're not helping,' said Mrs Irwin. She looked at me. 'Can't we just let this drop? Is it relevant?'

I sipped my coffee. It tasted bitter. Or perhaps that was just my mood. 'It could be, Mrs Irwin. We can only operate on the facts we know. And the parameters for this trip keep shifting.'

'Nobody ever listens to my side of the story,' whined Myles.

Something snapped in me. 'Look, I am not interested in your tawdry story. Not really. I think you are a generation whose entire social world is built around instant messaging and pornography. Maybe you really do believe that every woman secretly wants to be Barbie-smooth all over and is always up for rough anal sex, preferably with multiple partners and a little light throttling, and always finishing with their faces covered in cum.'

From the corner of my eye I saw Konrad's eyebrows go up in surprise.

'Oh, and then have images of those activities shared with the world. Does that sound like a regular Friday night in the Harrison household?'

That was the name he went by. Myles Harrison. It was why Nina had initially missed the connection between my client and the rape case.

'I don't care for your tone,' offered Mrs Irwin.

'Right now, I don't care for your son.' I was sailing very close to the wind with her, I knew. PPOs didn't say such things. Maybe it was time I looked for another job.

'You don't understand,' Myles said.

'Which part?'

When he looked at me his face was screwed up like a fist. Disdain dripped from every word. 'Any of it. You don't understand how modern life works, how we hook up with girls, what girls expect. You are still thinking like, like dinosaurs. You keep judging us by your world. Your ways of doing things. But this is our world now.'

God help us, but he might have been right.

'Yet there is still a dead girl at the heart of all this. I think that's a bad outcome in anybody's world.'

A huff, as if she were a mere irritation, a cancelled date or an undercooked hamburger. 'Yeah, well, maybe they should look at her old man a little more closely on that one.'

I got a strong whiff of a can of worms.

'OK, this isn't a court of law,' I said.

'I'm glad to hear it,' said Mrs Irwin. 'I was beginning to wonder.'

Konrad got up to make a second cup of coffee. He hadn't said a word, so far. 'I think what Miss Wylde here is worrying about is this: do the events in the United States have any relevance to our situation here?'

I nodded to thank him for pulling me off my soap-box and back to the situation in hand. He indicated I was meant to say something.

'Sorry,' I said to Mrs Irwin. 'This isn't quite going according to plan. New developments don't help. You have my apologies.'

Her lips pursed together tighter than a whale's anus. After a few moments, she relaxed a little. 'Accepted.'

'So, let me stress, what Miss Wylde is concerned with is not the case in the States. It is not our job to judge.' His eyes flicked to me and I nodded my agreement. 'It is how it impacts here. Have you skipped bail? Is there a warrant out for your arrest in the US?

Could they request you be detained? Extradited? We have one Red Notice and an EAW for a white-collar crime. This one could be different. A cop who might not worry about financial skulduggery might well have stronger views on rape.'

'He is not a criminal,' his mother clucked again. I kept my mouth shut. 'Nor is he a fugitive. Look, there was always a compelling case for Myles coming over. We have financial arrangements to make and I want Myles to take responsibility for some of the funds. He needs to be there for certain legal proceedings. When this story broke, there was something of a media frenzy. There has been a reporter from the *New Yorker* pestering us, day and night. Not just us, all the boys and their parents involved. The girls, too, I would imagine. I have spoken to this woman. She had already made up her mind to crucify our boys. So it seemed sensible to change plans about Myles flying out later and for him to come with me.'

I looked at Myles. 'You don't share the fear of flying?'

It was Mrs Irwin who answered. 'No. He doesn't. I had a brother who died ...' The memory seemed to choke her for a moment. 'You'll never get me up in one again.'

'I don't have a problem with flying,' said Myles. 'Safest way to travel. But I wanted to keep Mom company. And those journalists who were hangin'

227

around. Just fuckin' assholes, man. Like . . . like, lice.' He scratched his arm to make the point.

I turned to Konrad.

'You don't think we've been looking over our shoulders and seeing the wrong bad guys?' he said. 'In fact, not bad guys at all. You think I might have shot two reporters from the *New Yorker* by mistake?' He came and sat back down with his second cup of coffee. 'Is that a joke?'

'It's just a thought,' I said.

'Does the *New Yorker* normally send its people out with guns to get the story?' he asked.

'Not that I've heard,' I admitted.

'They weren't reporters for anyone. They didn't look like they could write their name, let alone a story. And journalism has changed a little if they also murder drivers, just to get our attention.'

To my shame, I'd forgotten about the poor guy probably being extracted from under a rotting rowing boat as we spoke. 'Unless we have two separate parties interested. One for Mrs Irwin, one for Myles.'

'Again, unlikely.'

I hoped so. I only had one Principal – Mrs Irwin. Myles was just excess baggage.

'I'm just running through the options,' I said.

'The simplest solution is usually the correct one,' he said. I felt as if I was trying his patience. Maybe I was barking up the wrong tree.

'I'd like to speak to Mr Konrad alone,' I said in a softer tone. 'Would you excuse us?'

'The water should be hot,' said Konrad. 'Have those showers.'

'And leave the cognac,' I said.

Myles looked at it with puppy eyes.

'Please. It won't help. We might have to move quickly. I want you sober, Myles.'

'Do as Miss Wylde suggests,' said Mrs Irwin.

'Sure.'

'And keep that tablet offline please. OK?' He scooped up the device without answering and I had to say. 'OK, Myles?'

'Yes. Whatever.'

Such a lovely, life-affirming word, 'whatever'. Warms the cockles whenever any teenager says it to me.

'It's for all our sakes,' I said to Mrs Irwin.

'I know. I'll make sure he does as he is told.'

Myles closed the door behind him and Mrs Irwin stood to follow. 'I can sense your distaste, Miss Wylde. But believe you me, if you had children of your own, you would know how conflicted I am in this. The mind says one thing, the heart another. I would be grateful if you did not bring this up again. I can't tell you how much it hurts to think my son had any part in those events or the death of a young lady.'

I didn't doubt her sincerity. 'We won't, Mrs Irwin, unless it turns out to have some relevance to our situation.'

'It hasn't. But thank you.'

When the mother had left, Konrad got up and started searching the wall cupboards. 'Where did that come from?'

'What?'

'The part about rough anal sex.'

It came, I thought, from having a daughter and the worry about the kind of society she was facing. *If you had children of your own*, indeed. I do. I have a beautiful daughter . . .

Fuck. You've done it now. Let her out of that box. What about the photo that the Colonel has? What about—

It was something of a struggle, but I managed to get the door to the compartment closed and put a mental foot against it.

'It came from a woman's perspective,' I said eventually. 'Was I shouting?'

He scratched at a pockmarked cheek and gave a half-smile. I couldn't tell what he was thinking behind those sunglasses. They were beginning to annoy me. Well, truth be told, everything was beginning to annoy me. 'I think I heard a round of applause from the Women's Committee of the European Parliament at one point.'

'Sorry.' I was well aware I had not just crossed the line but leaped over it like I was a regular Greg Rutherford. I was annoyed with myself. I was meant to be a professional.

'Ah. Here we are.' He put two glasses on the table. 'The kid could be right, you know.'

'About what?' He pulled the cork out of the brandy. I waved a hand. 'Not for me.'

'About the fact it's their world. It has to be at their age. One day he'll end up with bank loans, mortgages and alimony like the rest of us. Society swallows them in the end. You should feel sorry for Myles. One day he'll wake up and discover it's the same old shit world we all live in.'

'Tell that to the girl.'

'Ah,' he said softly. 'There's that. But we can't let her worry us. Not now.'

'No.'

He raised his glass and knocked the contents back. 'Medicinal. I didn't take the painkillers.' He pointed at my glass. 'Go on. One won't do any harm. The tyres will be here by late afternoon. Allow an hour to fit. We could be on our way by—'

He stopped.

'Sorry. Your call.'

I thought. 'I don't want to spend the night here.'

'Agreed. This place will be very vulnerable after dark.'

'You asked if they'd loan us a new car?'

'They couldn't spare one. At least, that's what they claimed.'

It was a big ask, a car with no papers. It would have been a lot easier to pick up a new hire car than the new tyres. But that meant passports, driving licences, credit cards, entry on a database. Even buying one, at least above board, was also out of the question. Too many footprints to be followed by those who were looking.

'What they are bringing is a fresh set of plates, ones registered to a 508.'

It was my turn to apologise. 'You're doing my job for me.' He pushed the drink across. 'No. I'll have a shower.'

'And maybe a nap. You must be tired after all that driving. 'I'll keep my eye on things.' He nodded towards the CCTV. 'I'll put Myles to work too.'

'If you can find any rocks he can break in the hot sun, that would be good.'

Konrad frowned. 'As I said, you have to let that go, now.'

I took a deep breath. I hadn't met such a bloody reasonable gunman in a long time. Or ever, come to think of it. Right, right, right again. You are a PPO. No opinions, no prejudice, just protect the Principal. And, if need be, her fuckwit of a son.

On impulse I took the drink and downed it, waiting for the burn. It didn't come. Just a soft, caressing

warmth that spread up my throat and to my cheeks.
'Wow.'

'I think young Myles found the good stuff.' He
splashed a few more millimetres in his own glass. 'One
more, then the cork goes in.' He proffered the bottle
to me.

I shook my head. I already felt like I'd been playing
truant by having the one. 'No, not for me.' I checked
my coffee. It was cold. 'You said there was tea?'

'Coming up.'

He stood back up. I almost missed the flicker of
pain across his face. He was overcompensating for the
wound. He didn't want me to think it had taken any
edge off him. *Nothing wrong with me, look. This? Just
a nick, ma'am. I've had worse scratches from my dog.*
He'd be doing handstands next. But I let him make the
tea if it made him happy. A shower and a power nap
sounded good.

'You want something to eat?'

We'd only had the pastries at breakfast. My stomach
did feel hollow. But that could wait. 'Later.'

Konrad knelt down in front of a cupboard and
began to read out names. 'We got Assam, Darjeeling,
Lapsang something, camomile, English Breakfast ...'
He turned and looked at me on the last one.

'Not with no milk. Darjeeling, please.'

I let my mind empty. I needed to refocus. We were
safe for the moment. Nobody could have guessed we

were coming to this chateau. Unless I had overlooked something, there were no telltale signals giving our position away. I could power down a little, down to yellow.

Konrad handed me a business card. For a moment I thought it was going to say: 'George Konrad: Have Gun Will Travel', but it was for Ronin International Film Services.

'Just in case,' he said. 'These are the guys bringing the tyres and plates. I've told them the password is De Niro.'

'As in Robert?'

'He was in *Ronin*. The movie? They worked on it. You see it? Great car chases.' He gave a smirk to show he was well aware of the irony.

'They'll ask if De Niro is here and I say, or you say if it comes to it, no, but Jean Reno is out back.'

'Seriously?'

'Why not?'

Boys, I thought. Give them a big gun, they're still kids at heart, playing their bang-bang games. Until, as my mother used to say, larks turn to linnets.

I never did understand what that meant.

I looked down at the card and ran my finger over the extravagant embossing. They were, as he said, based in Le Mans. As good a place as any for professional petrolheads.

'Here.'

I took the tea from him. 'Shower, then thirty minutes and you'll wake me?'

'Take an hour. It's what I'll need to be fresh,' he said truthfully. It was obviously painful to admit a weakness. 'I'll give you the same. It's only fair, *neska polita*.'

'What the hell does that mean?' I asked.

'Sweet dreams.'

'OK. No longer than an hour,' I warned him. 'And if anything happens ...'

Konrad whistled softly to himself as he put the brandy in one of the top cupboards and moved bottles of olive oil and white-wine vinegar to cover it. He turned and smiled. 'You'll be the last to know.'

At the time I thought it was an odd sort of East European humour. Only later did I realise he was telling the truth.

NINETEEN

Thursday

Sarah took me down to the bar last night and there was a policeman there with Matt. He was being very aggressive. I had to say to the policeman that I was fine and Matt was my dad. I thought we were all in trouble because someone had tracked us down or snaked us to the cops, but Dieter took the cop outside and sorted it with him. The cop came back in, ruffled my hair – ugh – and said he would see us all next week.

Saturday

Dieter and Aja have invited me on a boat for a picnic tomorrow. I asked Dad and he didn't seem too keen but Sarah was there and she said it would be a good idea for me to have some time out on the ocean. She said she will take me to the night market to buy a new bikini and T-shirt.

LATER: I got a SILVER one. It's really cute. And the T-shirt is old school Hannah Montana.

I used to watch that with Paul, my other dad. I had a dream about him the other night. Nice things – the weekend at Center Parcs when he said it was like a prison and we plotted a mass breakout. The chocolate room at Alton Towers. The day he was attacked by an ostrich at Paradise Wildlife Park and it stole his Cornish pasty.

I wonder sometimes what life would be like if he hadn't died.

The Jane Austen is so slooooooowwwww.

TWENTY

Normandy, France

Unease was spreading through me like ink climbing up blotting paper. My senses were coming online in a fitful way, as if there was a short-circuit in my wiring. My eyes refused to open. When I forced them, the light was like the flash from a thermonuclear device. When I closed them again, I could still see the solar-bright retinal burn.

My right side felt numb. My arm moved, but without direction, flapping like a freshly landed fish. My head was an enormous bell being struck by hammers.

I ran my good, responsive hand over my face. It was sticky, as if someone had thrown a can of Coke over it. Probably dried sweat. I carried on down, past my throat, over my breasts and onward.

I was naked.

I flung my arm out and patted. I was on a bed. On a bed and naked.

I tried to think how I had got there. Normally I could re-spool events like a DVD on fast rewind, stopping where I pleased. But now I was just looking at darkness. The disc was blank.

I rolled on my side and risked opening my eyes once more. It was still light, so it was the same day as . . . as what? Something had penetrated the blackness then, and slipped away, like a half-glimpsed figure in a fog.

The room was blurred and I felt a burning in my throat. I was in danger of vomiting. There was a glass on the bedside table and I reached for it with my left hand. It was empty apart from a smear of blue liquid in the bottom. Blue? Curaçao? I wouldn't drink that. I wouldn't drink on duty.

I never drink on duty. Do I?

I rolled back, closed my eyes again and let the nausea wash over me and retreat like an ebb tide. I was coming back to life. It would just take time. I mustn't rush it. Softly, softly. I steadied my breathing and watched multicoloured lights dance across the inside of my eyelids. Pins and needles began to shoot down my right arm. It was a good sign.

I was in a bedroom, of that much I was certain. I was probably upstairs in . . . the chateau. I was in the chateau. Rewind further. On the road with a woman, her son and Konrad. Hungarian gunman. Trouble on the way to Saint-Lo. Marigny? Yes, got that. Tyres.

Needed tyres for the car. Konrad suggested a chateau. I remember arriving, and then ... and then ...

What would I have done? If the SitRep was bad, I would have phoned whatshisname. In Geneva. No, Zürich. The Colonel. I would have phoned him. Did I make that call?

The haze swirled and shifted in my brain, like a Victorian peasouper. The lack of detail was frightening, as if I were lost at sea and I didn't even have a horizon. I tried to imagine myself on the phone. Hello? Colonel? It's me. But the image wouldn't take. It faded like a badly fixed photograph.

Naked and in a bed. What did that suggest?

I put my hand between my legs, feeling for any swelling or tenderness. There was none. I slipped a finger inside me. Nothing untoward I could detect. I sniffed it. It smelled of me.

That was a good sign, too.

I checked my armpits. Sour. Like I had run a marathon.

I tried the eyes again and this time I wasn't blinded, although I had to blink a lot to clear the film over my corneas.

Ornate ceiling with fancy plasterwork, chandelier. There were still flashes of light, like a migraine aura, but someone had put felt on the little hammers striking my skull. I could tolerate them now.

I shuffled up onto the pillows and looked down at

my body. As I did so I became aware of another pain, around my neck. I touched the left side and winced. Without a mirror I couldn't be sure, but it felt like a bruise. I used my fingers to explore and found a matching tender spot on the right side.

Had someone tried to strangle me?

I did a visual of the rest of me that I could see easily. No more damage. No scratches or impact marks. Just the neck, then.

It was another ten minutes before I managed to slide my feet off the bed and sit up. The world tilted a few times and I wasn't certain my legs could take my weight so I sat there for a while, still breathing as slow and steady as I could. My heart seemed to have other ideas. It had some sort of aerobic workout going on in my chest.

What the fuck had happened? And where were my clothes?

It was a woman walking through gloop who made it across to the bathroom and put her head around the door. Still no sign of any clothes. But the shower over the bath looked inviting and after a process that resembled the first moon landing, I managed to step in and get a stream of water coming out of the head. Several times I had to cling on to the slimy curtain for support. Eventually I got myself firmly under the spray. I began to feel like I never wanted to move again.

Jess. Most days the realisation that I no longer had

Jess dawned on me slowly. Then the full impact of what had happened to my daughter hit me like a truck. I let out a strangulated cry.

The Colonel was looking for the two photos she had sent to Saanvi. I recalled all that with absolute clarity. Had he found anything yet though? I had no idea. I became certain that I had called him, although I had no recollection of the actual event. Never mind, I could do it again. If I ever managed to get out of the shower. And once I figured out what the hell was going on. If that was possible in my state.

What about your Principal? Where is she? All this thought for yourself and not one for Mrs Irwin. *Protect the Principal?*

Shit, I couldn't even protect myself.

I staggered from the bath and found a towel in a cupboard. I wrapped it around me, then sat down on the lavatory, head in hands. I managed to stop myself crying. But I stayed there for some time, gathering my strength for what I had to do next, my mission to Mars. I had to go downstairs.

I had to assume the others were still in the house, maybe suffering like I was. When I went to the bedroom and threw open the shutters to let full daylight in I became convinced of one thing. It was the next day – the one after we arrived at the chateau. That was *morning* out there in the ragged garden. I had lost a whole night.

I returned to the bathroom, wiped the steam off the mirror over the sink and gave my neck a good look. Two bruises, one either side, each about the size of a two-pence piece. Someone had gripped my neck. Hard. Were they trying to occlude the carotids? Was that how I had passed out? I doubted it. Those kind of Vulcan death holds only work in movies.

I moved into the hallway and gingerly began to descend the curving stairs. I didn't even remember ascending them but, willingly or unwillingly, I clearly had. Either way, I soon decided that banisters were one of the greatest inventions known to man. I gripped this one like I never wanted to let it go.

'Hello?' I croaked when I was a third of the way down. Then, stronger: 'Anybody there?'

My voice moved along empty corridors and through deserted rooms, lost and lonely in the silence.

A short lifetime later I sat down at the bottom of the stairs to recover from the challenging descent. It didn't look like much but to me it was the Hillary Step. I felt like one of those newborn foals that can barely stand and I was wheezing like a consumptive.

There was a sense of barely contained panic threatening me now. A barrage of questions that could sweep through my brain and overwhelm me. I had to keep that locked down, safe behind my mental flood defences. The trick here was not to jump to any conclusions until I had solid evidence.

Until you find the bodies.

Yes, if that's what it comes down to. But I mustn't get ahead of myself. I only had fragments of a picture and at the moment it made no sense at all. I just had to hope the missing parts of my neural system would return at some point.

I found him in the kitchen. He was face down on the table. He'd been sick at some point. I knew this because most of his hair was in it. I crossed over and touched his neck looking for a pulse.

'Whatthefuck?'

He sat bolt upright like he'd been plugged into the mains, his hair flicking the vomit across the room. Luckily it only hit the towel I was clutching to my chest.

'Jesus,' I said. 'You OK?'

Myles tried to focus through a Nile delta of blood vessels in his eyes. I stepped closer and my toe hit a bottle that rolled lazily across the stone floor. Like an alcoholic game of boules it nudged into another, identical empty brandy bottle. No wonder he'd been sick.

He swayed woozily in his seat. A sentence came out of his mouth, but the meaning was known only to him and God. I fetched a glass of water from the sink and put it in front of him.

'Drink.'

He did as instructed. 'What timessssit?' The tongue was still thick in the mouth, but I got that one.

I looked at my wrist. Force of habit. I had already

ascertained that my watch was missing. Gone, along with my clothes? Shame, I liked that Omega. 'Not sure.'

The sight of Myles actually made me feel a little better. I felt rough but I didn't look like that. I fetched him more water and used a cloth to mop up the contents of his stomach. It was lucky he'd been sick. Consuming two bottles of brandy was grounds for severe alcohol poisoning. I used a rag from under the sink to get as much as possible out of his hair. Part of me was grateful they had used something other than booze to knock me out.

'You need a shower,' I said, as I scrubbed my hands under the tap. 'And soon.'

'Yeah.' He managed to get me in focus by moving his head back and forward like a turtle. That seemed to hurt a little. 'Where's your clothes? Why you wearin' that ...?' Something salacious swam into his eyes. I'm sure for a second he thought he was having a PornHub dream.

'Down, tiger. It's not for your benefit. Where's your mother?'

'She went to ...' A pause. Had he lost part of the last twenty-four hours too? 'To get the passport. With Konrad.'

'What? We ... didn't we dismiss that as a bad idea?' Or had we changed our minds and that had slipped away too?

'I guess. I was pretty wrecked by the time they left.'

'He let you drink?'

'Hell, yeah. He's a *good* guy.' He didn't actually say: not like you, you stuck-up … But I felt its presence. What had I done to him to make him dislike me? Something else that would emerge in due course, no doubt.

I pulled out a chair and sat. Myles wobbled to his feet. 'I'll take that shower.'

'Sit down!'

'Fuck,' he muttered. 'Don't drop a ball.'

'Look, I've got some gaps. I can't remember everything from yesterday.'

'What?'

'I've got a memory blank.'

'No shit.'

Thanks for caring, I thought. I suddenly got a flash of Jess – how she shut down when she was with her friends and embarrassed by her mum. I didn't have to say anything to cause her excruciating agony, I just had to be in the same room and breathing. 'Myles, I need your help. Can you kill the attitude.'

'Huh? What attitude?'

'That attitude.'

He scratched the side of his head, releasing flakes of dried sick. 'I don't have any attitude.'

'Imagine you are talking to someone who isn't as old as Methuselah and is dressed in more than a towel. Can you do that?'

'Methu-who?'

'It doesn't matter. I'm not your mum. You don't have to play the tortured teen shit with me. We need to figure out what the fuck has gone on. Just try not to be a cunt.'

As I had hoped, the word acted like a slap in the face. He probably thought I was too old to know it, let alone use it. 'OK ...' He swallowed hard and shook his head before adopting what I guess he thought of as his serious face. 'What parts can't you remember?'

'I dunno. Let me ... I guess much of what happened after we got here. It's a blank. I remember pulling up outside, going into the chateau, some of patching Konrad up and then ... nothing till now.'

'Je-sus. None of it?'

'I think there's a pretty big chunk still missing.' He seemed oddly pleased by that. He perked up a little and fetched himself some more water.

'That's a bummer.' He sounded almost concerned.

'Indeed it is a bummer. My job was to drive your mother. Now they've gone. When did they leave?'

He thought through the fuzz of his hangover. 'Last night.'

'What time?'

'Seven, eight ...' He looked around the table, confused. 'Hey. Where's my iPad?' Then down at his feet. 'And my sneakers?'

'There's a lot missing. All the luggage, my clothes.

Don't worry about that now. So, after we got here, what did we do?'

'I think ... you made some calls. Yeah, you did. To this guy called the Colonel. We had a talk in here. We went upstairs, Mom and me, I mean. Got freshened up. Then you went for a shower. Konrad and I had a drink. And a pizza. He explained what was going to happen once the guys with the tyres turned up—'

'Wait, they came with the tyres?'

'Yeah. It was arranged, remember?'

'That's the problem. I don't. I think I've been drugged. Maybe you too.'

'But I remember everything. Well, most things. I just feel like shit. But you ...' His eyes widened. 'You could've been. Spiked, I mean.'

'How could anyone spike me?'

'Lots of ways. Did you have a drink?'

'I don't know. I can't remember. If I did it was probably tea or coffee. I don't drink when ...' I let it tail off. I felt some uncertainty about my not-drinking-when-working rule. Had I broken it?

'Well, if they used a roofie on you it'd be blue. Well, the legal stuff is blue, you can get colourless.'

'Roofie? Rohypnol?'

'Yup. Like it totally fucks up your brain. You can't remember shit.'

I knew about retrograde amnesia from drugs, but not the fine details. 'For how long?'

'Like, the hour before you take it is pretty much frazzled.'

I tried to keep my voice level. 'There was a blue liquid in a glass next to my bed.'

'Son of a bitch. You've probably been RoHo'd.'

'But I think I was given that after being knocked out.' I pointed to the bruise on my neck. 'I reckon I got these while he was forcing me to swallow.'

'Konrad?'

I nodded. Who else? 'Well, it's either you or him ...'

His eyes widened at the accusation. 'Me? Please ...' He hesitated. 'What sort of guy do you think I am? Some kind of pervert?' He gave a smile I couldn't quite interpret and then fixed me with those bovine eyes of his.

'No. Sorry. Of course not. I'm not thinking straight. But how did I get knocked out?'

He thought for a minute. I fetched some more water and made him drink. He was rehydrating before my eyes. Youth has enviable powers of recovery.

'Any ideas?'

'I'm just running through some possibilities. None of them are good.'

'I'll take them all.'

'OK, let's just say I wanted to knock you out. Assuming I couldn't get you drunk.'

'Unlikely.'

'Right. So if, theoretically, it was me wanting to ...
Whoa!'

'Whoa what?'

'Man, he could have used the Devil's Breath on you
first.'

That was a new one on me. And I'd rather he didn't
sound so excited by it. 'The Devil's Breath?'

'It's a powder. Used in South America. Men would
blow it in the face of girls they wanted to drug. That's
how, y'know, it got its name. But these days it's all
over the world. And it's often on pieces of paper. Beer
mats, envelopes ...'

'We don't have any beer mats or envelopes.'

'And business cards.'

'Business cards? How does that work?'

'It's in the embossing. Think about it. Someone
hands you a business card, you always rub your thumb
over the raised letters. Everyone does it. Well, the
Devil's Breath is absorbed through the skin. It's the
same shit they use in anti-seasick patches, but a fuck
of a lot stronger.'

'How do you know all this?' I couldn't keep the
suspicion from my voice. How would he know about
how to deliver a drug unless he was part of this? But
why would he still be here if that was the case?

'Look, I didn't do anything to you,' he said. 'If that's
what you are suggesting.'

'I'm not suggesting anything. Just running down a

few stray thoughts. But you know all about the Devil's Breath or whatever it's called.'

He shrugged, some of his old indifference to my plight implicit in the movement. 'Jeesus, we all know about that. We get taught it at college. Security on and off campus one-oh-one. It's a compulsory unit. And it's not only girls who get drugged and raped these days, you know.'

'I suppose not,' I admitted. Equal opportunities had its downside.

'So, did he hand you anything to touch?'

'Touch?'

'Yeah, like I said, a business card? Or maybe even a letter. An envelope? A map?' Before I could answer he did it for me. 'You don't recall.'

'No, I don't. Look, I need to think. I feel like if I could just kick-start my brain it would all come flooding back. Go and have your shower. And drink more water.'

'Is Mom in trouble?'

Well, that took its own sweet time to surface. 'Honestly? I don't know.' But I did. She was in bad, bad trouble. I could only imagine that Konrad had been turned by the opposition. That's the trouble with guns for hire. There's always someone who can go higher on the wages front.

'Right. But we'll go and get her, huh?'

Time to play the wildly optimistic card. 'Of course we will. Don't worry.'

'Cool.'

He gave a lopsided smile as he got up and went to find a shower. I told him he would have to re-dress in the clothes he had on but that we'd have to pick up some new clothes for him later. The ones he was wearing stank. I had the impression I had been a little hard on him when we first met and perhaps just a few moments ago. Irritated that he had come along in the first place, annoyed to find him here and pretty useless. Apart from filling me in on what might have happened to me.

Now, I reckoned, having another warm body along wouldn't be so terrible. It was someone to talk to, someone who would recall more than I did about our time at the chateau. And, of course, it was possible he wasn't such a bad kid after all.

He can be fun. Funny. Wasn't that what his mother had said?

But I was left with the feeling that there was something else I should ask him. Or perhaps something else I should know about him. Something important. But it was just out of my grasp, somewhere below the surface of the deep pool of black, featureless oil that was my short-term memory.

I refixed my towel with a more secure knot and put the kettle on. I knew I had to try to stay calm. Looking into my immediate past was like standing on the ledge of a very tall building, where the ground was covered in mist. I had no idea how far I would fall if I stepped off. It wasn't a bad analogy because I also had real head-spinning vertigo every time I moved too quickly. Even when I was at my most drink-sodden, in the wake of my husband's murder, I had never felt this shit.

So, very gingerly indeed, I searched cupboards till I found some more cleaning cloths and bleach and scoured what was left of the vomit off the table, holding my breath as I did so. I knew that by now I would probably have done this several times for Jess. It was what teenage girls did. Test the boundaries. They drink fruit-flavoured cider and cheap, possibly counterfeit, corner-shop vodka and throw it back up over their parents' dining tables or, if we are lucky, bathrooms. *Oh Lord, give me Jess back and I promise I'll never complain about clearing up her sick.*

I made such deals with the deity on a daily basis. Apparently my offers hadn't quite hit the spot yet. When I had finished and scrubbed my hands, I slumped back at the table with a black coffee in one of those French breakfast cups you could do laps in. The rust-spotted clock on the wall told me it wasn't yet seven o'clock. I had a whole day ahead of me to sort this mess out.

Protect the Principal.

I didn't need to be reminded by that admonishing

little voice in my damaged head. I knew I had fucked up. Not just failed to protect – I'd lost her entirely.

I heard the thump of the boy's feet on the stairs. He pushed his head in the door. 'My backpack has gone.'

'I told you. All my stuff has gone too.'

'What about the phones? Mine and Mom's?'

'They were in the boot of the car.'

The boy's face crumpled in despair. 'Why didn't he just kill us, the motherfucker?'

Interesting weighting of events, I thought. He could take possibly being drugged, certainly being drunk enough to vomit, me being roofied and stripped naked, all our gear stolen, but take away his phone? Now you're really pissing me off, dude.

'Do me a favour. Go and check the landline, it's ...' I almost had it for a second, but the image danced away before it could solidify from its wraith-like state.

'I know where it is.'

And I knew before he pounded up those stairs and returned, a little more slowly, what he would say. 'Dead.'

Of course it was. No phones. No car. No luggage. No gear. No money. No hope.

'At least you have the clothes on your back. Go and wash your hair, I can smell you from here.'

'What are you going to do?'

'I'm going to think,' I promised.

*

The trick was to start this from the beginning. Trying to remember recent events was only going to cause anguish and frustration, as I had already discovered. I put Myles out of my mind, drank some more coffee and went back to the time when I first met Konrad. The obvious conclusion came quickly.

Konrad hadn't defected for money. He hadn't been turned by the opposition. Konrad *was* the opposition.

He had always been the opposition.

And now he had my client. The Euribor charge against her was probably his doing. The idea of people trying to ... Re-wind. I needed to go further back, to before I met Konrad.

The NOP account. The one in Luxembourg, where all this started. The man who held all Mrs Irwin's dirty-money secrets in his head had been the victim of a hit-and-run driver. That triggered the crisis that brought her over. What if the driver of the car had been Konrad? Or, possibly, a hired associate? Then made sure that Mrs Irwin's security missed the boat. She would need cover in Europe. Chances are she would go to a certain outfit in Zürich. There aren't that many trustworthy guns-for-hire in Europe. Konrad could easily have got himself to the top of the Colonel's go-to list. Well, not easily, but it was certainly possible.

So who'd killed the delivery driver and put him in the boot?

Konrad had.

Why? There were two possible answers. One was that the driver had rumbled him. Perhaps knew him of old. Realised there was something else going on. The second scenario was that Konrad had to throw me off-balance, wrong-foot me. If I thought that the opposition was right behind us, and had killed one of our own, I was more likely to panic. No, not panic, but not think as straight or as logically as I might. Certainly, I was more likely to listen to what Konrad suggested. After all, gunplay was his thing.

But wait. What about the gunmen on the square at the village? There had been an exchange of gunfire.

I took a sip of my by-now lukewarm coffee.

Or had there?

Konrad had been shot. That much couldn't be faked. It was a clean wound but for some powder burns. No material in the trough along his side. Lucky, I had thought. And he had said the perp was close, that he'd managed to knock the gun aside.

Bullshit.

He had shot himself. He had enough spare flesh around his middle to take a shot. Yes, it would hurt. But what better way to sell a story that there are bad men after you?

And the tyre punctures? That could easily have been him too. All ploys designed to get us to this house, this place, and to separate us from Mrs Irwin. How much was pre-planned and how much was improvised, I

couldn't be sure. But all this didn't answer one important question.

Why?

Why did he want Mrs Irwin, and what was he going
to do with her?

I heard the voice of my old sergeant in my head.
Rough, unpitying, practical: *Just get it sorted*.

The answers would come later. Right now I had to
take charge of the situation. I had to find my Principal.
I stood up and gripped the table as the room did its
Tower of Terror impression. I still had that shit in my
bloodstream. I wondered how long it would take to
clear completely. I would be below par until then. Who
was I kidding? I'd been outfoxed all the way.

I waited until everything steadied and headed for
the stairs. I could look for answers while I searched for
clothes. There was one very big question that needed
addressing.

Who was George Konrad?

PART FIVE

TWENTY-ONE

I found a dress in a wardrobe in a dusty under-the-eaves bedroom at the far end of the top floor. It was clearly a forgotten prop, thick yellow brocade with a tightly cinched waist, puffed shoulders and massive skirts. It had a squared-off neckline low enough to need better breasts – or a better bra – than I could supply.

Nevertheless, beggars and choosers came to mind. I took it down to the kitchen, found a blunt pair of scissors and began to hack at the skirts and petticoats. By the time I had finished and put it on I looked like a punk version of Marie Antoinette. With no knickers. Although that was probably true of the real Marie Antoinette as well.

I heard Myles shout my name and went back into the hallway and up to the ground floor. He was standing by the front door, his hands behind his back, a very-pleased-with-himself grin across his face. It got wider when he saw me and the result of my attempt at dressmaking.

'Wow. That's quite the party piece. Little Bo Peep?'

'That is the last we shall speak of it,' I said with all the menace I could muster. 'What is it?'

'I found something.'

'What?'

'A gun.'

I'd rather have a phone than a gun. 'Let me see.'

'Left or right?' he asked, a lopsided grin skewered across his face.

'What?'

'Left hand or right hand.'

I took a step towards him and he got the picture. I was in no mood for guessing games. From behind his back he whipped out what might have been what they called a gun once, but to my mind was something you put on the wall in a glass case.

I took it off him. It was fine if you wanted to play highwaymen – 'Stand and deliver!' – but would be more practical as a club.

'I don't suppose there was any powder or bullets?' I asked.

'I think they used balls in those days.'

'All right – any balls?'

If he'd come back with a smart answer I think I might have beaten him to death with the butt, just as a lesson in good manners. I took a breath, which wasn't easy in that bodice, and told myself to calm down.

'No balls.' It was most likely just another film prop, not intended for inflicting serious injury.

'Where did you find it?'

'There are some buildings out back. Stables, I guess.'

'Anything else in there?' I asked.

'Nah.' He thought for a second. 'Well, there's some kinda old car.'

I pulled the tarpaulin off and stepped outside, waiting for the dust to settle and the grumpy moths and other insects to flutter away. A platoon of spiders scuttled over the cement floor, looking for some replacement peace and quiet.

We were about 100 metres from the back of the chateau. It was a lawn that sloped uphill to the stable compound. Once, judging by the low walls and pediments that intersected it, this had been a formal garden similar to the one out front, but it was dotted with explosions of unruly wildflowers. The stable block was brick-built, topped with rococo plasterwork that had once been as ornate as any on the main building, but was now crumbling and split. Two cherubs who looked like they had been the victims of acid attacks stared down at me dolefully, only a few years away from toppling headfirst onto the brick apron that fronted the block.

Myles was still holding the useless flintlock pistol, thumbing back the hammer, aiming it and pulling the trigger to produce a loud snapping sound.

'Stop that.'

He did it again and I snatched it from him. He bunched his fists and snarled as if he wanted to make something of it and I squared off against him. I would almost welcome a physical attack. I felt like I needed something to release the fury that had built up inside me. But it was probably better to wait until I found someone who really deserved my full rage. George Konrad for one. Still, I think my come-on-if-you-think-you're-hard-enough expression was clear enough, and he took a step back, letting some of the puff out of his chest.

'You don't seem too upset,' I said.

'About what?'

'Your mother.'

It was another shrug, but this one had a strange sinuous, serpentine movement that rippled from head to toe. 'My mom can look after herself. Look, we're not that close. I don't even have the same name. I was brought up by an aunt in Boston. My dad died when I was just a kid. A baby. She's kept her distance, really. It was only when . . .'

I waited.

'I got into a little trouble. In college.'

'What kind of trouble?'

There was a lengthy pause, as if he was summoning up the courage for confession. 'You know, I dealt a little weed. No big deal. But everyone acted like

I was something out of *Narcos*. Mom decided she'd been a bad parent. So she thought it was a good idea for me to come along, so we'd get to know each other.'

And also give the kid a few million from the Luxembourg account? It didn't seem like totally bad parenting to me. 'And did you? Get to know each other?'

'Not so much. God, it was boring. All that fuckin' sea, day in, day out. I mostly played on the computers. And the fuckin' boat is owned by a Mormon friend of hers. It was a dry ship. I had to smuggle Coca-Cola on board. She spent much of the time on the sat phone to her bank. So, it wasn't the full mother-and-son bonding experience.'

Child cruelty. 'This fear of flying. It's genuine?'

'Oh, yes. Scared shitless. When her brother died in a crash, it freaked her out. Me, I still think it's the safest way to travel.' He rolled his eyes. 'Way better than fuckin' boats.'

A flurry of cackling crows took to the air from the woods beyond the stable. I waited to see what had spooked them, but after a minute they began to return to their perches. It reminded me I had business other than the Irwin family's history.

'OK, we haven't got a boat or a plane. But let's take a look at this car.'

*

The stable was a single large space, more garage than home to horses. The stalls had been ripped out and workbenches and cupboards put along the rear wall. This was where Myles had found the pistol. An inspection showed a few rusted tools, but little of practical use. And definitely no ammunition or powder for an antique flintlock. A cement floor had been laid at some point and, judging from the Rorschach assortment of oil stains on it, work had been done on a variety of vehicles over the years. As well as the car there was a four-wheeled carriage, down on its luck. It had even lost its traces and the interior was covered in what looked like mouse droppings. I turned my attention to its rather classier neighbour.

'Handsome', I would guess was the right word for the car. There had been one for sale in Monaco, at the official auction, and there had been a lot of interest in it. A Facel Vega. The car, so the brochure had said, that killed Albert Camus. Well, not the actual one, but the same type. It seemed a somewhat morbid boast to me. But then I guess Porsche had the same sort of relationship with James Dean.

The model before me had a European elegance coupled with design cues that suggested the brashness of old Detroit – a hint of fins, an oversized grimacing front grill – but also Motor City power: as I recalled there was a big thumping V8 under the bonnet. Yet it was very much made in France, albeit a France in thrall to the USA.

And author Albert Camus really had died in one, although it was being driven by his publisher at the time. I was thankful for my time at the Historique GP in Monaco and for Keegan's thorough briefing documents. I thought going through all the old cars being sold off was overengineering the whole deal. But how was I to know I would come up against a Facel Vega? Thank God I hadn't skipped the Historic Car Market folder.

I walked around the vehicle, sizing it up. The bodywork had been subject to some restoration, but the wire wheels were in need of care and attention. The tyres, too, were perished around the walls, judging by the capillary bed of fissures over the word 'Dunlop'. I opened the door on the driver's side. The once-opulent red leather interior was scuffed and split, the windscreen had a crack in one corner. Cobwebs hung from the ceiling. The dash was a painted burr-walnut effect over metal, although it was chipped and peeling in parts.

I tucked myself in behind the huge ivory-coloured steering wheel, careful not to give Myles too much of a view up my dress, and gripped the circumference.

'You don't think this thing will go?' Myles asked.

'It only has to go as far as the nearest village,' I said. I wasn't sure how far that was. It was just on the border of my memory, at the point where my mind lost focus. It was quite a few kilometres, of that much I was sure. And the prospect of walking that distance barefoot dressed – as Myles would have it – as Little Bo Peep didn't appeal.

I looked down at the dash. There was the slot for the key. What I didn't have was the key to go in it. I yanked down the sun visors, scaring a few more spiders, but there was no sign.

I pulled the bonnet lever and said to Myles, 'See if there is a spare key taped under there.'

He got the bonnet up and came back. 'No key.'

'No worries, I can hot-wire it.'

For once he looked impressed. 'Can you?'

'On a car of this age?' I said, possibly smugly. 'Easy.'

Then, a sneer of a smile. 'Even without a battery?'

I spent a long time looking for a car battery in those stables. I spent almost as long glaring at the rusty tray where it should have stood, as if I could will it to teleport in. It remained stubbornly empty.

Everything else on the electrical system looked OK. There were plugs, plug leads that hadn't cracked or perished, a distributor, a big generator the size of a turbine, the fan belt was OK, the points seemed in reasonable nick and . . .

A generator.

Why was that important? It had a generator, not an

alternator. I knew that was significant, but couldn't recall why. It was a throwaway remark from someone. One-Eyed Jack, my car guru.

Think!

I closed my eyes, and summoned up that distinctive south London growl.

'In the old day, you could bump-start a car with a generator, even without a battery. Now they all got alternators, which need a spark from a battery to wake them up.'

Or words to that effect. And something else. I knew this part myself: you can't bump-start an engine attached to an automatic gearbox.

I poked my head back into the cabin and rattled the gear lever. I felt a surge of relief. Four-speed manual. Good.

'OK, Myles, time to do something useful.'

'What?'

'Push.'

He looked at the bulk of the car. 'Push that?'

'I'm not sure about this, but I recall a friend of mine saying something about being able to bump-start a car with a generator and no battery.'

His look was as blank as a fresh fall of snow. 'You're shittin' me.'

I might have been. Sometimes I only half-listened to One-Eyed Jack when he lectured me on the finer points of mechanics. 'It won't work on modern cars because alternators need . . .' I improvised. 'They need power from the battery initially to, um, prime them. But once you get a generator turning, you've got all the power you need.'

Just don't stall it, that's all, because you'll be dead.

'Fuck. Who knew? What's the difference—?' he began, but I was at the limit of my knowledge.

'Not now,' I snapped at him. 'We've got work to do.'

I went back and looked for a set of wire strippers or pliers in the workbenches. Nothing. 'You're going to have to help me hot-wire it,' I told him.

'How?'

'All that expensive dentistry you keep flashing.'

Never use your teeth as tools, the army dentists used to tell us. Because if a wire needed stripping, a jammed bottle freed or stitches cut when you had no scissors, we all had a tendency to call on our teeth. Well, sometimes there was nothing else available. Like now. My only tool was a twenty-year-old kid with lovely dentition.

I used the handle of the pistol to crack away at the shroud of the steering column, but the butt began to splinter before it had done much more than put a few scratches on the metal. If there had been a battery there would have been an easier way to do this by rewiring in the engine bay, but that wasn't an option. I found the screws that held the cowling in place. Slots rather than Phillips or Pozidriv. Not that it mattered – I didn't have a screwdriver of any description. I'd checked the boot for a factory-fitted tool kit, but there was nothing. Just a couple of red warning triangles tossed in as an afterthought and a spare wheel, neither of which were much use.

I pulled out the ramrod from the pistol. One end of it was flattened, so that it could be used to unscrew the lock plate and the hammer mechanism. It was too big for the ones on the column shroud, but Myles watched and I rubbed it on the cement floor to wear down the head.

One screw came out easily, the second with some swearing and the third stripped. I put my fingers into the gap I had created and pulled. The screw stayed put but the metal around it tore and I twisted the shroud free. Tendrils of wire tumbled out in a faded rainbow of colours.

I imagined the auctioneer at Bonhams blanching at my methods.

'How old is this thing?' Myles asked.

'Fifties.' I pulled the wires so they spilled out further. 'I think this is the ignition bundle ... battery, starter, ignition.' I hoped I sounded more confident than I felt. 'What we need to do is get a live feed from the generator to the ignition. So, Myles, I want you to bite these two here.' I pointed at the suspects. 'Strip the wire, and be generous, we need a good connection, and then twist them together.'

'Bite?' He said it as if I'd asked him to eat his own shit. They were pretty filthy. I used my fingers to clean them off a little.

'Yes. With your teeth. Those two, the red wires. Don't worry, there's no power. Not while the generator isn't turning. You won't get a nasty little shock.'

'What are you going to do?'

'Check something else.'

I went to the rear of the car and unscrewed the petrol cap. The Facel dated from the days (and the class of owner) when siphoning fuel out of cars wasn't an issue and so there was no locking mechanism. I put my ear to the aperture and tried to shake the car. It was like moving a stubborn elephant. I couldn't get it to rock. Still, there were fumes coming out of the tank and stinging my nose and eyes, so there was some petrol in there.

It took me a while to fashion a small leather cup out of what was left of the harness of the four-wheeler carriage and make a handle from the wire springs in the mouse-chewed seats. By that time Myles had finished the wiring and was looking thrilled with himself. I didn't mention the smear of dirt and oil that now streaked his face or that he now had what looked like Shane McGowan's teeth.

I undid the top of the air filter – thanking God for the wingnuts as I did so. Then, using my makeshift ladle, I carefully extracted a scoop of petrol from the tank. I slopped a little as I poured it into the bowl of the carburettor, but enough got in there for my needs. I dropped the bonnet and replaced the petrol cap. I couldn't think of anything else.

'I think we're good to go,' I said.

Myles frowned.

'I'll help you with the initial push, don't worry. We've just got to get it rolling.'

'It's not that. Listen.'

I listened.

'There's a car coming.'

TWENTY-TWO

Monday

*Yesterday started really well. There was Dieter,
Aja, a guy called Theo who owned the yacht
and his girlfriend who was called Rose. And
two local crew who never spoke, just served
drinks and snacks all day, when they weren't
putting sails up or down. We left harbour really
early – it was about eight o'clock. I had been up
since SIX. We had to drive for an hour to get
to the boat. Such a trek. It is a pretty big boat,
a sailboat, called* Princess Mona. *All white. We
had to motor out before we could do the sails.
Well, I didn't do anything. Rose, Aja and me just
sat below while the men did it all. The girls were
really nice but spoke a lot in their own language.
Tagalog – they are from the Philippines. It's
funny to listen to. Like birds chirping. They*

gave me a coffee and then insisted on rubbing like factor 50 all over me. They said it could get really hot up top.

Once we were under sail we went back up and the girls moved to the front of the boat (the foredeck) where there were loungers and a fridge full of drink and cold towels. The guys stayed at the back for the most part, smoking and drinking.

When we lay down Aja and Rose both took their bikini tops off. They didn't say anything. But I could feel the pressure. But they both had lovely brown boobs. I'm still flat as an ironing board. Well, compared to those two. It was a bit cringe.

But I am so relieved I didn't because the men came up then with champagne. They talked to me for a bit about how they knew my dad – they met Matt on Ibiza years ago. Said he was a real character – used to party for weeks on end. But his party days were over now he had me to care for. He was all grown-up and sensible. Then that one Theo, who I didn't really like, said something about me being a shy girl. He was looking at my top when he said it. Dieter elbowed him in the ribs and told him to stop being a creep.

I drank a glass of champagne (OK, maybe two!), but with the up and down of the boat it made me feel a bit sick. Well, more than a bit. I threw up. So I didn't feel like eating when the crew said that lunch was ready. I went downstairs and lay on a bunk. Dieter and Aja came to check I was OK. I was but still didn't feel like eating or drinking anything, even though there was tons of food.

I only came out on deck when we were heading home. The girls were back on the sunloungers, giggling like mad. I knew why, of course. I could smell it. Theo offered me some because it would 'settle my stomach', as he said, but I didn't fancy going round and round as well as up and down. Every time I have it, it makes me so dizzy. I think they were a little disappointed in me. I don't think I was much fun. But if they were disappointed, they didn't show it and Dieter said we could do it again, I just had to get my sea legs. Aja gave me a kiss on the cheek when they dropped me off, probably to show there were no hard feelings. All I wanted to do was clean my teeth and go to bed.

Sarah was at the house when I got back. Her and Matt said they were discussing my education.

Yeah, right.

TWENTY-THREE

Normandy, France

I pulled the doors to the stable shut and pulled the tarp back over the Facel, leaving the passenger side uncovered for now. I peered out through the crack in the stable doors. The sound of the car's engine had stopped. Whoever it was, they were outside the chateau. Or perhaps in it by now.

The crows rose from the trees again in alarm. A bit bloody late, I thought.

'What if it's Mom?' Myles said.

'Shush. Keep your voice down. That was a diesel. The Peugeot was petrol.'

'They might have switched cars. What if it is her and Konrad and they've come for us?' he whispered.

'Well, they have some explaining to do, that's for sure. Like why I was drugged and stripped naked.'

'There might be a simple explanation.'

'I'm all ears.'

He kept quiet after that. I watched the building, but there was no sign of movement. And then, something on the first floor. Curtains being pulled back. A silhouetted figure, but there was sunlight reflecting off the window and I couldn't make out any details.

'Look, if it's the cavalry, I'll go out. You stay here, OK? Lay low until I say it's all right. It might just be a caretaker. Hold up.'

'What?'

One of the French windows at the rear of the property had opened up. A second later a man stepped through into the gardens. He had close-cropped hair, with a well-trimmed beard. He was wearing a leather blouson, jeans and black trainers. He had his hand in one pocket of the jacket.

He looked from right to left, scanning the grounds. When his head stopped moving, he was facing the stable block. I froze, resisting the temptation to snatch my head away from the crack. Even at that distance, some movement might register.

I heard a voice shout something in the house and he turned. I backed away from the stable doors and herded Myles towards the car. He started to protest and I hissed in his ear.

'It's not the cavalry, boy. It's fucking Cochise and his Apaches. OK?'

It took me a second to find the release catch, but I pulled the seat forward and pushed Myles in the back.

I returned it to the upright position and sat in, getting ready to pull the tarp down, when I realised I had left the pistol on the cement floor. I rolled back out, found it and my home-made leather cup. The latter I slid under the car, but I put the pistol on my lap, once I had managed to close the door and pull the tarp down. I was relieved this model didn't have electric windows, which would have made life more difficult. I cranked the door glass back into place and cradled the sharpened ramrod like a knife.

'Do not say a word. Do not breathe,' I warned. Although, given the sharp-sour smell emanating from his booze-and-sick-spattered clothes, it was good advice all round. 'No matter what happens. You understand?'

Myles let out a small groan, which I took as a yes.

I reached over and touched his arm. He was shaking like a wet puppy. 'It'll be all right,' I said.

His hand found mine over the back of the seat. It was clammy. I felt our fingers intertwining. I squeezed, as reassuringly as I could.

'I'm sorry,' he whispered.

'What for?'

'Being an a-hole.'

'When?'

A pause. 'Pretty much up till now, I guess.'

'We can all be arseholes,' I said. 'I'm sorry I was so hard on you. Water under the bridge. We're in this together now. And I'm glad you're here. Now shush.'

The leather squeaked as he leaned over and rested his head on my shoulder. It was all I could do not to ruffle his hair. Maybe I should get a dog when I got back. Or was that my mythical maternal instinct cutting in? I untangled my hand from his. I just might need both of them very shortly.

Apparently time slows when your brain is making fresh memories, trying to store all the details of a trip, an accident, a fight, a new lover. It speeds up when it is deprived of fresh stimulation, running like an engine at fast tickover. It's why the journey back from a new destination can seem so much quicker than the trip there – the memories have already been made and to the brain the landmarks are now numbingly familiar. Your nervous system is like a junkie for new experiences, an attention-deficit organ.

So, theoretically, time should have dragged its feet while we were sitting there in a greenish gloom, waiting for someone to come. But it seemed to me I had only just got the window back into place when the stable door creaked and I heard tentative footsteps on the cement.

Times like this you always imagine your heart is banging hard enough to be heard several villages away, so I ignored that. It was only that loud in my ears.

I heard a sniff. Of course, he would smell the petrol I had spilled. Then, the flap of a corner of the tarp being thrown back.

I placed my hand on the door handle, ready to put my shoulder against it and knock anyone who might be standing there off balance.

'Jules!'

The shout came from or near the house.

'Jules?'

I heard a little grunt of annoyance. Steps moved away from the car.

'You got something?' our man yelled back. French, with no foreign accent as far as I could tell.

'No, it's empty. You?'

'A nice car.'

'We're not here to look at nice cars. He won't be happy.'

'Fuck him.' This, though, was said under his breath. His chum at the house would never have heard. Then louder: 'We're wasting our time.'

'What did you say?'

'It's a waste of time.'

'You want to tell the boss that?'

'No.'

'You coming?'

'Sure.'

He walked back into the stable and I heard the scrape of the heavy material on the Facel's body once more. But he was pulling it off further, not re-covering. A strip of daylight appeared at the bottom of the windscreen. I flattened myself against the seat, staying as still as I could, while I watched a sliver of the man move around the bonnet. He placed a hand on it, as if checking for the warmth of a recently run engine.

'Jules!'

'Jesus.' Then, louder: 'OK, OK.'

The thin corridor of light disappeared as the tarp was roughly pulled back into place. The stable doors' hinges gave their little squeak as they were closed again and I heard a tuneless whistle, fading as the man walked back towards the chateau.

'Stay where you are. Say nothing,' I said as softly as I could.

Now the brain did what it was supposed to do. Time stuttered and stopped. I counted my heartbeats to keep some kind of score. Five hundred and I'd go. That would be enough time.

At just before one hundred I heard the cough of a car starting and then the gear change as it drove away.

'OK,' I said eventually, 'you can breathe.'

Myles exhaled and then gulped a big lungful of air. 'Thank you.'

I wasn't sure what I'd done to be thanked for. Hiding isn't the most pro-active option for a PPO.

'Who were they?' he asked.

'I have no idea. I didn't like the look of the one I saw, though. I think he was carrying. A gun, I mean. And he was dressed as if he binge-watched *The Sopranos*.'

That got a polite laugh. 'They could have been cleaners sent by Konrad.'

'Cleaners?'

'Yeah. Not the kind who come with hoovers and J-cloths. The other sort.'

It took a while for the penny to drop. 'Oh. But it's only a guess, eh?' There was a tremor in his voice.

'I don't know. I think Konrad had this set up all along. To get your mother here and make her his prisoner.'

'Fuck. Why?'

'I hate to keep saying the same thing, but I don't know. Did she say anything to you? About enemies?'

'No. Well, she has said there are people who are jealous, but, fuck, no. Nothing like someone ... will he hurt her?'

My silence told him yet again, I didn't have a clue.

'So what do we do now?'

'We have some options. I need to get us out of here. I need to speak to the Colonel. I need some clothes and we need some money.'

'OK.'

'You up for this? Getting this monster going?'

'Yeah. Fuck, bring it on.' He banged the back of the seat. With his fist. It was pure bravado. He was scared. I was worried, verging on scared. But it seemed to me we had very little choice in what to do now.

I felt his hand grip me and squeeze. 'It'll be easier if you don't have your hand on my shoulder.'

'Sorry.'

By now it must have gone nine and the heat of the day was building. After extracting myself from the Vega, I threw open the stable doors once more and dragged the cover off. Myles emerged blinking like a newborn lamb. 'So, how do we do this?'

I didn't answer for a while. I surveyed the house again, making sure we really were alone and they hadn't left a watchman behind. After all, I only heard two voices. That didn't mean there'd only been two of them.

Once I was satisfied I turned to the boy.

'OK, we try and roll it. The main problem is breaking the inertia. When we are out of the stables, the slope of the garden will help momentum. I'll aim for that path there.' Which wouldn't be easy without the power steering I hoped the brute had when it was up and running. *If* it got up and running. 'I'll jump in, gravity should do the rest, I'll put it in second, drop the clutch and if you've wired it properly—'

'Hey. I only did what you said.'

'Myles,' I said quietly. 'If this doesn't work, we're going to need a scapegoat. You're it. So man up.'

'Is that British humour?'

'Best you're going to get with me dressed like this. Come on.'

A cold dash of reality hit him and his shoulders went down. 'It'll be a fuckin' miracle if this works.'

'Trust me, I'm overdue in the miracle department.'

I released the handbrake, which didn't cause the headlong rush for the door I had been hoping for, then took up position at the rear. All I had to do was start it moving, then I'd switch my position to the driver's door.

We both put our backs to it, got as much purchase on the floor as we could and pushed. It was like trying to move the stable block itself. I just hoped the brakes hadn't seized. Or the handbrake cable. For all I knew it hadn't released at all.

'Are you putting your back into it?'

'Sure. Are you?'

I felt the sinews in my neck bulge out of my skin as I strained. 'Jesus, why couldn't I have got the captain of the school football team rather than the college dope dealer . . .'

'I'm stronger than you.'

'It's not enough,' I goaded.

He let out an almighty grunt and the Facel gave the barest of twitches. I scrabbled my bare feet until I had something like grip and leaned into the boot. The panel dented with a loud pop but I ignored it.

The car gave another grudging inch. 'Keep pushing,' I yelled, while I ran around to the open door on the off-side. I flung myself at the intersection of door frame and roof and pushed. She was creaking now, finally accepting that she was going to have to move. 'Keep going!'

The nose was out of the stable, the sun bouncing off the pocked brightwork. Then, the slope of ground in the small yard had me and I felt the machine begin to roll of its own accord, despite the shrieks and groans coming from the axles or wheel bearings or both. 'OK, don't stop, we need as much speed as we can get for this to work.'

I risked a glance at Myles. He had his hands splayed on the boot now and was almost horizontal, his face traffic-light red. A for effort.

I jumped in as best I could, all idea of modesty forgotten as the skirt flipped up to my waist. I slammed the door shut and got into position. Clutch down, second gear. I yanked at the wheel but it was like trying to move a supertanker. In dry dock. I bore down on one of the spokes with all my strength and the under-inflated tyres inched around as I rolled out off the brick frontage and on to grass. There was a scrape as I touched one of the low walls – another fifty grand off the value – but I was more or less on the dusty gravel-strewn path that led down to the house. I straightened her and, as I did so, felt the bodice of my dress rip.

A glance in the mirror. Myles was still there, his face set in a grimace, but the slab of a car had serious momentum now. I realised I was heading straight for a chateau in something that weighed two tons. Did the brakes even work? I daren't try an exploratory jab, because it would cut my speed. We only had one go at this – we could barely push when it was on the level, let alone back uphill.

The rumbling of the tyres filled the cabin. I watched Myles stop and fall back, his outline blurred by the dust the old Dunlops were kicking up. The rear of the mansion was growing large in the windscreen.

'Now!' Myles's yell drifted through the open window.

I waited another three seconds and let the clutch in. The Facel bucked like I had given it electro-convulsive therapy. A series of rattles came from under the bonnet, as if the V8 had been replaced by a collection of saucepans.

I dipped the clutch again. 'Come on, you bitch,' I said, thumping the dash.

I'd lost some edge, but there was still enough speed to make any other car catch. I must have got the wiring wrong. And I was running out of road. I could make out the details of the handles and the cracks in some of the panes on the French doors now.

Clutch up. Again, the sound of gargling metal from under the bonnet and then a juddering and a kind of harrumphing sound. Two out of eight cylinders, maybe. Three at most. I felt her slow slightly. I blipped the throttle. I heard One-Eyed Jack yell in my ear.

Don't flood her.

Five, maybe six cylinders, but now the Facel was

apparently having an epileptic fit, threatening to shake the teeth from my skull.

I'd left it too late.

You've left it too late.

Thanks, Jack. I hit the brakes and felt my foot go to the floor. I pumped as fast as I could and they began to bite. But not quickly enough. One last stamp on the flaccid pedal, then a splintering of glass, wood and metal as the Facel Vega hit the doors dead centre, the impact snapping me forward to head-butt the steering wheel and into oblivion.

TWENTY-FOUR

Tuesday

'I declare after all there is no enjoyment like reading! How much sooner one tires of any thing than of a book! – When I have a house of my own, I shall be miserable if I have not an excellent library.'

That's from the Jane Austen book. Written before anyone had the internet.

Thursday

Putu let me ride out on a delivery with him. I had been asking him for days. He was going up to one of the really big villas the rich people rent. With servants and big pools and stuff. Dieter said I could go, but not to tell my dad, who was in

town getting some more booze for the bar. But
I had to wear a crash helmet. Even though Putu
wore one on the back of his head and didn't even
do the straps up.

It was a SCARY ride, I had to hold on tight as
he weaved in and out of the traffic. I thought we
were going to die a couple of times he was SO
CLOSE. But we made it. Mind you, it took about
thirty minutes. The pizzas must have been cold by
the time we got there.

I had to wait at the gate while he went in to
deliver the two pizzas – an American Hot with
extra pepperoni and a Four Seasons. He was
counting the money as he came back. They have
to pay in cash. They must be better pizzas than I
thought because Putu said business is booming.

Friday

OK, so Sarah and Dad are definitely at it. I
FaceTimed Laura yesterday and she kept going on
about Dad and mentioning Sarah. She definitely
thinks something is up. And she's right. Last night
I heard them through the walls … They thought
they were being quiet but they kept laughing and
then shushing. I don't know how to write the
appropriate noise. So gross. Imagine me with my
fingers down my throat. Only not so happy as that.

She wasn't there at breakfast, but I bet she soon will be here, buttering his toast. That might be what Mrs Rodak used to call a euphemism. (I wonder if she is still at the school? After that thing with Mr Horton.)

I might blackmail Sarah. Tell her that I'll tell Laura about her and Dad if she makes me finish Pride & fucking Prejudice.

I keep wondering how Mum is doing.

TWENTY-FIVE

Normandy, France

I could only have been out for a few seconds. I felt Myles's hands shaking me and his voice whining in my ear like a mosquito.

'You OK? Sam, you OK? Speak to me.'

'Don't,' I snapped. Except my thick tongue made it come out like some other word altogether. I pulled my head back from the wheel but kept both hands at ten to two. 'Don't ever shake someone who has hit their head.'

I released my right hand and touched my forehead. No blood but the brush of my fingertips felt like an explosion of needles. 'Ow.'

'What can I do?'

I focused on him, followed the flick of his eyes and realised my skirt was doing a very poor job of covering me and that my left breast had escaped from captivity and was running free. 'You can turn around.'

He did so and I rearranged my clothing towards some sort of decorum. 'OK.'

He crouched down next to me. 'You feel all right?'

I wasn't sure. There was a rumbling in my head I couldn't place and a pain behind my eyes. The world seemed very bright all of a sudden. There would be a chance of concussion. 'Just don't let me go to sleep,' I said, although the very word sounded inviting. 'Anyway, I'm in better shape than the wall.'

The French doors were like a couple of drunks hanging on to lampposts for support. Most of their panes of glass had gone. One of the curtains lay across the bonnet of the Facel. The car hadn't ploughed very far into the room – the brakes must have finally bitten – and the doors had been wide enough that I hadn't hit the brick walls on either side. So whoever the owner was wouldn't come back to find that his restoration project was a total write-off. But that didn't help me right now.

'Give me a minute,' I said. 'I'll get out slow.'

'Sure. You know, Sam, I didn't think you could do it.'

I didn't need a told-you-so speech from the kid. 'OK, no need to gloat. I'm the one with the bruised head. It was a long shot.'

'What do you mean? You're a fuckin' genius.'

It was only then I appreciated the rumble wasn't in

my skull. It was coming up through my body, from the seat, and through my arms from the wheel.

The big Chrysler V8 was running.

I wasn't sure how I had knocked it into neutral. Maybe I hadn't. Maybe the impact had done it for me. Either way, the engine was ticking over, relatively smoothly. I found the manual choke and eased it out a notch. This was the tricky bit. One stall and it was all over.

'I'm sorry,' I said, tapping the dash, 'that I called you a bitch.'

I dipped the clutch, selected reverse and kept the revs reasonably high as I let my left foot lift up the pedal. I had no idea about the bite point of the clutch, but it didn't snatch and let the power in smoothly. The car gave a shiver along its length, then extricated itself from the wreckage of the doors with a tinkling of glass that sounded like ice falling. The curtain drew out after me for a few yards, billowing like a sail, then gave up, recoiling from the bonnet.

When I was clear enough to turn and drive around the house, I shouted to Myles to get in.

'What now?' he asked, suddenly keen as a puppy dog.

'Town.'

'You OK to drive?' He pointed to his own forehead. I glanced in the rear-view mirror. I looked like I was part Smurf – there was a blue-black bruise running just below my hairline. No wonder I had a headache.

'Can you drive a stick shift?'

'I can try. Can't be that hard.'

Wrong answer. 'Now probably isn't the best time to learn.'

It was a little like manoeuvring a barge compared to a modern car. The power steering was light and not progressive, so it was very easy to overcompensate. What should have been a straight line became a sine wave as I tried to get a feel for her. Frisky was the best adjective I could come up with to describe her. I took her around the side of the house in second. The engine burbled with only the occasional hiccup. One cylinder had a slight misfire. Probably a plug, but I wasn't about to try diagnostics. I got the Facel into third along the drive and it seemed to clear.

Maybe it needs higher revs to come on cam.

My mental One-Eyed Jack had lost me now, so I ignored the voice. I slowed for the gates. The pedal went far too close to the floor for my liking and the front end shook. It felt like it had bottle tops instead of drum brakes. No wonder I had hit the French doors. 'Can you see if there's an anchor in the back seat?'

Myles half turned before he realised I wasn't entirely serious. 'The brakes bad?'

'You remember the gate code?' I asked when we had finally pulled level with the black box on a stalk that held a keypad. I remembered stopping outside, but the time around the actual input numbers was another cerebral lacuna.

'Ten sixty-six,' he said.

I laughed. Fucking French, still gloating. 'Of course it is.'

I punched it in and the gates swung towards us. I crept forward and pulled us to a halt with the nose sticking out in the road. I was sweating with the exertion of coping with the heavy steering and clutch, coupled with brakes that faded faster than a snowflake in hell. 'Christ, no wonder Camus copped it.'

'Who?'

'Doesn't matter. Is there a map in the glove compartment?' I'd only been interested in a key when I had gone through it.

He popped the walnut flap and rifled through some papers.

'Nothing?'

'No map that I can see. An owner's manual.'

I pulled out onto the road and accelerated gingerly up the hill. I eased the choke in a little. The gates swung closed behind me. I would imagine the chateau was glad to see the back of us.

'Listen to this,' he said. 'It's in the owner's manual. In English. "*Driving your Facel Vega. At high speed drivers are warned to be careful to hold the steering wheel with both hands except when shifting gears; to keep as close as possible to the centre of the road;*

not to overtake on the brow of a hill; to reduce speed over the brow of a hill as a car might have stopped on the far side; not to look at anything else but the road; not to change the radio programme; not to smoke".'

'I'll bear all that in mind.' Although I felt like lighting up just to spite the nannying tone. 'Nothing useful?'

'Some cash.'

Now he was talking. 'How much?'

'I don't know. It's foreign.'

Against all the advice of the owner's manual I stole a glance at the money on his lap as we crested the hill. Nothing was coming my way. 'Fuck.'

'What?'

'It's probably as old as the car itself. Francs.'

'No good?'

'No good.' Not unless we went to the central bank in Paris. And I wasn't going to do that for the sake of a few euros.

'Bummer.' Before I could say anything, he wound down the window and flung it out. I watched the bills flutter like demented bats in our slipstream.

'What did you do that for?'

'You said they were no good.'

'For our purposes, right now. You could have just put them back.'

He jutted out his lower lip and folded his arms.

'Next time you want to see what it feels like to throw money away, ask me first.'

'Yes, Mommy.'

I glared at him. His real mommy was somewhere, probably many miles away, with a very clever maniac whom I suspected intended to do her harm. Why else take her? Money. That was usually the reason. He wanted the cash she had hidden away in Luxembourg. But why not wait until we were a little closer to Luxembourg City to make his move? Still, he could well be there by now, walking into a strongroom while we thrashed around trying to reclaim a little bit of modern life. Clothes, money, phone, that sort of thing. Underwear. Shoes would be good, too. My soles were stinging from pushing on that gravelly path.

I pulled over a little to let an Audi pass, which it did with a leonine growl. It was a lovely road, wide enough for three cars abreast, lined by plane trees, with plenty of blind brows and bends to add a little excitement. It was the kind of route I could drive for hours. In something less lethal than the Facel Vega, that is.

I could sense the other drivers admiring the sleek lines of the car as they approached us. I once said cruising round London in a Rolls-Royce Ghost was like driving with your bollocks hanging out. I felt like I had my tits out too. Which, given the dress, wasn't all that far from the truth. If the police stopped us my best hope was to claim we had run away from the circus. Anyone would fall for that one.

But there was one big problem with the Facel. Once seen, not forgotten. And I knew of one man who had admired its lines who would remember that the last time he saw this car it was under canvas.

'Berlot, three kilometres,' said Myles, reading off a sign. 'Is that where we're going?'

'We'll see what Berlot has to offer.'

Not a lot was the answer. There was no proper post office from where I might have been able to make a reverse charge call and the linear main street had a high proportion of antique shops, all of which were closed. Which didn't matter, because we certainly weren't in the market for the kitchen dressers that dominated most window displays.

I saw the bank coming up on the left and stomped on the brake pedal well in advance, but even so over-shot the mark by a few yards. I was going to end up with a right thigh like one of Popeye's arms at this rate.

'Wait here,' I instructed Myles. 'I want you to get in the driver's seat.'

'I told you, I don't do stick shifts.'

'I don't want you to. I don't want you to touch any-thing. But I have to leave it running. If it sounds like it might stall – you know, begins to run rough – pull this out. Just a gnat's.'

'A gnat's?'

'A gnat's cock.' I realised I was speaking like One-Eyed Jack. 'A tiny amount. OK? Pull it out too much and it'll flood the carb. And don't touch anything else.'

'Or speak to strangers?'

'Especially that.'

They didn't so much raise their eyebrows in the bank as crank them up by crane. I waited in the queue, acting as if I didn't look like the survivor of a particularly bad road accident, and when I went to the cashier's window I tried to use all my best charm and bad French. She was a middle-aged woman with a chilly, businesslike attitude. Her hair was dyed ginger – at least I guessed it was, I'd never seen a natural colour quite like it – and coiffured into an elaborate helmet.

I explained that we had been robbed. No, I hadn't been to the police. It happened while we were asleep, so we had no description to give them.

What exactly did I want? Could she contact my bank and transfer me some money, I suggested. I had a sort code and an account number. I could remember that OK.

She looked as if I had asked her to cook and eat her own children.

C'est impossible, apparently. But perhaps if I let her have my passport.

No passport.

Or driving licence.

Nope.

No proof of identity at all? she asked.

I explained I seemed to be all out of recent utility bills, credit cards or Oyster cards. She couldn't help then. After all, how could she be sure I was who I said I was? I had to appreciate the need for security. There was more along those lines before she told me the local police station was in the next village. I asked where the nearest British consulate was located. Le Havre. I did a quick mental calculation. A ninety-minute drive? A little less, she suggested. Not by Facel Vega, I thought. I'd have to start braking somewhere around Caen.

I thanked her and left, trying to ignore the stress coming my way. I stepped into the street and stopped to gather my thoughts. The British consulate might help. Money, documents. There would be a lot of explaining to do, but from there I could make phone calls and then ... then what? Luxembourg popped into my head again. It all began in Luxembourg with the hit-and-run on the NOP bank guy. Maybe that's where it was all meant to end. But, I realised, I had some way to go yet.

Especially as the Facel Vega had gone.

I looked up and down the length of the main road. No sign of the car. It wasn't like I could miss it. Had that idiot man-child tried to prove something to me by driving off? But I didn't think that was it. Two kangaroo leaps and a stall would have been the most likely outcome of him trying to master a manual.

It was then I spotted the man in the blouson. Jules? Yes, Jules. The guy from the stables. He was leaning into a shop window, his eyes cupped to the glass as if looking into the interior for something. Or someone.

When he turned away, he had his back to me, and he had slipped his hands into the pockets of his leather jacket. I did another scan of the immediate area. There were very few people about. Not enough to worry me, anyway. Certainly no cops or anyone official-looking. Not even anyone whom I reckoned could take care of themselves. Jules excepted. Oh, and me.

I launched myself along the pavement, my shoeless feet making barely a sound as I accelerated. I pumped my arms, ignoring the protests from my much-abused body and the hammering behind my eyes. I was a few yards away from him when I jumped, turning sideways and pulling my knees up, as if I were making a tuck dive from the high board.

It meant I hit him like a giant clenched fist, high on his back, sending him sprawling. Do this properly and your momentum will carry you over the victim, enabling you to roll up into a defensive position. But I wasn't match-fit and I landed heavily, knocking my wrist back with a force that made me gasp.

But he was worse. He'd gone straight down and hadn't quite got his hands out of his pockets in time to fully break his fall. I leaped up, ignoring the shouts from an outraged old man over the road, and dropped onto his back, pulling at the pockets of the blouson and extracting what I needed. A wallet. And in the other? A phone.

Bingo.

I did a quick frisk. No gun. Odd.

He started to shift under me, so I placed a knee between his shoulder blades and raised my fist to deliver the blow to the back of his head that would break his nose on the pavement and render him unconscious.

'Miss Wylde!'

I became aware of the deep, slow thrum of the V8 over my shoulder.

'Would you mind not inflicting any more damage on my son?'

TWENTY-SIX

'I'm sorry.'

Jules touched his nose. 'It's been broken before. Rugby.' Like his father, his English was good, although Bruno, the dad, had the stronger and stranger accent. He had looked ridiculous in the Facel Vega, barely able to see over the wheel. He was a shrunken version of his son – bald, bearded, but with a deep, nut-brown skin colour. He had scooped us up and driven us to a rough pit-stop next to a petrol station, used by the sort of *camionneur* who would only have one thought when he looked at me in my bedraggled state: *I bet she comes cheap*.

The four of us were sitting in the corner of the overlit room, which was decorated with framed pages from Pirelli calendars of yore and posters from ancient kung fu films. I had my back to the wall – and the four-sheet for *King Boxer* – from where I could watch the door. I was opposite Jules, Bruno was next to him, across the table from Myles.

A waitress delivered four coffees and a pile of pastries that looked as plastic as the chairs we were sitting on. It didn't matter. I was so hungry I'd probably move on to the chairs later. I broke off half a croissant.

'I'm sorry,' I repeated, but to both of them this time. 'When you came looking at the chateau, I thought you were from Konrad. That he'd sent you to clear up some loose ends. Us.'

'So you said.' Bruno poured a stream of sugar in his coffee. 'But when you failed to turn up at my, um, workshop, I telephoned the Colonel. He said he was worried too. He didn't have any heavyweights in the area, so he sent us along to check out what was going on. We are not muscle.'

I was only too aware of that now. Bruno was the 'inker', the man we were meant to meet to pick up the new passport for Mrs Irwin.

Myles beat me to it. 'How did you know where we were?'

'Because I only gave him rough directions,' I added.

'Your friend Freddie told the Colonel where the chateau was. Apparently you have some code between you for sharing co-ordinates.'

That was true. We used old army slang, a means of obfuscation when talking on an open channel, just in case Al-Qaeda or similar was eavesdropping. But when exactly did I give her our location?

'Freddie?' I realised I sounded as bright as Homer Simpson. 'You spoke to Freddie?'

'Yes. You made a call to her when you arrived at the chateau. Saying something was off. That you might need back-up.'

Did I?

My expression must have betrayed my confusion. 'After you called the Colonel.'

'Look ... I think ... I don't remember too well. Any of it.'

Bruno and his son exchanged concerned glances.

'I think Konrad drugged me,' I said tentatively.

'Fuckin' A, he did,' said Myles, spraying bits of *pain aux raisins* over the table. I wanted to tell him not to speak with his mouth full but thought better of it. *Yes, Mommy.*

'It's left me with some memory gaps. Forgive me. Freddie phoned the Colonel after I did?'

'No, she phoned him after she had been to the chateau.'

'Whoa.' Myles articulated my thoughts precisely.

'She was at the chateau?'

Jules took up the story. I found it hard to look at him without feeling a pang of guilt, because his right eye was getting bluer by the second. 'As far as we can gather, your friend arrived in time to see Konrad leave with the Principal. She followed him.'

'What? Really?' Without coming in to check on me?

There's friendship for you. It didn't sound like Freddie. But it could wait until I had the full picture. Which may be never, given the state of my recall systems. 'Where is she now?'

'Still following him, as far as I know.'

'Shit.' This was good news and bad. A solo tail is really, really difficult. I was not sure I could pull it off. And it was hours since Konrad left. They could be many, many miles away.

On the other hand, even knowing Freddie was in the country gave me a little glow of confidence. I just wished I could remember those damned calls I had apparently made.

'I guess they are on the way to Luxembourg?' I asked.

'I don't know.'

'I need a phone.' I'd given Jules his once back.

'All in good time,' said Bruno.

I shook my head as if it would clear it, but all it did was ramp up the thumping behind my eyes. I poured and drank a glass of tap water. What else had I forgotten? And what made Freddie follow the Peugeot instead of coming in to check on me? I might have been dead or dying – or drugged to the eyeballs. But if she hadn't, we might have no idea of where Mrs Irwin was. I could imagine it was a very tough call for her to make. The professional or the personal? She went pro. I was proud of her. On the other hand, I was slightly pissed off she hadn't come to check me out, given the state I was in.

'Your friend is good?' Jules asked.

'Ex-army,' I said. 'She knows her stuff.'

'Special Forces?'

'Something like that.' She had been a Combat Medical Technician like me, but I didn't think a little mystique would go amiss. 'Give me a minute.'

I ate some more of the pastries, trying to put everything together as I did so. Freddie was in France. Good. I had no idea where. Bad. I looked like a battered junkie-whore. Not good in any light.

'I need some things,' I said.

'Such as?' asked Bruno.

'Clothes for a start. Some ID.'

'I have the passport I prepared for Mrs Irwin with me. If we can find somewhere to shoot a photograph.'

'Best to pick up the clothes in a market,' said Jules. 'No CCTV or receipts. It won't be high fashion . . .'

'I know. Five pairs of knickers for ten euros sort of thing.'

Bruno laughed. 'Round here it is more like ten pairs for five euros.'

'Sorry. I'm used to the high life. I need some other things.'

'What?' asked Bruno.

'A knife, a torch, a first-aid kit, phone, phone

charger ...' I gave him a list that re-created my RTG kit. When I had finished, Bruno stood.

'Where are you going?'

'To the ATM at the garage,' he said. 'You are a very expensive young woman.'

After he had left, I said to Jules: 'Thank you. For helping.'

'I do it for my father.'

'You're not ...' I mimed writing.

'A forger? No, I'm a guitarist. In a rock band. And I have a small garage in Saint-Lo. My father came from Algeria in the Sixties. A *pied noir*. You know this phrase? He was a lawyer. He helped represent other *pieds noirs* with papers, with tax, with getting compensation. But after a few years, he became ... what is the word? Not happy ...'

'Disillusioned?' Myles offered.

'*Oui*. Disillusioned with the French legal system. He began to help people coming over in other ways. With some papers. Then maybe a passport.'

'And now he works for the Colonel?'

'Well, they are old friends. The Colonel was in Algeria during the unrest.' Even I knew that was a euphemism for what went on in the French colony. 'They stayed in touch. My dad helps him out when he can. And, as you know, the Colonel pays well.'

'Why did he send you two to the chateau? If Konrad

had been there . . .' I didn't finish the thought. He was well aware of what I was getting at.

'I know. We are not . . . not professionals in that department, you understand.' Not gunmen or PPOs, he meant. 'He knows that. Which is why he hesitated to ask us. But we were the nearest people the Colonel had to the place. And we were only to report what we found. We thought we had found nothing.'

'You almost had us.'

'And if I had found you hiding in the car like you say you were? What would you have done then?'

I had a flash image of me plunging a sharpened ramrod into his eye socket. But I said nothing.

'Judging from how you greeted me in the street, I think I am lucky I didn't find you in those stables.'

'Maybe,' I admitted. 'Have I said I'm sorry for that hello yet?'

He smiled and finished his coffee. 'Enough times I think.'

'I know you are not in that field of work, but there is one thing I didn't ask your father about.'

'You would like a weapon.'

'A pistol,' I said.

'We have a hunting rifle, that's all. We are not in that game. But you are welcome to borrow it.'

'I want something I can put in my pocket.' I pulled at the ragged hem of my dress. 'Just as soon as I get one.'

Jules stirred his coffee for a few moments. Then he

appeared to come to a decision. 'There is a man who might be able to help. In Rennes. He runs a bicycle repair shop. He might have something.'

Rennes might not be in the right direction for Luxembourg, but it wasn't too far a detour. I would feel a lot safer with a Glock or a Colt under my belt. 'Can you give me a contact number?'

'I'll give you the address. I'll call him. Let him know you are coming. Tell him Big Thrash sent you.'

'Stage name?'

He flashed a bashful smile. 'Be careful. He is not to be trusted on price. If he senses you are desperate . . .'

I laughed. 'That's gun dealers the world over.'

'How do you know this guy if you're not in the, y'know, the business?' Myles asked.

'Ach. Moby might be a greedy arsehole, but he's also a pretty good drummer.'

'Moby?' I asked. 'Like the whale?'

'Like the drum solo,' he said.

Before I could ask for clarification, Bruno returned and slid back into his seat. 'I have been thinking. I am afraid I can't allow you to continue.'

I stiffened. I felt what was left of my adrenaline trickle into my bloodstream. I sat up straighter. Gripped the edge of the table, ready for the push back. I take Bruno first. A fork to the throat, maybe. The old man was small and wiry, but not with much strength.

So, a good thrust with the heel of my hand, knocking him backwards off the chair.

I looked down at the table. The cutlery was plastic. The eye, then. Even a plastic tine in the eye—

'Until you have rested,' he finished. 'And are fully organised. From here, we go to the market. Get clothes.'

I exhaled, letting some of the tension go from my muscles. I was getting jumpy. Which meant I was tired.

'I could do with some new gear, too,' said Myles.

'As the man said, it won't be American Apparel,' I warned, 'But he'll live,' I said to Bruno before Myles could chip in. 'But the rest of us won't unless he changes his boxers soon.'

'Then, there is a Formule hotel about five kilometres away,' said Bruno. 'No staff, all done by cards. Jules will book in under his name and get us in. There I use a Polaroid to take the photo for the passport, maybe an hour to work on it. You'll be an American citizen, though. I only brought the one blank.'

'Swell,' I offered.

'I can always do the talking,' offered Myles with a look of disgust. 'At least my accent is authentic.'

Great. One real accent and one phoney passport between us.

'I want you to get some rest while I work on it.'

We would see about that. 'We'll need a car,' I said. 'I can't take that Facel any distance.'

'Besides, it is like driving with your cock hanging out,' said Jules. 'Everyone remembers what they saw and where.' Maybe he really was a mechanic after all. 'Which is why we moved it from the high street. But I can whistle up a less conspicuous one from Saint-Lo. I'll make sure it has all-drivers insurance.'

'Thank you. And if you can make it an auto?' His eyebrows asked the question. 'Just in case I need both hands free. Myles here can manage an auto, but not a manual. I'll pay, of course.'

'The Colonel will cover it,' said Bruno.

'For now.'

'Of course.' At this rate my expenses deductions were going to be a doozy. 'Have you thought that, perhaps, the boy should stay with us?'

'No fuckin' way.'

'No, I hadn't,' I admitted. 'But it's a good idea.'

'It's a pile of horseshit idea. Look, as you just said, I can drive if we get a proper gearbox.'

'I'll manage that alone.'

He leaned in and stabbed a finger at me. 'And my mom is out there, alone and frightened with some maniac planning God knows what. And you want me to what? Just go off with these guys? Wait for your call? Excuse me, Sam, but your batting averages this season haven't been so great, have they? And, if you leave me I'll be straight into a police station and tell them there are people with guns running around after someone with a European arrest warrant on her head.'

His face had flushed while he was talking.

Well, he had talked himself into a stay in a wardrobe with his hands tied and mouth taped if any of us felt so inclined. You don't try to blackmail until you hold all the cards. 'I didn't know you cared quite so much,' I said, '... about your mum.'

'I'm not the boo-hoo kind. I thought you'd figured that. But of course I do.'

I looked at Bruno. 'The boy stays with me.'

'Very well. While I was out I telephoned your friend Freddie, to say you'd be in touch soon. Once we get everything together. No rush, she said.'

'Where is she?'

'Ustaritz.'

'Where's that?' I asked.

'South. The Basque Country.'

TWENTY-SEVEN

There were hands on my breasts. Lots of hands, or so it seemed, but moving lightly, fluttering almost, merely brushing my nipples, which, nevertheless, had hardened. I wasn't sure whether I should be embarrassed or not, but something about me felt brazen, enjoying the feeling of being pawed. Groped with sensitivity, that's what it was. The pressure increased and I realised I was being massaged, not assaulted. I felt the guilt slough off me like a used skin.

I was lying in a room that glowed with an ethereal light. Or was it sepulchral? It was like the finest Carrara marble, yet it was as if the stone itself was glowing from within. My masseurs – no, masseuses, I was sure they were women – were dressed in robes as if they were part of a holy order. The light emanating from the walls was so bright I had trouble making out their features, these women whose fingertips were dancing over my skin, stroking my jaw, kneading at my temple, sliding down over my belly.

I tried to speak, but words would not form. As one of the hands slid between my legs I let out a low growl of ... pleasure? Displeasure? Stop? Go on?

Those fingers were inside me now. One, then two as I yielded. But did I want to yield? One of the women put a hand on my forehead and it felt cool and soothing. And it was as if the hand spoke to me, some kind of wordless communication. *Let go*, it said. *Let go, you need this.*

My back arched up from the table. My knees had bent, pushing my hips up, inviting them to explore more. I didn't care. I was wanton. Careless. Hungry. Something cold, metallic, entered me and began to buzz. A moan escaped my lips.

She must be cheap.

I heard the voice in my ear, a sneering hiss.

Fuck off out of my dream.

Cheap.

I tried to ignore it, but it came again with a banging, rhythmic sound this time: *cheap, cheap, cheap.*

That wonderful, translucent light faded, replaced by something flat, cold and enervating. I was enveloped in beige. The banging, though, was still there. Someone was at the door. I wasn't in some Sapphic temple after all, but a hotel room. A very cheap hotel room, appropriately enough, with the blinds drawn and fissures of daylight leaking around the edges.

I tried to bring myself back to full reality, to slough

of the memories of that temple, to ignore the peevish woman speaking in my skull. *You didn't even let me come.*

Oh, that was me.

'I'll get it.'

I moved up the bed, pulling the sheets with me. I wasn't naked. I had on a T-shirt and . . . yes, knickers. It was Myles going for the door. Myles who had been sitting in the armchair next to me. Watching me sleep?

Christ, what sort of noises had I made during that dream? I didn't want to give the boy the wrong idea. I felt myself redden as Bruno and Jules stepped into the room. I had the feeling I used to have as a child – what if they could read my mind? What if they know my every thought? What if they could see from my expression that I had been pleasured – well, almost pleasured – by some strange race of Amazonian women who only lived to serve the goddess Inanna?

Seeing Bruno and Jules gave me some clarity and reassurance that my frazzled brain was working again. I checked and the memories of the money, the market, the clothes, the shower, the photographs they had taken and how they had repaired to a second room to produce my new passport were all present and correct.

I blinked away the feverish dream, trying to ignore what spin Freddie might put on it. You didn't have to be Freud to get to the bottom of that. All I knew was, I needed another shower before we went on our way.

'Sorry, how long was I out?'

'About ninety minutes,' said Myles. 'I'm sorry. You were making some strange noises, so I thought I ought to stay.'

'Iraq dreams,' I lied. 'Bit of PTSD.'

'You were in Iraq?' He pronounced it Eye-rak.

'Yeah. Long story.' One I didn't feel like sharing at that moment. 'It comes back now and then.'

'You OK now?' asked Jules.

I was, but I felt hot and sticky here and there. Again, I had the sense that I was missing something, a fact or facts that were important. Was the dream trying to tell me something? I would go mad thinking that. It was just a mildly horny dream. That was all.

'You OK?' Myles repeated.

'What?'

'You just zoned out on me.'

'Yes ... sorry.' I licked dry lips. 'Myles, can you get me some water? And open the window.'

'They don't open.'

'Turn up the air con, then. Thanks.'

I moved my feet as Bruno sat on the bed. 'The Colonel wants you to call.'

'The Colonel wants to pull me,' I said.

Bruno shook his head in a way that wasn't entirely convincing. 'He just wants a chat.'

'About what?'

'Your situation.'

'Not my daughter?'

'He didn't mention that, no. Just a review of the facts, he said.'

'No, he wants to pull me off this,' I said, taking the water from Myles and gulping it down. I handed it back for a refill. 'Look, she's my Principal. I lost her. It's up to me to sort this mess out.'

'The Colonel said it might be in your best interests to speak to him.' The words had a cold, devious undertone I knew only too well. 'Best interests' my gold-plated arse.

Was he threatening me with withholding information about Jess? The devious, octogenarian fucker was capable of anything. Part of me was screaming inside that I should call him, just in case he had any news. What was Mrs Irwin to me?

Nothing.

Except professional pride. If I returned to Zürich empty-handed, then I'd never get a Grade-A security or PPO job again. You only get to lose one Principal and that's it. No second chances. And I had lost mine.

There was something else. There was a time when I would have seen straight through Konrad. Well, maybe I wouldn't have been that prescient, but some instinct would have alerted me to him being 'off'. This time: nothing. Why? Because my attention, my concerns, were split between the job in hand and Jess. Turns out

319

I couldn't multitask after all. So it boiled down to this: I make it right by going after Mrs Irwin and Konrad and then I turn my full attention to Jess.

Sorry, darling. But I am coming for you. Right after I've gone up against the man who left me naked and humiliated. And amnesiac, I mustn't forget about that. 'You tell the Colonel I'll come up there and dangle him from the thirty-sixth floor of his power eyrie if he tries to screw me over.'

'That is between the two of you,' said Bruno diplomatically. 'I am only passing on the message.'

'Pass that on and then this: I'll call him when I have Mrs Irwin safe and sound. In the meantime, he is to continue doing his utmost to locate my daughter. You got that?'

He spread out his hands in a conciliatory gesture. 'As you wish.'

Jules tossed some keys on the bed. 'There's a Renault Megane downstairs. Silver. Four-door. Automatic. It says it's an Expression on the back, but it's a GT Nav. Everything you requested is in the boot.' He winked to show me this included the address of a certain bike shop in Rennes.

'And the passport is finished,' said Bruno. 'I am not sure you'll fool homeland security with it, but a French traffic cop? I think so. You sure about the Colonel? He doesn't like bad news.'

There was the outside chance that he had some news

about Jess. Maybe his pet troll had tracked down the images from Snapchat. But I suspected it wasn't that he was so keen to talk about. Having an operation go tits-up wasn't good for business. He would have to throw a spanner in the Circuit's first-class rumour mill as soon as possible.

'Look, Bruno. He won't put a new team in the field while I am still active. That always ends up in a shit storm. Blue-on-blue is a real possibility. While I am still live he'll keep everyone else off the grid. I deserve one chance to fix this. And besides, it's my girl out there on his tail. Freddie might just have pulled all our fingers out of the fire.'

Bruno nodded. Even though that 'our' didn't include him. 'Let us hope so. Is there anything else?'

'Yes, can you all fuck off and let me have one more shower?'

But there was something else. There's always something else. I was just too dumb to know it.

With a freshly minted passport, a new car with insurance, and no woman with a Red Notice pinned to her back, I was free to use the main roads and the motorway system. I had asked for, and been given, 3,000 euros by Bruno. Not all of it would go on tolls. It was early afternoon when we pulled away from the hotel and I did some crude circling and bluffing – including a detour down a one-way street, the wrong way – before hitting the A84 to Rennes. Nothing came after me. We had a clean set of heels.

I was dressed in a denim jacket over a T-shirt and black jeans with blue-black knock-off Adidas trainers. Not surprisingly, you couldn't get ProTex bras in the market, so I settled for something athletic and black that squashed my tits flat.

Myles had opted for baggy-crotched jeans, which he complained were five years out of fashion, a button-down shirt, a baseball jacket and what claimed to be Converse high-tops. Maybe they all said 'Covnerse' on the heel patch. At least they were less memorable than the acid-yellow numbers he had arrived in. It all meant he looked like a French kid pretending to be American. Which worked for me.

I pulled over outside a coffee shop in what was the last sizeable town before the autoroute, at least according to the satnav. I sent Myles in to get us coffee and sandwiches. Then I called Freddie.

'It's me,' I said. 'New phone. Save the number.'

'Already done.'

'Look, Freddie, thanks for coming across. I—'

'You OK? You sound fucked up.' It was good to hear her no-nonsense voice. I cherished the little glow of confidence it gave me. Stuck in a ditch in Iraq, you always felt better when Freddie slid in beside you. You always knew that, somehow, you'd get out of that ditch alive.

'I wouldn't go that far. I'm functioning.'

'Look, Buster,' she said, using my old army nickname. I'm sorry I didn't stick around with you ...'

I knew what she was apologising for immediately. 'You did the right thing. Follow the Principal. Just tell me why.'

'They drove out of the gate, just as I arrived. You'd told me what make and model of car you were driving, remember?'

'No. Actually I don't.'

'Ah. Right. Bruno told me you'd had some tapes wiped.'

'You can say that again.'

'Anyway, the Peugeot came out. I thought it must be you at the wheel, I tucked in behind.'

'Go on.'

'I called your mobile. It rang. Then I saw the driver dump a phone out of the car. Well, toss it, into some bushes.'

Of course, I'd left my phone charging in the centre console.

'I reckoned there was something funny going on. I stuck with it.'

'You were right. Listen, Freddie, my memory really is pretty fucked up.'

'So the guy said. But why?'

A combination of drugs and too many blows to the head. 'It doesn't matter. I don't remember calling you—'

'Hold on. They're turning.'

'You're still following?'

'Yup, but I'm going to have to drop back a little. Small roads now. Pretty damn obvious I'm on his tail. Or it soon will be. I'm mainly using the dust he's throwing up to guide me.'

'Where are you?'

'Spain.'

'Spain?' I blurted. 'You've left France altogether?'

'Yup. We're just over the border.'

That was my theory about Luxembourg dead in the water. 'Listen, I have one small detour and I'm coming to you.'

'OK. Download the FMF app on your phone. I'll tag you, you do the same for me.' That way we could keep track of each other's progress.

'Will do. How is Mrs Irwin? Can you tell?'

'I think he's drugged her. She's had a bathroom break, but she was pretty wobbly on her pins.'

'But he let her go in the toilet? Alone? He trusted her not to try and run or raise the alarm?'

'No. He's not that daft. The woman went with him.'

'Woman? What woman?'

'The one who was driving the Peugeot. The one who wasn't you. She's the reason I thought you were in the car. It was only when she dumped the phone I realised it was someone else. I was kind of committed by then.'

'Fuck.' Now I knew why she hadn't come into the

chateau to check on me. She had thought I was in the Peugeot.

'You didn't know?'

'I don't know if I knew. I might have once. I don't think so. I don't recall any other woman. As I said, my memory is pretty fucked up. Does she look like she's on the Circuit?'

'Hard to say. Drab clothes. Probably scrub up OK.'

'Age?'

'Over thirty, under forty, would be my guess.'

I sucked my bottom lip. 'OK, so he's doubled the opposition.'

'And so have you. You have me, remember?'

'I didn't mean to sound ungrateful.'

'Don't worry, it just comes naturally to you.'

'I'm glad you came.'

She laughed. 'Of course I came. I'm just jerking your chain. What else would I be doing, apart from having a pair of handsome young men, one on each breast?'

'I prefer mine weaned.'

'You are so conventional, Buster. Where are you now?'

'About to head for Rennes.'

'Why?'

I didn't want to tell her over the phone. 'As I said, a small detour. Just some business to take care of. I'm going to see a man about a bike.'

'You've lost me.'

'I'll explain later. I'll get to you as soon as I can.'

The door opened and Myles slid in holding a cardboard tray of coffee and two baguettes that had ham and cheese lolling out like tongues. He dumped the change next to the gear selector.

'As I said, we're only just over the border. It's about eight hours from there I would guess.'

'I'll do it in six.'

'Either way, it'll be dark by the time you get here.'

'Good. I do my best work after dark. I'll call again. Stay safe.'

I took the coffee from Myles and started the car.

'That your friend?'

'Yes. She's still on him. And your mom is OK.'

So far, I almost added. So far. But Konrad had something in mind for Mrs Irwin, that much I was certain. And it was unlikely to be anything good. I just hoped we got there in time.

TWENTY-EIGHT

Rennes, France

We found – or rather the satnav did – the bicycle repair shop with ease. It was a surprisingly grand affair, double-fronted, with rows of serious road bikes outside, all with finger-light frames and tyres as thick as a two-pence piece. I drove past and parked around the corner. I didn't want anyone to see what car we had arrived in.

I didn't make the mistake of leaving Myles in the car this time, but I did warn him not to open his mouth or act surprised at anything that should go down. We entered a shop full of more bikes, lined with posters of great racers – or at least great foreign racers like Eddy Merckx and Bernard Hinault; no Froome, Hoy or Wiggins, I noted – and breathed in an atmosphere that was as much rubber and plastic as oxygen. The man behind the counter was thick-set, small-eyed, with hair down to his shoulders to compensate for the fact he had little on top. He was wearing a collarless shirt and a leather waistcoat covered in silver studs. On his right bicep was a skull-and-roses tattoo. He looked like a heavy-metal monk.

'You're Moby?' I asked in my clunky French.

He nodded.

'Big Thrash sent me.'

'Not here. Out the back. I'll be through in a minute.'

We stepped through the door he had indicated into a workshop, where the skeletal frames of bicycles were hung on the walls, along with pegboards of tools and racks of tyres and inner tubes. There was also a drum kit, set back in the corner on a wheeled pallet, so it could be pulled out to allow for some thrashing practice. I went over and flicked a fingernail at one of the cymbals. It shimmered and hissed, like I had disturbed the nest of some strange insect species.

'Zildjian,' said Moby as he came through the door and closed it behind him. He had switched to English, which was a relief. 'Created by alchemy in the seventeenth century. The exact formula for creating the alloy is still a family secret.'

'Like Coke?' asked Myles.

Moby shot him a look of disdain. I guessed drummers didn't like their precious, expensive cymbals being compared to a fizzy drink. He turned to me.

'How can I help?' he asked.

'I need some accessories.'

'What kind of accessories?'

He knew damn well I wasn't after a clip-on water bottle, but I played along. 'The nine-millimetre kind.'

He rubbed his chin as if I'd asked him the distance from earth to the sun and it was on the tip of his tongue. 'Might have something.'

'And something to put in it.'

'Yes. I don't keep stock here, though. I need to make a call.'

'How much?'

'You'll want to see it first?'

'I will before I hand any money over. But I don't want any surprises. And I don't want it to have a list of credits longer than *Star Wars*. No history.'

He laughed at that. 'They're clean. From when the Swiss Army switched from Sigs to Glocks.'

'So it's the P220?' A lot of those came onto the second-hand market when the change was made.

'The Swiss called it the P75. Same gun.'

'Chambered for?'

'Nine-mil Parabellum.'

I thought back to my ballistics tutorials in Slovakia. Nine Para was good. It meant I could also use a Luger or a NATO round. 'So how much?'

'A thousand euros.'

Ouch. It was more than twice the price you could pick one up for in the USA.

'It's a good gun. You won't be disappointed.'

Myles snorted. 'For that price I expect it to wake me up in the mornings with a coffee and handjob.'

I flashed him a look that told him to leave the smart-arse comments to me. I turned back to Moby. 'I can give you seven-fifty.'

The man's top lip curled. 'You can keep your seven-fifty then.'

I made a pretence of mentally re-counting my stash. We both knew that he was in the stronger bargaining position. I needed a gun. He didn't need to sell me one. 'Eight-fifty?'

'Nine.'

I thought for a minute. It didn't leave me much spare cash. And there was the little surprise gun people always spring on you. Guns are pretty useless without bullets. 'Nine with a box of ammo?'

He gave a shake of the head that set the fringe of hair whirling. 'Nine-fifty with ammo.'

One last roll of the dice. 'Do I get a discount if I take two?'

Moby watched impassively as I field-stripped one of the Sigs and checked it. Clearly I wasn't going to be able to fire it in the shop. There were customers out front he had to keep leaving to attend to. He told me there was a small section of forest in Saint-Jacque-de-la-Lande where I could put a few rounds to test them. If I was unhappy, I could come back for a refund.

I doubted that was going to happen. Nothing rattled when it was shaken. There was no rust (more of a problem than you might think on guns) or pitting. Everything that was adjustable adjusted but the fixed sights were well fixed. The slide worked well, the trigger pull was good and smooth, with no snagging. There were no visible tool marks – meaning it had been worked on or modified – and no wear on the grip. No screws were stripped. The hammer engaged in half-cock and stayed where it was put. The barrel wasn't new – it had some wear marks around the locking points and a gouge on the feed ramp – but it wasn't on its last legs and the rifling was intact. The recoil spring was in good nick, too. When I had reassembled it I put a plastic pen down the barrel, cocked the hammer and pulled. The pen shot out of the barrel for a few feet. The firing pin worked.

I did the same to the second one. It wasn't quite as pristine – whoever did the last strip of the slide had a none-too-steady hand judging by the scratches around the screw holes. But it would do. Finally I slid a magazine into the first gun, chambered a round and pointed it at Moby's head.

He flinched and stepped back. 'Hey. Fuck.' His hands automatically went up.

'Give me the keys to the shop.'

'What?'

'The keys.'

'Look, there's only like two hundred euros in the till. We do everything on cards now.'

'I don't want your money. I just want some breathing space.'

'What you talking about?'

'Just in case you told your pals in the police where they could find a woman firing an unlicensed Sig, which you will eventually get back when it disappears from the evidence room.'

'Fuck, you're kidding me? This is bullshit. I don't have friends in the police department.'

'Maybe not . . . but best to make sure.'

'Stop pointing that thing at me.'

I lowered the gun, but kept it aimed in his general direction. 'I can't be too careful. The keys?'

'I'm going to reach into my pocket.'

He extracted a bunch of keys. 'Toss them to the boy.' Moby did so and I took them from Myles.

'Which one locks this workshop door?'

'The gold one.'

'And the rear door?'

'Same.'

'Go and lock the back door,' I said to Myles, giving him the bunch back.

'I'm going to lock you in here,' I said to Moby. 'I'll

leave the keys on the counter outside. You can shout to the next customer who comes in. But for the next five minutes I'll be outside waiting to shoot you if you try to get out. You got a cellphone?'

'No. It's out front.'

'Good. It's just a precaution, you understand. Nothing personal.'

'It is shit. Shit way to treat me.'

So was charging me close to two thousand euros. I don't trust greedy men. They never know when to call it a day. 'Sit down. There.'

He did so. I gave the Sig to Myles, who held it in a two-handed movie-style grip. I fetched a small-diameter tyre from the collection on the wall. 'Arms by side.'

'Fuck you, woman.'

'Just do it.'

He did as he was told. I forced the rubber over his broad shoulders and down over his body and also over the back of the chair. It wasn't much, but it'd slow him down, which was all I needed. Then I took the pistol back.

'And you can tell your friend Big Thrash he is a shit guitarist,' said Moby with some considerable venom. 'Shit!'

Two minutes later we were walking quickly but unobtrusively to the turning at the end of the street where the Renault was parked up, me carrying a bag with 'Rapha' written on the side, but stretched with the weight of two Sigs and their bullets.

'You really think he was going to turn us in?' Myles asked.

'No. But I couldn't be certain. The main thing is, I didn't want him to see what make or model of car we are driving. And before you ask, no, we aren't going to the forest to test-fire the guns.'

'I'd like to know mine works.'

'Yours?' I asked, appalled at the thought. 'It isn't for you.'

'What? Why not? You trusted me back there.'

'For a second. Don't think it's a permanent arrangement, Hawkeye.'

'Why the fuck not, huh? We're in this together.'

'Look, partner, it's for Freddie. Someone who knows how to handle a gun.'

'I can shoot.'

'Get in the car.'

'I can. My uncle in Virginia taught me.' At a firing range, no doubt. Shooting back while being shot at is something entirely different. 'I have a permit to carry a concealed weapon in the state of Vermont.'

'We're not in Vermont now, Toto. I want someone I know I can trust on the other end of that Sig. Not Justin Bieber with attitude. Get in the car.'

He shook his head in dismay, but opened the door. 'Fucksake.'

'What?'

'And I thought my mom was paranoid.'

I waited until we were well clear of Rennes and the irate bicycle salesman before I pulled over at a service station. I sent Myles in to get water and any snacks he wanted, and made a call. Not to the Colonel, but to Nina.

'Any excitement yet?' she asked once I had got through.

'Oh, this and that,' I said.

'You confront the boy?'

'Myles? Confront him with what?'

'The frat-house business I told you about.'

I assumed she meant the dope dealing that Myles had confessed to. 'No, not yet. Too busy herding cats.'

'Well, just watch your back.'

'I will. Listen . . .'

A sigh. 'Ach. What is it this time?'

'A name. I want you to do a search beyond the usual sources. Film magazines and the like.'

'Who for?'

'George Konrad.'

'Your bodyguard?'

'Yes. I think there might be more than meets the eye there.' Queen of Understatement, that was me. 'But I think he works in the movie business. It's Konrad with a "K".'

'Give me a second.'

I heard her humming and the tap of keys. 'There's an entry in *Variety*. Legendary film armourer George Konrad. Famous for his work on war movies. *Dirty Dozen, Kelly's Heroes, The English Patient* . . .'

'*Saving Private Ryan*?'

'Yes, that's here. *Fury* was the last one.'

'Anything else about him?'

'Yes. He's dead.'

PART SIX

TWENTY-NINE

Wednesday

There was trouble at the bar last night. Two guys came in with baseball bats and smashed some of it up. They terrified the customers, most of who ran away. Matt got a black eye fighting them off. I didn't see it till this morning, but there was a lot of glass everywhere. The two guys were Russians, so Sarah said. Everyone was very glum. That policeman who had questioned me came down and Matt asked him, 'What the fuck am I paying you for?'

After that, Dieter told me it was no place for me to be hanging around. It was just a problem with the pizza delivery business.

I told him I didn't think they were that *bad.*

He thought that was funny.

That night Putu stayed with us and slept

downstairs, just in case, they said. I had trouble getting to sleep.

Friday

They have stopped doing pizzas. Maybe they trod on Domino's toes. It was pizza wars. That was what I said to Matt. And he said yes. That was precisely it. A turf war.

I could tell he was lying.

I'm not that stupid. I knew what was really going on. I just didn't want to face up to it. There wasn't just American Hots and Four Seasons in those pizza boxes. Why would people miles away in fancy villas with chefs and everything pay big bundles of cash for lukewarm pizzas with very soggy bottoms. It had to be drugs.

Mum once said Dad had done this sort of thing before. In Ibiza. Which is where he met Dieter and Theo.

I went to the surf club. I got hit on by one of the beach boys for the first time. A pretty buff one too. Normally they try and pick up older, rich women who can buy them drinks and dinner. He said he'd go with me for free. I told him to piss off.

Monday

Boring day of lessons but then Sarah announced her and Matt were going on a 'mini-break' together. Over to the island next door. Just as friends. But would I not tell Laura? Please. I feel like I should tell her so she'll come back. But I think that might cause a shit storm, too. Best stay out of it. Aja is going to look after me for the weekend. Like I need 'looking after'. That's OK, I like Aja and I don't think she'll 'look after' me too closely.

THIRTY

Basque Country, France

I didn't stop again until the last of the autoroute service stations before we had to turn off to the minor roads. We were south of Bayonne. I had been driving for six hours and it felt like my bladder was the size of a hot-air balloon. My need to urinate when in action was where I got my army nickname. 'Buster' was from the old quiz show *Blockbusters* – 'Can I have a pee, please, Bob?' And, Bob, I really needed one at that moment. Dusk was coming on strong when I pulled into a service station that advertised its WCs.

I parked up close to the entrance to the food court/ shop, went in and bought a detailed map of the region, a can of black spray paint from the car accessory stand, and a six-pack of Red Bull. I got the code for the lavatory block usually reserved for the lorry drivers from the cashier and drove over and parked near it. Regular drivers used the internal toilets in the main service area concourse, which were smarter. But I didn't want to be in there with the regular folk. For a start, I was carrying heavy weaponry – I had taken the guns with me when I went into the shop and did the same with the *Dames WC*, a belated acceptance that some HGV drivers were women – just in case Myles had any ideas about purloining one for himself.

The toilets were almost clean enough for me to sit down, but out of habit I didn't. When I had emptied the contents of the Aswan dam, I examined myself in the mirror. Maybe it was the flickering neon tube that made me look as if I could draw a pension, but I didn't think so. My skin was sallow and my eyes gritty with lack of sleep. I ought to find another hotel, get some decent drug-free sleep. But that wasn't going to happen. I left the lavatories, told Myles to go to the *Messieurs* and broke open the pack of Red Bull.

I was in no hurry to get back in the Megane, so I drank one as I spread the map out on the bonnet and angled it so that some light fell on it. I located the service area, and the road that would lead me to Freddie. Except I was fairly certain I couldn't take the direct route. Not now.

As casually as I could, I ran my gaze over the parking area, picking out the coming and going of the cars. It didn't tell me anything, except plenty of people on the road need gas, food and lavatories. Myles came and joined me, flicking water off his hands.

'Dryer bust,' he explained.

I offered him one of the cans and he took it.

'How far now?'

I had already checked Freddie's location on the phone. 'About ninety minutes, give or take.'

'Want me to drive?'

I hesitated.

'I got some sleep back there.' Which was true, he had nodded off before we got to Bordeaux. And it was a good idea to go into enemy territory with both hands free. And I had asked for an auto for just that reason.

'You can do the last hour, when we go to meet Freddie.'

He nodded, pleased to be contributing something. 'What's Freddie like? I mean, is she like you?'

'Well, we were both in Iraq. Combat Medical Technicians – medics.'

'Cool.'

'It sounds cooler than it was. It . . .'

It broke my heart, I was going to say, all those kids maimed and killed for a mission that had no clear end game. I wasn't one of those who thought certain politicians should be put on trial for what they did. It wasn't going to bring back Jones or Carroll or give Withers his leg back. But I was one of those who wouldn't trust any of them ever again when it came to sending young men and women off to die without a watertight case for a real threat to our country and some idea of an exit strategy. I don't think there is any room for playing the Lone Ranger with other people's countries. Not any more. The game has changed since 1939.

'It was rough. But Freddie's very capable. If she's got eyes on your mum, then your mum is OK.'

I crumpled my can and tossed it into a nearby bin. He tried the same and missed. He shook his head. 'And I shoot hoops.' He walked over, picked it up and threw it in, hard, like a slam-dunk.

'You ever bodyguard anyone famous?'

It is what they all want to know, sooner or later. And there are PPOs who do nothing but the celebrity circuit. Incidents like Kim Kardashian West's ordeal in Paris cause a big uptick in requests, and every time an *EastEnders* actor or a reality-TV star is mugged for his or her Rolex in their driveway, there is a surge in demand for protection. It never lasts though. After a few weeks of shelling out for someone to walk with them to and from the house, the client realises it's easier and cheaper just to hand over the watch and buy a new one each time.

'I'm not a BG,' I said. 'PPO. Personal Protection.'

'Well, whatever you do, you ever do it with anyone I'd've heard of?'

'Probably. But I can't talk about clients.'

'Seriously? They probably talk about you.'

I laughed. 'I doubt it. Clients barely notice you when you are there, unless something happens to spook them. They certainly don't think about you when you've gone.'

'Yeah, but come on. There must be someone ...'

I threw him a bone. 'There was this one pop star, I guess you'd call him. An English rocker with a penchant for blondes. Been around since the Seventies. Sixties, maybe. I did his wedding. Well, one of them.'

He took a few wild stabs before he got the name. 'And?'

'And nothing. I was close protection for the wife, who was lovely. Well, we had one thing happened. The wedding was at a villa in Italy. We were there three days before the guests arrived. And every night I'd go out on the terrace and feel like I had an itch I couldn't scratch. Just a sense of being watched. Then, on the night before the ceremony, I caught it, a flash of light from the hillside. Just from the corner of my eye. Next morning we went up there and found a paparazzo who had dug in like it was the end of the world. He'd made a cave with enough food to survive for weeks, a chemical toilet, and, of course, cameras with the longest lenses I'd ever seen. There was a door made of twigs and ferns that blended in perfectly. But he'd opened it with a light burning inside and I'd caught it.'

'You get him arrested?'

'Nope. When the groom heard, he let the guy take one photo of him and his bride posing at the villa. Said his ingenuity was impressive. Then he punched him on the nose.'

'Fuck. Did he sue?'

'You kidding? That one picture earned him thousands. It was worth a swollen nose for a few days.'

I folded up the map. 'We going?' he asked.

'In a minute.'

'I thought we were in a hurry.'

I decided to share something with him. 'You know that feeling I said I had at the wedding?'

'The one about feeling you're being watched?'

I nodded. 'I don't want you to react in any way. Certainly do not turn your head. But I have it now.'

His body stiffened a little, but that was all. He put the can to his lips and drank before he spoke. 'Where?'

'I don't know. Sometimes, like with the light from the hills, you pick up a subliminal signal. Someone holds a look at you for a second too long, you see the same car twice. I've had it for a while now. It isn't going away.'

'You sure you don't want to give me a gun?'

'I am positive. We are not going to have a shootout at a service station,' I assured him. At least, I hoped not. But it reminded me I had to prep the guns, just in case. 'Get in. I have something to do.'

Once we were inside, I took out one of the pistol's magazines, emptied it of shells and began reloading them. Bullets left too long in a mag tend to become sticky, used to each other's company. It was a good way to cause a jam. Myles watched intently as I slid the rounds home with my thumb.

'You really shoot?' I asked.

'I'm an American. It's in the constitution and my DNA.'

I smiled. 'Yeah, I was forgetting. You still can't have one.'

He gave a grunt of annoyance. I suspected he wasn't used to being denied anything he wanted.

'OK, can you do the same to this one for me, though?' I asked, passing him the second Sig. 'Take the bullets out, mix them up, reload.'

He did so, admirably cautious with the loaded weapon, and dextrous when it came to handling the ammunition. He completed the task in a faster time than I did. I still wasn't going to change my mind about arming him, though.

When we finally left, I was behind the wheel. 'You going to get gas?'

'I am. I'm just going to forget for a moment.'

'What?'

'Just stay calm, no matter what happens.' I tossed him the can of spray paint. 'Give that a good shake.'

The little ball bearing inside rattled as he shook.

'I hope you have a steady hand.'

'You are fuckin' weird, you know.'

With luck, just weird and unpredictable enough to throw someone off my scent.

I started the car and set off, taking the lane that indicated the fuel stop. Myles said nothing when I passed the entry to the pumps and apparently sailed on by. I waited until I had passed the 'Exit Only' sign of the petrol station and stomped on the brakes. A car behind me hooted and swung by. Another crawled past. I waited for two more to pass, watching in the mirror for anyone who had stopped to observe what the hell I was doing. None had. I engaged reverse and steered my way into that 'Exit Only' gap, then over to the furthest row of pumps.

'Oops,' I said to Myles. 'I forgot I was meant to get petrol. At least, that's what I hope it looked like.'

He shook his head in disbelief. 'Really? Is that the best you have?'

Sadly, yes, I was tempted to say. 'For now. Look, while I am filling up, I want you to fuck up the licence plates with the spray. Change one letter, obscure it, I don't care. Slide out your side and keep low. The pumps should mask you.'

'What the fuck is happening?'

'If we were being followed, it was one of those cars that went by. Now, they are waiting down there.' I pointed towards the slip road that fed into the autoroute, most of it hidden behind trees. 'I mean, there's only one way we can go, isn't there?'

'Is there?' he asked, unsure of the answer.

'No, there's not. OK? Let's go.'

I wasn't certain we had been tagged – if we had, a pissed-off Moby the bicycle repairman was my best guess – but it always paid to trust your instincts. While I pumped in petrol, Myles altered the number plates. I paid, we got back in the car and I turned to him. 'Ready?'

He belted up. 'Ready.'

I pressed on the hazard lights, engaged reverse and reversed out of the in lane. I kept close in to the side, hugging the low bushes. Even so, several drivers flashed me. Some hooted. I just hoped whoever was waiting for us didn't realise what was going on. But who would expect this?

Once we were out onto the main parking area I carried on, one hand on the wheel, my body half-turned so I could see clearly out of the rear window. And then I floored it. Not enough to cause any wheel spin, but fast enough to get us out of there and, with a twitch of the wheel, down the autoroute slipway the wrong way, heading back onto the motorway into traffic coming straight for us.

I risked a glance at Myles. He had gone pale. Which meant he realised I was planning on driving along the highway the way we had come. Only backwards.

Control and confidence was the key. I'd done this scenario a dozen times when I was on my defensive driving courses. It only works if there is a short distance between the service station and the autoroute intersection. In this case it was about two kilometres. But it was two kilometres full of angry stabs of horns and furious blinking of lights and, I could imagine, outbursts of choice language.

I pressed as close to the barrier as I dared, but the hard shoulder on the ramp was narrower than usual, and so I had to barge the approaching cars aside. I snatched the wheel to avoid a lorry that wasn't minded to get out of my way, running up his inside. The enormous wheel arch loomed large in the passenger window, snagged the wing mirror and tore it off with a short, sharp screech. Myles swore. I corrected the car and kept going, onto the autoroute proper.

By now I was sure a CCTV operator was staring at his screen, wondering if he was seeing this correctly. This is the footage that would be on YouTube: 'Watch Deranged Woman REVERSE down French Motorway at HIGH SPEED'. But I was hoping the obscured number plate might throw them. And that there were no cops hungry for an arrest within hailing distance to stop me.

'Nearly there,' I said, yanking the wheel so that we powered up onto the 'on' ramp and up towards the roundabout of the intersection. He didn't respond. Another quick look across at him confirmed he had his eyes shut. I couldn't blame him.

The cabin filled with the lights of another truck, followed by the blast of an air horn that sounded like the *Titanic* was bearing down on us. And we were no iceberg.

Another spin of the wheel and he was gliding by us, but I could feel the back end of the Renault breaking away. The last thump of his slipstream was all it needed to spin us round. The boot caught the barrier and we lost a tail light in a flurry of red plastic. The car began to slow. As it squeaked to a halt along the Armco, I engaged drive and gunned the engine. The front wheels juddered alarmingly, several dash lights flashed at me, but finally I had grip and forward momentum. Now we were going the right way, but still against the flow of traffic. I put the headlamps to full beam and leaned on and off my horn to create an urgent honking sound. I reckoned they'd assume I was a cop coming at them. Who else would be stupid enough to do this?

At the top of the ramp, I barged a Citroen out of the way with a gentle nudge and fishtailed into the flow of traffic on the roundabout, finally pointing in the right direction. I saw the sign for the turning I needed to take, towards Villefranque, and steered us onto that road in as sedate a manner as I could. I flicked off the high beam. Swallowed. Took a breath. Turned to Myles.

'There,' I said to him. 'That wasn't so difficult was it?'

*

I pulled over so we could change drivers once we had passed Villefranque and I was certain we hadn't picked up any outraged traffic police. I gave the car a walk-around before I got back in. Apart from the missing mirror, the cracked taillight, a big ding in the boot and a smaller dent in the offside wing, we were OK. The Megane wouldn't be winning any concourse shows, but it was driveable. And me? My heart was still running a little fast, but that was to be expected, given the amount of adrenaline that must have been dumped in my bloodstream. I felt a flare of craving for a cigarette, but ignored it. This was no time for relaxing and blowing smoke rings.

I used the phone's torch to check under the wheel arches, in case we had picked up a tracker. There was nothing untoward under there. But I was pretty sure someone had been at that service station, eyeing us up. But who? And how?

Eventually I put those questions out of my mind. It was no good worrying at them when no answer would be forthcoming. I had to concentrate on things I could control. Getting to Freddie, for example.

Finally, I used a pair of fabric gloves – intended for tyre-changing duties and the like – from the boot to wipe the still-wet spray paint off the licence plates.

'OK, all good. Can you manage without the door mirror?' I asked Myles as I settled into the passenger seat.

'I guess,' he said. 'As long as you can promise we'll only be going forward from now on.'

'I'll try my best. Can't say for sure.'

He made a noisy swallow. He was obviously short of saliva after that little jaunt. 'I'm starting to think weird doesn't even begin to cover it with you.'

'Look, this is all about finding your mother. By any means possible. I didn't do that for fun. We should be OK now, because I doubt anybody followed us up the off ramp.'

'Me too. There can't be two people that fuckin' mad.'

'That's what I am counting on. You're taking a right at the next junction.'

'Yes, ma'am.'

The road became narrow and darker as we dog-legged onto minor routes. Dusk was definitely nudging into night. He switched back to full beam. He was driving confidently and surprisingly well. I laid the phone on my lap and the plastic Rapha bag with the guns at my feet.

'When you said your mother was paranoid, what did you mean?'

'When?'

'In Rennes. When we picked up the guns.'

'Ah, just sayin'. When I was growing up, after my dad died, she parked me with my aunt and moved around a lot. Even changed names every few years.

She said that there were always people out to take everything away from us.'

'It doesn't sound very relaxing.'

'You don't notice as a kid. It was only when I went to college that I realised I'd had a weird childhood. Nice drive.' He stabbed at the throttle and we went into a bend fast enough to make both me and the car's body lean. He came out of it flat and smoothly.

'Keep it down. Country cops love city boys who are speeding through their villages.'

'OK. Just seeing what she can do.'

'Just stick to whatever I say. OK?'

'Yes, chief.' He was silent for a minute. 'And then, I remember, once she came to see me and was very upset. She told me an uncle I never knew I had had died. Uncle Ronnie Corrigan.'

'Died how?'

'Well, I only found this out later. On the internet. But he had been murdered. Shot in the head.'

I didn't speak for a while. I was too busy trying to build some kind of coherent picture from the scraps I had. But this jigsaw had too many missing pieces.

'You think Konrad might have something to do with that?' asked Myles eventually.

'I don't know. People bear grudges for a long time. I have this friend . . .'

I let it tail off.

'Go on,' he prompted. 'Or I'll put the radio on again.' We'd already tried French pop music. It was an underhand threat to subject me to it again.

So I told the story of Tom Buchan again, and the Albanian gangster he had let live in Kosovo, who was now out to avenge his family.

'Wow, it's just like *Saving Private Ryan*.' That again.

'Really? I missed the part with the amphibious landing and the slaughter on the beach in my version.'

'Nah. Doesn't Tom Hanks let a German prisoner go who comes back and bites his ass?'

'Missed that, too.'

'You know what I mean. The German ends up shooting Tom Hanks. If he hadn't let him go earlier in the movie . . .' He shrugged.

I said nothing. Was he saying Tom and Paul should have executed the Albanian lad? I didn't want to think too hard about the morality of that. Nor the film, because Konrad had said he worked on that movie. Which George Konrad had, according to Nina. But Konrad was dead. The man I knew as George Konrad had borrowed his identity and chunks of his biography, although the imposter was clearly younger than the real thing.

How had he got past the Colonel? More to the point, how had he got past me? And there was still the enigma of the woman. Where had she come from?

'When we were at the chateau, did you see anyone else?' I asked. 'Another person?'

'Other than?'

'You, me, Konrad and your mother.'

'The guys who came to change the tyres. I saw them out of the window.'

'No woman?'

He shook his head. 'Not that I recall. Why?'

'We think he has a woman with him. Konrad. An accomplice in all this. Whatever this is.'

'News to me.'

The road began to climb towards the stars that were coming out. The houses strung along the way seemed to melt away into a darkness pierced only by the odd porch light. The headlamps grew brighter, stronger, picking out the deep black of smooth new tarmac in front of us. We passed through a small community apparently denuded of inhabitants except for one hole-in-the-wall bar. Myles slowed as if we were taking a look at it. The yellow and brown interior seemed inviting enough. Maybe we should just pull in and ...

'OK, let's go,' I said, killing the temptation. We picked up speed as we left the village, our route now hemmed in by drystone walls that were designed to stop the twisted trees beyond marching into our path. Or at least, they looked as if they were capable of ambulation in that last glimmer of twilight that often gives forest the look of ancient giants.

I texted Freddie and told her we had less than an hour to run.

No change, she came back. *Three pax. Two well dressed.*

It wasn't a sartorial comment. It meant that two of three were armed, the third being the hostage or prisoner or whatever Mrs Irwin was.

I reached down and checked each of Moby's Sigs again, just to be on the safe side.

I laughed at that thought. If it came to a gunfight, there wasn't going to be a safe side.

I am wearing my best bib and tucker, too, I texted. *And I have some spare clothes for you.*

Good, because I am feeling very underdressed, Buster.

I left it at that. At least she knew I was coming tooled up.

The road began to snake as well as steepen now and the auto box had to work harder, hunting for the right gear. To our left, the stone walls gave way to rough-hewn cliffs, netting, and signs warning of the dangers of rockfall. A light rain started as we gained altitude and Myles, after a little fumbling, found the wipers. In the minutes and hours before something like this, I always thought the same thing: *What the fuck am I doing here?*

Why aren't I at home, sitting up in bed with Jess, watching inappropriate TV and scoffing on funsize Mars Bars?

Because you haven't got a daughter, remember? You are here for her.

Yeah, thanks for that.

I checked the map. We were travelling through one of the lower passes towards Spain. The border, I hoped, would be just a line on the map. It might not be. This would be one crossing easy to police.

Spanish lorries appeared, coming down the hillside towards us, buffeting the car as they passed in a flare of headlights and a rush of impatient wind.

'You nervous?' Myles asked.

'About?'

'This Konrad. He's a professional gunman. And he's got a sidekick now. You really going to try and free my mom?'

'You got any better ideas? Call the cops, maybe?'

'Maybe not.'

'We'll play it by ear, OK? Do me a favour. Shut up and drive.'

It came out harsher than I intended. I guess I was a little rattled, after all. And irritated that the kid was right. I was going up against someone who did all this on a regular basis. I was a PPO. My job was to stop it getting this far. By those lights, I had failed. Just like I had failed Jess.

I texted Freddie some more, but the answers were terse now. *Yes. No. Get here asap.*

After thirty minutes I said, 'Left here. Looks like her car is about a mile ahead.'

There were no lights on the hillsides, they simply

rolled on upwards in a series of dark humps towards a row of jagged peaks, some glowing faintly with late snow. The road we turned onto wasn't much more than a stony path, one car wide in places. But it didn't look like it saw a lot of traffic.

The rain grew heavier. The wipers squeaked. Clouds had obscured some of the stars. The night was beginning to match my mood.

'Right here. Slowly. And keep it down.'

We saw the reflectors of Freddie's hire car ahead. A BMW. I didn't have to tell Myles to slow. He pulled in behind her in the little passing space and killed the engine.

I saw Freddie exit the car, hood up against the rain. She skipped around to my side and I opened the door.

'Hey—'

'Keep your hands where I can see them.' The accent was thick, Irish. The tone was aggressive. The gun steady, pointing right between my eyes.

One thing was certain. This wasn't Freddie.

THIRTY-ONE

Saturday

FUCK FUCK FUCK. *It is Saturday, now, just after midnight. Matt and Sarah are away for their 'mini-break' and Aja came but she had to go again. Someone phoned her – a man I think – and she said whatever it was was too good an opportunity to miss. She told me just to watch TV, which I did, and that someone would come and check on me. Maybe Putu. That would be good I said. I liked Putu.*

But it was DIETER who turned up. And he is well drunk. He's more than drunk. He chopped out a bloody big line of cocaine on our table, did about two thirds of it and asked if I wanted to try the rest.

Nooooo, I said. I'm good. So he did it. All.

I am in my bedroom now and I can hear him

stomping about. He's calling my name. I think he's pissed off because Aja has gone off to see another man. A rich c--- Dieter calls him. He says Aja is a kupa kupa malam. He's also mad at Matt, saying he has ruined the business. Dick-for-brains he called him.

He's phoned that Theo from the boat and asked him if he wants to come over to the house to party. That they might as well finish up the stock as they can't sell it. So I was right about the pizza business.

I told him my dad wouldn't like that, but he didn't answer, just made a funny noise.

I've just tried Dad but he isn't picking up and I can't remember the name of the hotel Sarah said they were going to. I left a voicemail but he never listens to that and I've sent a text. But he probably won't see that till the morning. He never looks at his phone before ten. I could call the police but that one from the bar might turn up. I even tried Mum, but the old number seems to be dead. How could she do that?

If anyone finds this, then it was DIETER who was here. I am going back out to try and calm him down. Just in case, if anyone is reading this:
DIETER DID IT!!!!!!!!!!!!

THIRTY-TWO

Basque Country, Spain

'You know those scenes in the movies where they jump the gunman?' I said to Myles quietly. 'Well, it doesn't work like that in real life. You end up shot. And most likely dead. Just do as she says, very slowly.'

'You too,' said the woman, taking a pace back. 'Take your own advice. Very slow. Get out. Keep your fuckin' hands where I can see them.'

Myles leaned over to take a look at her as I levered myself out of the passenger side. 'What the fuck—?'

'Quiet,' I said to him, before she could.

I did as I was told, into a slanting rain that made me shiver. At least, I think it was the rain. She didn't take her eyes off me, figuring I was more of a threat than the kid. It was what I would have done.

'Where's Freddie?' I asked the woman.

'Your friend? Ah, she's been gone a while now. Not as good as she thought she was, that one.'

363

I closed my eyes for a second as the use of the past tense sank in. Colours swirled behind my eyelids and a strange whistling started up in one ear. My brain was cooking. It had just appreciated that, for at least some of the time on the road – probably since the last time she called me Buster – I'd been texting this woman with the crazy eyes staring out from beneath the hood. Hence the brevity of her answers on the phone. And Freddie? Oh, God, no. My world slipped off its axis for a second and I made a monumental effort to pull it back. Jesus, I'm sorry, Freddie. You'll forgive me if I wait a while to mourn you.

'Tsk, tsk. You thought we wouldn't spot her? Trying to tail with a single car. I'm surprised at you, Sam, a woman of your experience.'

I turned to see Konrad coming out of the gloom, boots crunching on gravel, better dressed for the weather than either me or Myles, who had now exited the vehicle and was hoisting up those low-slung jeans. Konrad had on a Belstaff jacket and thick trousers, with hiking boots. He moved with a slight stiffness, no doubt because of that self-inflicted gunshot. I had to give him some grudging respect for that. It sounds easy on paper, but once you have seen what a bullet can do, it isn't easy to pull that trigger against your own skin and bone.

The thought of bullets reminded me about those two expensive Sigs in the car, but I dismissed any idea of going for them. Konrad was holding an over-under shotgun. He wouldn't even have to make the effort to aim to do me serious damage. And I was fairly certain the Irish woman knew what she was about.

Konrad began to whistle as he approached, the same atonal sound I recalled from his inspection of the Peugeot. I wasn't sure whether he couldn't actually whistle or he had some strange Hungarian tune going through his head. Either way, it wasn't a pleasant sound.

'What's your game, Konrad?'

A lance of bright light shot out from his arm, straight into my face, and I closed my eyes. Too late. Bastard. He'd ruined my night vision.

As he came closer, still waving the torch at me, I turned my head away. When I sensed him standing close to me, I turned and let out a little gasp. He didn't look like the Konrad I had last seen in the kitchen back at the chateau. His jowls had shrunk, the beard had gone and the skin on his face was smooth. No pock-marks. Yet the voice was the same.

'What happened to you?'

'You know, working in the movie business you meet all sorts of interesting people. Make-up artists, for example. Useful when it is important that someone doesn't recognise you.'

'I still don't,' I said. 'I've never seen you before this job.'

'Not you, that bitch up there. Who should be wide awake by now.' I assumed he meant Mrs Irwin. So they had face-to-face history together. Hence the disguise. And those bloody dark glasses, which he had now jettisoned.

'Is Freddie up there with her?' I asked, more in desperate hope that I had misunderstood the woman than anything else.

Konrad shook his head as if it was heavy with sorrow. 'Sadly, no. It's a very intimate gathering we have here. No room for extras. Shall we?'

I stood my ground. 'Where is she?' I demanded, with a force I couldn't back up.

Konrad didn't answer, simply indicated I should move by pointing the end of the shotgun up the track.

'What have you done with Freddie?' I shouted.

Compared to me, he sounded calm and rational when he eventually spoke. 'We can end it here, right now, if you wish. You've always been surplus to requirements, Sam. Right from day one. I'd get moving if I were you.'

The woman had shifted to cover Myles and she, too, directed us up the track. Grudgingly, I began to put one leaden foot in front of the other.

When we were a few metres away, she dipped inside the Renault and pulled out the Rapha bag. A glance inside and she swung it around her head and flung it down the hillside, where it rustled away into the darkness. Hell of a way to treat a couple of reasonable Sigs. But I guessed they had all the weapons they needed.

'You've been very resourceful,' said Konrad from behind me. The accent was different now, softer, as if, now he had dumped the physical trickery, he was slowly morphing into his new self. It had taken on an Irish lilt, softer than the woman's, but still noticeable. 'Clothes, a car, a gun. Money, I assume. I thought you'd be banjaxed when I left you like that. I should probably have killed you on the beach or at the chateau. Still, you're here now. Let's get the party started.'

We began to walk, the sleety rain stinging my face, our two hosts bringing up the rear, the torch beam dancing about just in front of us so we didn't stumble. Myles looked at me with a 'what's going on?' expression. I shrugged. I knew we'd find out sooner or later. I had the feeling Konrad had something to get off his chest. Except, he wasn't Konrad, was he?

'Konrad, can you answer me something?' I asked, my breath coming ragged as the path steepened.

'What?'

'What's your real name? You're not Hungarian, are you?'

'No. But George Konrad was. The old man who taught me the armouring business.'

'Who is dead.'

'Sadly, yes. But it was useful to borrow his

background. Hungarian is the closest language to Basque. You know that? That and Maltese, so they tell me.'

'So you're Basque?'

'Well, as they say, I've got Basque in me somewhere.' He spoke in a much stronger mock-Irish brogue that might have been meant to amuse, but it didn't sound funny to me. It sounded like the voice of a killer. 'They used to call me Anjel McManus Garzia. But as we are amongst friends, Anjel will do.'

I couldn't help thinking that he didn't look much like any kind of angel to me. Unless it was an avenging one.

When I was sixteen, I decided to have some fun. My dad was a miserable bastard. He did it professionally. If miserable bastards had an SAS wing, he would have been the commander-in-chief. Life at home was joyless. Glasses weren't even half full. They were empty in my dad's world. Unlike most other parents, mine had never discovered social drinking. I swear they had the only drinks cabinet in the land that still held a bottle of South African sherry. It was brought out no more than three times a year. When the neighbours were gorging on Smirnoff Ice, Malibu and Black Tower, Mum and Dad were still living in the Babycham years.

So, when I was tall enough and curvy enough to pass for eighteen, my friend Egg and I launched a mission to explore the world of alcohol. And we wanted to find out about the real thing, not the alcopops, like the White Lightning and Bacardi Breezers our contemporaries were downing in the park. We had an advantage in that Egg's parents ran a pub. It didn't last long. The advantage, not the pub. It's still there. But after several clandestine visits where we got away with some sneaky sampling, we had a bet about who could have one shot from every optic in the bar. It ended in vomit and being barred.

Once we had recovered from the we'll-never-drink-again phase of alcohol abuse, we started to frequent pubs out of town where we had no chance of being recognised. In those days, they rarely asked for IDs, it was all a matter of confidence, which Egg had in spades. And clubs, diamonds and hearts.

We had two places that we knew were always a good bet: the Swan Inn, which was an old man's boozer, with a carpet so sticky you felt like you had Velcro soles on when you walked across it; and the Queen's, which was in the process of becoming what we would later call a gastropub. Both were low-lit, the Swan because most of the bulbs had blown and the landlord was too tight to replace them, whereas the Queen's was going for a soft, female/couple ambience and had real candles on the tables.

At the Queen's we would sit in a booth at the back, shrouded in shadow, only exposing ourselves when Egg ventured forth for a refill. She was bustier than me, which always distracted the barman. It was a battle to stop ourselves giggling at our audacity, but we saved that for the bus home.

One night, the door to the pub opened and a couple walked in. I didn't recognise him at first. He had on a brightly coloured shirt and jeans. Jeans! At his age. It was my dad. But that wasn't my mum with him. As the woman shucked her coat, I recognised her as Mrs Anderson from his office. Egg, who had followed my gaze, put her hand on my knee and squeezed.

Don't do anything stupid, it said.

I was transfixed though. It was my father's face that held my gaze. It was unrecognisable. It moved, changed, rearranged itself into strange, foreign (to me) shapes. He was grinning. Laughing. Offering quips. The fucker was having a good time.

We waited until he had gone to the bar before we slipped out. We crossed the Queen's off our list. Sticky carpets for us from then on. I worried for a week about how to tell Mum, but one night, over a typically glum dinner, Dad announced that Mrs Anderson was moving to Peterborough, and the office would need a new purchasing assistant.

I never saw him that happy again. But I learned a lesson that had stood me in good stead. That two, or more, very different people can occupy the same body. So the fact that Konrad had emerged as someone else didn't faze me the way it might have.

All that did worry me was this: how come Konrad had managed to fool me?

We trudged on, past fields of stunted trees to the left and right, the track still climbing, albeit very gradually. I didn't make the mistake of burning up my energy wondering about what lay ahead. It was what it was. Nothing I could do about it. Nothing I could do for Freddie if they'd ...

I shut it all down. If I was going to get us out of this, I really needed to concentrate on the matter at hand. I wiped away hair that was plastered to my forehead. The fine rain had penetrated through to my T-shirt and I was shivering, despite the exertion.

'Left here.'

As I turned I saw the building ahead, a dark block against the mountains, a single light burning on the ground floor and a lamp glowing above the door. It looked almost welcoming. Except I knew that was the last description of what was going to happen here. I could make out the familiar silhouette of the Peugeot, parked just to the side.

'Stop. Hands on heads. Kneel.' The woman used words like a whip, snaking out and snapping at us. I didn't like her one bit. In fact, every time I thought of Freddie, I wanted to break her neck. I was certain she would have done her, not Konrad. The woman would do the dirty work, and with some pleasure, I suspected.

'Now.'

'Do as she says,' I muttered to Myles, despite my fantasies of squeezing her carotids down to the thickness of pipettes. 'It's not what you think.'

I laced my fingers together, pressed them against my scalp and sank onto the damp gravel. I felt it press through the cloth and into my knees. Myles slumped down next to me with a peevish yelp. The Irishwoman came past – well out of grabbing distance – and unlocked the door, kicking it open with her heel. Her eyes had never left us. And I also knew that Konrad – Anjel – was behind us, keeping us covered.

The woman backed into the stone-built structure, gave a quick glance over her shoulder and, obviously satisfied, beckoned with her free hand. 'In ye come.'

We struggled to our feet and entered. There was a portable oil stove pumping out some heat, but even so it was as chill inside as outside. The thick walls and the high ceilings saw to that. There were bits of old agricultural or industrial machinery around, including some sort of press. The air was sharp with the smell of something organic from long ago. A fruit was my guess.

The woman had pushed back the hood and unzipped the jacket. I put her at mid to late thirties, with thick auburn hair cut to her shoulders and what in other circumstances might have been lovely green eyes. In fact, she was quite delicately featured, an effect only ruined by the curl of her lip.

There was a rough wooden table on the left-hand side of the room. Beyond it sat Mrs Irwin, one hand raised as if asking permission to go to the toilet. On closer inspection I could see that the wrist was hand-cuffed to the bracket of a hefty cast-iron pipe that ran down the wall. She was awake and seemed alert, although her left cheek was badly discoloured.

'Mom!' Myles cried, taking two steps forward.

'Stay where you are, Myles. We can do the teary reunion soon enough,' said Anjel, closing the door behind him. He flicked on a few more lights and the room brightened. Then he swung the shotgun at me. 'Strip.'

'Whathefuck?' asked Myles.

'She knows why.'

I knew why. Konrad reckoned the guns and the clothes might be the least of my resourcefulness.

'I'll catch my death in here,' I protested. It was a moment before I appreciated the horrible irony of those words.

The woman disappeared through a doorway and I heard a cupboard open and close. She came back with a thick grey blanket and threw it at my feet. 'Strip,' she repeated.

I began to pull damp clothes away from skin and over my head.

'Did you take the opportunity to have a feel of those tits?' Anjel asked Myles.

'Shuthefuckup,' the lad said.

'While she was out, I mean?' Anjel smirked. 'After all, old habits die hard.'

'Shut up!'

Anjel laughed. Then he saw the expression on my face. 'My God, I forgot. You don't remember, do you?'

I wasn't going to give him the satisfaction of admitting I didn't have a clue what he was talking about.

'Myles here, he likes his women comatose.'

'Shut up!' Myles bunched his fists but didn't shift.

I was beginning to suspect Myles might have done more at his college than smoke some weed. Was that what Nina had been talking about? But that could wait.

I stepped out of my shoes, peeled off the black jeans and threw them in a heap. Now I was down to my socks and underwear. 'Really?' I asked.

'Siobhan. Do the honours, will you?'

The once nameless woman stepped over and looked me up and down. She reached in and poked each of my breasts in turn and then ran her fingers around the elastic of my knickers. I looked down and saw something metal poking from beneath her sleeve. Something familiar.

'Nice watch,' I said.

'Shut up. Turn around. Slowly.'

I did so. Goose bumps started to rise on my arms and legs. I was fighting to keep my teeth from chattering. It was as if all my body heat was wicking away through the stone flags my stockinged feet were planted on.

Siobhan kicked at my pile of clothes, hoofing them away over the floor.

'OK, you're clean. Pick up your blanket.'

I did so, and wrapped it tightly around me. Sadly, Siobhan was spot on. I didn't have a weapon hidden anywhere about my person or in one of my pockets. I was not only clean, I was clean out of ideas.

Myles shrugged off his jacket and began to unbutton his shirt.

'You're OK,' said Anjel.

'No, he's not,' said Siobhan.

'I'm soaked, man,' said Myles through chattering teeth. 'I'll get pneu-fuckin'-monia.'

Siobhan snorted her derision but went and fetched him a blanket just the same. He stripped to the waist and wrapped it around his upper torso. Siobhan gave him a pat down but, as expected, the boy wasn't holding anything either.

'Let Myles go.' It was Mrs Irwin, her voice both croaky and thin. 'It's me you want.'

'And you I have.' Anjel pointed at the chairs around the table. 'Shall we sit and make ourselves comfortable?'

I shuffled over and sat down. Anjel gingerly lowered himself into place at one end, grimacing slightly. The gunshot wound again, no doubt. That dressing would need changing. I didn't feel much like volunteering.

Myles moved around the table and stood next to his mum. She was sitting in a high-backed oak chair. A belt ran around her waist, securing her to it. 'Can't you undo the cuffs?' Myles asked. 'Look, they're cutting into her skin.'

Anjel nodded to Siobhan, who released the arm. Mrs Irwin groaned with relief and began rubbing some life back into it.

'Why the charade?' she asked Anjel. 'All this Konrad shit. Why didn't you just kill me?'

'You're the last one,' he said, almost wistfully. 'It's been a long time. I didn't want to rush it. You changed things by bringing your son along. I had to ditch him. Then Snow White here,' he nodded at me, 'gets free and gets organised and so here we are.'

Mrs Irwin glared at me, which I thought was rather missing the point of who had caused all this. 'Sorry. Just doing my job. So was Freddie.'

'Your Freddie,' said Anjel, 'is no longer a player.'

The euphemism made me boil over, just for a second. 'Fuck you.'

Anjel simply smiled, as if indulging a childish tantrum. 'Well, Myles, I guess you're wondering why we are gathered here today. What exactly your mom has done to deserve what is going to happen to her.'

Myles was stroking his mother's hair. He, too,

looked like he would happily eviscerate Anjel given the chance.

'Jesus fucking Christ', I said, 'I'd like to know what this is all about, you sick fuck. Can we have the short version?'

'Siobhan, can you make some coffee? I'll be OK here for five minutes.'

Siobhan tucked the Ruger LCR in her waistband.

From the pocket of his waterproof jacket, Anjel fetched the big Brno pistol. He laid it down in front of him, but kept his hand next to it. He was at the far end of the table from me. He had nothing to worry about.

'Two sugars,' I said, as Siobhan turned to go.

I got two fingers instead.

'What is this all about?' I asked when she had left the room. Maybe now he was by himself the old, reasonable Konrad might return. Although I suspected that had been a construct for my benefit.

'It's about a flat battery.'

'Don't play games,' I said with all the exasperation I felt.

'It was a flat battery that killed Andrea,' Anjel said to me.

'Andrea?' I asked.

'It was an accident,' said Mrs Irwin before he could answer my question.

'You know, they all say that. The thing about

bombs, they are just a dumb device, they never know who they are *meant* to kill.'

'Like I said, it wasn't designed to kill her. She was an innocent bystander.'

'Yes. She was.'

'But you have a family history of bombs going bad, don't you, Anjel?' Mrs Irwin said with just a hint of vitriol. 'Maybe it's karma.'

Now Anjel looked at me. 'My mother was part of an IRA active service unit. She had been trying to bomb a British Army base in Cyprus. They were penetrated by the SAS and she had to go on the run. The IRA hid her in the Basque Country, where she met my father, an ETA activist. She was known as Eneca, the fiery one, because of her red hair. And a tendency to blow things up. They were both killed during an operation to plant a bomb in Majorca. The device went off prematurely. You see, as I said, you never know who is going to get killed, once you start making bombs.'

I sensed he wasn't finished.

'When I was a teenager my uncle brought me up here to this very place. An old cherry processing plant. The same uncle who used to take me fishing for velvet swimming crabs on the coast.' He winked at me. 'He explained to me what my life was going to be from then on. That I was of an age to carry on the family heritage. To join the struggle. Son of Eneca, the fiery one. I was to become a freedom fighter for ETA.'

Freedom fighter, patriot, murderer, terrorist, psycho-
path ... take your pick.

'I was meant to follow in my mother's hallowed
footsteps. But I wasn't having any of it. I didn't want to
be killing innocent people. So I wrote to my mother's
family in Ireland, asking if I could come over there and
live there. And I did.'

Mrs Irwin hawked up a great gob of spit and depos-
ited it noisily on the stone floor. 'And became a tout,'
she said, and smiled as sweetly as a woman with her
bruised face could. 'Sorry. Go on.'

'I did. Become a tout, as she puts it. I prefer the
word spy. Not immediately. But that family, it was as
steeped in violence as my Basque one. They used to
have a picture of Bobby Sands above the dining table.
Can you imagine him staring down at you while you
ate your roast lamb? When I had been there a year
or so, I was approached by a member of the security
services. A man who knew all about me and my "terrorist" family links, as he put it. I was on a watch list
somewhere, apparently. Anyway, he told me he knew
how my mother and father died. And it wasn't as a
hero of ETA or the IRA.'

'That's news to me,' said Mrs Irwin.

'Then shut your gobshite mouth and listen.'

She closed her eyes and said, 'I'm all ears, Anjel,' as
if he were about to tell a bedtime story.

'But there was a price for this information,' he

continued. 'Those fellas, there's always a price. They make Faust look like a market trader. In payment for the truth, I had to use my celebrity as Eneca's son to dig the dirt on the FIL. The Freedom for Ireland League, a fundraising group in the United States. You see, the Brits kept intercepting shipments of weapons bought by FIL. From anonymous tip-offs. What they couldn't understand was that the weapons were all shit. I mean, the kind of crap a kid soldier in the Congo might turn his nose up at. So it transpires that at least three people in the FIL, Sean Logan, Ronnie Corrigan and Marie Ronan, had a plan. It was the dog days of the struggle anyway, peace was coming. They were going to cash out before everyone turned into Martin McGuinness. So the FIL claimed the Ulster Constabulary – as they were then – and MI5 had intercepted a million dollars' worth of guns. Damn, what a shame. Except these were worth maybe ten grand as scrap.'

'Why didn't the police expose this?'

'Because taking a haul of weapons that were intended to kill had far more political clout than taking weapons that couldn't kill a rabbit. So the press releases would say that a major arms shipment worth a million or two had been intercepted. They'd show some weapons, but who was to say those nice shiny AKs were the ones they actually found?'

'And the rest of the money from the deal? The skim off the top?' I looked at Mrs Irwin, who still had her eyes closed. 'Let me guess. Luxembourg. An NOP account. Funding a new life in the USA.'

Myles gasped, as well he might.

'As a rich widow,' Anjel confirmed. 'With canny investments. Which, to be fair, she had made. But the seed money, that was blood money.'

'So it was a simple scam?' I asked Anjel. 'This FIL business?'

'Simple, yes. But also dangerous. In the end the security boys decided that, despite the evidence I had given them, it would imperil the peace process to prosecute them. Political expediency. But the TRU decided on a different approach. They let it be known to the IRA Army Council what was going on. That they were being used as a milch cow to feather someone's nests.' I let the mixed metaphor pass. 'The Brits reckoned the Squad would take out the embezzlers, saving them the trouble.'

Mrs Irwin turned her glare up to eleven once more, but kept quiet.

'The Squad?' I asked.

'The Internal Security Unit of the Provos. Also known, probably more accurately, as the Nutting Squad. They vetted new members, hunted out informers and carried out any punishments decreed by courts martial. Everything from kneecapping to killing. If you stole from the IRA, you had a week of being tortured with oxyacetylene or acid or worse. Castration if you were a man, and if you were a woman ... well, you didn't want to be a woman. The Brits thought the Squad would know how to deal with thieves.'

'And did they?'

'Aye, but there was a complication. One of the embezzlers was Ronnie Corrigan, a key figure in the Squad. A legend, just like my mother. The very man meant to punish such crimes had been culpable himself. Who polices the policemen? In the end, they let the FIL thieves live.'

'Unusual,' I said.

'Aye. But you remember the Northern Ireland bank raid?'

'Vaguely,' I admitted.

'Twenty-odd million it netted. Part organised by Sean Logan. Poor Sean. Anyway, a good chunk of that haul went to pay back the embezzled money. Once they had done that, the thieves were told to fuck off and never set foot in the old country again. Except in a wooden box.'

'And you?' I asked. 'What did you do?'

'Me? It made me realise that behind every great political cause, there is a group of venal men and women who are only in it for the excitement, the power and the prestige, and, when that goes, the money. In the end, I didn't give a fuck about what happened to them.

Not really. I was done. I went to make a new life, to forget ETA and the IRA and all that shite.'

Mrs Irwin made an unpleasant noise in her throat. 'Anjel has neglected to mention that, in order to protect his cover, he let Ronnie Corrigan and Sean Logan torture and shoot an innocent man. Stood outside a cottage in County Tyrone with me while they shot Jamie Brogan in the face, to make sure there couldn't be an open coffin.'

'Innocent?' Anjel asked. 'Who among us can say that? He was what he was. A soldier caught in the crossfire. Probably shouldn't have signed up.'

'You are a bastard,' she spat.

'You helped make me one.' Anjel turned his attention back to me. 'I was given a new identity. Michael Shannon. I'd met a girl, and a beautiful girl, too. Andrea. From Cork. In a pub in England, when the TRU was training me in covert operations. She didn't know that of course. Thought I was on a sales course. But we got on like ... we got on. But what was left of the FIL tracked me down through some arsehole of a tout and tried to blow me up. But there was a flat battery ... and just once, just that fuckin' once, Andrea, my wife, forgot what I had drummed into her over and over.'

Looking under the car, he meant, a daily routine that would have saved her life. You only had to forget once. As his wife discovered, bad luck would make sure that was the very day there was a mercury tilt mechanism or an electronic activation circuit attached to a bomb beneath your vehicle. No wonder Konrad had been so assiduous in his own inspections of that Peugeot.

'And Siobhan? Why is she here?' I made a guess. 'Sister? She's Andrea's sister?'

Anjel nodded. 'Aye. Andrea's younger sister, yes. My partner in . . .'

'Revenge,' Siobhan said as she entered carrying two mugs of coffee. Looked like I was being snubbed. 'We got her brother. And Corrigan. She's the third. The last of them. Then it's over.'

It's never really over. I knew that. Except for the dead. But for the living, closure is astonishingly hard to find. 'It won't help,' I said. 'All this. It won't help stop the voices in your head. Or the reliving of that moment when the bomb that killed your wife went off. Nothing stops that. Except time, maybe. You won't find peace by murdering more people. It never works.'

I didn't want to spell it out in front of Myles. About what they intended to do to their prisoner, and maybe us. But Siobhan knew what I meant. 'I'd like to find out for myself, if youse don't mind.'

Anjel stared at her for a minute, his face set in stone. Eventually he looked at me. 'I'm going to show you something that might explain this.' I said nothing. At least his talking kept us all alive for a while longer. From his pocket he took a clear plastic wallet. From it,

384

he took out several sheets of newsprint, clippings that had grown smudged with time. He carefully unfolded them and laid them on the table. 'That one first,' he said, as he pushed them across to me. It was from the *Cork Evening Echo*. About a 'local woman' killed by a car bomb, that old IRA favourite. Andrea Shannon. The police claimed there was no proven paramilitary connection.

'But of course there was a paramilitary connection,' Anjel said. Just not an official one. This was FIL's farewell to Ireland before they buggered off for good.' He pointed at another cutting. 'Now that one. The Belfast paper.'

This one was about a plane crash in Northern Ireland in which a certain Sean Logan died.

'Now Sean was easy to find. He placated the IRA by volunteering to do time in the Maze in place of someone above his pay grade and keeping his mouth shut. He was rewarded with a job and his life. So he got to stay in Ireland. Liked flying his wee plane, he did. Until it blew up.'

'I always knew it wasn't an accident,' said Mrs Irwin. 'Knew someone had murdered Sean.' That explained her being scared of flying. She thought they might explode under her. 'I thought it was belated revenge for the money we took. Not you.'

'Sorry to disappoint,' said Anjel. 'But it was me and Siobhan here. So, then, that last one.'

I picked it up. I knew what the gist of it would be before I read the words. A father by the name of Ronnie Corrigan shot dead in the street. That was the name of the uncle Myles had mentioned to me. Just nipping out for a pint. Back in time to cut the daughter's birthday cake.

'So there we are,' said Anjel with a sigh, as if he had just done a good day's work. 'There were one or two others along the way, but they never made the papers. Anyway, I've saved young Marie for last.'

'You killed these people?' I asked, flicking the cuttings. 'Logan and ...' I looked at the name again. 'Corrigan. These murders were all down to you?' I just wanted to hear him confirm it.

'Aye,' he said.

'Down to us,' said Siobhan, not wanting to be robbed of her credit.

'And you set up this whole scheme, just to get her over here to finish the job?'

'It was important,' said Anjel, 'that she was last. And that she knew why she was the last.'

I didn't have to ask. I knew he would tell us.

'Look at that first clipping again. The car bomb. Meant for me. It was little sweet Marie here, you see, who made the bomb that killed my wife.' He paused, as if struggling to say the next words. 'And my child.'

THIRTY-THREE

Cork, Ireland – 2000

Michael Shannon is shaving in the bathroom, looking through the tiny window over the rooftops, the slates freshly slicked with rain, a low, zinc sky keeping a lid on the city. He is thinking about Spain, and sunshine, and good food. Of velvet swimming crab soup, deep-fried elvers; of pâtés of *marmatiko* – bonito cooked with potatoes, garlic and red pepper – and glasses of light, lively *txakoli* in summer and deep draughts of cloudy cider on a winter's afternoon. Of the excavated cathedral high above Vittoria, the surfing beach at Donostia, the slippery, silvery form of the Guggenheim at Bilbao. There was a lot to show her. Lots to explain.

'I promised I'd pick Andrea up.'

He thinks, as he does most days, of his mother and father. Desperate to stop any further atrocities, bending to defuse the bomb cynically placed in a tourist café.

'*I'll take yours, then.*'

And the explosion, detonated by remote control by an ETA *comando* unit, that atomised them into motes of dust dancing in the sunlight.

'*I'll see you later.*'

Like one of those cheap hypnotism shows Andrea loves, Michael is now back in the bathroom, staring at a half-shaved face in the mirror. What did she say? What did Andrea just say?

'*You'll do what?*' he shouts.

His mind replays the conversation with her over the past five minutes, an exchange muted to muffled exchanges by his being in the square, watching those people die again.

Michael, are you taking your car?

No. Joe's giving me a lift.

You don't need it?

No, why?

My battery is fuckety-fucked again. I'll take yours then. I've got the keys. See you later.

NO!

He shouts it out, but he has no sense of how much time has passed since they first spoke. A few seconds? A few minutes?

Andrea! Wait.

He is out of the bathroom and running – almost falling – down the stairs when the house rocks as if a giant tidal wave has crashed over the city and broken against the outside wall. The staircase becomes fluid beneath his feet. A roaring fills his ears. For the second time that morning, a bomb, a cowardly bomb, has shattered lives as well as bodies.

Plural.

Although it is only after the postmortem that he discovers Andrea had been pregnant.

THIRTY-FOUR

Basque Country, Spain

There was a stunned silence once Anjel had finished his explanation. Myles looked at his mother with an expression like curdled milk on his face. I pulled the blanket tighter around myself, a sudden shudder taking me by surprise.

'The woman you know as Mrs Irwin, and I used to know as Marie Ronan, was bomb-maker to the active service units of the Provisional IRA. And very good she was, too.'

Mrs Irwin shook her head at her son, but it wasn't clear what she was trying to convey. She certainly wasn't denying the charge.

'Can we just get on with this?' asked Siobhan. 'All this gassin' is givin' me a headache.'

'Ach, hold your peace,' said Anjel. 'It's been almost twenty years. I think we can savour the moment. You might think I'd have more sympathy, wouldn't you?

Given my mother's story. But it turns out my mother was trying to defuse a bomb, not plant it, as the legend has it. My father stood by, covering her. ETA detonated it deliberately, to make two new martyrs.'

Eventually, after she had processed this, Mrs Irwin spoke. 'That's what they told you? The fuckin' Brits? That she was trying to *save* lives? And you believed it?'

'They had decided to support the peace initiative. The Zuba, the ETA high command, could not let them defect. They set them up.'

'You'd take the word of a TRU man? Even now, when we know they are lying scum?'

I didn't know much about the TRU, but I was convinced the security services were economical with the truth. But perhaps it is always easier to believe your mother was a force for good, rather than evil, even if she was a late convert to the cause of righteousness.

'Well, whatever the truth, at least you can't blame that one on me.'

'Not you personally. Just your kind.'

'What kind is that?' she asked.

'The hurting kind,' Anjel said.

'Me?' She sounded genuinely shocked. 'I'm the hurting kind? Sweet Jesus . . . who's got the guns here?'

'Can we just get on with it?' Siobhan repeated, even more impatiently. 'We'll be here all night at this rate.'

'Get on with what?' asked Myles. 'This is fuckin' insane.'

'Funny thing is, I'd grown up hating the violence that those people perpetrated. All of them, Basque and Irish. I thought I wasn't like them. And now, here I am. Ah well, maybe blood will out. Maybe it always will.'

He reached for the shotgun.

'You can't do it here. Not now.' Mrs Irwin's voice sounded stronger and there was a tinge of defiance in it. 'You'll never live with yourself.'

'We'll manage,' said Siobhan flatly.

'Not you. Him.' She pointed at Anjel. 'He'll never live with what he is about to do.'

'Why the fuck not?' asked Siobhan.

'That baby in your wife's belly? It wouldn't have been your firstborn, Anjel. You already had a child. And what sort of man kills the mother of his own son in front of the lad?'

It took a while for me to compute. It was like playing a game of Unhappy Families in my skull. The first one to move and speak was Siobhan, who strode over towards Mrs Irwin, gun raised to strike.

Mrs Irwin's voice was very small in that echoing space. 'You already had a child, Anjel, before the bomb.'

'You lying bitch!' Siobhan yelled.

'Stop!'

Anjel banged the table. I have never seen a man overcome by weariness in such a short space of time. His skin was sickly and wan, his shoulders slumped. Anjel Garzia sagged like a broken reed. He waved Siobhan away with the shotgun.

'Well, it's not fuckin' true, is it? Anjel? Is it?' Siobhan screeched.

He rubbed his eyes with his free hand. 'Well, now, it could be, Siobhan. It could well be.'

'No way,' said Myles. It was his turn to glare at his mother. 'You cannot be serious. You ... you told me ...'

Myles, I recalled, believed his father had died when he was a kid. And now there he apparently was, sitting at a table with a shotgun within his reach, which he intended to use on the boy's mother.

'I told you whatever needed to be said at the time,' she snapped. 'The truth is something different.'

'The truth, I find, is somewhat slippery to say the least,' said Anjel. 'We only have your word for this revelation. In the absence of a DNA test kit ...'

'You have the same eyes,' I offered.

'Fuck,' said Myles, squirming. 'Fuckin' mindfuck.'

I didn't think they had the same eyes at all. I couldn't see any resemblance. But if it kept us alive, I'd swear they were dead ringers, peas in a pod, Tweedledum and Tweedledee.

Myles stood, wrapping the blanket around his shoulders, and moved across the room, as if wanting to distance himself from us all. I could see his point.

'Don't go wandering off,' warned Siobhan, brandishing the Ruger at him. 'We aren't done with this.'

Myles positioned himself against a pillar and began to mutter to himself. I think he had a lot to mutter about.

'OK, Anjel, let me put it another way,' said Siobhan. '*Could* it be true?'

'That he is my son?' He frowned, as if calculating dates.

I watched Siobhan's spittle fly across the room when she yelled. 'What I mean is, did you *fuck* this piece of shit?'

'Ah, now there I'll have to say yes. It was only on the pillow she was going to let slip how FIL was getting its money, and how we could run away and live happily ever after. And where the money would come from. Pillow talk that found its way onto little cassette tapes. Needs must.'

Siobhan shook her head in dismay. I guessed what she had thought of as solid ground was now decidedly fluid. But Anjel was hardly the first undercover man to sleep with his quarry. Nor would he be the last.

'Look, it was the only way to get close to them. I was Eneca's son, she was the celebrity bomb-maker. People wanted it to be a perfect match. So, yes, I did fuck her.'

'And it didn't occur to you *that* was why she wanted you dead afterwards?' I said. 'A woman scorned?'

Anjel turned his attention to Mrs Irwin. He didn't have to ask the question.

'Of course I hated you for it,' Mrs Irwin said. 'To feel so *used*.'

'And carrying such guilt about what you had done,' I said. She glared at me, but I ploughed on. 'You gave him what the FIL were up to. Between the sheets. He gave it to the MI5 or whoever. In a way, you were the tout.'

She flinched at the hated word. The light in her eyes softened and she nodded. 'Guilt and shame, too, for that, yes.' She turned back to her old lover. 'But for God's sake, Anjel ... haven't you done enough damage? Leaving your boy an orphan? What sort of man does such a thing?'

I thought we'd already established that, but I needed to move it on. 'I think it ends here, Anjel,' I offered.

'No,' said Siobhan, sounding like she was about to cry. 'Not like that. Like this.'

She raised the gun so quickly, I knew I couldn't make the distance, but I had to try. I was half out of my chair when the shotgun boomed.

The sound seemed to fill the room like primeval thunder and for a few seconds it was as if someone had shoved rags in both my ears. Siobhan was still rooted to the spot, right arm out straight, pistol in hand. She slowly raised her head and looked at the hole in the ceiling, and the stream of debris spiralling down from it.

'Put it down,' said Anjel. 'And stop playing the maggot.'

She took a deep breath, as if making sure she still had lungs, lowered her gun arm and slumped back into a chair. I let the tension drain from my body, just a little, and sat back down. I glanced over at Myles, who had flattened himself against the pillar, as if hoping he could disappear within it. I wondered if there was room for two in there. Disappearing seemed like a good idea.

Mrs Irwin licked her lips, very slowly, as if any sudden move might provoke Siobhan into further action. She cleared her throat before she spoke. 'There must be another way out of this. It was a long time ago, Anjel. We were different people. I thought I loved you. It's why the hate was so intense. We both suffered from what our families did, what they expected of us. We both rebelled, in our own ways. But now, you're just … it's the same solution every time. This is what Ronnie would have done. Not you.'

'I tried to warn you,' said Anjel. 'That night at the hut when they executed Jamie Brogan. I told you to come here, to the Basque Country. I told you to get out of it there and then. But you didn't.'

She gave a bitter laugh. 'That's the thing about the freedom fighting – easy to get into, bastard to get out of.'

Anjel stood and began to pace. He began to tell the

story of the murder of an informer. Or a man that Anjel had convinced the others was an informer. 'It was almost midnight when we got him to Marie's cottage,' he began.

He reloaded the empty barrel of the shotgun as he talked. We weren't out of these deep, dark woods yet. 'You remember how it ended?' he asked Mrs Irwin as the tale drew to a close. 'The two shots? "There, it's over now," I said. But it wasn't was it?'

'You let him be murdered,' she said.

'Him or me. As I said, just another casualty of war. Soooooo . . .' He drew the word out like Elsa the masseuse. 'There might be a way out of this, keep everyone happy. And alive.'

I was suddenly all ears.

'How much is in that account in Luxembourg?' he asked, finally sitting down once more.

Siobhan's head snapped up. 'Anjel!'

'Shush. How much?'

'Several million,' she answered.

'Really? What about Corrigan's share? And Logan's?'

She cleared her throat, as if signalling the truth was coming this time. 'Eleven.'

He nodded as if satisfied. 'We want five million each. Siobhan and me. That leaves you a million there and however much you have legit back in the States. I wouldn't want you to starve.'

'Fuck your money,' said Siobhan, eyes downcast. 'It wasn't about the fuckin' money.' Her gaze flicked up to Anjel and I was glad I wasn't on the receiving end. 'Was it?'

Anjel gave a little shrug, as if he was certain his dead wife's sister would come round to his way of thinking. Judging by the black cloud of an expression she was still wearing, I wasn't so sure. But then, someone dumping five million in front of you can be like the sun coming out. Although, I reminded myself, five million wasn't what it once was. Would barely keep *Kubera* afloat for a year.

'I can get you that,' said Mrs Irwin – or, more accurately, Marie Ronan – quietly. 'No problem.'

'We keep the boy until you do,' Anjel said.

She went to protest, but realised it was inevitable. They wanted collateral. Myles was the best they could get.

'This sucks,' said Myles. 'Mom, don't do this.'

'I have no choice.' Her voice was laced with defeat. Then, to Anjel: 'Do I?'

'I could leave you alone with Siobhan for five minutes. That's a choice.'

Siobhan's face brightened and her shoulders went back at the thought. 'I've waited a long time for this. Half my life. The five million doesn't even begin to cover it.'

'It'll have to do.' Anjel began offering travel advice

like some RAC operator. 'You take the Peugeot. There's cash in the glove compartment. Go back over the border. There's a TGV station at Tarbes. Leave the car with the keys on one of the tyres. You go to Paris and switch to a TGV to Luxembourg City. Take nine, maybe ten hours.' He placed a card on the table. 'Phone this number, I'll tell you where to transfer the money. Once it is done we'll put Myles on another TGV to France.'

'What about the Red Notice and the EAW?' I asked.

'What Red Notice?' he smirked. 'She's not wanted for anything.'

I wasn't sure what to believe now. The Red Notice and the European Arrest Warrant had been fabrications? But how do you fuck with Europol and Interpol? That bothered me. Something didn't quite chime.

I stood. 'I should go with her.'

'Why?' asked Mrs Irwin, her voice taking on a mocking tone. 'Because you did such a bang-up job of protecting me last time? I'll be fine.'

She probably would be. After all, we knew who the opposition was now. He was standing right in front of us.

'Did you pick us up near Bayonne?' I asked Anjel. 'Is there a second team out there?'

'No second unit,' he said. 'We didn't need one. You came to us, remember? You must have been imagining things.'

All that driving in reverse, causing motorway chaos, all for nothing. I'd have to double-check the veracity of those infallible instincts of mine from now on.

'Undo her,' Anjel ordered Siobhan who, as sullen as a teenager, walked over and freed Marie Ronan from the chair.

She picked up the card from the table. I wanted to tell her not to run a thumb over it, but I guessed it wasn't one of those. He had no intention of drugging her. She pocketed it and held out her hand for the Peugeot keys. Anjel fished them from his pocket and tossed them over.

'I'll be in touch.' She walked over and kissed Myles on the cheek, then whispered something into his ear. His eyes glistened and his lower lip trembled.

As she left she threw me what I guess you'd call a withering look.

Five million isn't what it was.

I felt a strange sense of dislocation, like I was Alice down the rabbit hole. Nothing made sense here. Five million? Anjel, a man who had spent twenty years systematically tracking down and killing the men and the woman who had murdered his wife rolls over for five million after five minutes? And could look so relaxed about it?

He hadn't gone and inspected the car, I realised. Every time we went near that Peugeot, he had gone under the bonnet, under the dash ... but why would he think it was booby-trapped? After all, *he* was the bad guys. He'd know it wasn't rigged to blow.

Unless it was.

Anjel watched in detached bemusement as I leaped up and ran for the door, the blanket falling away behind me. 'Mrs Irwin. Marie! Marie! It's wired.'

He hadn't been looking for bombs when he was pulling that charade. He *knew* there was one in the car. He'd been making certain the one he installed was set to *off*. That was why the delivery driver died, perhaps. He had forgotten something and come back, only to find 'Konrad' wiring a bomb.

'Marie! Elizabeth! Ruth!' Too many names, too many lies.

I had reached the door when the room was filled with a pure, rinsed light, as if someone had switched on a battery of klieg lamps beyond the windows. I felt the blast wave hit the door, which bulged and creaked, but held. There was the pinging of metal and glass as debris hit the frontage like buckshot. The old stones shivered under the blast, windowpanes cracked with a sharp detonation and a fine rain of dust fell from the ceiling. But the building held. Then the sound of the fuel going up, like the roar of an angry giant.

I turned to Anjel. There was something wet on my lip. I touched my fingertips to it. They were bright red. My voice sounded like it came from another room. 'You sick fucker.'

'It was a nice try. But he's not my son,' he said flatly. 'Not a fuckin' chance.'

As if that made it all right.

But from the smug look on Siobhan's face I knew I had just witnessed a performance designed simply to get Marie Ronan to walk out to the car and blow herself up. Just like Andrea, all that time ago.

'I put a few seconds' delay on the timer. Just enough so she could hear it click. I mean, she's a bomb-maker. She would know exactly what was coming. But she wouldn't have enough time to get out before the detonation. There's some kind of poetic justice in there, somewhere.'

'No! No! No!'

The accompanying crack of the pistol seemed small and insignificant after the storm caused by the petrol detonation. The second seemed louder, the third louder still.

I watched Anjel fly backwards, still in his chair. He landed with a bone-jarring crash. He managed to get his head up and look down at his chest. It was spurting a small arc of blood, rising higher with each heartbeat. 'Je-sus,' he mouthed, but no words came.

Then Siobhan shot the shooter. Two rounds, spinning Myles away from the pillar and sending the gun skittering over the floor. Away from me.

I seemed to be the only one in the room without a weapon, but even before the bark of Siobhan's pistol had died I knew I had a window of opportunity. Her shot was a complete reflex. There would be a second or two while she would process what she had done. That was my time. My only chance before she shot me, just so she had the full set.

I was already on my feet, so I kicked off from the door behind me, running at her as fast and as low as I could, head down, ignoring the gun that was doubtless turning on me. I hit her hard and together we sprawled back into the chairs and across the table. She grabbed my hair with her left hand and pulled and my scalp became electrified with pain. I had to ignore that. I pinned her gun hand down on the table and punched her, hard, in the face, feeling something in my hand crack. As she went limp, I found the nerve in her wrist and pressed. The fingers went into spasm. I twisted the gun out of her hand. Then I slapped it across her face. It made a satisfying crunch.

'What have you done with Freddie?'

'In the boot of the car.' She smiled and there was blood on her teeth.

That's when I shot her. It seemed to be the fashionable thing to do in that part of the world.

It was only in the upper arm and I think I missed the bone. But it would hurt like fuck and I can't say I wasn't gratified when I saw her eyes roll to the whites as she screamed.

'You get up from there and the next bullet will leave

you like Anjel. Understood?' My voice was coming from underwater. The sound of the gunshots had battered my ears into submission. There was a thumping pain behind my eyes, but I ignored it. 'Do you understand?' I repeated at some volume.

She managed to nod. Her cheeks had taken on a bluish tinge and I turned her on her side, good arm downwards. I retrieved my T-shirt and wrapped one of the sleeves around the wound. She let out a tiny cry, like a baby's. Siobhan was out of the game. I pushed up a sleeve of her hoodie and unclipped the Omega.

'Mine, I think.'

I walked over and picked up the shotgun that Anjel had dropped. The walls were glowing from the residual fire that was burning in the Peugeot and the stench of burnt plastic, leather and flesh felt like it was leaking through the stone. Anjel was still alive, just, but in my army days I had never known anyone survive the kind of sucking noises coming out of his chest. He wasn't going to be the exception. Not even a SAM chest seal – which I didn't carry – could save him.

I crossed over to Myles. He was clutching his side and groaning. I knelt down and pulled the blanket away. One of Siobhan's shots must have missed because he only had a single wound, but it had messed up his ribs. His breathing was shallow and clearly painful. There was a deep gouge and bone was showing through, along with strings of tendon, a slice of muscle that had lifted away and the white of freshly exposed cartilage. I touched the area around it and blood welled from the wound, but not in alarming quantities. Not alarming to me, that is.

'Myles, listen, you'll live. It's bad but not fatal. Just don't look at it. It's better than it looks.' Which wouldn't be difficult.

He strung together every profanity he knew into one long, freeform sentence. I went to the kitchen and found a clean cloth.

'Press that against the wound,' I instructed him. 'Not too hard.'

Myles grimaced as he did so, then looked up at me. 'He wasn't. Was he? My father, I mean?'

The enormity of what he might have done was sinking in even as his blood leaked out. Had he killed his own dad? In truth, I didn't know, so I changed the subject.

'Where did you get the gun?'

'From the bag in the car. When we pulled up behind the BMW and you got out. I ...' Sweat broke out on his upper lip with the effort of talking. But I needed to hear this.

'Go on.'

'I put it down my jeans.'

'Where?'

'In the crotch.'

I'd never understood the point of low-slung jeans before. Maybe I'd just found it.

'You did well. They were going to kill us, like they did Freddie.' Hard words to say, even harder to process. But I was convinced we wouldn't have got out alive. Sooner or later Anjel would have realised we were loose ends. Surplus to requirements, as he so cogently put it. It would have been the logical thing to do, murder all of us and go and get on with the rest of his life.

'Fuck,' he muttered, but whether that was at the pain or the thought of how close we came to being the ones lying dead on the floor, I couldn't be certain. I knew there was a voice screaming in horror somewhere deep inside me, too, but I pretended to be deaf to that. Given the racket going on in my ears that wasn't much of a challenge.

'I am going to phone for help, OK? Using one of their mobiles.' If I could get a signal in that godforsaken place. 'But I have to do something first. OK?'

'What? What are you doing that's more important than fixing me up?'

I didn't answer.

'I thought you were a medic.'

'I was. Once.' These days I seemed to inflict pain just as much as alleviate it. I picked up his discarded Sig – I was rapidly becoming a one-woman arsenal – and headed for my clothes. I pulled on my jeans and slipped the jacket on over my bra. For some reason I was no longer cold.

'Hey. Ow. Fuck, this still hurts. You going to do something?'

'I said I'll get to you in a minute. I'll find my first-aid kit. It'll be around here somewhere. But like I said, I have to do something first.'

'You are a selfish bitch.'

I couldn't argue with that. A tired, pissed-off, selfish bitch whose mouth tasted like metal. My period was starting. It was one of my warning signs. That and, usually at least, a craving for chocolate. Maybe that would come later. It certainly wasn't the time or the place to be thinking about Dairy Milk. I headed for the door.

'Hey. Sam. Sam.' He waited until I had turned. 'You know, he was right. I did feel your tits. They were pretty nice.' There was a sneer and a swagger in the words and it wasn't just pain distorting his features. 'For an old lady.'

I wasn't sure whether to believe him. When, exactly, had he done it? It was possible he was just trying to piss me off. Well if so, he'd succeeded and I was now in no hurry to tend to that wound of his. Let him sweat. And if it was true, if he groped me while I was under, I might just break the little fucker's fingers.

There we go again. What did I say? That it was my job to make sure nobody gets hurt? I lied.

I put the pistols in my pockets, the shotgun over my shoulder and flexed a hand that was busy swelling up. Two of my fingers were already as fat as chocolate eclairs. Painkillers could wait, too.

I went to find what was left of Freddie.

THIRTY-FIVE

Zürich

'So this all goes back twenty years?' The Colonel shook his head as if he didn't believe a word of it. He had my notes in his hand and he shuffled them. 'It was all about revenge for a murder?'

'Two murders. Mother and unborn child. Marie, Corrigan and the others from FIL tracked Konrad down and, in revenge for blowing their little arms-dealing scam wide open, had planted a car bomb. A bomb made by Marie. It doesn't forgive what he did,' I said. 'But it might explain it. Anyway, that's all over now.' Apart from a few nightmares about what happened in that derelict cherry processing plant in the Basque Country, and the sight and smell of the Peugeot after the bomb had done its work. But they would fade. They nearly always do.

'Don't these people ever forget?'

It was a rhetorical question. He damned well knew

the answer. Long memories formed part of his stock in trade. And in the history of Ireland's troubles, two decades was the day before yesterday. But I said: 'They never forget. And they never forgive.'

'I am a great believer in truth and reconciliation.'

First I'd heard of it. I thought he was an honours graduate of the University of An-Eye-For-An-Eye. 'But you know there were two murders he was intent on avenging, although they were linked. To lose a mother to a bomb is bad enough. But then, almost twenty years later, his wife went the same way . . . I think it sent him over the edge.'

Think? I knew it did. I wasn't sure how I would react to anything happening to Jess like that. I was irrational enough now, when she was simply missing. *We are all damaged*, Konrad had said back when it all started. *And some of us are more damaged than others.* It was disconcerting to think that I was on a continuum with a man like him. But that didn't make it any less likely.

The Colonel frowned. 'But why didn't this Marie Ronan or Mrs Irwin recognise him? When you first picked him up.'

'Why didn't she know it was her old lover and betrayer? He was a changed man. He'd bulked up, he'd done some cosmetic changes and he nearly always wore those dark glasses. But most of all he was just a hired hand. She'd got used to having little people around her. She wouldn't have looked at him too closely.'

'And is Myles his son?'

'The dates fit. I think we let sleeping dogs lie on that.'

'You were lucky to get out of there in one piece.'

I held up my two strapped fingers. 'Almost in one piece. But I know. If she had accepted my offer to go with her, I'd be in a lot more than one piece.' It made me sweat when I think of how I had tried to persuade her to take me along to Luxembourg. Thank God I'd pissed her off.

He scratched at a mole on the side of his head. I had reminded him of something. 'It is the first time we have lost a Principal,' the Colonel said. 'If it gets out ...'

I sensed an undertow of accusation. I wanted to slap his face for that. 'Are you kidding me? It was you who sent the man who wanted to kill her as her bodyguard. What if that gets around the Circuit?'

He said nothing, simply consulted my notes again. 'You know your expenses on this are threatening to outdo our earnings.'

It always came down to the bottom line with the Colonel. And the clear-up of the carnage in the Basque Country can't have been cheap. 'How is the boy?' I asked.

'Recovering. As is the woman, Siobhan. Both in a private hospital.'

'Not in adjacent beds I hope.'

411

'Not even the same hospital. Both have been visited by lawyers who have laid out some very stark choices for them.'

'She is a murderer. Siobhan.'

'Accessory to murder.'

'She told me while we were waiting for your boys to turn up and bail me out. It was her who shot Ronnie Corrigan through the head. Anjel couldn't have got close, but a pretty young woman? Isn't that murder? It is by my definition.'

'When was this?'

I tried to recall the date on the cutting Anjel had shown me. 'Five or six years ago, I think.'

'It would be hard to find any forensics after all this time. And it'd just be your word ...'

'So she walks?'

'We'll see. But the lad certainly is a murderer, if what you say is true.'

Why did he have to throw doubts in like that? Now he sounded like a lawyer. 'It's true, Colonel. It's all true. I wish it wasn't. The boy killed Konrad, Anjel, whatever you want to call him. I think we can get self-defence on that.'

'If it ever comes to court.' He said it in a way that suggested the carpet was already lifted, the broom ready to go. 'They have to find a body first.'

'True.' I didn't ask for any details. Best not to know.

'Of course, if all goes well for him, Myles will be a very rich young man in a year or so.'

'Really?'

'If he can prove the account in Luxembourg was his mother's.'

'The NOP? The same one where the account manager suffered a hit and run?

'Yes. That one. If he can prove it, he will be due the contents of that account.'

'There's no justice in this world,' I said wearily. I now knew, from a long call with Nina, what she had originally told me about the boy and the frat parties. The manipulation charge for Mrs Irwin – Marie – might have been trumped up, but his one was 24-carat. And if I found out he really did squeeze my tits, as soon as he recovered from his gunshot wound I might just shoot him again.

And then I thought of what the desire for revenge had done to Anjel and Siobhan and countless others. As I had said, best let it lie.

But there was something nagging at me, like a stone in my shoe or grit in my eye. Something that hadn't yet clicked into place.

'Can we get back to Jess?' I said impatiently. I'd had enough of debriefing. 'Apparently you have recovered a photograph.' Something else I had no recollection of from my conversation at the chateau.

'Yes. And, you will be pleased to know, we have more news.'

I waited. He pressed a button on his old-fashioned intercom. 'I'll let Henri tell you. Coffee?'

'No thanks.'

Henri came in a couple of minutes later, with a red folder in his hands. 'Miss Wylde,' he said, giving a little bow. 'I am pleased to say Herr Gorrister made some progress. With the original photo.' From the folder he slid out an 8×4. It was a blurred picture of an ankle, with some writing above it.

'Poobag,' I said.

'Pardon?' asked Henri, adjusting his glasses as if that would make him hear better.

'It is a nickname. Saanvi told me. It says Poobag in Sanskrit or Thai.'

Henri reddened a little. 'No, it doesn't. It says ...' He cleared his throat. 'White slut.'

There was a moment of tension before I gave a little laugh. 'Well, that serves her right. I just hope it's not true.'

'There is more,' said the Colonel.

'There was some information in the picture, down at pixel level. A code identifying the cameraphone used. Gorrister did a search for images with the same unique alphanumerical sequence.'

'What, around the world?' How good was this guy? Or how many people did he employ?

'No, he was initially able to narrow it down. Because the tattoo isn't written in Sanskrit or Thai, Miss Wylde. It is in Balinese.'

'Balinese?'

'From Bali.'

'Yes, I gathered that,' I snapped. 'Jesus. She's in Bali?'

'She certainly was at some point.' Henri passed me several other photos, one taken in a bar that was clearly the one that had gone across on Snapchat to Saanvi. Jess with a young boy, a surfer type, with his arm round her, dangling over her shoulder, as if heading for ...

It hit me like a baseball bat around the head, in a way just the ankle shot couldn't. That was abstract. This was my Jess, out there in a world where people like Myles existed, across the other side of the world. A world of hook-ups and date-rape drugs and lost memories. I had known all along that was the slalom course of modern life she would have to navigate. But here was the pictorial evidence that she was already out of the starting gate.

The noise in my head was like water gushing down a pipe.

'Sam?'

I managed to say, 'Yes?'

'You all right? Please, Henri, fetch Miss Wylde some water.'

He went out and came back with a paper cup of water that I tossed back. 'Another, please.'

I was fighting being sick, struggling to keep from

screaming and absolutely determined not to break anything, although I felt like taking an axe to the desk.

I began to sort through the other photos.

'Sam, do you think that's a good—' the Colonel began.

'I want to see her. I want to see what she looks like.'

And I did, lying on a sunlounger next to a pool. At the beach, holding a surfboard. It was heartbreaking. Although at least there were no priapic boys draped over her.

I took the next cup of water and sipped. 'Any of these have a GPS tag?'

'No.'

'This one with the pool. Look at that background. And there's a monogram on the towel. Blow that up and we should be able to ID the hotel.'

'It is possible,' said the Colonel.

'Which might give us the location on the island.'

'Yes.'

'I'll get on to it,' said Henri.

'You know, the Red Notice and the EAW still bothers me,' I said.

The change of gear took the Colonel by surprise. 'What?'

'The EAW that was served on the woman we thought was Mrs Irwin. How did you know about that?'

Henri, sensing his work was done, started to excuse himself.

'No, stay here,' I said firmly. 'You might be able to help me with this. How do you get notified about a European Arrest Warrant?'

'There is a daily bulletin. It goes to all national police services across Europe. For a small fee, we get to see a copy,' said the Colonel.

'Every day?'

'Yes, it is emailed across to me. Well, to Henri.'

I looked up at Henri. 'How difficult would it be to intercept the bulletin and add an item of your own. Imitating the style and format? Like phishing?'

'I …'

'Not difficult for a man like Gorrister?'

Henri looked offended. 'Gorrister? Are you suggesting—'

'No, I'm not suggesting anything. I just mean any man with his skill set.'

'Not too difficult, I suppose.'

'What are you driving at?' asked the Colonel.

'Anjel told me that there had never been a warrant out for Mrs Irwin. But you thought so. She thought so …'

'Because we told her,' said the Colonel wearily.

'Because it was on the bulletin. Right?'

I looked at Henri, who indicated with a curt nod that it had been.

'Who is going to doubt an official Europol release?' I said, trying to make him feel better. 'Can you check the original bulletin against the one you received? To see if they are identical or if one of them has been, um, expanded? Tampered with in some way?'

'I suppose.' He didn't sound too thrilled about it. The thought that he might have been duped clearly rankled. Me, I was getting used to it.

'Ask Dujardin at the National Crime Agency. He owes me a favour,' suggested the Colonel. 'See if they match. See if they had Mrs Irwin down for this charge.'

When Henri had gone, he put his head in his hands. 'It just keeps getting better.'

'You know the next question, don't you?'

'I think so.'

'Who suggested George Konrad as the bodyguard for Mrs Irwin? Because whoever it was failed to perform the proper background checks. And I suspect that wasn't you, Colonel.'

He sniffed. 'The same person who brought the Red Notice to my attention.'

We both glanced at the door. 'Henri,' I said softly. 'Who suggested me?'

'How do you mean?'

'When we first met, Konrad said he had been expecting to fly solo. I had a feeling I was a late addition to the party.'

'It was my idea. I thought it was a two-person job.'

'Did Henri agree?'

I thought it was impossible for more wrinkles to appear on that face, but as he grasped the implications of what I was saying it crumpled a little, creating more crevices. 'No. He argued you were an unnecessary cost.'

'So we can assume that Henri was working for Konrad. He slipped in the phoney EAW and the Red Notice. He set it up so that Konrad was the only security. But first I turn up, and then the son. So Konrad is forced to improvise. He doesn't want to kill us, not at first, so he sets up the chateau and dumps us there. Agreed?'

I stared at the Colonel until he nodded. I went to rise but he shook his head. 'Please, Sam. Sit down. He's my son.'

'I won't hurt him.'

A flicker of pain crossed his face. 'You have a habit of hurting everyone, Sam.'

I sat back down, shocked at the thought. And perhaps recognising the truth of it. 'Did he do it for money?' I asked.

'Blackmail, perhaps. I can't say I know everything about him. Henri, I mean.'

'Who can say that about anyone?' I stood up and gathered the photos into the file Henri had brought. 'But he's a bad apple.'

'He's also flesh and blood. My flesh and blood.'

419

That was no excuse as far as I was concerned. 'Who almost got me killed. And is indirectly responsible for the deaths of both Marie Ronan and Konrad.'

'You will let me deal with this? I like to clean out my own stables. I'll get to the bottom of it.'

I let him sweat for a minute and then shrugged. 'If you wish.' I grabbed my bag and put it over my shoulder.

'Thank you.'

For a second I was looking not at the man who was at the centre of a web of operatives across Europe, but at a heartbroken old man. A father. 'I'm not going to touch him,' I said eventually. 'I promise. But you and he need to have a long talk. And let me know the upshot.'

'Thank you. Where are you going now?' he asked.

I looked at him like he had lost his mind. 'Where do you think?'

'Ah, yes. I'll be in touch, Sam. I promise. I'll give you chapter and verse.'

'I look forward to it.'

I left, closing the door behind me, leaving him to his crushing disappointment. I padded on springy carpet past Henri's office on the way to the lift. That door was also closed, the blinds down. I thought about kicking it down and dragging him across the desk by his Hermès tie, but I doubted that would achieve anything. Professional pride would mean that the Colonel would get to the truth, that much I was certain of.

For my part, I was going to Bali. I was going to find my daughter. And with a bit of luck, I wouldn't be alone on this one, if I played my cards right. I took the lift down to the ground floor. She was waiting for me in the café round the corner, face turned to the sun.

THIRTY-SIX

Wednesday

I'm trying not to think too much about what happened at the house the other night. It's enough to give me nightmares, worse than I get from The Walking Dead. *I REALLY don't want to imagine what would have happened if Dad and Sarah hadn't had a row on the Saturday afternoon. He stormed out of the hotel and caught a plane back home. Went to the bar, found it closing. Putu told him Dieter had come to see me after a stonking argument with Aja.*

Matt came home and found that Dieter was buzzing out of his mind and he BEAT THE SHIT out of Dieter. I had to pull him off the guy before he killed him. I'm not even joking.

I have never seen Matt like that. It helped that Dieter had done so many drugs and so much

*booze that he must have been seeing triple. Still,
I'm proud of Matt, because even shit-faced Dieter
was a bit of a scary guy.*

*Anyway, Matt panicked because Dieter has
some even scarier friends, apparently. Like that
cop from the bar. So we had to leave Bali real
quick. There, I can say it now. We were in Bali,
down near Jimbaran Bay, below Kuta. But we
had to get out by BOAT, can you believe. Vomit.
Well, I didn't, but almost.*

*But we are on dry land, now. We've got some
moving on to do. We have to cover our tracks.
Dad says Dieter is bound to come after us. I
think he might just be being paranoid. But as he
said, better safe than sorry. So it's back to hush-
hush again. Off to a 'secret location', as Matt
says.*

*Matt says we might not be away too much
longer. Mum is getting better, the court case is
nearly over and we should be back home soon –
Hurray!! Be good to see Mum again – and the
Poobags.*

But it's Bye for now.

THIRTY-SEVEN

Zürich

I explained what had just happened in the office. Freddie couldn't quite believe what she was hearing. I couldn't blame her. 'His own son?'

'That's my best guess,' I said.

'That's a pisser all round. If you are right, what will the Colonel do about him?'

I shook my head. 'I don't know. I wouldn't want to be in Henri's shoes. But I think we should move on. Leave and close the door behind us. Or, at least, I should. Tell me, do you think Konrad would have fooled me a year ago?'

'What?'

'The Basque phrases he used. *Neska* something. And bloody velvet swimming crabs – you don't get them in Hungary.'

'What are you talking about?'

I had been obsessing on this. 'When I was at my

best, I would have smelled a rat about Konrad from the off. The gourmet gunman? The considerate killer? Do me a favour. But I didn't. You know why? Jess. Part of my brain has been disengaged from the job, worrying away about her. It's cost me my edge.'

'You're being too hard on yourself. Konrad had nearly twenty years to get his act right. And how the fuck could you have known he was speaking Basque? It's some language from the Stone Age, isn't it?'

Nice of her to try to let me down easy, but I wasn't having it. Because I knew my version was the correct one. 'That's no excuse. And no consolation. I can't do this any more. The PPO stuff. I have to worry about Jess full-time now.'

'*We* have to worry about Jess full-time,' Freddie corrected.

'Thank you.'

I passed the folder to her. She pulled out the photos and examined each in turn. 'I hate to say this, but ... Jess looks well. My guess? We aren't exactly looking at an abused, unhappy child here.'

'I know.' Her looking happy was another stiletto in the heart. But what did I want – pictures of her looking miserable, depressed, anorexic, haunted? No, this was a good result. She had still been stolen from me, was still a prisoner, even if it was a prisoner in paradise.

Freddie sipped her coffee, making a squeaking noise as she did so. Her top lip was still cracked from where

Siobhan had hit her with a gun. Right before she bundled her into the car Freddie had driven down to Spain in. The BMW. Not the Peugeot that Marie Ronan died in. I'd gone out looking through the wreckage for her. It was only after I had burned my fingers and scorched my hair and tried not to look at the hideously blackened mannequin in the driver's seat I realised I'd made the wrong assumption.

I'd wept with joy when I had found her. She had wept because her lip hurt. Amazingly, she had forgiven me. She blamed herself for being outfoxed by Anjel and Siobhan, who had known they were being followed. Anything she had told the Colonel, the old man had doubtless passed on to Henri. And he to Konrad and Siobhan. The pair had been waiting for her all along.

I fantasised about going back in and thumping Henri a few times, but I simply ordered a coffee for myself. The Colonel would figure it all out. I had bigger fish to fry than Henri. I realised that the well of fury had been replaced by something else. A determination. Perhaps it was seeing how corrosive Anjel and Siobhan's bitterness had become over the years, distorting their worldview until the only thing that mattered was some sort of revenge. I didn't want to be eaten away like that. I had to get Jess back without destroying myself in the process.

Just get it sorted.

I watched two men approaching us from over the

square. There was something about the way they were heading towards us with laser-guided accuracy that made alarm bells ring. I sat up in the chair.

I relaxed just a little as I recognised the feline walk of one of them. Jean-Claude. The Frenchman from *Kubera*. And that was Keegan next to him. The retrievers. What the hell were they doing here?

'What now?' Freddie asked, not yet sensing my growing feeling of alarm.

'We go to Bali,' I said, but even as the word came out, and Jean-Claude raised an arm in greeting, I sensed that the two men rapidly closing on our table had other plans for me.

The pair came to the table and I made the introductions. Sensing they had something to say, Freddie went in to use the toilet and to rustle up a waiter. They sat down.

'I heard you had some excitement,' said Keegan.

'News travels fast,' I said.

'Well, we were almost close enough to witness some of it. The stunt on the highway? Impressive.'

A sort of tingling started in one of my hands. I shook it. But it wasn't pins and needles in my fingers. It was alarm bells.

'Bayonne? That was you on my tail?' Perhaps all that fancy wheelwork hadn't been a complete waste of time after all.

'We picked you up earlier than that. But we figured out you'd end up here eventually.'

'If I lived.'

'Well, we didn't know exactly what was going to happen in Spain, did we?'

'What the hell are you doing chasing me down to Zürich?'

Jean-Claude leaned forward. 'That man you told us about. The Albanian who may have killed your husband.'

'Leka?'

'Yes. We tracked him down. He is one of the biggest people-traffickers in Europe. And not a man to cross, even for us.'

'Meaning?'

'He made us an offer,' said Keegan.

Status: orange. 'What kind of offer?'

'An offer of work,' said Jean-Claude, and as his jacket fell open I could see the Smith & Wesson on his belt.

'A retrieval,' offered Keegan.

'What has he hired you to retrieve?' I asked.

But I knew the answer even before Jean-Claude spoke and the day suddenly turned very chill. Behind him I saw the steel anti-terrorist bollards that ringed the public space sink into the ground and a blacked-out Range Rover bounce over them onto the plaza, heading our way. Status: very, very red.

Keegan's hand clamped onto my wrist.

'You.'

THIRTY-EIGHT

You never forget the sound of a soft human body hitting hard earth from a great height. It stayed with me for days in Iraq. A patrol had managed to capture a local warlord, code-named Desert Cobra after the lightning strikes he organised. He was believed to be behind the constant mortar raids on our camp. Anyway, you could probably have heard the cheers of the Intel lads in Baghdad when they were told he was being brought in by chopper, wounded but alive.

At that point there were two ways for the helicopter pilots to approach the camp to avoid missile attacks and small-arms fire, and they liked to mix them up. One was a low-level dash, over the ridge and down onto the landing zone. The other was to come in at some considerable altitude and drop like a stone.

That day they chose the latter. There was always a moment before the descent when the helicopter hesitated. The crew liked this, because most passengers got shit-scared in those brief seconds before the machine dropped like a rock. Stomachs were always in mouths. Screams not uncommon. Vomiting a well-known hazard. It was just like when the roller coaster crests the top of the ride, a heartbeat of what-are-we-doing-here-again?

It was in that tiniest of windows that the Desert Cobra broke free and jumped.

Freddie was standing next to me when he went out and she grabbed my arm and squeezed, pointing to the sky with her free hand. We watched the tiny black dot grow into a human being. He wasn't flailing as one might expect – his hands were cuffed, but even his legs stayed still. I always imagined he was quite calm, waiting to be welcomed in the arms of Allah as the unforgiving soil of his home country rushed towards him. The Desert Cobra struck the earth with a deep thud that seemed to vibrate through the soles of our boots, the impact obscured by a thick cloud of yellow dust. Only later did we wonder: *did he fall or was he pushed?*

They say the noise of a human body hitting a pavement is worse. Like a giant steak thrown onto a griddle with all the force the chef can muster, wet and sickening. It is hard to imagine it was more extreme than the sounds I experienced that day in the plaza.

He hit the Range Rover at the junction between the bonnet and the windscreen with an almighty slap. The latter deformed into an opaque spider's web, the former creased like crumpled paper with a sharp squeal of protest. Inside, every airbag detonated with an explosive rush of compressed air. Then the alarm began to honk like a wounded animal. I could just make out the driver's flailing arms through the tinted side windows. Trapped. And in shock, no doubt. I wouldn't have to worry about him.

'Fuckin' hell!' Keegan spoke – or rather yelled – for all of us.

I found the three of us were on our feet, backing away from the shattered flesh and bone that was Henri, the Colonel's son. Keegan, appalled and perplexed by what he was seeing, had loosened his grip on me. I used the opportunity to break one of his fingers. He yelped, but the incessant honking of the Range Rover's alarm drowned him out. He drew back a fist to punch me and I stamped one of the metal legs of the café chairs into his foot, just above the tassel of his loafer. Another cry of pain. The punch sailed by and with my good hand I gave him a short sharp blow to the ribs. Now he hurt in three places. He'd keep.

I turned towards Jean-Claude. I had expected him to act by that point. He might not pull a gun – the cops would be all over the place soon – but the fact he was rooted to the spot surprised me. Then I saw the reason for his inaction, leaning round to shout in his ear.

'This is a steak knife pressed against your spine,' Freddie said. 'And I know what I am doing with

431

spines. And knife blades come to think of it. One false move and you'll be booking your place in the next Paralympics. Understand?'

Jean-Claude looked pale. 'Yes.'

She tossed me a blade, which I caught by the handle. 'I brought a spare.'

The business end was nasty and serrated and I was glad the Swiss don't like plastic cutlery. I grabbed my bag and opened it. 'Put your weapons in here. Carefully.'

Jean-Claude did as he was told. Keegan shook his head to show he wasn't carrying. I slipped the bag onto my shoulder. The new heft from J-C's Smith & Wesson felt good.

'What now?' asked Keegan, nursing his damaged hand.

'We are going across to that other café over there and we'll sit. We will order coffee. Then we'll wait for the police. Give our witness statements.'

Did he jump or was he pushed? I wondered. Had Henri jumped because he was ashamed of something he had done or had the Colonel lost his temper at his son's treachery and tossed him overboard? But that was one for the cops. Not my concern, sad as it was either way.

'And if you try anything, Keegan, I'm going to put this knife in your thigh and twist and dig until I find the femoral artery and Zürich will have a brand-new fountain. Do you believe me?'

A nod.

'Good. Get going. We need to talk about Leka.'

As he limped off with me at his back I heard Freddie laugh.

'What?' I asked.

She prodded Jean-Claude forward as the plaza began to fill with blue lights and sirens and she flashed me a grin.

'What's so funny?'

'Nothing,' she said. 'But welcome back, Sam.'

What will Sam Wylde's next assignment be?

We are looking for a PPO to accompany our well-known International Celebrity client on a visit to Hong Kong for personal reasons.

- The successful applicant will be discreet and well versed in defensive surveillance.
- The client has received kidnap threats that she – and we – takes seriously.
- The successful applicant will be part of a team offering 24-hour protection for the duration of the trip.
- Client stipulation is for at least one female to cover all possibilities.
- Mandarin or Cantonese an advantage.
- Clean passport essential.
- Proof of self-defence skills expected.
- Must be willing to submit to random drug testing.
- Salary negotiable.

ACKNOWLEDGEMENTS

Author's Note

The core of *Nobody Gets Hurt* was suggested by a true story, related to us by a relative over a few pints of Guinness. Sadly, we cannot identify him, as he would get into trouble for breaking a confidence. It is well documented that the FRU (here known by its alternative name of TRU) used informers and double agents and that, in some cases, informers/touts were exposed and murdered.

This is from an article by journalist Robert Stevens, published online in in 2001:

> During the past three weeks, the *Guardian* newspaper has run several articles on the Force Research Unit (FRU), an undercover security operation financed and run by the British state in Northern Ireland for more than two decades.

The articles detail how this terror network – involving up to 100 soldiers and double agents – organised a series of covert intelligence and military operations and authorised their agents to carry out numerous illegal activities including bomb–making, murder, and the shooting of Royal Ulster Constabulary (RUC) officers.

Through interviews with alleged former members of the FRU, the *Guardian* reports that the FRU was in active operation until the British and Irish governments signed the Northern Ireland Agreement three years ago. Afterwards ex-FRU members complain they were discarded by the British secret services and left without any protection.

Elsewhere, thanks are due to Jean-Francois Gourdon for decoding Monaco for us, Salvatore Madonna of the Hotel Byron in Forte di Marmi for plugging us in there, the Facel Vega Car Club for technical assistance and, of course, Lisa Baldwin for PPO advice. Also to Neola for help with photoshoots – www.neolaapparel.com. The eagle-eyed Mike Gostick helped with Sam's military background in this and *Safe From Harm*. Thank you also to Jo Dickinson and Sam Copeland for their enthusiasm and help in developing Ms Wylde's world. For this one, Bella and Gina Ryan assisted with the tone and language of Jess's diary.

RJ Bailey
Safe From Harm

YOU CAN RUN
Sam Wylde is a Close Protection Officer to the rich
and powerful. In a world dominated by men, being a
woman has been an advantage. And she is the best
in the business at what she does.

YOU CAN HIDE
She takes a job protecting the daughter of the Sharifs –
Pakistani textile tycoons – but she realises that there is
more to their organisation than meets the eye and
suddenly she finds herself in danger.

BUT ONLY ONE PERSON WILL KEEP
YOU SAFE FROM HARM
Now she is trapped underground, with no light, no signal
and no escape. Dangerous men are coming to hurt her, and
the young charge she is meant to be protecting. With time
running out, can she channel everything she knows to keep
them safe from harm …?

**'Sam Wylde is a hero for our times … RJ Bailey has
created a serial hero to rival Jack Reacher himself'
Tony Parsons**

**PAPERBACK ISBN 978-1-4711-5716-5
EBOOK ISBN 978-1-4711-5718-9**

THE
DARK
PAGES

Visit The Dark Pages to discover a community of like-minded readers and crime fiction fans.

If you would like more news, exclusive content and the chance to receive advance reading copies of our books before they are published, find us on Facebook, Twitter (**@dark_pages**) or at **www.thedarkpages.co.uk**